P9-BJV-869

# THE SECRET WEDDING

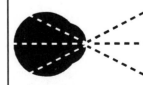 This Large Print Book carries the
Seal of Approval of N.A.V.H.

# THE SECRET WEDDING

## JO BEVERLEY

**THORNDIKE PRESS**
*A part of Gale, Cengage Learning*

GALE
CENGAGE Learning

Detroit • New York • San Francisco • New Haven, Conn • Waterville, Maine • London

GALE
CENGAGE Learning™

Copyright © Jo Beverley Publications, Inc., 2009.
Thorndike Press, a part of Gale, Cengage Learning.

ALL RIGHTS RESERVED
This is a work of fiction. Names, characters, places, and incidents are either the product of the author's imagination or are used fictitiously, and any resemblance to actual persons, living or dead, business establishments, events, or locales is entirely coincidental.
The publisher does not have any control over and does not assume any responsibility for author or third-party websites or their content.
Thorndike Press® Large Print Basic.
The text of this Large Print edition is unabridged.
Other aspects of the book may vary from the original edition.
Set in 16 pt. Plantin.
Printed on permanent paper.

LIBRARY OF CONGRESS CATALOGING-IN-PUBLICATION DATA

Beverley, Jo.
    The secret wedding / by Jo Beverley.
        p. cm.
    "Thorndike Press Large Print Basic"—T.p. verso.
    ISBN-13: 978-1-4104-1688-9 (hardcover : alk. paper)
    ISBN-10: 1-4104-1688-7 (hardcover : alk. paper)
    1. Large type books. I. Title.
    PR9199.3.B424S43 2009
    813'.54—dc22                                           2009011384

Published in 2009 by arrangement with NAL Signet, a member of Penguin Group (USA) Inc.

Printed in the United States of America
1 2 3 4 5 6 7 13 12 11 10 09

# ACKNOWLEDGMENTS

Special thanks go to Doncaster Local Studies Library, which gave me generous assistance with details and maps of the town in the eighteenth century, in particular about the various inns and their ages. Isn't the Internet wonderful?

I also made use of the library of the Canadian War Museum in Ottawa. In another benefit of modern technology I was able to digitally photograph pages of old books about the Life Guards and Horse Guards. I remember the days of handwritten notes — and not being able to read them clearly later.

As is usually the case, the material in the finished book is only the tip of the iceberg, but it's lovely to have the depth beneath.

Thanks also to Sharyn Cerniglia for taking the time to read through a partial draft to see if the story was flowing properly.

# PROLOGUE

*February 1754*
*The Tup's Byre, Nether Greasley, Yorkshire*
The scarlet-coated officer stalked into the low-ceilinged inn, heels harsh against the flagstone floor. "Lieutenant Moore?" he demanded.

The innkeeper hurried forward, bobbing his round, bald head. "The gentleman's summat busy, sir. Would you care for some ale as you wait?"

If he sounded nervous, it wasn't surprising. The invading officer was young, but the taut lines of his fine-boned face said danger, and striplings could be the worst. Impeccable uniform and white powdered hair didn't help, either, especially when he had a sword at his side.

"I carry an important message," the officer said in that clipped Southern accent. "What room?"

Jacob Hood was used to dealing with the

roughest drunks, but when he was confronted by armed authority, what could he do but say, "Upstairs, sir, first door on your right"?

The officer ran lightly up the stairs, spurs and sword hanger jingling, high boots thumping ominously. Hood moved to follow, but then thought better of it and hurried to summon his potboys and grooms, muttering about people who brought trouble to a respectable inn.

He'd known, though, when that couple had turned up — another young officer, though not so young as that one, with his "wife" swathed in a cloak. Wife to this other man, perhaps, though he seemed young to be shackled. Not yet twenty, even. But that'd be a fine kettle of fish.

On the upper floor, Lieutenant Christian Hill opened the first door to his right without pause. The room was low-ceilinged and poorly lit from a small window, but it stank of what was happening here. The man on the bed jerked up, cursed, and rolled off the woman beneath him.

Hill could spare only an appalled glance at the white-eyed victim because Bart Moore swooped up his sword belt, discarded on the floor with his outer clothing, and drew. He was a broad-built, robust man with sandy hair and a square jaw, and mostly dressed other than his flap, which hung over to reveal an exhausted penis.

"Damnation, Moore —"

But the man's sword swung viciously without warning. Swung to kill.

Hill ducked, then rolled under the bed to rise dusty on the other side, his own sword in hand. "Don't be a fool, man. You don't want to do this."

"Don't tell me what I want to do, pipsqueak!" Moore yelled. "Get out while you can!"

Hill was more lightly built and softer in the face, but he spoke with noble determination. "Only with the lady."

"Fancy yourself Sir Galahad?" Moore sneered. "She doesn't want to go. We're about to be married, aren't we, sweetheart? Especially now."

The girl — and she was a girl, hardly budding yet — made no sound, but she shook her head frantically, pushing her skirt back down over thin, pale legs.

Hill turned on Moore. "You disgusting —"

Moore's face engorged with fury and he raced around the bed to slash viciously at Hill's head. Hill ducked, but the blow took a chip out of a massive oaken bedpost.

9

The girl gave a muffled scream then, but neither man could pay her any attention. Their swords clashed until Hill got the oaken table between them.

"Have sense!" Hill gasped. "Do you want to die over this?"

"Scared to fight, stripling?"

Fueled by new outrage, Hill vaulted the table, kicking out to drive his opponent back and then attacking ferociously. Bed hangings parted; more chips of wood flew. Moore retaliated with wild murder in his eyes.

Hill pushed a chair at Moore's legs. "Think, you madman!"

Moore kicked the chair across the room. "Get out, get out, or I'll spit you like a chicken." His sword shot forward.

Hill lifted the second chair so Moore's blade point drove inches into the wood — where it stuck.

Hill could have killed him then, but stepped back, breathing hard. "Now will you see sense?"

Moore placed a foot on the chair and wrenched his blade free and swung with snarling, deadly force. Hill blocked, then slashed back. Blood spurted from Moore's arm and Hill retreated again, but his opponent howled with rage, blood spraying

10

from his wound. He charged, blade point driving for the heart.

Hill jumped aside and turned the blade, but not quickly enough. The point sliced through his open jacket and into his waist-coated torso. He staggered back, a hand to his wound.

Moore cried out in triumph and raised his sword over his head to deal a final blow.

But at that crucial moment the door burst open and inn servants rushed in. Moore hesitated for a small but fatal second. Hill drove his sword, right through his opponent's heart.

"Murder!" someone gasped, and then everyone leapt into action.

Three men seized and disarmed the panting victor without care for the bloody slash in his white waistcoat.

Two others ran to the fallen man.

The innkeeper shouted, "Liza! Liza! Run fetch the magistrate, girl. There's been murder done!"

So much, thought Lieutenant Christian Hill, for trying to rescue a damsel in distress. And that was his first death. What a pointless one.

He was thrust into the heavy, scarred chair and kept there by threat of a dirty kitchen knife — a knife able to slash off his head in one stroke, held by a man who looked as if he'd be happy to do it.

One of the men kneeling by Moore said, "Dead and gone, Mr. Hood. Didn't have a chance."

"Of course he did," Christian said, pressing a hand to his wounded side. A glimmer of good news there. It seemed to be a mere slash. "Moore attacked me first, and he was at least as good a swordsman."

"So you say," the innkeeper interrupted. "And who's to pay for all the damage?"

"I will." Money was the least of Christian's worries right now. He needed a witness to the fight. He risked turning his head to look toward the bed.

It was empty.

"Where's the girl?" he asked.

"The wench who came with him?" the innkeeper said. "Long gone, by the looks of it."

"She was there. On the bed."

Christian moved to look. The kitchen knife stung. He jerked back, glaring at the scrawny man, who clearly hadn't moved an inch to avoid cutting him.

He rolled his head sideways to look at the bed again. He couldn't have imagined her, but other than the dragged-back sheets and general rumpling, there was no sign of her at all.

Clattering feet and a variety of voices said that someone else was coming. Christian prayed for the magistrate. A gentleman seemed a better bet than these ferocious yokels. He couldn't turn toward the door, but he could see part of it in the reflection of a small mirror.

The person who entered was not a magistrate. A middle-aged woman invaded like a man-o'-war, her bolster of bosom and belly like wind-full sails. Christian had no idea who she might be, but he assessed her as if his life depended on it.

It very well might.

She wasn't alone. Two men took up position behind her, muscular men with ominous, big-knuckled fists. She didn't look as if she'd need protection. He'd take her for a man in a dress if not for the immense bosom. Her jaw was heavy and bracketed with jowls. Her eyes, mere slits in sagging folds, managed to be both cold and angry at the same time as she scanned the room.

Eventually, she said, "Where's me niece?" in the flat accent of this part of Yorkshire.

The innkeeper was bobbing anxious bows. "The lady who arrived with the officer, ma'am? Left, ma'am. Gone before this disaster."

The eyes turned on Christian. "You this Moore?"

"Neither moor nor dale, dear lady. Only a Hill."

She was not amused and her steely gaze moved on to the body. "That's Moore?" she demanded.

The innkeeper shuffled forward. "Yes, ma'am. At least, that was the name he gave."

"Half-undressed and indecently exposed. You 'ave many guests arrive in the afternoon and strip like that when alone?"

"Er, no, ma'am."

"Dorcas!" the woman commanded, slapping her riding crop against the palm of her gloved hand.

There was a scuffling noise and a dusty head appeared from beneath the far side of the bed, looking, if possible, even more terrified than before.

"Don't bully her," Christian said, weak with relief. He had his witness. "She's been through enough —"

"Do you think so? Anything she's suffered 'as been entirely 'er own fault, and now a man lies dead for it. Get up, girl!"

This Dorcas scrambled to her feet and hugged herself, tears trickling through the dust on her cheeks.

If her aunt's shape was aggressively female, the girl's was the opposite. Despite rouge on her cheeks, she was as flat as a boy. Her mousy hair had been pinned up, but now straggled in wavy rats' tails around her thin face.

What had Moore seen in her?

Money. At least that was the gossip that had sent Christian on this mad venture. Moore planned to ruin a besotted heiress to force a marriage. He must have been desperate to need whatever funds this waif owned.

"You've ruined y'self, y'silly twit," the woman said. "That woman as runs that fancy-dancy school your mother insisted on 'as made a great alarm of your running off."

The girl whispered, "I'm sorry. . . . I thought . . ."

"Thought what?" the terrifying aunt snapped. "That he *luvved* you? A scrawny piece of nothin' like you? Lord save me from fools. And 'ere 'e is dead, so you'll have to marry 'im."

The girl's wide eyes went to the corpse and the whites showed. Christian stared at the woman, wondering if she were mad.

"Not 'im, y'dope. 'Im." She was pointing at Christian.

"Ma'am —"

15

"Shut up." Formidable jowls turned on Christian. "You killed 'im, young man, so you'll take 'is place."

"The devil I will!" Christian surged forward. The knife bit again. "Damn and blast you all!"

One of her henchmen moved forward, fist ready, but the woman commanded, "No." Into the frozen silence, she spoke with flat calm. "I don't bear with profanity, lad, so guard your tongue. Now, be sensible. You've no choice 'ere but the gallows."

Breathing hard, rage in every sinew, Christian snapped, "I'll take my chance with the law, then."

"Will you, now? I don't know anything about duels, but this doesn't seem to 'ave been a proper un." When Christian had no answer to that, she pulled a leather money pouch out of her pocket and addressed the room, chinking it. "Didn't I 'ear it declared cold-blooded murder?"

After a moment, one man said, "It was indeed, ma'am. T'other man looked to the door, and this un ran 'im straight through."

"Struck to kill," said the innkeeper, "as God's me witness, ma'am. Struck to kill. No doubt about it."

"Likely wanted the girl for 'imself," called a woman from the back of the crowd, eager

16

for her bit of the reward.

"Then 'e'll get 'is wish, won't he?" the aunt said, turning to look at Christian with something that might have been a grim smile.

Christian could almost feel a noose around his neck, but he still wanted his day in court. If he could once get out of this madhouse, he could summon help from his family. He burned with embarrassed fury at the thought of having to tell his father about this fiasco, but that was better than hanging.

He fired a glance at the girl, demanding her witness, but she was staring into space, shivering and hugging herself. Just his luck. She'd been terrified out of her wits.

Christian unclenched his teeth and tried for a reasonable tone. "Perhaps, ma'am, we can talk about this more temperately and without so many listeners."

"They know what they know and they know you killed 'im."

A murmur of assent ran around the room.

"Ask her," Christian said, glaring at the girl. "She'll tell you it was as fair a fight as possible!"

"It doesn't matter. Dorcas needs a husband."

"And to marry like this won't be a scandal

in itself?"

"A marriage papers over anything."

That was unfortunately true.

"But it can't be achieved in moments," Christian argued desperately. "There are laws. . . ." He had no idea what they were. "I'm only sixteen!" he protested. Plague take it, that sounded pathetic. "I'm a military officer," he said with more dignity, "and may not marry without my colonel's consent."

"Then don't tell 'im," the woman said, unimpressed.

Christian gaped at her. "What?"

Before he could explain how outrageous she was, a stir in the doorway behind him suggested a new arrival. A magistrate at last? He tried to turn, but the knife bit again. Muttering curses, he watched in the mirror, praying for help.

He saw a short fat man in a short fat wig, dressed in clergyman's black. Where the devil had he come from? He might as well be a hangman in Christian's eyes.

The clergyman stopped at the sight of the corpse and began to retreat, but the gawking audience had closed in behind him.

"You 'ere to perform a marriage?" the woman asked.

"Er . . . for a Lieutenant Moore, yes,

ma'am . . ." His eyes, tiny currants in a red, glossy moon face, darted around and fixed on Christian. He stared, swallowed, but then said, "You are Lieutenant Moore, sir?"

"No," Christian said.

The eyes moved on to the corpse. "Oh dear, oh dear, oh dear . . ." The clergyman pulled out a handkerchief to dab at glistening sweat. Christian was damn hot, too, both from fury and the press in the room.

"You 'ave a license with you?" the woman asked.

The man turned to her. "Er . . . yes, ma'am. I am . . . I am authorized by law to provide them, and . . . er . . . to perform marriages. Though normally speaking, in a church. I was told the bride was confined to her bed."

"She can be if you insist on it," the aunt said.

Had "confined to her bed" been grim humor on Moore's part? What the devil had been the plan? How had he intended to force the girl to marry him?

But then Christian considered the aunt's determination. If Moore were still alive, the girl would be married to him by now.

The clergyman was still dabbing his face and clearly wishing himself anywhere else in the world. Christian prayed he'd balk, but given the demeanor of the aunt and her two men, and the mood of the entrapping crowd, Christian wasn't surprised when he said, "Of course, if all is in order . . ."

He looked at the girl, but took her frozen state for consent. Christian had heard of brides and sometimes grooms dragged to the altar bound and gagged, forced into a nod as agreement to the vows. Hadn't there recently been a change in the laws about things like that? If so, word hadn't reached this nether end of nowhere.

The clergyman went to the small table and took a folded document out of a battered portfolio. He smoothed out the paper, extracted a pen and a capped inkpot, and began to amend the license.

Christian watched in disbelief. The whole world knew there were clergymen willing to overlook nearly every impediment and marry almost anyone for a fee, but this couldn't be happening to him.

The man turned his head toward Christian. "Your name, sir?"

"This is monstrous," Christian protested. "I've done nothing wrong. I heard of Moore's plans and came here to rescue the girl."

He saw no change in the expression of anyone around him. The inn servants didn't seem hostile, more like people enjoying a play, in fact, but determined that it go on. Or like a Roman mob, Christian thought grimly, keen to see someone fed to the lions.

"If you want money for your witness," Christian said to the audience, "I'll outbid her."

He saw some reaction, but then one man said, "Let's see your gold, then."

Of course, he didn't have more than a few coins on him, and not much gold of his own at all, if truth be told. He was his father's heir, but his father wasn't a rich man and had many obligations.

He tried reason again. "The girl can go home and forget about this. Marriage to me locks her up for life."

"Don't be daft," the woman said, turning from where she was supervising the alteration of the license. "A marriage like this is easy to end."

Christian wanted to believe her flat certainty, but in his experience a wedding took place in the parish church by license or after banns and was then indissoluble.

People did go to court sometimes to end marriages. He thought bigamy was the main cause, but he remembered one case of a man who'd drunk too much and woken up married. This felt like a similar nightmare, but he couldn't remember the outcome of that court case.

"Dorcas will return 'ome married," the woman stated. "I won't be balked on that, so give us your name."

Christian would still prefer to take his chance with the magistrates, but his mind was working furiously, spinning out grim alternatives. If he ended up before the magistrates, he'd have a dozen people swearing he'd committed murder and it seemed the girl would be no help.

Once he summoned help from his colonel and his family, he wouldn't hang, but the affair would embarrass him forever and could easily ruin his newborn military career. His regiment was set to leave for Canada within days, where they'd oppose the French. No bunch of yokels was going to block his way to adventure, or prevent him fighting for king and country.

Moore was dead. That couldn't be covered up, but he could probably convince Colonel Howard of his side of the story. A plaguey mistake, but when he glanced at the pale and shaking girl, he could only wish he'd arrived sooner.

"Someone put a blanket around her," he snapped.

His words seemed to startle everyone, but

one of the henchmen pulled the coverlet off the bed and draped it around the girl, helping her to a seat on a bench.

"Yer name, lad!" the woman barked, snapping Christian back to his intolerable situation. If he wanted to escape, he was going to have to go through with this farce. As she'd said, no need to tell anyone about it, and surely such a forced affair would be set aside. If there were witnesses to his killing Moore, there were as many to this abuse.

And, he thought, no need to give his real name . . .

He was inventing wildly when he remembered that quip about moors and hills. Damn his flippant tongue! And now his mind had gone blank and he could do no better than change "Christian" for something more common.

"Jack Hill," he said. There must be hundreds of Jack Hills.

Whether the woman believed him or not, she nodded and turned her attention back to where the clergyman continued to tamper with the document. Christian glanced again at the girl, who was huddled in the coverlet like a bird trying to keep warm. She reminded him of his younger sisters and he hoped Moore was roasting in hell. No matter how great her folly in running off with a scoundrel, she hadn't deserved this.

The aunt was right about the magical healing power of marriage. One of his cousins had run off with a rascal last year, then been brought back and married off, and now everyone politely forgot about her error.

In contrast, a Miss Barstowe had also disappeared with a rascal at about the same time. When she returned to her family, she claimed to have been abducted, and had refused to marry the man. Or had it been some other man, as in this case? Reasonable enough, but last Christian had heard, she was living a penumbral life, officially still part of her local society, but rarely appearing and not truly accepted anywhere.

Of course this Dorcas and her aunt weren't of the gentry, but if there was a school and some money, they were a respectable family in their own way, with a place and reputation to preserve.

"Father's name?" the clergyman asked.

Sons were often named for their father, so Christian said, "John Hill." In fact, it was James.

"I assume you're not already married, lad?" the woman asked, her tone implying it would be the worst for him if he was.

"I'm only sixteen, if you remember."

24

"A lad can marry at that age. Let's get on with it."

"Can we dispense with the knife at my throat?" Christian asked, with careful calm. At least he could go to his execution with dignity.

"What?" She seemed to see it for the first time. "Oh, take that away. 'E couldn't escape now unless 'e sprouts wings."

As soon as the knife wielder retreated, Christian stood and straightened his uniform. He felt the wound in his side, but it was a mere scratch and seemed to have stopped bleeding. Ruined a perfectly good waistcoat, however.

He demanded his sword, and when it was warily returned to him, he cleaned it as best he could and sheathed it. Then he pulled free a sheet and spread it over Moore's corpse.

Now he had more command of affairs, his tension eased. If the woman insisted on this sham and it helped the girl preserve some fragment of her reputation, so be it. A marriage performed in an inn involving a groom who used a false name, with an altered marriage certificate . . . it would collapse as soon as it was blown on.

He turned to the woman. "Your name, ma'am? And my bride's?"

"I'm Abigail Froggatt, and she's Dorcas Froggatt."

Dorcas Froggatt. Christian shuddered. Gathering himself, he asked, "From?"

The woman's eyes narrowed as if she was considering ordering him back in the chair with a knife at his throat. "Sheffield, if it's any concern of yours. Let's get this done."

The girl was extracted from the quilt by the henchman. He attempted to put his arm around her, so perhaps he wasn't unkind. She pushed him away, however, then walked forward, chin up in an attempt at dignity. There was still little to recommend her — she was bony, pale, and straggle-haired, and the heavy paint she'd applied to attempt to look older was a streaky mess — but Christian appreciated her courage.

He found it hard to make himself speak the necessary vows, for his word was his honor and he had no intention of cherishing this creature till death did them part, but he reminded himself that this was merely a formality to salvage the girl's reputation.

His bride seemed to choke on the vows, but the dreadful woman barked, "I, Dorcas Froggatt . . ." and she repeated that and managed the rest. When he had to take her hand, it was cold and seemed fragile as a

26

sparrow's wing. He slid on a cheap metal ring the clergyman provided. Clearly the man performed irregular marriages for a living and came equipped.

Christian signed the documents, as did his bride, the aunt, and one of her men. The clergyman made a great show of recording the marriage in a decrepit book and then smiled as if this were a happy occasion. "God's blessings upon the happy couple!"

Mistress Froggatt turned to the audience. "Off you go now and toast the bride and groom." She gave the innkeeper some coins and the crowd pushed out to be the first downstairs.

That left only six people in the room, if one didn't count the corpse.

"May I go now?" Christian asked coolly.

"Not quite. You," the formidable Froggatt said to the clergyman, "write me a document."

"I am not a clerk, ma'am!"

Abigail Froggatt put three guineas on the table.

The clergyman uncapped his ink, picked up his pen again, and wrote as she dictated what seemed to be a brief marriage contract. Contracts were usually drawn up and signed before the wedding, and Christian realized that as the girl's husband he now had a great deal of power over her and whatever property she possessed.

He didn't give much for his chances of wielding it.

He glanced to where his bride had resumed her huddled position on the bench, and a protective instinct twitched. He stamped on it. The sooner he was free of Froggatts, the better.

He paid attention to the document, however. He'd sign nothing blind. He read it over to make sure it said what he'd heard dictated. It did.

His bride's property would remain as disposed in her father's will. So she was an heiress of sorts. In lieu of his rights thereto, her family would provide him an income of thirty guineas a quarter as long as he remained in the army.

He paused over that. A hundred and twenty guineas a year was a substantial sum to someone like himself, who was living on his officer's pay. Pride made him strike that section out, however. "I'll make no profit from this," he said, signing.

That gesture would probably please the monstrous woman, but he wanted nothing of this event to linger in his life. He'd leave the country with his regiment as planned and never think of it again. Perhaps, he thought philosophically, the hazards of war would end this misbegotten marriage without need of courts.

If not, it could be dealt with later. A false name, irregular circumstances, and lack of consummation must explode it. Hades, the greasy clergyman was probably defrocked.

"Your name?" Christian demanded.

The man's slack mouth moved as if he'd rather not give it. "Walmsly, sir. Walmsly."

Doubtless a lie, but that made this even less valid.

Mistress Froggatt signed the contract as the girl's guardian. Then she said to Christian, "Now you can go."

From sheer bloody-mindedness, Christian turned to the girl, thinking to at least kiss her cheek, but she was such an image of hopeless misery he couldn't. Again, he felt he should rescue her. He was, after all, her husband. . . .

To Hades with that.

He turned and left the room, determined to put the past hour out of his mind.

He was done forever with playing Galahad to damsels in distress.

# CHAPTER 1

*Ten years later*
*London*

"Grandiston!"

The call penetrated even the laughter and chatter of the Guards' Officers' Mess.

Christian had been Viscount Grandiston for nearly a year, which was long enough for him to respond to it but not long enough to be pleased about it. He was also just leaving with a group of friends to go to the theater.

At the second bellow he turned to look across the crowded room misted by pipe smoke.

"Hades," he muttered. Middle-aged, bulldog-jawed Major Delahew was beckoning him. These days, Delahew was a paper pusher in the regimental administration, but he was a tough old soldier with an honorable career, and a superior officer to boot. He couldn't be ignored.

"Don't leave without me," Christian said to his friends, and worked his way through the crowded room. What bit of paperwork had he bungled this time? Peacetime soldiering was a devilish bore, perhaps especially when a man had known nothing but action in his career.

"Yes, sir?"

Delahew's glare turned into a rueful smile. "Sorry, didn't mean to bellow an order. So demmed noisy in here. Drink?"

Christian had to accept the offer and sit at the man's table.

Delahew eased into his chair, arranging his wooden leg at an angle. Such things were sobering evidence of the consequences of war, but these days Christian could almost find thought of wounds exciting.

He was coming to regret transferring to the elite Life Guards. When his father had inherited the earldom of Royland, he'd urged the move. He'd seemed to think it would be a treat for Christian, though he hadn't been blind to the advantages of his heir in the palace guard.

With the French and Indian War over, Christian had been ready for lighter times, and playing the military beau in London had promised amusement. London was the center of the world, full of good company and lovely ladies. He'd be close to old friends, especially Robin Fitzvitry, now Earl of Huntersdown, and Thorn, the most eminent Duke of Ithorne.

His new life had amused for a while, but he was beginning to itch for action, any action, near or far. Delahew would hardly choose this moment to discuss some adventurous posting, alas.

Christian took the glass of wine and sipped, hoping he could cut this short. There was a wager running to do with the reigning actress, Betty Prickett, with Christian the favorite.

"Got a relative by the name Jack Hill, Grandiston?"

Christian returned his attention to Delahew. "Yes, sir."

"Dead?"

"Gads, I hope not." A spark of alarm fizzled. No one would send Delahew to inform him of a death in the family. "Younger brother. About seven years of age."

"Ah." Delahew drank. "Thought you might be able to cut through a knot."

"Sorry not to be able to help, sir." Christian drained his glass and declined more, hoping that was it. "I could ask my father. There might be a family reason he called a son John — that's Jack's baptismal name — though now I think of it, he'd been reduced to using the evangelists by the twelfth child."

"Twelve?" Delahew stared.

"Ninth was Matt, sir, then Mark, Luke, and Jack."

"All surviving?"

"My parents haven't lost a one."

"Twelve," Delahew said, shaking his head. It could have been admiring, but Christian suspected he was thinking it unnatural in the extreme.

"Thirteen, actually, sir," Christian said, to rub the salt in. "Benjamin, aged three."

Silence fell. Christian glanced at the door. His friends were leaving. "This other Hill in trouble, sir?"

"No, no." Delahew worked his heavy jaw as if chewing stringy meat. "Letter came from York asking for any information about a Jack Hill, regiment unknown, rank unknown, but an officer said to have died at Quebec. No one of that name in the casualty lists there. Probably an inheritance issue, but I'm not about to order a search of records on a fool's chase like that."

"No, of course not. Get many like that, sir?"

The offices of the Horse Guards had become the headquarters for administration of the whole army.

"Every now and then. Even more difficult if it's one of the common men. Many are illiterate, so their names end up spelled by guess, and they often enlist under a false one, trying to escape the law or some woman." He drained his glass. "Charging the enemy's guns is a damned sight easier than paper pushing, I can tell you."

"I'm sure it is, sir." Christian judged the moment right and rose. "I'll ask my father, but 'Hill' is such a common name. There might be no connection at all."

"My regards to Lord Royland. Sorry to have bothered you."

Christian lied and assured him it had been no bother at all, and caught up with his friends as they were climbing into a carriage.

"Come on!" Balderson called, and dragged him into the overcrowded coach just before it lurched off. "Even though you'll capture the citadel, you handsome bastard, and a future earl to boot."

"If I were a bastard, I wouldn't be in line to inherit, would I? Which would make my life a damned sight easier. I wouldn't be a prime target of all those husband hunters."

The young men all gave theatrical groans.

"And we can't even avoid them," said

plump Lavalley. "Plaguey hostesses seem to think Guards officers exist for their convenience."

"Wouldn't mind being caught by a rich husband hunter," said Greatorix, "but they want to buy a title."

True enough, Christian thought, squeezed into a corner with an elbow sticking into his ribs. What's more, an impoverished title beckoned a predatory heiress like a wounded rabbit appealed to a fox.

He was certainly no richer than he'd ever been. The earldom had increased his father's income, but when a man has thirteen sons and daughters all needing their start in the world, he needs every penny.

That was why Christian's presence at court and in the upper circles of power should serve the family. Juicy posts, privileges, and sinecures were always floating around. He was willing to do his best there, but he was balking at his father's latest strategy — using Christian as bait to bring a rich heiress into the fold.

He put that out of mind and turned his attention to enjoying the evening. The play was excellent and the farce suitably ribald. In the greenroom he made progress with the pretty Prickett, but she wasn't willing to be captured yet.

It was only later, rolling home drunk and merry in another overcrowded carriage, that Delahew's question popped into his mind again.

"Zeus!"

It was too noisy for most to hear, but Arniston, crushed up against him, slurred, "If you're going to puke, Hill, turn the other way."

Christian ignored him, the name "Jack Hill" echoing in his mind. The name he'd given for that ridiculous marriage — how long ago? His sozzled brain protested arithmetic, but it had been just before he sailed. A bit over ten years, then.

But in all that time, it had been as if it hadn't happened.

Moore's death had been reported as a drunken brawl with an anonymous opponent. The Froggatt woman's doing, he supposed, and he was grateful to her for that, at least. No one in the regiment had doubted the story. Everyone assumed that the girl's vengeful relatives had done for him, and the news that she was only fourteen had meant everyone applauded the deed.

Fourteen.

When a vague story had circulated that a wedding had been involved, it had been assumed that Moore had married her and that his death had ended it. Within days, the regiment had begun its preparations for departure, and that had been that.

There'd been the long sea voyage, with him sick as a dog for half of it, and then the excitement of a new world and the demands of learning to lead and fight. Somewhere in the midst of it he'd received a letter from the aunt to inform him that the girl was dead. He'd been sorry for her short life, but he couldn't claim any deep concern.

After that, he'd given it not a thought. Until now.

Someone in Yorkshire was inquiring about Jack Hill.

There couldn't be any connection, but an icy worm was creeping down his back, and he'd learned to pay heed to it.

What if the letter had been a lie, and his bride still lived?

He didn't want to be married. Growing up in a modest manor house bursting with infants cured a man of that, and one advantage of having seven healthy brothers was that his father had never pressed him on the matter.

Until now — not to secure the line, but to ensure the family's fortunes by hooking wealth through marriage.

Christian knew his father wasn't motivated only by money. When the earl came to Town for Parliament, he shook his head over his son's "solitary state" — struth, did he not understand barracks life? — and lack of wifely comforts. Christian didn't think his father could be as naive as to assume him celibate, so he assumed he meant a well-managed household. And children.

Christian shuddered.

His father, both his parents, were dear souls and a loving couple. So much so that they produced children constantly. After him had come Mary, Sara, Tom, Margaret, Anne, Elizabeth, and Kit. Then the easily remembered Matthew, Mark, Luke, and John, and finally, he hoped, Benjamin. Surely his mother must be past childbearing age now.

He had no memory of his solitary reign as eldest, but a clear one of a new baby every couple of years, demanding attention and filling the house fuller and fuller. No wonder he'd been keen to escape when the opportunity presented.

He'd been ten, and Lisa was squalling in her cradle when his father had been approached by the guardians of the young Duke of Ithorne, one of whom had been Christian's uncle. Thorn's father had died before he was born, so he'd been born a duke and an only child. His guardians had belatedly realized he needed a companion of his own age, and Christian had been the lucky choice.

He remembered his parents' tears, but they'd seen the value of the opportunity. With boyhood callousness, Christian had felt nothing but the thrill of adventure. He'd traveled to Ithorne Castle to become the young duke's foster brother with all the space anyone could want, and everything else as well — horses, boats, weapons, travel.

Thorn.

He was in Town at the moment, and his level head could be useful. Christian would stroll around for a visit tomorrow and talk this over. Delahew's query had to be some wild coincidence. His long-forgotten bride couldn't be stirring from the grave.

"Hill, m'man!" Someone poked him hard. "Wake up."

"Not asleep, and it's Grandiston."

"Well, I beg your pardon, your damned grandstandandiston!"

Struth, it was Pauley and he was a fighting drunk.

"No offense, Pauley. As you say, half-asleep and with weird dreams. Dreamt I was married."

The whole coach rocked with the cries of alarm, and as it pulled to a stop, the bunch of young bachelors tumbled out laughing to stagger off to their beds.

# CHAPTER 2

The next day Christian walked to Thorn's mansion near St. James's Square. He was still one of the family and found his own way to the ducal study, where Thorn was giving orders to three harried clerks. He was a dark-haired man who'd managed from boyhood to be neat and tidy and make that unnatural state look comfortable.

Christian was neat at the moment because his rank and duties required it — polished boots, braided uniform, sash, powdered wig, and all the rest — but off duty he enjoyed a more relaxed style.

He surveyed the busy scene. "Ah, the blessings of not being a duke."

"Wait until you're an earl." Thorn shot a few more orders, then took Christian off to a small library he'd made his private sanctum. "Problems, or you just wanted to gloat over my slavery? Wine, tea, coffee?"

"Tea," Christian said. He preferred coffee

or chocolate in the morning, but didn't mind tea. As Thorn was a devotee, it was a small thing to do for a friend.

As usual, he had to listen to a short paean to a new variety and observe the careful preparation before he could get to business. He sipped. It was pleasant enough, but didn't taste different from most other teas he'd drunk here.

"Well?" Thorn asked, relaxing back in his chair.

It was hard to put it into words. Christian spat it out. "I might be married."

Thorn froze with the cup at his lips. "It does tend to be a thing one either is or is not."

"You'd think so, wouldn't you? Don't suppose you know the finer details of the marriage laws that came into effect about ten years ago?"

"The Hardwicke Act?" Thorn put down his cup untasted. Remarkable. "No, except that it makes clandestine marriages invalid. You're of age, so that's not an issue, but the act also dictates that marriages have to be by license or banns, and almost always in a church between nine in the morning and noon. So if you went through a drunken ceremony last night at some inn, you're probably still free."

"A good law, for once. But no, it's not that. Rather, I did once go through a wedding ceremony."

"Only once. What a wonder."

"I mean," said Christian, jaw tightening, "once upon a time. Not long before the regiment left for America. There were no banns, and it wasn't in a church, so if the act was in force . . ."

"But dammit, Christian, the act was passed more than a decade ago. In 1753, I think. You were sixteen!"

"The ceremony was in 1754. Does that mean it was in effect?"

"Laws don't always come into force immediately." He rose and tugged on a bell-pull. When a footman entered, he simply said, "Overstone, if you please."

Overstone was Thorn's dull but extremely efficient Town secretary. The plump man quickly appeared.

"The 1753 Marriage Act," Thorn said. "Exactly when did it come into effect?"

"If I may consult some books, Your Grace?"

Thorn waved him on his way. "If it was in effect, you're free and clear, yes."

"God bless Lord Hardwicke!"

"It isn't an entirely godly law. Before, a man who made promises and seduced could

44

be deemed to have married, ceremony or not."

"Damn it all to Hades, I made no promises and certainly didn't seduce!"

Thorn returned to his seat and tea. "Then why not tell me what you did do?"

Christian sighed and obliged, recounting the strange events of ten years ago.

"Struth! But why barge into that kind of mess?"

"Surely you remember sixteen, when a youth feels a man, but invincible and immortal? I was a newly fledged lieutenant in His Majesty's army, master of the world, and thus, by obligation, a gallant rescuer of fair maidens."

Thorn gave a short laugh. "A fair maiden called Dorcas Froggatt."

The sneer in Thorn's voice tempted Christian to defend the thin, frightened girl, but Thorn went on. "If it weren't you telling the story, I wouldn't believe a word of it. You've kept this secret all these years?"

"What point in telling anyone?"

"I'm thinking," said Thorne, "of a certain vow."

"Ah, I'd overlooked that."

Christian had returned to England twice in the past decade, on the most recent occasion to deliver dispatches and recover from being wounded by a hatchet in the shoulder. Once fit, he'd been primed to rip wild, and Thorn and Thorn's cousin Robin Fitzvitry had been willing accessories.

Grand times, and not entirely divorced from the war because Thorn had been doing some smuggling in the cause on his yacht, the *Black Swan.* Thorn had been Captain Rose and Robin, Lieutenant Sparrow, both plays on their names. Christian had declared himself Pagan the Pirate.

Good times, and some useful work done against the French.

One evening over wine, when Thorn had protested the continual pressure on him to marry, Christian and Robin had decided to support his resistance. They'd drawn up and signed a vow not to marry before thirty.

To bolster their will, they'd created a penalty — any of them who succumbed would have to pay a thousand guineas to the least worthy cause they could think of, Lady Fowler's Fund for the Moral Reform of London Society.

That sour lady worked to close the theaters, and ban dancing — especially masquerade balls — and prosecute anyone who gambled with cards or dice. She and her followers even took station outside masquerades bearing a banner declaring that London would burn like Sodom and Gomorrah.

Giving the madwoman money was anathema, but poor Robin had already had to do so. After much tormenting, Christian and Thorn had taken pity and allowed him to do so anonymously. However, as Christian had already been married when he'd taken the vow, it wasn't surprising that Thorn was questioning him now.

"I drew up that document, if you'll remember, being the soberest at the time. Amid the flowery phrasing I inserted a bit about not marrying from that day hence."

"Unworthy!"

"Necessary. There was no other way to join in the game."

"You could have told us the story. That would have amused."

"Reason enough not to. I felt a damned fool about the whole thing, and I've always regretted Moore's death. He was a foul sort, but he didn't have to die for it. If I'd been older, I'd have managed it better. In any case, by that time I'd been told my bride was dead and the whole matter buried."

Overstone returned. "The twenty-ninth of March, 1754, Your Grace."

Thorn shot Christian a question and Christian grimaced in response. "We sailed mid-March."

Overstone said, "I could have Poultney lay out the finer parts of the law, sir, if it would be of use."

"Thank you," Thorn said, and waved his secretary away.

"Poultney?" Christian asked.

"Lawyer I use for legislative and theoretical matters."

"How many lawyers do you have?"

"I lose count."

Christian shuddered.

"You'll come to it one day," Thorn said unsympathetically.

"Unlikely. Royland's a very minor earldom, whereas Ithorne's a very major dukedom. Besides, Father must be good for decades, whereas I'll probably die young — with God's blessing, in a cloud of noble glory."

"Damn you, Christian."

"Sorry, one becomes accustomed to the idea."

"It looks as if you'd better become accustomed to being married. Except that you thought she was dead?"

"I received a letter in 'fifty-six to inform me of that."

"Then why are you disturbing me with it?"

"Because someone from Yorkshire is inquiring about Jack Hill." He described the encounter with Delahew.

"You have a very unruly way of telling a story." Thorn picked up his teacup and drank. "This inquiry might be nothing to do with you."

"True. Or the letter announcing her death might have been false."

"For what reason?"

"The poor girl had been taken by force and then witnessed a bloody death. If she wanted nothing more to do with me, I'm not surprised."

Thorn nodded. "Then let the dead bride rest in peace, on earth or in heaven. It's not as if you have plans to marry another." Perhaps Christian twitched, for Thorn focused on him. "Have you?"

"Absolutely not, but my father's beginning to push."

"Why? He's not short of sons."

"But, as always, short of money and he's realized that promise of a future countess's coronet is worth a lot in the marriage market."

"Gads." Thorn might even have shuddered. "There, you do have my deepest sympathy. And I suppose being in the Guards makes it hard to lie low."

"Impossible. Hostesses think we exist for their convenience. It hasn't been so bad in the duller days of summer, but when the winter season starts . . ."

"Indeed. But at least the Marriage Act means that some scheming piece can't trick you into foolish words and embraces and claim the coronet that way."

"Or you," Christian said.

"Or me."

"God bless Lord Hardwicke."

"Amen. As for your father, his whim will pass."

Christian considered the linen at his wrists. "Unfortunately there's already a bidder."

"For your hand in marriage?"

Christian looked up. "Psyche Jessingham."

Thorn's face became still. "Ah."

"Your mistress, I believe?"

Thorn met his eyes. "Not now she's a widow."

"Ah," Christian said. As the wife of an older and obliging husband, Lady Jessingham had been the perfect mistress, but her husband's death changed everything.

"I knew she was looking for a new husband," Thorn said, "and this time one of her own choice. I, of course, would have been perfect, but I made my position clear.

I do feel I should try to ensure that my heir is of my blood. I'm surprised your father thinks her suitable."

"He won't know her reputation."

"He doesn't have to know that to recognize that she'd be an eagle in the nest."

"You know Father," Christian said. "When I hinted at that, he assured me that my charms and devotion as a true husband will mellow her. I think he imagines her cozily at Royle Chart putting up jam with Mother. And, of course, he's convinced that as soon as she meets the bounteous hillocks, she'll adore them, every one."

"It's not a fault to love one's children."

"Of course not, but I intend to avoid adding to the problem by not marrying at all."

"Not marrying again," Thorn said with relish.

"Damn you to Hades." But then Christian said, "My God . . ."

"What?" Thorn was alert.

"Legitimacy. Marriage. Children. In the unlikely event that Dorcas Froggatt is still alive, wouldn't any child of hers be legally mine?"

"Including a son," Thorn said, putting down his cup, "who would then be in line for the earldom. But there has to be the possibility of the husband fathering the child.

You've never been near the woman in ten years."

Christian got only a moment's comfort from that. "It looked as if Moore consummated the marriage a bit early."

"You left immediately."

"But was definitely in the area at the time."

"So she could claim you came together in the following days and you'd have no way to disprove it," Thorn said. "And even if the wife's dead, someone could be trying to act on behalf of the child, not even sure what the truth is."

Christian swore. "But why now? Why would anyone be digging this all up ten years later?"

Thorn refilled his cup. He offered more to Christian.

"I could do with something stronger."

Thorn rose and poured brandy from a decanter. He gave it to Christian, saying, "Consider the earldom. It was in all the newspapers because of the long search up the family tree to discover the next in line. Someone in Yorkshire reads that Sir James Hill has become the new Earl of Royland, and wonders."

"Hill's a common name," Christian protested.

Thorn sat down again. "But even as a youth you weren't a common man. It wouldn't be that difficult to find the names of the new earl's children. . . ."

"I gave the name Jack."

Thorn nodded. "Some protection, but even so, inquiries might be made about a young military officer called Hill."

"Over a year after the event?" Christian was liking this picture less and less by the moment. He drained his glass and went to refill it.

"News can travel slowly to the provinces," Thorn said. "The inquirer could be Dorcas herself, perhaps living in reduced circumstances. She realizes she might be a viscountess. Her son, if she has one, might have a claim on an earldom. . . ."

"Viscountess she may be, but I'll see her in hell before she foists Moore's bastard on me."

"Assuredly, and this query from Yorkshire suggests that something's stirring. We need to move quickly to discover whether Dorcas is alive or dead, and if she bore a child. My people will know someone in Yorkshire who can make inquiries."

Christian put down his glass. "I'm not going to cower in a hole waiting for trouble to find me. I have to do something."

53

"And get another hatchet in your shoulder?"

"Hazard of war."

"This is not a war," Thorn said, "and doesn't require that sort of action. Leave it in my hands."

"What can you do if you find Dorcas alive?"

"Buy her off."

"Not if that aunt's still on the scene. Dammit, she's probably the one behind all this. She looms in my memory as a monstrous creature with a Yorkshire accent that could grind wheat, and vicious henchmen who'd slit a throat at her orders."

"A trifle medieval, don't you think?"

"That's Yorkshire for you."

"I've met civilized Yorkshiremen. And women. The Countess of Arradale, for example."

"Equally terrifying, especially now she's Marchioness of Rothgar as well. I like my women pleasing and pliant."

Thorn's lips twitched. "Perhaps your Dorcas is that. What then?"

"A lackwit, I can believe, but pliant — no. Not from that stable."

Thorn rose, too. "Let me deal with this, Christian. You're the one for action, not delicate investigation and negotiation."

Christian paced the room. "I need action. All very well for you, always in command of life, everything neat and in order."

"Thank you," Thorn said drily.

"Deuce take it, that wasn't a criticism!"

They both brushed off the moment, but perhaps it had been a criticism of sorts.

Thorn had always had unnatural control. It probably came of being born a duke and without true family. His young mother had remarried when he was three, and as she'd married a Frenchman, she'd not been allowed to take such an eminent son out of the country with her.

Thorne had been raised impeccably by conscientious guardians and trustees who'd even gone to the trouble of providing him with a foster brother, but it was a strange way to grow up. Though Christian often rolled his eyes at his own enormous family, there was a lot to be said for growing up with parents and a few brothers and sisters to knock around with.

To break the awkward silence, Christian said, "If I am married, it has to be voidable. There was force on both sides."

Thorn shook his head. "It's never easy. There might be something about consummation being necessary when the vows take place outside of a church. . . ."

"We definitely did not."

"If someone took her virginity, that's hard to prove."

"I didn't have my father's consent," Christian said. "Surely that counts for something."

"No. That was the main point of Hardwicke's reform — to give parents control over the marriage of minors, and prevent secret weddings through banns, openness, and true consent." He gripped Christian's arm. "Don't worry. We'll sort this out. Now, what documents do you have?"

Christian thought about it. "None."

"None?"

"I stalked out of there in high dudgeon without a scrap of paper. I can't even remember the name of the parson who did the deed."

Thorn rolled his eyes.

"I was sixteen!"

"If they hanged people for arrant stupidity — which might be a good idea — you'd still hang. God only knows where any record is lodged, or even if the man bothered to pass his records on to a bishop. What about witnesses? Who were they?"

"Half the people in the damn inn. What was it called? The Tup, I think. Somewhere near Doncaster."

"I am positively drowning in useful details."

"The aunt was there," Christian said. "If she's still a Froggatt, she'll be easily found. No sane man would marry her, that's for sure."

"It's astonishing who will marry whom, but if the aunt is behind the inquiries, we may not want to go directly to her. If that clergyman didn't file his records, you could deny the marriage took place."

"Lie?" Christian said. "In any case, there were all those witnesses."

"Ah, yes. Pity, that."

"You'd feel no honorable qualms?"

"You didn't bed her," Thorn said, "you haven't sired children on her who'd be bastardized, and the alternatives are disastrous." He went to his desk to make notes. "Where exactly did this happen? The Tup, you said? In Doncaster?"

"No, near. Hell, I don't remember." Christian tried to run his hand through his hair but only dislodged the damn powdered wig. "We were billeted in Doncaster and it was a few miles away in the direction of Sheffield. Nether something or other."

"The back end of somewhere?" Thorn queried, brows raised.

"Or privy parts. Greasy ones . . ."

"What?"

Christian pulled his wits together. "Nether Greasebutt!"

"Nether Greasebutt?" Thorn echoed.

"Something like that. Damn funny names up there. But don't worry about that. I'll recognize it. I'm going to investigate the nether regions for myself."

Thorn straightened. "Unwise."

"Look, either I'm legally married or I'm not. Going there won't change that. But someone needs to make inquiries on the spot, and it might as well be me. I can get leave. I might remember more when I'm there."

"This could stir the very corpse you're trying to keep interred."

"How? I'm not going there as Jack Hill. I'm Lord Grandiston now. No one will know I'm in the army when I'm wearing civilian clothes."

"And if Dorcas and her aunt know or suspect that Jack Hill is now Lord Grandiston, heir to the Earl of Royland?"

"Devil take it." Christian paced again. "Very well, I'll be *Mr.* Grandiston. If they do recognize the name, I'll have reason for my investigations. I'm a concerned relative of Jack Hill, seeking the truth of an old incident."

"Ever the hothead," Thorn sighed. "If you encounter the Froggatts — Abigail or Dorcas — won't they recognize you?"

"I was a stripling in uniform with powdered hair."

"Your eyes?"

Christian knew what Thorn meant. His eyes were a green-gold hazel that women tended to remember.

"Half the family has 'em. But in any case, I doubt anyone in that debacle was noting eyes."

# CHAPTER 3

*Luttrell House, near Sheffield, Yorkshire*
"He had extraordinary eyes," said Caro Hill, putting aside the letter from the Horse Guards and picking up her chocolate cup.

She was with her companion, Ellen Spencer, in the elegant morning room of her home, where sun shone in through the diamond-paned windows that provided a tranquil view of orderly gardens. In her mind, however, she saw a squalid, crowded inn room, a bloody corpse, and the blood-stained young officer who had been forced to marry her.

"I wonder what he remembers of me."

"Nothing," said Ellen, without looking up from her own correspondence. "He's dead."

Caro grimaced. There Ellen sat, in perfect order from her brown hair beneath a neat cap to side-by-side feet in polished shoes, insisting that everything else in the world was as neatly arranged as she, when it

60

clearly wasn't. Perhaps passing forty brought placidity, though Caro couldn't help believing that Ellen had been born that way.

"Ellen, I want to marry, so I must be sure of that."

Ellen glanced up, looking over half-moon glasses. "You received a letter of condolence from his colonel."

"As I've said before, anyone can write a letter."

"And as I have said before, your aunt Abigail was capable of a great many things, but even she would not falsify an official document."

But Caro wondered, and had wondered for some time. To Abigail Froggatt, everything was like the crucible steel that made the family fortune — malleable if one applied the right force.

"Do you really believe that?" she asked quietly.

Ellen looked up again, lips pursed, perhaps in irritation. "She did have her own notions of what was right."

"Like forcing that marriage. Even she admitted that it might have been a mistake."

"Did she? How odd. If there'd been a child, marriage would have been salvation for you and the little one. She acted decisively, as she did in business matters. You must never forget that she ensured the comfort we enjoy today."

It was the stern voice of the governess, which Ellen had been in Caro's younger years, and it was the truth. Caro wouldn't be living the life of a lady on a lovely estate without her aunt's grim determination and hard work.

Because of Aunt Abigail, Froggatt's cutlery works had been one of the first in Sheffield to adopt crucible steel, which others said was too hard to shape. It proved worth it, however, because it made stronger blades, and soon money had begun to pour in.

Aunt Abigail had not approved of Caro's father attempting to join the gentry by buying Luttrell House and moving his wife and daughter there. Or when he'd enrolled Caro in the Doncaster Academy for the Daughters of Gentlemen. Or when Caro had begun using her second name instead of her grandmother's name — Dorcas. Aunt Abigail had called her Dorcas to her dying day.

Perhaps Abigail Froggatt had been right to disapprove. Only a year after moving to Luttrell House, Caro's mother had died of pneumonia. "That big drafty place," had been Aunt Abigail's opinion. Not long afterward, her father had followed from an apoplexy Aunt Abigail had put down to too much rich food. At that point Froggatt's looked likely to collapse.

Abigail Froggatt had taken over the management. Everyone had predicted disaster, but the works had increased in prosperity, helped by the long war with France. Froggatt blades were shipped around the world, and even then, Aunt Abigail had been introducing the manufacture of excellent steel springs, looking ahead to times of peace.

Aunt Abigail had lived out her life in the small house by the works, but she'd been grimly determined to fulfill her brother's dreams. Luttrell House had been retained, "Dorcas" had continued at school, and after the Moore disaster, a suitable governess had been hired.

Ellen Spencer was the impoverished widow of a clergyman, but she came from a gentry family and had a brother who was a dean at York Cathedral. She'd been able to teach Caro basic subjects, but also to continue her education in the ways of the gentry. In that respect, Ellen's training had been limited, as she disapproved of social frivolities, but Aunt Abigail had also engaged music and art instructors, and even a French dancing master.

*If a thing's worth doing,* she always said, *it's*

*worth doing well.*

Yes, having forced that marriage, Aunt Abigail had been capable of doing anything to do it well — even forgery.

"What exactly does the letter say?" Ellen asked, putting aside her own reading with a slightly martyred air. Caro knew it was the latest letter from the social reformer Lady Fowler. Ellen always read those with avid attention.

"That I've given them insufficient information. I don't see why."

" 'Jack Hill' is a common name."

"How many Jack Hills were officers? How many Jack Hills were sixteen in 1754 and died 1756 in Canada?"

"Cogent points," Ellen agreed, frowning.

"There's something else. Aunt Abigail constantly advised me against marriage."

"And very odd it was, too. Quite unchristian."

"But based on reason. A woman such as myself, with independent control of a substantial income, risks losing everything that way."

"Women are not supposed to have independent control of their income," said Ellen.

"You control yours."

"A pittance."

"I pay you more than a pittance." Caro turned from that diversion. "My point is that when I attracted suitors, she became quite fierce about it. She used to point out every story of an oppressed wife, or of a husband who lost all at dice or cards. On her deathbed, she even tried to compel me to promise never to marry."

"Caro! You never mentioned that."

"What point? I refused, of course. It distressed her, which I regretted, but I would not bend. But what if her urgency, her distress, was because she'd fabricated the news of Hill's death?"

"And feared *bigamy?* Oh dear, oh dear. You must consult Sir Eyam."

"Tell the sordid truth to the man I want to marry?" Caro protested. "Bad enough that he knows the official story, that I eloped with a young officer who died soon after in the service of the king. To question that death is to question all."

"Perhaps it's time to trust him with the truth."

"No," Caro said. "And you must not, either."

She dearly wished Ellen didn't know, but it had probably been necessary. She'd been such a distressed waif when Ellen had first come here.

"Of course not," Ellen said, but though discretion was sacred to her, so was truth. If anyone directly questioned her, could she lie?

"Give me that letter," Ellen said with the manner of one who could sort this out in a moment. She read it quickly. "They ask about Hill's regiment. Why didn't you tell them?"

"I don't remember it. Moore didn't march around announcing it."

"Caro, it will be in the letter informing you of his death."

"Lud, so it will!" Caro rose, but then said, "I don't know where it is." She put a hand to her head, trying to remember. "It was so many years ago. I recall Aunt Abigail came up here with it. . . ."

"She insisted on speaking with you privately," Ellen said. "I remember that."

"I read it. . . ."

"And?"

"And I felt nothing. I was ashamed of that. No — of feeling relief. Dead so young, and he had dashed in to save me." She twisted the wedding ring on her finger. Not the one Jack Hill had put there in the ceremony. That had been cheap metal and had left a mark even after only a few hours' wear.

"I mean," said Ellen, irritated, "what

became of the letter?"

Caro came back to the present, picturing the event. "Aunt Abigail took it back. Yes. I didn't want it, so she took it away with her."

"Where would she have put it?"

"With her own letters, I assume. Where did we put them?" Caro thought back two years to the time when she'd dealt with all her aunt's possessions. "In the library!"

She ran across the hall, removed the wooden box from a cupboard, and carried it to the central table to search. This didn't contain any business papers — they were stored at Froggatt's — but it held her aunt's letters and other personal papers.

She put aside invoices, lists, and household account books to concentrate on letters. There weren't many.

Ellen came in. "Have you found it?"

Caro put aside another letter from someone called Mary, who had written from Bristol, and who seemed to have married a ship captain.

"No. And now I'm at letters twenty years old and more. Where else could it be?"

Ellen began to search for herself, but then stood back. "Perhaps she destroyed it. Once it had served its purpose."

Caro sank into the wooden chair. "Because it didn't bear close scrutiny."

Ellen rested a hand on her shoulder, consolation in a time of tragedy.

Caro rebelled. She rose to her feet, saying, "I won't give up hope. How do I find out which regiment? It was stationed around Doncaster for some months. . . . I'll visit Phyllis and make inquiries."

Her friend Phyllis Ossington had recently moved to Doncaster with her husband, a solicitor.

Ellen began to tidy the papers back into the box. "It will look strange that a widow not know. Why not use Hambledon again?"

Hambledon, Truscott and Bull were the York solicitors Aunt Abigail had chosen to manage Caro's affairs.

"I will," Caro said, "but it will be easier for me to visit Doncaster, and I can be discreet. Oh, why, why, *why* does this have to be such a tangle?"

"Because you allowed yourself to be fooled by a rascally charmer," Ellen said, locking the box and replacing it in its place.

Caro wanted to protest, but it was true. "Moore was buried in Nether Greasley."

"Moore?" Ellen asked, as if she'd never heard the name.

"The rascally charmer. I remember Aunt Abigail saying that no one had claimed his body — with relish. She was never a good enemy. His sister, my teacher at the academy, had fled the area."

"Overcome with shame and grief at having encouraged such wickedness."

"Perhaps, but she'd also been dismissed from her post and had Abigail Froggatt out for her blood. So with no one to claim his body, Moore was buried there. There may not be a stone, but the church records should contain the details."

Ellen nodded. "There, see. Easy enough. If you had only thought before . . ."

Caro cut that off. "I can't bear to wait. We'll travel to Doncaster today."

"So impulsive, Caro. But it will be good to have it settled so we may all be comfortable."

"That will only be the first step. What if Horse Guards have no record of Hill's death?"

"Caro, stop poking around this as if it were a wasps' nest."

Caro whirled to face her. "But that's exactly what it feels like! Have you thought of the implications? If Hill is alive, he's my *husband.* Jack Hill, stranger, could walk in here and take complete control of my life. The business, my money, myself. He could be a drunkard, or gamester, or foully diseased, and I would have *absolutely no re-*

*course!*"

Ellen blanched. "Oh, dear. But isn't the business protected, at least?"

"How can you worry about the *business?*" Caro shrieked, then put a hand to her face.

"Caro, my dear —"

"I'm sorry, I'm sorry," Caro said, lowering her hand. "But though you might have pleasant memories of marital matters, Ellen, I cannot."

"I would not say quite pleasant," Ellen said, pink in her cheeks. "Oh, dear. But nothing to fuss about, I assure you. I'm sure what happened to you wasn't pleasant at all. . . ."

"Ellen —"

"And Sir Eyam . . ."

"Ellen!"

"Very well, very well. But before rushing off to Doncaster, why not look through the papers at Froggatt's? Your aunt might have put the letter there."

Caro was convinced by now that the letter had been a forgery, but she had to try. "An excellent idea. I'll do that now. I'll do my monthly inspection of the works and the books at the same time. Then we can travel on —"

But then she heard wheels on the gravel drive.

70

Caro hurried to the window. As she'd feared, it was Sir Eyam Colne in his stylish curricle. "Perish it," she muttered.

Normally she'd be delighted, but today she felt Sir Eyam would read all her secrets in her face. He was such a perfect gentleman, and she an imperfect lady.

"Oh, it's Sir Eyam!" Ellen declared. "And you all over dust, Caro. Hurry, hurry to tidy yourself. I'll entertain him." She bustled out, and Caro ran upstairs to her bedchamber.

There was only cold water in her jug, but that sufficed for her hands and dust-smudged face. Caro checked her hair in the mirror, but it was so curly she had to dress it in plaits and use many pins to keep it tidy, and it rarely escaped. She hadn't dressed for guests, so her outfit was a plain brown skirt with no hoops beneath and a warm caraco jacket. The jacket was woven in pretty autumn colors, however, and was one of her favorites. It would do.

She looked nothing like that poor child. For a year or so she'd stayed thin despite fortifying broths and jellies, but then like a bud in warm weather, she'd blossomed. She'd gradually developed womanly curves and a healthier complexion. Her first reaction had been dismay, she remembered, for it had drawn the attention of men. She'd outgrown that discomfort, too, and now, at last, she was ready for the culmination — marriage.

She *wanted* to marry, and she'd found the perfect man. Sir Eyam was everything she respected in a gentleman, and yet . . .

It was as if her probing into that painful event had stirred fears.

To overcome dark memories, she'd acquired some books — the sort ladies were not supposed to even know about. They were embarrassing and at times odd, but they did suggest that there was more to the matter than short, brutal pain. Considering peculiar illustrations, Caro sometimes thought short would be preferable as long as she was willing and Eyam was gentle.

It was, after all, necessary for children.

That was her goal. She had two friends now who were married with little ones, and any visit made her longings worse. She'd begun to have strange dreams in which she was seeking lost babies, or suddenly acquiring them and not knowing how to care for them. Once it had been a plaster baby that she left out in the rain. . . .

She shook all that from her mind and went downstairs. She would marry Eyam, become Lady Colne of Colne Court, and fill a nursery with happy, healthy children. Eyam would be a perfect husband, and as he was quite wealthy himself, she was certain he wasn't wooing her for her fortune.

She paused halfway down the stairs. What had happened to that short marriage settlement drawn up after her wedding? Where had Aunt Abigail put that? If Hill was alive, did it at least safeguard her fortune? If not, the business built by her father and grandfather, and by Aunt Abigail, could be lost in one night on a hand of cards.

Something similar had happened to a wealthy widow only a few years ago. Harriet Webley had succumbed to a charming gallant and wedded him without legal safeguards. He'd spent everything and then run off, leaving poor Harriet to eke out her life in one small room on the charity of friends.

Caro didn't want to see Eyam with her mind in such a state, but she must. She forced a bright smile and went to the morning room. Her smile turned genuine as she went to her suitor, hands held out.

He was only a little taller than herself, but well made. His dark brown hair was neatly dressed and tied back. He was always elegantly dressed, but she could see he'd taken special care for this courting visit. His cobalt blue coat and breeches and ecru waistcoat were a little too fine for a country drive.

He took both hands and raised them to within an inch of his lips — correct in everything. If she could only say yes, his lips would finally touch, and all would be perfect.

"I have come unannounced, I know," he said, "but are you free to drive out with me? Some trees at Colne are just beginning to show color and present a pretty vista on a sunny day."

Caro wavered. The search for the document could wait another day — but if she went, Eyam would propose again and she couldn't say yes until she was sure she was free.

"I do wish I could," she said, "but I'm about to visit the works."

He frowned slightly. "Do you not do that at the end of the month?"

"Normally, yes, but there are some special matters to discuss." She realized that there were. She must not leave the family business vulnerable to a rapacious Hill. "I want to sell my half of Froggatt and Skellow."

She saw Ellen stare, which wasn't surprising when Caro had never mentioned such a thing, but Eyam smiled. He assumed it was in preparation for marriage, and so it would be, she hoped.

"Any part I play is merely symbolic," Caro said. "I wasn't raised to run the business, so since my aunt's death, Sam Skellow has been doing all the work. It's only right to offer him the chance to own it all."

"Then I surrender my claim," Eyam said graciously. "The trees will be as pretty tomorrow."

"I knew you'd understand." But then Caro thought about Doncaster. If she didn't find the letter at Froggatt's, she must go there. "But alas, tomorrow won't do, either. I'm to visit my friend Phyllis Ossington in Doncaster."

He frowned. "Do you have to go?"

She linked arms with him and led him out. "She's with child again and they haven't been in Doncaster for many months." Both were true, but Phyllis was in robust health and was enjoying her new home.

"And you have a kind heart," he said, smiling again. "I suppose I must grow used to sharing you a little of the time."

The hint of their future made her blush. "Not too often, I hope."

He looked at her intently. "Caro, my dear . . ."

She'd opened the way to this.

". . . when will you make me the happiest

of men?"

Life would be perfect if she could say "now." "Soon, Eyam, I hope."

"What can I say to wipe away your doubts?"

"Nothing. It's . . . I must be sure."

"I know you loved your youthful husband. You must have, to have acted so rashly. But it's been ten years."

"I know. Please, Eyam. You see that I'm putting my affairs in order."

He chuckled. "Caro, my dear, that sounds as if you expect to die."

"Oh, you. But indeed, Caro Hill will cease to be when she becomes Caro, Lady Colne. Soon," she added, then realized it was more of a promise than she could make. "Soon we will talk seriously about all this. When I return from Doncaster."

He sighed. "I must agree, then. Return soon, Caro."

"I will," she said.

She waved him off, ordered her carriage brought round, and returned to Ellen. "We'll have our valises packed and be off."

Ellen picked up her letter. "I shall take this to Joan Cross. I know she'll find it interesting."

Caro suppressed a grimace. Lady Fowler collected money and supporters for her movement to reform London society. Ellen had been introduced to it earlier in the year and become quite avid. Caro wouldn't mind, but Ellen kept attempting to convert her and get her to donate large sums to the cause. Caro was as willing as anyone, perhaps more so, to abhor wastrels, seducers, and fornicators, but she liked the theater and dancing and even card games, when played for modest sums.

All she said, however, was, "You to your worthy work, Ellen, I to mine."

Worthy work, Caro thought later, as she finished her tour of the hot and noisy building, and dirty as well. She kept a plain overdress and mobcap in the adjoining house to cover her clothes and hair during these visits, and they were needed. Aunt Abigail would turn in her grave, but Caro would be delighted never to visit again.

She finished, as always, in the offices, reviewing the account books, and then she asked Sam Skellow to bring any papers her aunt had left here.

He didn't question her. He never did. Though he was her partner here, he'd started out as an apprentice to her grandfather and worked his way up. To him, the Froggatts were still the masters.

Earlier, she'd hunted through the house her aunt had lived in. As expected, she'd found no papers there at all. Though it was kept ready for use by herself or Sam Skellow, it was a furnished shell.

Sam brought a box of papers and left her with them. They were in such excellent order that it didn't take Caro a quarter hour to be sure that a letter announcing Jack Hill's death wasn't there, nor was the marriage settlement.

But now she realized such a settlement might be in the hands of her lawyers. Perhaps the letter was, too. She'd write to Hambledon.

Sam Skellow returned. "Sommat the matter, dear?"

Caro looked up. "Only a small family matter I was hoping to sort out. The business is in fine order, as always."

He bobbed his head in a gesture much closer to touching his forelock to her than a bow. He still spoke with the local accent, but his sons had attended the grammar school and were moving into gentry ways. Perhaps Henry Skellow's children would dance at assemblies in York with hers and Eyam's.

Caro turned completely to face him. "If I were to offer to sell my share, Uncle Sam, would you be able to buy it? Or is there someone else you'd want as partner?"

His eyes widened, and a touch of color in his cheeks might be anger, enthusiasm, or embarrassment. "Thee doesn't want to sell, does thee, dear?"

Brushing dirt off her overgown and aware of the endless din of the place, Caro meant it when she said, "Yes."

"But thee could marry. Thee sons . . ."

". . . are likely to be gentlemen with no knowledge of the trade. You'd not want them dabbling here, would you?"

He didn't argue. It was probably a nightmare thought. Even so, he shook his head. "It'll be a reet sad day not to have a Froggatt involved, but if thee's sure, then yes, I could find t'money. My Elizabeth's husband would probably join us."

Caroline hadn't thought of that. Uncle Sam's oldest daughter was Caro's age but four years married to a master cutler with a small company of his own.

"Skellow and Bramley. A good match."

"Aye, but think it over carefully afore doing sommat to regret."

"I will, I promise, but my interests lie elsewhere."

"In a fine baronet?" Sam asked, his eyes twinkling.

Caroline knew she blushed. "Perhaps."

Caro left the works through a door that led into the adjoining house, feeling as if she'd shed one burden. Yes, whatever the outcome of her marital entanglements, she'd made one right decision and she'd complete the matter as quickly as possible. If — heaven forfend — Jack Hill was alive and attempted to claim her assets, Froggatt's would be safe.

She'd include this house in her share of the business. Three servants maintained it because Caro hadn't been willing to let it fall into neglect, but it needed a family here. As she followed a narrow, gloomy corridor toward the front hall and the stairs up to the bedchambers, she wondered if the works foreman would like to live here.

She had turned to go up the stairs when behind her the door knocker rapped.

"I'll get it!" she called to the housemaid in the distant kitchen, and opened the door.

A man stood there.

Tall, fashionably dressed, sword on hip — but Caro truly saw only eyes of green, gold, and brown.

She shut the door in the man's face, leaning back against it, her heart hammering with panic.

Aunt Abigail had lied.

80

Jack Hill wasn't dead.

Instead, like a demon summoned from hell, he was knocking at her door!

# CHAPTER 4

The man at the door wasn't in uniform, she told herself, recalling that brief glimpse. He was tall and robust, not slender and young.

But she *recognized* those eyes.

She couldn't think.

She couldn't think. . . .

Had he recognized her? Why should he? Her gray overdress and mobcap must make her look like a maid, and she had no such distinguishing features. Dare she take another look? Maybe she was so wrapped up in this matter that she'd imagined the eyes? She inhaled a few times, gathered her nerve, and opened the door again.

The man was still there, brows raised in haughty surprise.

Blond hair. He'd been powdered back then.

A man's strong-boned face, not a youth's. But time had passed.

Tall. Had that young soldier been so tall?

But the eyes, the eyes. She wasn't imagining the eyes.

She had to say something. "Yes, sir?" she asked in the flattest local accent she could summon.

He was staring, but she could tell it was because of her strange behavior and not recognition.

"I wish to speak to Miss Froggatt."

He spoke in a cool, crisp accent, as she remembered Jack Hill had done. A voice from the south, and from the upper reaches of society, where power dwelled.

"She's dead," Caro said, and began to close the door.

He put out a hand to block her. "When?"

"Two years back."

"Then I wish to speak to whoever lives here now."

"None does." She pushed the door, but against his strength she couldn't budge it. "I'll yell for some o't'lads from t'works!" Caro cried, pushing harder. "Geroff it."

His lips tightened, but he was stepping back when Ellen came out of the parlor. "What's going on?"

Caro whirled to face her, grimacing desperately as a clue. "Some gentlemun as wants Miss Froggatt, m'um. I told 'im she were dead, that none lives 'ere anymore, but 'e won't go away."

Ellen stood there, clearly at a loss, but deep-rooted propriety took over. "That is correct, sir. Miss Abigail Froggatt is sadly deceased. May I be of assistance?"

"Thank you, ma'am. My name is Grandiston. . . ."

Caro turned to stare at him before she thought better of it. Not Hill? She hastily looked away before he noticed her attention.

". . . though in truth, I'm seeking the lady's niece, Dorcas Froggatt."

Ellen blinked and glanced once toward Caro. Caro grimaced again, wishing she could violently shake her head. Not Hill, but who?

Remarkably, Ellen bent the truth. "She's not here, either."

"Also dead?"

*Say yes, say yes, say yes!*

A bald lie was beyond Ellen, however. "I must know your business, sir, before answering."

"Then perhaps we could discuss this out of the doorway, ma'am?"

True, they were all clustered around the open door, and in the street two shawled women had paused to see if anything interesting was going on.

Ellen glanced helplessly at Caro, but then turned and led the way into the parlor. The man followed, and Caro closed the front door. She longed to flee, but if she behaved oddly, he might notice and wonder just who the maid had been.

He said his name was Grandiston, not Hill.

Those eyes? She hadn't dared study them, but that first impression couldn't have been entirely wrong.

The only logical explanation was that he was a relation. Not wonderful, but not her husband here to seize her. But what could he want? She inched forward to hover by the door.

Ellen was saying, ". . . your interest in the Froggatt family?"

"A personal matter, ma'am."

Caro moved another step so she could see.

Ellen had sat on the settee and Grandiston was in the chair opposite. He was wearing brown leather riding breeches and boots, a snuff brown jacket, paler waistcoat, and a soft cravat without lace. A very ordinary outfit, but not an ordinary gentleman. He was highborn, as Hill had been, and he sought her.

Perhaps she moved, for he glanced to the side and saw her.

Those eyes!

Ellen followed his gaze. "Oh, Ca— Carrie! Do you think tea is ready?"

Caro was both relieved and frustrated. Ellen had covered Caro's hovering and her own mistake with the name, but now Caro would have to go for the tea and miss what was said.

She bobbed a curtsy and hurried toward the kitchens. Sukey Grubb, eleven years old and fresh from the foundling home, was scrubbing a pot under the supervision of ancient Hannah Lovetott in her rocking chair. Hannah had worked here for thirty years, and nowadays her position as housekeeper was more of a pension than a job. Both servants stared at her dress.

"I'm playing a trick on a guest," Caro said. "The tea tray, please, and I'm going to serve it."

The old woman looked heavenward, but she told the girl to pour boiling water into the waiting pot. Everything was ready save that and cakes to be put on a plate. Caro did that, trying to think things through.

Was Grandiston here on behalf of Jack Hill? Or was he Jack Hill himself, hiding behind a false name? If the name was false, it suited him. There was grandeur in every line of his large body, in the way he sat, in the sword at his hip and his direct eyes. He expected by right to be master, even here in someone else's home.

She looked at the back door.

She could escape. Be safe.

But that might make him wonder, and she couldn't abandon Ellen.

No, he couldn't be her husband, for he'd have no reason to use a false name. He had all the power on his side.

The tray was ready and she picked it up. She was going to find out what was going on, but until she was sure she was a widow and free of all entanglements, the arrogant Mr. Grandiston must have no idea who she was.

Ellen Spencer had entered the parlor powerfully aware of the man behind her. She was not a fanciful woman, but it had been like having danger at one's back. He might lack a title, but he was highest of the high or she was a bishop's widow.

What had Caro been up to, to throw her into such a panic?

There was a streak of wildness in Caro — only consider her youthful folly! — and an element Ellen could think of only as earthy. It came from her Froggatt blood, and Ellen feared that no amount of training would remove it.

It had been wrong for Daniel Froggatt to want his daughter to move in high circles, for they were rife with idleness and sin, as Lady Fowler illustrated again and again in her missives. Society gave too many opportunities for folly and clearly Caro had succumbed. It was for Ellen to save her.

She sat and gestured Mr. Grandiston to a chair. "Now, sir, your business?"

But as he faced her directly for the first time, she saw green-gold eyes of a very uncommon sort. Angels of mercy — was this monster Caro's long-lost husband? But the name . . .

"As I said, ma'am, a personal matter. Therefore I need to know your name, ma'am, and your connection to the Froggatts."

She saw no way to refuse. "I am Mistress Spencer, Mistress Hill's companion. Mistress Hill was once Dorcas Froggatt."

"Mistress Hill," he repeated. His eyes had widened in a way that sent a shiver down her spine. She wished there were a man in the house to summon if this one turned violent.

*Caro, come back and tell me what to do!*

"You and Mistress Hill live here?" he asked. "The maid indicated that this house was uninhabited."

Ellen opened her mouth to explain, but she mustn't tell him about Luttrell House or he'd be banging on that door next. She was going to have to lie.

Begging forgiveness ahead of time, she said, "You must have misunderstood, sir. She doubtless meant only that Mistress Hill is away. Now, your purpose?"

Ellen tried to make that a demand, to be formidable. She even tried to resurrect memories of Abigail Froggatt, who would doubtless not have allowed this man over the threshold, and certainly wouldn't have tolerated this bullying. He wasn't daunted at all and she braced for attack.

However, he merely said, "I have come to discuss some legal matters with the lady. Legal matters arising out of her marriage to Lieutenant Jack Hill."

Legal matters. It had to be a will. Jack Hill's will, and the way he'd phrased the statement meant that he wasn't Jack Hill himself. Whether Abigail Froggatt had lied or not, Caro was free now. Safe, and able to marry Sir Eyam. Ellen felt quite breathless with relief.

"Thus, I must speak with Mistress Hill," he reminded her.

What to do, what to say? Impossible to

89

reveal Caro's presence in the house without her permission. "I'm afraid that isn't possible at this moment."

"Why not?"

Ellen's mind went blank. "Because I don't know where she is."

That was true. She could be upstairs or downstairs, or already escaped elsewhere.

His brows rose in doubt. Oh dear, oh dear. She was going to have to lie again. "She is traveling," Ellen said.

"Where?"

"I'm not sure. She likes to wander."

The brows rose higher.

*Caro, help!*

Suddenly he smiled — a slightly rueful smile that was almost boyish. "I'm distressing you, Mistress Spencer, and that wasn't my intent. Please forgive me. It is only that I have little time to complete my errand. Of your kindness, can you assist me?"

Ellen experienced an extraordinary melting effect that slid her toward doing anything, absolutely anything, she could to oblige him. And realized that was precisely his intent!

"I'm sure I would if I could, sir," she said frostily, "but all I can promise is that as soon as I hear from Mistress Hill, I will inform her of your request. What direction should I give her?"

"I'm currently at the Angel."

"Here? In Sheffield? I mean to say . . . you said you had little time."

"I can afford a few days. Will contacting Mistress Hill take longer?"

"How can I tell?" Ellen wished she had some ancient power to drive him out of Yorkshire. She tried a smile of her own. "Can you not give me a hint of the situation, sir? After all, Mistress Hill has been a widow for some years and to the best of my knowledge has heard nothing from her husband's family. It was, I gather, a foolish elopement."

Because she was watching him carefully, she saw something — a blink, no more.

"She was informed of his death, then," he said.

"But of course. By his colonel."

"Ah. Yet she made no attempt to contact his family."

"No?" Ellen said vaguely. "She was very young when she married, and the union was sadly brief."

"True, but the need to speak to the lady remains. Even wandering, she must have some destination." Even smiling, he was like a hunting dog sniffing the wind.

Ellen wanted him far, far away. "London,"

she said. "She is on her way to visit a friend there."

"How may I contact her there?"

The only London address Ellen knew was Lady Fowler's. . . .

At that moment Caro came in, bearing the large tea tray, still in her dusty, works-inspection overdress, mobcap pulled down so the brim flopped over her face.

"Here thee be, m'um!" she said, vastly overdoing the gormless servant. "Where'll I put it, then?"

Ellen would rather like to faint. "On the table by my hand, er . . . Carrie." She smiled at Grandiston, hoping it didn't look like a grimace. "I do apologize, sir. Carrie is newly arrived from a . . . local institution. We're training her in domestic service."

Caro had her back to him — or her posterior, to be more precise, as she was bending to place the tray. She shot Ellen a wild-eyed, laughter-filled look.

Ellen felt heat rush to her cheeks. She'd almost said "foundling home," but Caro was far too old for that. Her hesitation and the word "institution" had probably led him to think she'd been rescued from a life of sin!

"From the local Bedlam," Ellen corrected brightly. Then knew that was even worse.

Caro backed away, biting her cheeks

against laughter, but instead of leaving, she took up a station against the wall behind Grandiston's chair. Outrageously bold! But Ellen could understand her need to know what was said here. As she stirred the pot, Ellen planned how to share the excellent news.

"Milk, sir? Sugar?"

At his request she added a little milk. Next, she offered him currant cake. He took a piece.

"As Jack Hill is *dead*," Ellen said, for Caro's benefit, "I assume your business here relates to his will?"

"To a number of matters," he countered, drinking tea. "As the lady is still Mistress Hill, I assume she hasn't married again?"

"Oh, no."

Ellen risked a quick glance at Caro, who was in rapt attention. Ellen set to squeezing more information. "You are a cousin, sir?"

"One of the family. London, you say. Do you have her direction there?"

"She was to send it. You've traveled up from the south, I gather?"

"Perhaps I passed Mistress Hill en route." He took a bite of currant cake, revealing strong, straight teeth.

"Perhaps," Ellen agreed. She glanced at

93

Caro, hoping she'd reveal herself, but she didn't.

"You must enjoy this area while you're here," Ellen said, and embarked on a list of local features, not allowing him any opportunity to interrupt. As soon as he'd finished his tea, she rose. "If you give me your direction in the south, Mr. Grandiston, I will inform Mistress Hill how to reach you. When I hear from her, of course."

He also rose, as he must, but she'd forgotten how tall and broad he was. Now he loomed and his eyes commanded. "What is the name of the friend Mistress Hill is to visit in London?"

Ellen was tempted to say, "The Marchioness of Rothgar" to scare him off. Caro did know that great lady through her charity work, but Ellen doubted even that name would make him quake.

"I don't know," she said.

"I find that hard to believe."

"Well, really! I will not be badgered, sir. Please leave."

Instead, he stepped forward. "And I will not abandon my mission." Ellen tried to step back, but the settee was right behind her. "You, ma'am, are concealing Mistress Hill's whereabouts from me, and I will not allow it."

"Well, really!" Ellen expostulated again, feeling the phrase's inadequacy.

"For what reason?"

*"Reason?"* Ellen exclaimed. "Given your atrocious bullying manner, sir, I see *every* reason. When I do hear from Mistress Hill, I shall warn her to avoid you at all cost!"

Behind him, Caro mouthed, *Bravo!*

Grandiston's jaw clenched. "Perhaps you have reason for your discretion, ma'am. I was given to understand that the lady might be somewhat lacking in her faculties. If so, I do understand, but —"

Ellen had been gaping, but now she shrieked, *"How dare you?"* Punctuating the word with a straight-armed, pointing finger, she snapped, *"Leave!"*

For a moment she thought he would refuse, that he might even seize her, but then he grabbed his hat and gloves and stalked out of the room. A moment later, the front door slammed.

Ellen collapsed back onto the settee, close to a faint, but Caro smothered a whoop of triumph and dashed to the window. "He's truly left!" She came back to sit on the chair he'd vacated. "You were splendid, Ellen! I didn't know you had it in you."

Hand to thumping chest, Ellen said, "I didn't, either. I don't know what came over me. So intemperate. But what an appalling bully of a man. I'm sure he's exactly the sort of specimen Lady Fowler describes as haunting fashionable London and seducing maids to their ruin. Thank heavens he's not your husband."

Caro tensed. "You're sure of that?"

"Oh, yes, yes. The name. And he as good as said that Hill is dead. Such good news."

"That a man is dead?"

"I know a death must sadden us, but it was long ago, and you are *free*."

Caro took a piece of currant cake, frowning. "What of the eyes?"

"Plate, dear." Ellen pushed one over. "Such things are often a family trait."

Caro ate. "I was wondering whether he might have given a false name at the ceremony."

"Surely not."

"No one could blame him."

"For lying on oath? For that is what marriage vows amount to."

"He had just killed a man."

Ellen shuddered. "Vile, vile. You must not fall into his hands."

"All very well, but how do I avoid it?" Caro picked up another cake and took a bite. She had the weakness of eating when under strain, but perhaps it was excusable now. "If he asks questions in town — and he will — he'll soon know Mistress Hill isn't away. He'll find out about Luttrell House and hound me there."

"Oh, dear. But if he's not your husband, he has no power."

"But why is he here, then? After ten years?"

"Perhaps Hill has only just died. Or his family has only just learned of the wedding. As Hill's widow you could be entitled to part of his estate."

"That would be appalling!"

"What very strange things you find appalling."

"To inherit family money or property, simply because that poor young man was forced into marrying me?"

"Really, Caro —"

But Caro frowned into the distance. "I feel I should grieve. No, I am grieving. Jack Hill saved me, and he seemed an honorable young man, and now he's dead."

"But now you're free to marry Sir Eyam. You should meet with this Grandiston and sort it all out."

Caro took another bite of cake. "What if he's Jack Hill's heir? You point out that as widow I might have rights, but a husband also has rights to his wife's property." The cake threatened to choke her. "Dear Lord, he *owns* her property. His heir might inherit it!"

Ellen gaped. "Everything? Are you suggesting that if Grandiston is Hill's heir, he might have inherited everything you own? Might be able to throw us out of Luttrell House?"

"Might own my share of Froggatt and Skellow."

"You must go instantly to Sir Eyam, Caro. Tell him all. You need a man's advice."

"I need a *lawyer's* advice." Caro tossed down the fragment of cake. "I'm going to York, to Mr. Hambledon."

"Oh, yes. Just the thing. We can order a chaise immediately."

"No." Caro went back to the window to peer around the edge. "He could be watching the house."

"Surely not."

"Would you say it was past him?"

"Oh dear. No."

"If you leave here with another lady, he'll instantly guess the truth. He seems capable of taking me captive and carrying me away south."

"That would never be allowed."

Caro wished that were true, but she remembered the Marchioness of Rothgar's

98

situation. That great lady of Yorkshire had become a friend of sorts as she and Caro had worked together on a number of charities directed at women. She'd held a title before her marriage, for she'd been Countess of Arradale then, in her own right. It was one of the few titles that could descend to a daughter. High rank had not protected her, however.

"Remember Diana Arradale," she said to Ellen. "She was forced to London and threatened with incarceration in an institution for the insane simply because she balked at marrying the man the king chose."

Ellen put a hand over her mouth. "And she is one of the most powerful women in England. But then what can we do?"

"Leave separately. You by the front door, I through the works. I'll go to Doncaster first. To Phyllis. That's on the York Road."

Ellen nodded. "Yes, that will do. We can be off shortly."

"Not us, Ellen. I told you, I can't be seen leaving here with you. Besides, I need you to return to Luttrell House and hold the fort."

"Caro, you can't travel alone!"

"I won't. I'm going by public coach."

"Caro!"

But Caro had grabbed the coaching guide

that sat on a table by the door. It opened to the Sheffield page. "The Doncaster coach leaves from the Angel."

"But that man's staying at the Angel."

"The wretch. But he doesn't know Caro Hill by sight."

"Everyone else does," Ellen pointed out.

Caro growled with frustration. "Someone would be sure to speak to me, address me by name. . . ." She turned slowly toward the mirror and studied herself. "No one would recognize Carrie, though."

"What do you mean?"

"I'm going to travel as Carrie the maid."

"Go abroad dressed like that. Caro, you can't."

"No one will know it's me. That's the point."

"But, but . . . what if that man questions you? Really . . ."

"I have to. You return to Luttrell House, but first send the clothes I packed for Doncaster on to Phyllis."

"But that man will invade again. Bully me again."

"You managed him splendidly, and there are ample servants at Luttrell. Quickly, give me some money."

Ellen pulled out her knit purse and poured out some coins, but she tried to impose reason. "If that man is Hill, there's no escape. Sometimes we must resign ourselves to divine will."

"Not," Caro said, "without a fight. I'm a wealthy woman with excellent advisers and I will not be handed over like a shackled slave." She looked in the mirror again and pulled her mobcap lower on her head, then headed for the door. "I'll leave through the works."

"Oh, dear, oh, dear. Be careful, Caro. On the coach, I mean. Unescorted . . ."

"Traveling alone on the coach is the least of my hazards," Caro said grimly, and ran off.

# CHAPTER 5

Christian stalked down the grimy street assailed by the din of the surrounding manufactories. They were presumably all cutlery forges, but they bore no resemblance to the village blacksmiths he was accustomed to, or even to the smithies associated with the army, constantly dinging with the repair of metal and blades.

He paused to look back at the Froggatt house and the nearby wall on which the name FROGGATT AND SKELLOW was declared in white paint. Gray paint, to be exact, because the whole of Sheffield was drawn in shades of gray and black by the never-ending smoke that seemed to be trapped by the surrounding hills. What a hellish place this was, and what a hellish situation he was in.

He was a married man.

He'd gone to the house merely to gather information, but he'd instead been stunned by the fact that his wife was alive. He might have doubted the lunatic maid, but not the other woman — the companion, Mistress Spencer.

He was married to Dorcas Froggatt, resident of that ugly, narrow house, a woman content to live surrounded by dirty air and the constant clamor of hammer on steel. She must have grown into a copy of her fearsome Froggatt aunt, right down to the belligerent manner and corn-grinding voice.

He sped his pace and broke free into a wider street, a normal street, lined with shops and traveled by vehicles of all kinds. Though he knew the air couldn't be significantly cleaner, he inhaled as if escaping fumes, and his head did clear. He began to assess what he'd learned like a military tactician instead of a panicked raw recruit. Facts were facts and could no more be denied than a cannonball.

Fact: Dorcas was alive.

Fact: she lived in that house.

But fact: she had a paid companion. A prim-faced middle-aged woman and somewhat timid until roused, but clearly a lady born and bred. That argued some gentility. And hadn't Moore seduced her away from school?

Mistress Spencer had become enraged at the suggestion that Dorcas was a lackwit, but it wouldn't be surprising after the events a decade ago, and truth sometimes enraged more than lies.

Insanity in a prominent family couldn't be hidden from a community, and despite the house, clearly the Froggatts were of some importance here. When he got back to the Angel, he'd set his servant, Barleyman, to poke and pry. He was a dab hand at getting common folk to talk.

He found Barleyman in the low-beamed taproom sipping from a tankard and chatting to the barman. Already on the job. Christian left him to it and went up to his room. He tossed his gloves and three-cornered hat onto a chair, and took off his sword belt, considering what to do next. Thorn's secretary had given him the name of a solicitor here. He'd go there and ask about Froggatts.

Barleyman came in. "Good fortune, sir?"

"Devil a bit. My wife's alive."

"Unfortunate, sir. You met the lady?"

"No. She's either insane and concealed, or off a-wandering."

"A-wandering, sir? Like the fool on the moor?"

"Traveling," Christian clarified, "probably

to London, but with no fixed itinerary. It's all very fishy. I spoke with a Mistress Spencer, who claimed to be her companion. Definitely a lady, yet they live in a mean house attached to the Froggatt cutlery works."

"Perhaps why your wife travels, sir."

"More sensible to move elsewhere. The Spencer woman was hiding something."

"Perhaps not unreasonable with an unexpected husband on the doorstep, sir."

"Except that I presented as Mr. Grandiston, a connection only, seeking Mistress Hill on a legal matter."

"Legal matters are naturally alarming to the weaker sex, sir."

"Weaker sex," Christian snorted. "You're too old for delusions."

"No chance the lady you spoke to was your wife, sir?"

Christian had to think for only a second. "None. She's in her forties at least. A timid type until she turned tiger and ordered me out of the house."

"Indeed, sir?" Barleyman had the impudence to disapprove.

"I did nothing wrong. Oh, very well, I was trying to bully my way past her barricade."

"Perhaps not the best approach to take, sir."

"Of course it wasn't, but I'd had a shock and she was infuriating. Stick to the point. Dorcas Froggatt is my wife and I need to find her."

"Lady Grandiston," Barleyman corrected, like a torturer driving something sharp beneath a fingernail.

Christian glared at him.

"Begging your pardon, sir, but if the lady is alive, she *is* Viscountess Grandiston."

"Hades!" Christian stalked to the window, tempted to smash the diamond panes.

A coach was loading out in the busy yard. Christian had an irrational urge to buy a ticket and leave with it. Perhaps to escape, or perhaps to attempt a wild-goose chase after his errant bride.

He turned back. "What did you find out downstairs?"

"Only a little, sir. Until I had your full instructions, I didn't want to show my interest. Word gets back."

"Good man."

"Fortunately, Froggatt and Skellow is a well-known business, having prospered by early adoption of some special steelmaking process."

"Crucible steel." Barleyman looked impressed, so Christian confessed. "I read up on Sheffield in preparation for this."

106

"Daniel Froggatt, the one who started to use the steel, unfortunately had no son. In fact he had only one child, she who is now known as Mistress Hill, having run away with an officer as a girl and been widowed by war not long afterward."

"No hint of murder and mayhem?"

"None, sir."

"The Fearsome Froggatt at work. At least Dorcas hasn't remarried. Any hint that she has bats in her belfry?"

"None, sir, but people do tend to be discreet about such things. The Froggatt family seems well respected. They're patrons of a number of benevolent causes hereabouts — a charity hospital, a foundling home, and an asylum for insane females."

"Aha!"

"I doubt they'd put a family member in such a place, sir."

"No, but they might take servants from it. No mention of where the lady is?"

"No, sir, but a question occurs to me. If the lady is traveling, why isn't her companion with her?"

Christian hit his head with his hand. "The shock addled my brains. Dorcas might have been in the house all the time? Get over there and see what you can discover."

Barleyman grabbed his hat. "I'm to report

back, or send a message?"

"Use your judgment. If there's any action worth following, follow. I'll make more inquiries here."

Barleyman paused at the door. "The barman described the Froggatts as 'warm' and I gather that means rich, sir. Perhaps the marriage won't be so intolerable."

"No one with real money would live in that house. Unless they truly were mad. Go."

Barleyman hurried out and Christian found the card with the address of the solicitor. He went downstairs to ask for directions, hoping to pry about Froggatts at the same time.

Not finding anyone in the hall, he went out to the coach yard, but it was a busy moment. The coach he'd observed loading was pulling out beneath the stone arch with a rattle of hooves and harness and a blast on the horn to warn traffic in the street. Another had recently arrived and passengers were climbing out, demanding their luggage as ostlers ran to tend to the horses.

On the far side of the yard servants were strapping trunks on top of a private coach while a man in a leather apron inspected a wheel with concern.

Christian prepared to wait a few moments, but then a woman hurried into the yard from the street. She was plainly dressed and wore a mobcap and an apron. She could be any servant, but he immediately recognized the dim-witted maid from the Froggatt house. What was the name?

Carrie.

She joined the short queue at the ticket booth and Christian moved closer. When she reached the clerk, she asked for a ticket on the Doncaster coach.

Doncaster — a place name carved on his heart. That was where he'd shared a house with Moore and six other young officers, the place he'd left to ride to Nether Greasley intent on noble rescue.

Why was Dorcas's maid buying a single ticket to Doncaster?

For the companion to join Dorcas there?

Or for Dorcas herself?

The maid took the ticket and stepped aside. Christian moved almost out of sight, expecting her to leave to deliver it. Instead, she stood near the wall. Waiting for her mistress? Energy rose in Christian as it did before battle. Was he within moments of victory? He assessed the area, planning how he would approach his wife, how he'd prevent her from running away but without creating a furor.

They had to talk and come to some agreement.

Steaming horses came through the arch, hauling another coach loaded on top with goods and luggage. The clerk called, "Doncaster. All for Doncaster. Five minutes!"

The maid did not look around anxiously for her mistress, but took some steps forward, joining two others who were preparing to board.

The ticket was for her?

Such a servant could never afford to travel by coach. She might, however, be sent by coach in an emergency to deliver an important message. He'd not choose such a dimwit for the job, but perhaps Mistress Spencer had little choice. Perhaps Dorcas was in Doncaster and the maid would lead him to her.

He grabbed a passing ostler. "My horse. I need it."

The sight of a shilling ensured fast service, and Christian raced back to his rooms. He scrawled a note for Barleyman telling him to follow unless he had some other promising trail. Then he grabbed his sword and pistols and returned to the yard just as the new cry sounded.

"All aboard! All aboard for Doncaster."

He apologized to Buck for asking more

work from him so shortly after arrival, staying out of sight until the coach had left. No need to follow close when he knew the maid's destination.

The yard was relatively quiet as Christian rode out, though a somber group still inspected the suspect wheel, and a lad was chasing a dog who'd apparently grabbed some scrap of meat. He took his time on the busy street, for the Doncaster coach went slowly there.

When they left the town, he decided dawdling made him too obvious, so he guided Buck through an open gate into an empty field and dismounted, letting the horse crop the grass along the edge of the harvested field.

He realized it was the sort of magical day that sometimes comes in an English autumn. The sky was clear blue but with a slight mistiness to soften it, just as the green of the countryside was mellowing under the first touches of autumn gold. So quickly the black town and its noisy industry seemed another world. Since joining the army, he'd spent little time in country idleness, and recently, being stuck in St. James, none at all.

He slid a grass stem out of its sheath and chewed on it.

A cart labored by, the carter walking beside. Another cart passed, this time loaded with pungent manure. Even that seemed right and wholesome, which was a strange thought for him. Since joining the army at sixteen, he'd left country matters behind him.

It had seemed so essential to go to fight the foe. He'd been unable to tolerate any other thought. He remembered how mature and ready he'd felt. These days when he saw the fresh-faced ensigns and cornets, he both wondered at their youth and was touched by their bright-eyed enthusiasm.

Ah yes, that bright-eyed enthusiasm and lofty ideals. Hardly surprising that he'd tumbled into the marriage mess, bringing him here, today. And now, today, his future had become as certain as a weathercock in a gale.

What in God's name was he to do with a wife?

A wife meant a home. A wife meant a nursery.

He should be ready for that. He should have sold his commission and taken up his position as heir to the earldom, learning all the skills that weren't part of war.

That would mean living with his family, however, and though he loved them, he couldn't bear to live in the midst of them with his mother fussing, his father beaming, and all the little hillocks clamoring for his attention.

But now he had a wife, what else could he do?

Perhaps she was in an institution in Doncaster. In that case, he could ensure her proper care and carry on his bachelor life.

He tossed aside the grass and remounted.

Time to find out.

He kept the coach in sight but at a distance until a signpost told him it was two miles to Doncaster. He drew closer then in case the maid got down on the outskirts. Two people did leave by some cottages, but neither was his target.

As they entered the busy town, he had to move close, for they joined the Great North Road now, becoming part of a river of vehicles of all kinds, pushing north to Scotland or south to London.

Once in town, he was surprised to find how little had changed. There was the bun shop much favored by hungry young men, and down there, the White Swan, which he recalled had employed a very pretty barmaid. Betsy was probably a plump mother of five by now.

They skirted the edge of a market square

and turned into the yard of a place called the Woolpack. He didn't remember it, and it looked quite new. He followed the coach beneath the arch, pleased to find the yard crowded. He dismounted behind a wagon and held up a coin, which instantly brought an ostler.

"You staying 'ere, sir?" the lad asked.

"Tonight, at least."

The lad nodded and took away the horse. Christian found a vantage point and observed, his heart beating faster with anticipation. He could be face-to-face with Dorcas and destiny within the hour.

The maid climbed out third, marked among the inside passengers by her shabby appearance. The woman who followed sniffed and hurried to separate herself, whereupon the maid cast her a surprisingly sour look. Not a lackwit after all. Perhaps she had been rescued from a life of sin, not a lunatic asylum.

Hard to tell her attributes beneath the dull layers.

Having no luggage, the maidservant didn't dawdle. She set off through the arch and into the street, clearly knowing where she was going. Christian followed, noticing how light and brisk her walk was. Most dimwits were dim in action as well as thought, so

114

that was another count against.

She turned into a narrow street lined with dismal houses. It was no more than four feet wide, so Christian held back, but she didn't look behind before turning right at the end. He hurried to catch up and found himself in a handsome, modern street with tall, terraced houses on each side, each with a railinged enclosure at the front that would hold steep stairs down to the servants' quarters.

This was a street of homes for prosperous professionals or even town houses for local gentry. For Mistress Dorcas Hill, part of the "warm" Froggatts? Was the Sheffield house not her home at all?

The maid crossed the street toward one house, but instead of going down the steps to the servants' area, she went to the door and firmly rapped the brass knocker. Christian wasn't surprised that the maid who opened the door frowned and pointed to the lower entrance. But then she opened the door and Ellen Spencer's messenger disappeared inside.

So, the message was so urgent that the lowly maid was entitled to use the main entrance. Christian burned to ply the knocker and invade, but Dorcas might flee through the back door.

Better to watch and wait, but this was the sort of street with biddies peering from front windows, so he strolled along as if seeking a particular house. When he reached the corner, he found the street name neatly picked out in squares of white tile — Silver Street. He walked back and looked for the image that would identify the house. A pair of doves.

He had a direction — at the Pair of Doves, Silver Street — but he was still too noticeable. This was a time when it would be useful to be short and ordinary.

He hovered, hoping to see some action — someone leaving, or a message being sent. Instead, a well-dressed woman turned out of the lane into the street, her smiling attention on the chatter of the two young children, one on either side.

As she drew closer, Christian stepped forward to bow. "Beg pardon, ma'am. May I be so bold as to ask your assistance?"

She wasn't immune to good looks and a courtly manner, but was sensibly wary. "I will assist you if I can, sir."

"I'm seeking the house of Mr. Bollinger, the Greek scholar. Do you know which one it is?"

"I'm sorry, sir, but I don't know the name."

"You live on this street, ma'am?"

"I do."

He sighed and wrinkled his brow — looking, he hoped, harmless and put out.

"I have a commission from my grandfather to deliver some papers to this Bollinger. I have done the same errand once before and confess I trusted to memory. In short," he confided, "I was so sure that I would remember the house that I didn't write down the direction. It was birds, however. I'm sure of it. Is it perhaps that one there?" He pointed to the doves.

The woman glanced that way. "Oh, no, sir. The Ossingtons live there, and Mr. Ossington is a solicitor, not a scholar. A pleasant young couple, recently removed here from Sheffield. In fact," she added with a smile, "they changed the emblem. It was the Black Pig."

Christian wasn't interested in the delicacies of emblems.

Could Mistress Ossington be Dorcas herself? That would be the devil of a mess.

# CHAPTER 6

"How?" Caro exclaimed, staring out at the street.

"What?" Phyllis Ossington asked. She was petite and a pure blonde. Caro had always envied her that.

"He's out there," Caro said.

"Who?"

"Grandiston!"

Phyllis hurried to join her at the window. "Where?"

"Stand back," Caro hissed, pulling her friend aside. "He's looking this way."

"Why are you whispering?"

"I don't know. Because I'm afraid! How can he be here? I've only been here myself long enough to give you the bare bones."

"I will not be prevented from standing at my own window," Phyllis said, moving to get a clear view. "The man talking to Sara Dawson? My, my. If he were my husband, I might not be running away."

"Yes, you would. Imagine being ready to marry Fred, then compelled to take that one instead."

"Ah, yes. But you can't deny he's handsome, and he seems a perfect gentleman. Lud, only look at that bow!"

Caro looked, but grumbled, "He didn't bow to me."

"You were pretending to be a maid. Thank heavens you've taken off that overdress and cap. Appalling!"

"He didn't bow to Ellen, either. At least, not like that. He's duplicitous, conniving. . . ."

"Splendid," Phyllis said, almost purred.

"That is not an appropriate sentiment for a married woman with one child and another on the way."

"A thing of beauty should always be admired."

"Beautiful! He's too tall, too broad, and ugly in temperament."

"He's smiling."

"Like a wolf."

Phyllis turned away from the window, shaking her head. "Calm down, Caro."

"Calm?" Caro echoed. "That man invaded my house and bullied my companion. Now he's followed me here and is preparing to invade again."

"If he tries to invade here, he'll get a flea in his ear."

"Words won't stop him," Caro warned, and edged back to observe the enemy.

The woman and children had gone on their way, and Grandiston was looking directly at the house. Caro knew she couldn't be seen, but still, she shivered.

Phyllis returned to the center of the window. She'd always had a resolute attitude — and an eye for the men. "See, he's leaving now. No sign of him battering down the door."

"Perish the man."

"You want him to batter down the door?"

"I don't want him here. Why is he here? Do you think he knows?"

"That Carrie the maid is Caro Hill? How could he? I scarcely recognized you, and he doesn't know you at all. Ah," she said at a knock on the drawing room door, "here's the tea. Sit and be soothed and we'll decide what's best."

Phyllis resumed her seat on the settee and the maid put the tray on the table. As she straightened, she shot a curious glance at Caro, and no wonder. It was the same maid that had opened the door to her. If she didn't provide some story, her reputation could be in shreds.

"Your maid must wonder why I was so oddly dressed," Caro said to Phyllis in a light tone.

Phyllis's eyes asked questions, but she played along. "I suppose she must."

"Perhaps we should tell her the story." Caro sent the maid a conspiratorial smile. "I am plagued by a very insistent suitor, you see, who has taken to lurking near my house in a manner to drive me distracted. So I decided to escape. I put on those clothes and slipped away, but somehow he's followed me. A tall blond man in a brown coat and riding breeches."

"So don't admit him, Mary," Phyllis instructed.

"And please," said Caro, "ask the other servants not to reveal that I'm here."

Phyllis added, "I know none of you will gossip to strangers, Mary. Especially a Southerner."

"Oh, a *Southerner,* is he, ma'am? Don't you worry, then. He'll get nothing from none of us."

As soon as the maid left, Caro said, "A masterly stroke."

Phyllis grinned. "We all know Southerners are not to be trusted. Now, try to make more sense of your story. At one point you implied that man was your husband."

Caro took the tea and a piece of buttered crumpet, trying to decide what to say. Phyllis didn't know the truth of her wedding, only the story of the rash elopement with the young soldier killed soon after in action.

"That was when I first saw him. Because of the eyes. It cast me in a panic. After all, I thought Hill dead. *Think* him dead," she amended. "As Ellen pointed out, the eyes could be a family trait."

"And you think he wished to speak to you about your husband's will? Strange that he'd follow a maid to another town."

"Exactly."

"What do you fear, Caro?"

Caro took another crumpet. "I fear that Grandiston is Hill's heir and has inherited part of my fortune. Or even all of it. And maybe even a husband's right to control my movements."

"Oh, I doubt that, but the property is a concern. What a shame that Fred's away, for he'd know. But you're safe here for now."

Caro smiled, but she wished she felt so sure. Clearly Phyllis couldn't imagine anyone breaking into the sanctity of her home, but Caro could. To make matters worse, Phyllis was to leave shortly to join her husband in Rotherham. Of course she'd said Caro could stay here, but she'd feel

122

vulnerable.

She rose to pace the room. "How could everything become so complicated so quickly? I rose this morning to a perfectly normal day, and look at me. Driven from my home, from my town, even, and skulking in fear of another visit from an overbearing brute who, I am sure, has no purpose that's to my benefit."

"There's no need —"

But Caro swept on. "He has me cowering like a mouse in a hole. What would Aunt Abigail say?"

Phyllis smiled. "To confront him, but armed to the teeth."

"Diana Arradale would say the same. I wish I could turn on him and roar."

"Delicious," said Phyllis with a chuckle. "But impossible."

Caro contemplated an alarming plan. "Perhaps not with a roar . . ."

"Caro, what are you thinking?"

She inhaled, thought again, then said, "A little masquerade." She sat down again, facing her friend. "I need to get to my lawyer in York, so I need to take the coach first thing tomorrow. Why don't I go to an inn tonight instead of staying here? And to the very inn where Grandiston lodges."

"But he'll recognize you."

"How? He doesn't know what Caro Hill looks like, and in my normal clothes, he'll never suspect I'm Carrie the maid. But if I can strike up an acquaintance with him, perhaps I can learn the details of his purpose here."

"Strike up an acquaintance with a stranger at an inn?"

"Why not? He might even attempt to flirt. Mingling in Yorkshire society, I've become quite accomplished at that. It's my experience that when a man wants to please a lady, he talks and talks and talks. I'll have his secrets in an hour."

"When a man wants to please a lady he's just met," Phyllis said, "it's with dishonorable intentions."

Caro laughed. "Oh, very likely. But nothing's going to happen. I do need to know what inn he's at. Probably the Woolpack, as that's where the coach arrived, but do you have a servant you can trust to find out?"

Phyllis rolled her eyes, but said, "Anne, my maid. I'll go and speak to her."

"And I'll need to borrow some things for my journey. Ellen is sending on my luggage, but it won't arrive for a while. A hat and gloves. Some undergarments, a nightgown, and a spare gown."

"Very well," Phyllis said. "The gown will

be tight and short."

"I'll not need to wear it. Thank you."

"I'm not sure I should help you in this."

"Phyllis, I have no choice. I must get to York, so I must leave this house, and I'll feel safer at an inn than here alone."

"There are the servants."

"But they're not my servants."

Phyllis gave her a look. "You want to do this."

Caro smiled. "You know me too well. I truly would rather be at home, my life flowing as it should, but I'm accustomed to being in charge of my life. I need more information to take to Hambledon, but I also need to take charge."

"You'll be careful?"

"Of course. I have too much to lose."

Phyllis left, giving Caro time to think about her plan. Despite her bold words, she quivered inside at the thought of what she was about to do. She must, though, so she worked out the finer details.

Phyllis returned with the items, and Caro went to the mirror to put on a neat lace cap, and pin a straw hat on top. "Charming. I like the jaunty feather." She cocked her head. "I wonder if I can attract a man's interest when he doesn't know I'm rich."

"They gather around you like flies around jam."

"The jam being my money."

"Caro," Phyllis said, "what if this Grandiston is Jack Hill, your husband? Won't he recognize you?"

"I'm convinced now that he isn't, but why should he ever imagine this stylish lady to be that frightened child? I need a new name, though." She turned to the mirror again and adjusted the hat to a more jaunty angle. "I'll take a name to suit the game. Behold, Mistress Katherine Hunter, solicitor's wife of York. Kat Hunter on the prowl."

Phyllis groaned. "Turning yourself into a cat will not turn that man into a mouse, Caro. I predict disaster."

Christian returned to the Woolpack and sent a message by groom to Barleyman to remove here instantly with all their possessions. Every instinct told him his wife was in Silver Street, or the people there knew where she was.

He could do nothing until Barleyman arrived, however, so he took a room and followed the soldier's rule — eat when there's the chance. He'd get a faster meal down in the ordinary, where a quick meal was always ready for ongoing passengers given twenty

126

minutes at most for their refreshment. He'd also be able to observe comings and goings in case that maid appeared again, or even his wife taking a coach elsewhere. Though how he'd recognize her, he'd no idea.

Light brown hair, he thought, trying to remember from ten years ago.

Eye color? He had no memory of that.

Thin and flat, but she could be round as a ball by now. He realized he could have passed her on the street. Plague take it, he should have told Barleyman to get a description of the woman before leaving Sheffield. Too late for that now.

As he sat at the long table, he greeted the miscellany of diners. Some had sat down recently and were enjoying soup. Others had clearly been here longer and were on to the roast beef. Four were attacking damson pie with haste, for the call had already gone out that a York coach would leave in three minutes.

The pair just finishing their soup were a bright-eyed youth of about fifteen accompanied by a rotund, black-clad cleric who seemed to be his tutor. Both were eager to talk. Christian soon learned that Master Gray was a younger son of Lord Garforth, whose seat lay near Wakefield in North Yorkshire.

Christian had already supplied the name Grandiston, and could only trust to fate that neither lad nor tutor recognized that it could be a title. It seemed not, but nor were they a source of local information. Like all youths, Master Gray was completely absorbed in his own situation. He was on his way to Oxford to first prepare for, then enter, the university.

"Did you go up to university, sir?" he asked as Christian's soup arrived.

"No, but I'm sure it'll be a grand opportunity for you."

"Are you from the south, sir? I've never been south of Lincoln before. I expect it to be tremendous."

"It's not so different," Christian warned, amused, but recognizing much of himself at that age.

"You're teasing me, sir. Aren't you?"

"Now, now, Master Gray," murmured the tutor. "Cease your prattling."

The youth subsided obediently and Christian attended to his chicken soup while considering the middle-aged couple eating roast beef. They seemed set apart in some way, though their clothing was suitable for middling people on a journey. The woman wore a little too much face paint, but she seemed sallow and was perhaps trying to hide that.

The man caught his scrutiny; after a moment, he nodded.

"Grandiston," Christian said again. "In Doncaster on business."

"Silcock," the man said. Again, there was a slight pause, as if all words must be considered before spoken. "From Pennsylvania."

Christian almost said he'd visited the place, but best to keep his military career out of this. "Then you're a long way from home, sir. Returned to England to stay?"

"I was born there, sir, and proud to say so." With his solemn manner it was hard to tell whether he was offended. "My wife, however, is from the north of England. That is why we are in this locality."

"Ah." Christian smiled and inclined his head to the woman. She reciprocated, but as if she'd rather he ceased his prattling.

Christian was fishing around for a topic that might draw out the strange couple when a new person entered the room. This woman hesitated, which wasn't surprising as she seemed to be unescorted.

Christian and the other men rose, and he smiled encouragement at her. "There are ample seats, ma'am, and the food is excellent."

She smiled back and perhaps blushed a little, then surveyed the empty seats, including the ones on either side of him. She chose a chair on the opposite side of the table, however, and the look she flickered at him seemed both searching and nervous.

Struth, was she the sort to think any man likely to attack?

She wished them all good afternoon. "As I gather informality is the norm in these situations, I will take liberty to introduce myself. I am Mistress Hunter from York, cast here alone by a predicament."

"What has occurred, ma'am?" asked Protheroe, the tutor.

A maidservant took away Christian's empty soup plate as another servant put a full one in front of her. She smiled thanks to the server and picked up her spoon to take a sip.

All in all she was ordinary, with a slightly long face and no notable features except the excellent complexion common in the north. It was said to arise from the damp air and shortage of sunshine. A steep price to pay, in his mind. Her hair, showing at the edges of a white cap worn beneath a straw hat, was a mousy blond. And yet, she was immediately the center of attention, and he felt that attraction. A very interesting woman.

She glanced around. "My husband and I were traveling here, you see, but not far out of York, our coach lost a wheel. The dear man would try to help the coachman with the horses and has injured his back. Nothing serious," she assured them, "but the doctor insisted that he not travel all the way here."

"You didn't stay to tend him, ma'am?" asked Silcock, with clear condemnation.

Color rose in her cheeks in an admirably natural manner. "Sir, that was my deepest desire, but Mr. Hunter was bringing some important documents to Doncaster. When a passing vehicle offered assistance, he asked me to complete his duty while he made his slow way back to our home. I will, of course, return to his side by the first coach tomorrow."

"I commend your fortitude, ma'am," said Protheroe.

"A wife's duty, sir," she said demurely, and turned her attention to her soup.

As he enjoyed excellent roast beef and told a story of a traveling disaster, Christian observed Mistress Hunter. The roses in her cheeks might be honest, but he'd go odds her story wasn't. He couldn't say why, but he had a fine instinct for such things.

Was she spying for likely victims of highway robbery? Would she discover her purse left behind and wheedle a loan, never to be repaid? Or was she simply a sneak thief or pickpocket? He'd watch his purse and pockets, but was prepared to be amused — especially as Mistress Hunter seemed particularly interested in him. Oh, she was paying due attention to the grim American couple, the unctuous tutor, and the smitten lad, but he often caught her looking at him.

The next time their eyes met, she let her gaze linger a moment, then turned away, that blush rising.

Was her mischief as simple as a dutiful wife let off the leash and seeking adventure? By gad, he hoped so. He'd adventure her as she'd never been adventured before.

# CHAPTER 7

Christian had ordered a bottle of wine with his meal. When her beef arrived, he offered her some.

Her eyes met his again in that lingering, promising way. "Thank you, sir. Most kind."

He returned the look as he poured.

She sipped, then inclined her head. "An excellent claret."

It was, but how interesting that she recognize that. Was she a highborn lady seeking low adventures? He thought not, but she wasn't in the normal run of solicitors' wives, either.

"From York, you said, ma'am. That is your home?"

"Yes, sir."

"Have you lived all your life there, or are you country bred?"

"Not at all," she replied, rather ambiguously. "And you, sir? Not from the north, I think."

"Born and bred in Oxfordshire."

He'd forgotten the others, but the youth interrupted now. "Oxfordshire, sir! Can you tell me about the sport near Oxford? My father says he'll support a horse for me if I apply to my studies, and I have my guns with me."

The idea of the stripling with weapons alarmed, but then he'd been using weapons with deadly purpose at about that age. He obligingly discussed sporting possibilities near the university, but kept half an eye on Mistress Hunter.

She was pretending a flattering interest in his Oxfordshire boyhood. Her eyes frequently met his. Did she realize how revealing they were?

Perhaps she did, for she turned to the Silcocks with polite questions. By that, she revealed a blemish. On her jawline, just below her left ear was a pale, jagged scar. A tearing wound rather than a clean cut. She was lucky it wasn't larger or in a more prominent spot, but as is often the case, that small flaw increased her allure.

Christian reminded himself that he was here to catch his wife. But he couldn't do anything until Barleyman arrived in a couple of hours at best, and she was delightfully intriguing.

Mistress Hunter's charms drew little more response from the Silcocks than his own attempts at conversation had done. Mistress Silcock admitted to being born in County Durham rather than Yorkshire, and Silcock to being a farmer. She turned away and let the lad capture her attention again.

No poet would write sonnets to her ordinary lips, but they pulled in at the corners when she concealed laughter, creating sweet dimples. As Master Gray was trying to impress her with gallantry, the dimples appeared frequently, but she was gentle with him.

Protheroe rose, claiming their timetable as reason to leave. More likely because of his charge's interest in the lady, and very wise, too. The Silcocks took their leave as well. Christian stayed. He could hardly abandon a lady to solitude.

"Were you born and bred in York?" he asked.

She glanced around as if nervous, but then smiled at him again. "Yes. And you? Oxfordshire, you said? In Oxford?"

"No, in the country. York's a famous place. Should I visit?"

She looked up at him through her lashes. "Oh, most certainly, sir. I only wish I could be your guide."

He smiled encouragingly. "Perhaps you can. You tempt me to travel there."

"Alas, my husband will require all my care for a little while."

The neckline of her long-sleeved jacket was just high enough to completely conceal her breasts, but they seemed full, which was his preference. The full-length sleeves drew attention to her long, pale hands. He could imagine them cool on his hot body. She wore a wedding ring, of course, but that was for her conscience, not his.

But he was taken aback by the realization that he, too, was married. It felt as believable as being told he was Greek, but it was true. Strangely in his circle, he believed in marital fidelity, which was another reason he'd intended never to marry. Did his forced marriage vows bind him?

They hadn't done so for ten years, so to hell with that.

She cradled her wineglass and looked at him over the rim. "So, Mr. Grandiston, what brings a man from Oxfordshire to Doncaster?"

"Family business, ma'am."

"You have family here?"

"A very distant connection."

"Am I keeping you from your business?"

"Not at all. I'm waiting for someone. Am

I keeping you from your husband's business?"

"No, I only linger in case there is a message or document to take back. It's a matter of a will, I think."

The maid brought her damson pie. Mistress Hunter drained her glass, deliberately licking the last crimson drop from her lips. Christian shifted in his seat.

She picked up her spoon, saying, "Is your business a will?"

"Why think that, ma'am?"

She chuckled. "Forgive me. I like guessing games. Will your business keep you in Yorkshire long?"

"That depends on many things."

A fluttering glance and a rising blush showed she'd understood. She concentrated on her pie, but showed no affront and didn't attempt to leave.

How delightful.

After a mouthful, she looked up again. "This is excellent. You should have had some."

"You distracted me from other sweets, Mistress Hunter."

A hint of purple damson juice stained her lips. She licked it away. "If I may be so bold, sir, do I detect a little of the military about you?"

"I don't know. Do you?"

She chuckled. "Are we jousting, sir?"

He smiled. "Not yet."

Her lids lowered, showing that she understood the other meaning of "joust," too. "I'm sorry if you found my question impertinent."

"No. But I'm curious about your curiosity."

"But you are a very interesting man."

Christian said the expected line. "And you are a very interesting woman. Perhaps you would care for an after-dinner stroll."

"Why, thank you. So good for the digestion, but I would not want to walk about such a busy town alone."

She put the last morsel of pie into her mouth, dabbed her mouth with her table napkin, and rose. By then, Christian was around the table to assist her.

He admired the smooth line of the back of her neck, and the roundness of her buttocks beneath simple skirts, but made himself consider the hazards of this siren. He doubted she was any kind of thief, for he was an unlikely mark, but she could be intending to lure him to her bed so her enraged husband could burst in demanding recompense in money or blood. It was a trick played on many a traveler.

He was an unlikely mark for that, too, however, for he'd choose blood.

He needed to leave a note in case Barleyman made more speed than expected, so he excused himself for a moment and requested paper and pen.

First orders — go to the sign of the Two Doves, Silver Street, and see what you can find out from the servants, especially about comings and goings today. Is Mistress Hill in residence? Has she been there recently, or is she expected? Has she or anyone else left this afternoon? Fish for a description if you can. Slight chance Mistress Ossington is she.

The Froggatt maid went into the house at about two o'clock. What was her stated purpose? If possible, what was in the message she carried? Where is she now?

And anything else.

Yours,
CG

He heated wax and sealed it without any mark. Unlikely that anyone here would recognize Lord Grandiston's crest, but best not to take risks. He wrote "Joseph Barleyman" on the front, left the note with the innkeeper, and rejoined the intriguing lady.

He caught her frowning at the doorway to the street. He turned to look and saw the Silcocks leaving to enter a waiting carriage. Not a vehicle for long distances, but an open one-horse chair for a local journey.

"The Americans annoy you?" he asked.

"What? Oh, no, not at all." She hooked a hand over his offered arm. "Sometimes strangers catch our interest for no reason, don't you find?"

"In some cases," Christian returned, "it's not strange at all."

She fluttered her lashes. Could she be any more blatant? Or promising.

As they left the inn, she said, "Have you ever thought you recognized someone only to find them a complete stranger?"

"I met a man abroad who I mistook for a moment for one of my closest friends. He didn't even speak English. But upon discussion, we found there was a distant family connection."

"How interesting. Do you resemble your family?"

"It would be very odd if I didn't."

She colored and laughed. "Of course, how foolish of me. I meant all your family. I know one family with both blonds and brunets, and a number with different eye colors. I couldn't help but notice the color of yours, sir." She looked fetchingly into his eyes. "Are they a family feature?"

Christian steered them away from a collision with a party hurrying to the inn. "The Great North Road is a poor place for the digestion, ma'am. Perhaps we could go this way and find a quieter street?"

She hesitated but then said, "Of course, an excellent idea."

Another sign of eagerness. Christian chose a direction that should take them to Silver Street. He'd like another look at the house, and now he'd be less obtrusive.

After a few steps she said, "Your eyes, sir?" looking into them again.

"As you say, a family feature."

"Do all your family have them?"

"Some of my brothers and sisters don't." If this was the best she could do at flirtatious conversation, perhaps it would be better to progress directly to bed.

"And what of others?" she asked. "Cousins and such."

"The eyes come down my mother's line, so are scattered through the Dales."

"Dales?" she said, wrinkling her brow. "You mean as in Swaledale and Wensleydale?"

He chuckled. "A gruesome image. I mean

Dale, my mother's family name."

"Oh," she said, laughing with him. "What a relief."

Caro was genuinely amused, but she was making a mess of her flirtation. She must seem a complete idiot.

On the other hand, perhaps a complete idiot was what he wanted. He seemed to believe he could seduce her on a public street in broad daylight. It was as if he expected her to return to the inn and go straight to bed with him.

Yes, *expected.*

With a chance-met lady. She'd never have imagined such a thing possible, not even in scandalous London.

But, she reminded herself, if he had hopes, he'd keep talking. Like Scheherazade, she must keep him dangling until he'd told all his tales.

No, that was the wrong way round, but it had to be her general plan.

If she had brain enough to plan anything.

They unlinked arms to look in the window of a china shop, and when they moved on, he touched her back. It was so light a touch she wasn't sure it had happened, but her body knew. Sparkles were traveling up and down her spine, invading her brain even,

142

making it so hard to think. She was constantly aware of his presence at her side. Aware of him as she'd never been aware of a man before, of his strength, his long legs, his smiling eyes.

She was outmatched at this game, but she smiled back and tried another question. "Do your family connections live in Doncaster, Mr. Grandiston, or nearby?"

"I'm not entirely sure. I'm searching for them."

"Are they Grandistons? It's an uncommon name."

"No, their name is Hill."

Something struck her. "And your mother's maiden name is Dale? Are you inventing all this?"

He smiled. "Now, why would I do that?"

"I'm sure I have no idea. But tell me the truth, please."

"Why?"

She tried a pout. "Because you're being elusive, sir, and I do not find it charming."

"I'm not at all elusive, Mistress Hunter. Try me."

Shivers went through her at his tone, at the look in his eyes. She had to look away, and she saw they had the attention of three women gossiping in a doorway, their children playing nearby. Or rather, he had their attention. Of course. They looked as if they'd go to his bed at a crooked finger!

Caro desperately tried to recall the frightening, angry man in Froggatt Lane, but he could be a different person.

She caught one woman looking at her, and could interpret that expression, too: *What's a fine specimen like that doing with such a dull bird?*

Caro knew she was ordinary and he was not, but she shot the woman a look. *Dull bird or not, for the moment, he's mine.*

Now, however, she was aware of the general attention they were attracting, and none of it was due to her. It wasn't only his good looks. It was his carriage and easy confidence, signs that he was well-bred and highborn.

As Hill had been. Even at that terrible time, she'd known Hill was highborn in a way that Moore was not, but this was not good news. When ordinary people like herself clashed with the aristocracy, the aristocracy won.

"You're very bold, Mr. Grandiston," she said, making it a flirtatious tease. "Almost lordly in your expectations. Is there a title in your family?"

"Will it be to my credit or my shame?"

"Who could be ashamed of a title?"

"The Darien one is dubious, and the new Earl Ferrers has something to live down."

"Darien?"

"A positive stew of vileness."

"Ferrers?"

"His execution for murder escaped notice in the north?"

"Oh, that!" Caro said, realizing she'd been lost in her concerns. "No. The case is often mentioned as proof that there's equality before the law."

"You sound cynical, Mistress Hunter."

She probably had. "I merely think that the proportion of peers punished for their crimes is somewhat less than the proportion of paupers."

"A hit, I grant you. But that unfairness extends to all people of property. I'm sure you would fare better from the law than your ragged counterpart over there."

Caro watched an old humpbacked woman scurry out to scoop up the droppings of a passing horse and add it to a bucket. She'd sell her haul to a market gardener for a few pennies.

"Alas, sir, you're right, and that poor creature should be in an almshouse."

"You have a kind heart."

"Do you not care?"

He met her eyes ruefully. "I rarely notice.

That doubtless confirms your low opinion of the aristocracy."

There, confirmation, but she mustn't show her dismay. But, heavens, they were entering Silver Street. No one here knew her, but it still felt dangerous.

"I don't have a low opinion of all aristocrats," she said. "The Countess of Arradale is known in Yorkshire for her charitable work — she's Marchioness of Rothgar now, of course. But there are the other sort. The stories one hears. Quite shocking."

"And the lower orders are unfailingly virtuous?"

"No, of course not. I'm sorry," she said, distracted. What if one of Phyllis's servants emerged and recognized her?

"I see good and bad at all levels," he said. "For example, many of the aristocracy are idle, but some work responsibly in government and in managing their estates. Then there are their other interests. There's a fashion for science, and for industrial developments and even mechanical inventions, such as accurate clocks. A number of aristocrats — Ashart, Ithorne, Rothgar, and even the new Earl Ferrers — are in a grand fizz about the transit of Venus."

Caro almost exploded her deception by questioning the cool Marquess of Rothgar being in a fizz about anything. "Not, I assume, as improper as it sounds?"

"Not at all, which is probably why it doesn't interest me."

"Mr. Grandiston, you should be ashamed. What is it?"

"From the little I know, ma'am, ships are to be sent to observe the transit of the planet Venus across the sun from various locations around the world. That will enable a more precise calculation of something. Perhaps the size of the earth."

"Why does one need to know that?"

"There you have me, ma'am."

They were approaching Phyllis's house. All seemed quiet. Phyllis would be on her way to Fred, and Caro wondered why her life couldn't be as simple. It would be once she'd sorted out her problems, which meant discovering why Grandiston was seeking Jack Hill's bride. If only she could ask him straight out.

She smiled at him. "You were going to tell me more about your search for Hills," she said.

"Was I? Venus is much more interesting, I think."

"You're being naughty, sir. I won't permit it."

"Then perhaps I won't satisfy your curiosity."

Caro pouted again, and it was partly genuine. For some reason, he wouldn't talk about things that interested her. Men usually prattled on and on about their new horses, or their improved carriage springs, or their view on how the country's finances should be managed, but not Grandiston. Oh, no. And he really was too dangerous to dally with longer.

The church clock struck, offering her escape. "Oh my, I think I should return to the inn."

"Yes," he said, "I, too, think it time."

Lord save her! She'd like to hurry away from him, but she'd have to let him escort her back to the Woolpack. Given that, she'd have one more try.

"So you have Hills and Dales in your family tree, sir. Any Peaks or Vales?"

He smiled. "No, but I have to confess to a Plain."

"Truly? How lovely."

"And you, ma'am, any other occupations? A Fletcher or Smith?"

"No, I don't think so. But 'Katherine' is a traditional name in my family. Are there Christian names in yours that repeat?"

He seemed to find that amusing, but he

said, "None that I can think of. I have brothers called Matthew, Mark, Luke, and John."

"Your family is biblical?" she asked, though she couldn't see how this thread was leading to her goal.

"Not particularly. My parents were merely looking for simplicity. Do you have brothers and sisters?"

"Yes," she lied. "A sister called Mary and a brother called Jack."

She saw no twitch on his face at the name Jack.

"And your maiden name?" he asked. "It would be amusing if it were, for example, Fox."

She laughed. "It would, but I'm afraid it was the very boring Brown."

They were approaching the Woolpack again, and she'd learned very little.

"I'm curious about one thing," she said, trying to make it idle.

"I'm sure you are," he said.

"If your mother's maiden name was Dale, where do the Hills come from?"

"What a very geographical question, to be sure. Perhaps they're built by giant moles."

"Mr. Grandiston!"

"You expect me to be serious about such a dull question? Why not tell me instead what your purpose is here?"

That was ambiguous, but Caro said, "I am about my husband's business."

"How biblical. Remember the dire consequences."

"Mr. Grandiston, kindly do not flirt with sacrilege."

"Much sweeter to flirt with you."

They'd stopped, and Caro was snared by his smiling eyes, suddenly assailed by the impossible sweetness of this being real — of enjoying a playful, flirtatious bit of nonsense with a wondrously handsome man. One, moreover, capable of toying with her emotions with a look, of exciting her body with a touch . . .

Eyam!

She stepped back. "Remember, sir, that I am married."

"In Yorkshire married women don't flirt?"

"Not with serious intent."

"Am I serious?" he asked. "Are you?"

"Of course not." She turned to hurry toward the inn.

"Thus, we are merely amusing each other in an idle hour," he said, keeping up without effort, "which is harmless enough. Wait."

She stopped before she thought better of it, and saw him beckoning a flower seller. He bought a posy of country flowers and turned back to her.

Caro didn't want to accept them. It seemed like Persephone taking a bite out of the pomegranate, though she wasn't sure what underworld she'd be obliged to dwell in for six months. . . .

Instead of holding the posy out to be taken, he raised it to her nose. "Are they sweet?"

Caro inhaled. "Stock, verbena, rosemary . . ." Then he moved them slightly so they brushed her cheek, while his eyes — those eyes — held hers.

Eyes, perfume, butterfly touch.

Only that, but the bottom dropped out of her stomach.

"Well?" he asked softly, and she knew what he asked.

The answer was no, but perhaps she could go a little further. Perhaps she could experience more of this wicked fun and at the same time learn what she needed to know. What risk was there? Be he bold as Beelzebub and she weak as Eve, he couldn't achieve his purpose in an hour, and that was the most she'd give him. After that, she'd retreat to her room and lock the door.

She took the posy, saying, "Perhaps the news you expect will be waiting for you."

"That might be a shame."

She slid him a look. "Duty comes before pleasure, sir."

"How virtuous. But if duty can be postponed?"

"Can yours?"

"You want another guessing game? I'll give you the usual ten questions, but in my room, over wine."

She met his eyes. "That would be most improper, Mr. Grandiston."

"To take a glass of wine together in the afternoon? A little improper perhaps, ma'am, but not 'most.' "

Caro swallowed. Normally she'd not consider such a thing, but no one would know, it was daylight, and he was going to answer ten questions. They entered the hall of the inn and walked past the roaring fire, which seemed particularly hot.

"What a pity you're traveling to York, not London, Mistress Hunter. We might meet again there."

"London's a wicked place."

"But with a splendor of delights that I would unfurl for your pleasure."

Caro was lost in the vision of his promise. Grandiston was a wicked rascal, but she was sure he could do exactly as he'd promised and show her splendors of delights. . . .

What was she thinking?

She wasn't free to go to London. She didn't *want* to go to London. At least, not now. Perhaps she'd go with Eyam, for their wedding trip. A terrible little voice said, *It won't be nearly as splendid as with this man.*

He suddenly touched her cheek. "What caused that?"

Caro stepped back, covering the spot with her hand. "Oh, the scar?" She lowered her hand. "I stumbled as a child." She'd almost said ". . . in the works."

"Something sharp but jagged." He traced the spot again, and this time she let him.

"A jagged piece of metal," she said, her words merely breath.

"A pity, but it doesn't detract from your charms. Come south with me."

"You can't be serious." She looked around nervously, but there were only two people in the hall and they were paying no attention to them.

"Can't I?" he asked.

"No. And if you were, it would still be no. My home is here."

"With your husband."

"With my husband," she agreed. "I thank you for a pleasant walk, Mr. Grandiston."

He bowed. "I'm enchanted to have pleased." But he added, "You still don't know my purpose here. I might still tell you,

153

but you'll have to pay."

"Pay?" she asked, her heart fluttering.

"By letting loose some of your secrets . . ."

"Secrets? I have no secrets."

". . . layer by layer."

He somehow infused those words with notions of hot kisses, and of clothing sliding away, piece by piece.

As if to seal that impression, he added, "We may even, eventually, come down to the naked truth."

Caro closed her mouth, but was dumbstruck.

"Wine?" he asked.

Caro knew she should refuse, should flee to her room now and lock the door, but she couldn't bear to abandon this just yet. She'd never imagined anything like it.

And it couldn't go too far. An inn room in the afternoon wasn't an orgy in London, and more intimacy, especially in the privacy of a room, would create more Scheherazade opportunities. Of course, she might have to allow him some liberties. Some kisses, perhaps even some slightly improper touches . . .

Various improper places tingled and her faster-beating heart warned of danger, but she needed to do this. For a great many reasons, she had to do this.

As calmly as she could, she said, "By all means. This promises to be amusing."

"It will be whatever you wish, ma'am," he said, and turned to order a passing maid to bring wine to his room.

As they went upstairs, he rested his hand lightly on her back again, but lower this time. In the small of her back. Why did that feel so very, very wicked?

He opened his door and gestured her in. Caro saw the big bed and paused.

*Don't be a ninny. You're not fourteen, and Grandiston, for all his faults, is not a man like Moore. In any case, you went to the Tup expecting marriage and all it involved, though not so brutally. This is more like taking tea in a drawing room.*

All the same, as Caro walked in, she kept as far as possible from the bed. That wasn't difficult as the room was quite spacious, and this side held a modest dining table, four wooden chairs, and two upholstered ones here by the hearth, each with a piecrust table to hand.

"To talk of secrets, what is your first name?" he asked, unbuckling his sword belt.

Lud, was he *undressing?* Caro prepared to flee, but he put the scabbarded sword on the table and came to join her. "Well?"

"Katherine," she said with a dry mouth.

155

"Ah, yes, the family name. And are you truly married?"

"Why doubt that?" She stripped off her glove to show her ring.

He took her hand as if to inspect the gold band. If he expected to detect that it was new or recently put on, he'd be disappointed. He raised her hand to lightly brush his lips across her knuckles, touching, as Eyam had not done. As he did so, he looked at her, his eyes full of sinful promise.

*Look what I can do with lips on your hand, dear lady, and imagine what I could do with lips elsewhere. . . .*

"The first nakedness," he said softly.

She really should leave . . . but something was bubbling up inside her, a desire to enjoy this wickedness, to learn more about it. She'd flirted, but always so safely and with safe men. This man wasn't safe.

But nor was he truly dangerous. She could sense that about him, and even were he a foul brute, he'd not go further than she allowed in a respectable, bustling place like the Woolpack. The slightly open window let in voices outside and the bustle of coaches coming and going.

Caro pulled her hand free, attempting a playful manner. "And the last," she said.

"The alpha and omega of our interaction?"

"Precisely. You couldn't imagine more on such brief acquaintance."

"It grows less brief all the time. Ah, our wine. Do please be seated, ma'am."

He went to the door to take the tray and Caro sat, placing her gloves on the table by her hand. She saw the maid look in and smiled at the woman. The maid would see that everything was decent in here.

As if to emphasize that point, he left the door slightly open. He poured wine and brought it to her, then took the opposite chair, smiling in a supremely harmless way.

Excited expectation popped like a bubble. There'd be no dangerous, wicked games here. He'd been teasing, that was all. Despite some dissatisfied quivers deep inside, Caro told herself that suited her to perfection.

Indeed, why had she expected anything else? Was she the sort of woman to cause a stranger to burn with lust? Did she look like the sort of woman who'd fall into sin with a stranger in broad daylight?

Of course she didn't.

And she was wearing her hat.

No woman was ever ravished in her hat.

# CHAPTER 8

Christian knew he should be doing other things, but his errant wife was far less interesting than Mr. Hunter's. Especially as she was looking like a woman awaiting a tooth puller rather than a seduction. He wondered again about the lurking husband, ready to burst in. If so, this could be disappointing, but entertaining in other ways.

"How far away is your husband's resting place?" he asked.

"Lud, sir, you make it sound like a tomb."

"My apologies, but we can hope that he rests."

"Why do you want to know?" she asked.

*Why don't you want to tell me?* She did have secrets, and he hoped to learn them if nothing else.

"Secrets," he reminded her. "Layer by layer."

She blushed. "As I said, the accident occurred just outside York, and he might already be returning slowly home."

"But you expect to stay the night here," he said. "How delightful."

Her blush deepened and the wine in her glass trembled a little.

"I mean only," he said, "that we might spend some time together later, playing cards perhaps? Dear lady, you wouldn't abandon me to the Silcocks."

"Perhaps they'll return from their journey in better spirits."

"I sense intractable gloom, but I am an optimist by nature. As you see."

Suddenly those dimples formed at the corner of her lips, accompanied by a flashing look of naughty amusement. "Some optimism proves unwarranted," she said.

"Yet you are here."

"To ask questions."

"Ah, yes. Are you a wicked adventuress?"

"I?" She laughed, and it seemed genuine. "I'm the most commonplace of women."

"I doubt that. After all," he pointed out, "you are here."

She sipped her wine. "You're a more likely villain, sir. Have you inveigled me here to steal my trinkets?"

"My pardon if I offend, but your trinkets don't seem worth hanging for. Mistress Silcock's rings, however, are. Perhaps I'm merely passing the time until I can attempt them."

"Your chances of getting Mistress Silcock alone in a room are slim, Mr. Grandiston, despite all your charms."

He grinned. "Ah, so you've noticed my charms."

"But of course. You ply them so obviously."

He laughed. The lady had teeth when she cared to use them.

"Only on you," he pointed out.

"At the moment. But if my trinkets aren't worth the risk . . ."

"You might be."

Her eyes widened, but she didn't make even a token protest.

Both willing and nervous? A virtuous wife who found herself free of husband and familiar surroundings and inclined to take advantage of it, perhaps for the first time? Talk of risk. He should converse until the wine was drunk and then ease her back to her own room.

He rarely did what he should in these matters, but he offered a warning. "The risk would be largely on your side, Mistress Hunter."

"Mine?"

"From your husband. To your reputation."

"Oh," she said, "no need to worry about that."

Caro had merely meant to keep the conversation going, to return to questions, but she realized too late what an invitation her words had sent. He put aside his wine and rose to shut the door. He took her wine from her unresisting hand, but then instead of putting it on the table, he raised it to his lips and, watching her, drank from it, from the place where she'd sipped.

Why did that make her quiver from the toes up?

He tossed the empty glass to roll on the carpet. Her eyes followed it with alarm, and then she was in his arms, held tight against him.

Oh, dear. Oh, no.

But every part of her body instantly said *yes!*

Caro stared at the tight weave of his brown cloth jacket, so dazzled by sensations that she had no idea what to do. She knew what she *should* do, but her natural sense of propriety had fled.

He was raising her chin and she had to look up, up into those eyes. He was so close, she could see the green and gold and brown as distinct fragments around the deep, dark center.

And then he kissed her.

Caro allowed it. She wasn't capable of more than allowing, but she wasn't capable of less. She wanted to taste, to experience the things she'd wondered about for years.

Her first real kiss.

Eyam had not yet kissed more than her hand. A few other gentlemen had stolen kisses from her lips, but only in the most playful way, such as under a mistletoe bough. This man *took* her lips. That was the phrase for it. He took them, claimed them, captured them, and his capture was masterful.

That pressure, those movements, almost as if he spoke to her in a heated language she could barely understand. Teasing, tempting, coaxing. His tongue . . .

Like a blow, she remembered Moore.

Grandiston moved back an inch, his eyes intent. "No?"

It had to be no. "I'm sorry. I don't know. . . . We're strangers. We shouldn't. . . ."

She pulled against his arms. He neither released her nor drew her back against him. "We shouldn't," he agreed. He turned her face back to his, his big hand gentle and warm where it cupped her cheek. "But do you want to?"

*No.* That was what Caro should say, but he was nothing like Moore, his carefulness, his gentleness, wildly different, and every sensation different, too. Anticipation instead of fear, delight instead of disgust.

"Then relax, my dear, and let me pleasure you."

He drew her back against his body. He kissed her again, teasing her mouth open, angling her head for the invasion. At first she tensed, but then every sense sparkled with delighted anticipation.

She was his to do with as he wished, it seemed. Even as they kissed, he sat, taking her on his lap without breaking the sizzling connection. She moved, too, but not to struggle free. She pressed closer, raising a hand to cup the back of his head, to dig her fingers into his crisp hair, to hold him to her for her own thrilled exploration.

Incredible. Intoxicating! She could do this forever and die happy. At last she began to understand the books. . . .

His hand was on her leg. Beneath her skirts, even as she kissed, and kissed, and kissed!

Caro tensed, following the course of that invasion: warm hand traveling upward past her garter to the bare skin of her thigh, stroking there, squeezing there, and still he kissed. . . .

Sliding over and then — oh, my stars! — between. Shivers ran up and into her soul. She should protest now, push apart, escape. . . .

She couldn't bear to.

Not yet, at least.

Their mouths were still connected, but now his lips only teased, as if in deliberate contrast to the boldness of his other exploration, to his touch on a spot so sensitive that her whole body twitched.

His fingers slid deeper and any trace of rebellion collapsed. Her body clenched around him as if to keep him there. Her heart was galloping fit to kill her, and she was panting as if ready to expire.

This was shocking, sinful.

"You want me to stop?"

Caro realized Grandiston had gone still and was regarding her, puzzled. But his hand still rested deeply between her thighs, his fingers still inside her. Possessing her. But gently, oh so gently.

Sweetly, even, both causing and soothing an intense ache.

"Yes or no?" Those fingers circled and she inhaled, losing all power of speech.

He did it again.

She whimpered, but it wasn't in protest, and he knew it.

He pushed deeper into her inner place. Her muscles down there clenched again, with a hungry yet thrilling ache. "Oh my, oh my," she breathed.

He smiled — a devil's smile, an angel's smile, a supremely confident seducer's smile — as he kissed the side of her neck — so sensitive! — and the rough scar beneath her ear.

His lips played down the edge of her neckline to the skin just above her breast, and all the while his fingers stroked and swirled and she quivered and melted, incapable of any resistant thought.

She heard the little sounds she was making and thought of the open window. But if anyone heard, they'd never imagine them protests. This was the most extraordinary thing that had ever happened to her, something beyond any imagining, and she wanted it to never stop.

Then he thrust deeper — her thighs fell wide to encourage him — and moved his hand harder, faster. Eyes closed, lost in a dark, hot maelstrom, Caro simply experienced with gasps and cries and a madly pounding heart as waves of tight pleasure swelled and ebbed, building higher and higher, and then crested, shattering her to pieces.

She lay sprawled, aware of ripples of pleasure still pulsing in her, of tingling heat and the sweat to go with it. And his hand was still there, between her thighs, his fingers still inside her in intimate possession.

He stirred them a little. "If we were to undress a little, dear lady, we could soar to even greater heights."

Caro opened her eyes, blinking at him, trying to make sense of his words. Distantly, weakly, some part of her was trying to regain sanity and decency.

His fingers moved again, blasting away any such thoughts. But she was exquisitely sensitive now.

"I don't think . . ."

"Much the best idea," he said, beginning to unfasten her jacket.

She clutched his hand.

"Trust me, sweetheart, you'll like what I can do to your breasts."

"My breasts?" she said, suddenly aware of them as never before. Of their fullness, their heat, and the way her nipples tingled. With hunger? For what he could do?

"What sort of lover is your husband?" He undid the first hook at the bottom. "A quick fumble beneath nightclothes? Let me show you splendor and delight."

The second hook came undone.

Caro almost said, *I shouldn't,* but she was too honest to do that when she knew she would. She had to experience just a little more.

"I must at least know your name," she managed, with no calculation at all.

"Grandiston." Another hook.

"Your Christian name."

"You have it," he said.

She clutched his hand to keep it still. "What? Speak sense."

"I can't imagine why," he said, evading her grasp, "but my Christian name is 'Christian.'"

"Truly?"

"If that's too holy for this moment, try Pagan."

Caro pushed at him. "I demand the truth."

He laughed, gorgeous, rumpled, his neck bare. When had she disheveled his cravat?

"Why?" he asked.

"Why?" she asked back, with no idea what they were talking about.

"Why this obsession with truth? But if you want it, you have it. My baptismal name is Christian, but I sometimes go by Pagan. So is your name truly Katherine?"

Caro was so befuddled that she almost spilled the truth, but she caught herself in time. "Yes."

"Does anyone call you Kat?"

She wanted to be a Kat. "Yes."

His smile turned wicked. "Do you scratch? I might like that." He pushed her jacket off her shoulders. When had he completed the unfastening?

"You wretch!" she protested, but she let him draw the garment down her unresisting arms, even though it revealed her stays and the shift beneath.

One of her plainest shifts.

Why hadn't she worn one trimmed with lace?

"Pagans usually are wretches," he said, dropping the jacket to the floor. "Or so the churchmen would have us believe. Fornicators, every one. Cannibals, even." His gaze lowered. "You do look very tasty, Kat."

Caro looked down and saw her full breasts swelling above the top of her stays and the plain, narrow white frill. He turned her to face the whitewashed wall and began to unknot her stay laces.

She made one last attempt. "This is wrong. . . ."

"Not to a pagan."

"I'm no pagan!"

"Become one. Pagans are more honest, more true to natural forms. Your form is entrancing, you know." He ran a hand swiftly down her side and over her hip, then around to squeeze her bottom.

"Sir!" It came out as a gasp.

"If you feel obliged to protest," he said with laughter in his voice, "wouldn't it be better to try a name?"

"Christian? This is the most unchristian thing imaginable!"

"Don't be silly."

He turned her again, this time to face the fly-specked mirror. Through the wavering glass she saw a most unchristian sight.

Her skirt was intact. As for the rest, she was still mostly dressed, but so very, very undressed. Her plain buff stays were sagging forward as he unlaced them, exposing more of her breasts beneath fine lawn.

She clutched the stays back to herself. "We can't. . . . I can't. . . ."

He smiled at her, but didn't so much as pause in his work, and why should he? Her verbal protests were not accompanied by any meaningful action.

Why was he able to do this to her?

Why couldn't she resist as she knew she ought?

He was handsome — that was true —

especially now, in such disorder, but the conquerors here were his confidence and skill.

That should revolt her, but skill was skill and he was sweeping her into madness as a gale might sweep up a sheet and carry it away.

He looked up again, smiled at her again, then leaned to trace warm butterfly kisses at the back of her neck and then down the center of her spine. How could she not have known how beautifully sensitive her back was, how made for pleasure?

She arched, inhaling, but still managed a faint protest. "It's still daylight."

"You think too much."

He put his hands at her waist and picked her up. Before Caro had time to protest or panic, he put her down again — now straddling his thigh. He'd put his foot up on the bench in front of the dressing table.

"What are you doing?" she gasped to his reflection, alarmed but excited by hard pressure — down there, where she seemed so very sensitive. She squirmed, which made it worse.

"Distracting you as I complete your return to nature. Lean forward."

When she simply stared at his reflection, he took her hands from her clutch on her

170

stays and put them down flat on the dressing table, his body pressing down over hers, allowing no escape, intensifying the pressure.

"Angels of mercy!" Caro gasped, closing her eyes. But that made it worse. She looked at his reflection again. "You are too skilled at this!"

"You complain?"

"It's wicked!"

"It's pagan, and it's pleasure." He bounced his thigh slightly so that logic evaporated. "Pagan pleasures. Why deny yourself?"

And Caro could find no response.

He straightened, smiling, to complete his liberation, still moving his leg in that subtle, devastating way. He discarded the corset and slid both hands to claim her shift-covered breasts. Thumbs flicked hard nipples, sending a jolt through Caro such as she'd never imagined possible.

Braced on her arms, head hanging, tormented below and above, Caro moaned, but by the stars, this was the most delicious state of fever and desperation. How had she never known this was possible?

He leaned forward, so big and hot against her buttocks, and took both nipples between thumb and fingers. At the pinch, Caro stiffened, but then he began to roll and stretch them. A wave of something went through her, widening her eyes and mouth in the mirror as if in a silent scream, but stabbing her down in her private place. Stabbing her with desperate need.

He set his teeth into her shoulder. Not to truly bite, she could tell, but the hard pressure there completed her destruction. Caro muttered a prayer that God would certainly ignore and surrendered as a new, body-racking explosion built and built, and destroyed her again.

Before she could put back the pieces, he carried her to the bed and placed her there. Eyes hot but still smiling, he bent to capture her lips again, tongue plunging a command to surrender.

Unnecessary command. She wanted to kiss him. Needed to kiss him. To open her mouth and explore his as he explored hers — yes, almost like trying to eat each other.

Cannibals.

He slowly took his lips away. Panting, sweating, Caro stared up as he straightened, as those smiling, wicked, pagan eyes traveled over her, as if she were a rich dish he was about to consume.

He began to strip off his clothes. "My beautiful Kat. All rumpled skirts and loose linen, and glowing, delicious skin." Jacket and waistcoat gone. He pulled his shirt loose and unfastened lace-edged cuffs. "With your lips cherry red and wet — yes, lick them again. Just like that. And your nipples swollen with wanting more."

Caro instinctively covered them, feeling the truth of his words. He laughed, but not at her. He really seemed brimming over with delight, at her.

Wanting her.

*Her.*

He pulled his shirt up over his head and she absorbed, dry-mouthed, a perfect sculpted torso, hard with muscle. Then she saw the rough, white scar high on his chest.

"What did that?" she gasped, rising up on her elbows in shock.

"A hatchet."

"A hatchet? How?"

"Someone wanted to kill me, and they had a hatchet in their hand."

"An outraged husband, perhaps?" Caro asked, a glimmer of sanity poking at her. He was a rake. A hardened, practiced rake — with a very big bulge at the front of his breeches.

Caro edged back. "I don't think . . ."

He fell over her on hands and knees like a big cat. "Pagans never think. They thrive on natural impulses." He kissed her again, pressing her back into the pillows. Caro resisted for a moment, but she couldn't resist the heat of potent natural impulses.

When he raised his lips, she only wanted. Even his size, his muscles, the breadth of his shoulders seemed only wondrous to her now.

But the scar still shocked her. Such an ugly blemish on perfection. She placed a hand over it, feeling the hard ridges. "It must have been very painful," she said, "in the receiving and the treatment."

"True. As must this." He dropped a kiss on her scar.

"There's no comparison. It was an angry husband, wasn't it?"

Supporting himself on one arm, he played with her right breast. "Is yours likely to attack me with an ax?"

She thought of poor Hill. "No."

"With a pistol?"

"No."

"With a sword?"

Hill fighting with his sword. Skillful despite youth. Risking death for her.

"No," she said sadly. They were speaking of one of his family, and he didn't know. That seemed dishonorable in some way.

"A feeble sort of fellow, then," he said dismissively.

She shook her head. "Don't speak of what you don't know."

He raised a hand. "My apologies. A terrible breach of etiquette to talk of a husband at a time like this."

"There's etiquette to this?"

"Oh, yes. Both complex and important." He drew her closer, cupping one breast. "This is when you tell me what more you want."

He was smiling so confidently that Caro suddenly felt ashamed of herself. She pushed free. "Are all women such easy prey for you? Do we all lose virtue and willpower at your clever touch?"

He simply lay there, unmoved. "Not unless you want to."

"You think I want —"

"You're here, Kat," he interrupted, "and you enjoyed what we did. Deny it if you dare."

She wanted to, desperately, but in a day of lies, she couldn't form this one. Just as she couldn't make herself leave this bed as she ought.

She'd deflected, and if necessary repulsed, a dozen insistent men. Why not this one? It had to be his skill and experience, and that should disgust her. Instead, she hungered for more of it.

She wanted his knowing touch, his skillful kisses, his guidance through strange waters. She wanted to know and touch and learn, learn more. To put her mouth to the sleek muscles that made his flat, manly breasts, to run her tongue along the ridges of strong bones.

To experience more.

More of these mysteries.

All of them.

Now.

# CHAPTER 9

Caro looked up and saw that he knew her desires beyond hope of denial. That perhaps this interlude had been designed to bring her to full acceptance of them. Another skillful touch.

As was the way he pushed her gently back down on the pillows and placed his hand on her body again. But not on her breast. Instead on her hip, which should be safer but didn't feel that way.

"Shall we do more?"

Caro licked dry, hungry lips. "I must not conceive a child."

"You won't."

"Then there's little more we can do."

"More than a little. A great deal more. May I show you?"

He was tempting as the serpent in Eden and she was a very foolish Eve, but yes, please. She wanted to discover everything.

His hand still teased her hip, like a low

fire keeping a pot on the simmer, but he was seducing her with smiling eyes and subtle voice, assuring her that she had nothing to fear, that all he offered was more safe delirium.

Lies, all lies, but she said, "Perhaps a little more," her voice husky.

"Little by little," he agreed, which wasn't the same thing, but when he took his hand off her, she moved as if to follow it.

He began to unbutton the flap of his bulging breeches. He unfastened his drawers beneath, and released his phallus — thick, long, and pointing right up at her.

She'd thought the pictures in books exaggerated.

Caro looked up into his amused eyes. Her gaze skittered to the side and found the mirror, which thank heaven didn't show anything of this.

He grasped her hand and closed it around his hard hotness.

Which quivered.

Heat seared all over her skin, but after a moment, she had to look again. Moisture glimmered at the dark tip.

"Oh, dear . . ." But between her thighs, her private place didn't know it was too long, too thick, too much of everything.

His hand still covering hers, he guided

her, sliding over the rock hardness beneath. "You haven't done this before, have you? Your husband is a fool. Or is he poorly endowed? I know, I know, terrible breach of etiquette, but it's a crime to leave a venturesome lady so undereducated. Explore as you will, sweet Kat, as I play cannibal."

He removed his hand from hers, but coiled over to put his mouth to her breast.

At the new intense sensation, Caro let out a small cry, but she continued to fondle him as long as she could. Until passion surged to overwhelm her, to whirl her again into mindless, stormy pleasure.

But then he plunged into her, huge and hard. Filling her, stretching her —

Memory hit like a lightning bolt.

Moore!

She pushed up violently, trying to heave him off her. "No! Stop!"

His hand clapped over her mouth. "Struth, ma'am!"

The formal "ma'am" shocked Caro, and then made her laugh. Which was madness, but it sent dark memories scuttling back into their pit.

Leaving her fully aware of her situation.

Transfixed in all ways.

And ruined.

Watching her carefully, he removed his

silencing hand.

Caro swallowed, almost blinded to reason by that deep connection below. "You said you wouldn't do this. Risk a child."

"I'll pull out before I spill my seed. Come, Kat. Heaven is in reach." He slid out a little, then in again, slick as grease. New sensations exploded.

"Pagans don't go to heaven."

Continuing the slow movement, he said, "They have their own heaven. One that's a great deal more exciting than harp playing."

"That's heresy . . . or something."

"And this is sin. But wonderful, isn't it?" He moved again, slowly, almost gently, like a stroke against sizzling, secret places, and Caro's body recognized the one thing above all that it wanted.

Was it possible that he do as he said?

Was she safe?

The very idea was laughable. He filled her so completely, moved so confidently. His big body was her whole world, making nonsense of any idea that she could escape unless he allowed it.

And yet she felt safe, and in some way cherished, as if encircled in protective warmth.

Fulfilled, or with true fulfillment in reach.

"Isn't it?" he repeated, his voice deep and

soft as he slid a hand beneath one buttock, locking her to him, capturing her for his pleasure.

For their pleasure.

"Wonderful," he repeated again, "isn't it?"

He wanted her assent, demanded it.

Something strangely like a gurgle came out of Caro's throat, but then she managed, "Yes." She followed it with a vague "I think . . ." but it was lost in a kiss and the rhythm of their connection.

Caro surrendered. And kept surrendering until he was pounding her into a heart-galloping intensity that fired her into a dimension she had never imagined could exist.

It seemed a long, hot time before she could think again, a time of clutching and kissing and sweaty, pungent heat. She blinked her eyes open, astonished to find daylight still filling the room and faint noises that said that somewhere the world went on as normal.

Such sinful passion was surely meant for quiet night.

She was half over his strong chest, his arm around her. Safe. Protected.

Ravished.

Yes, she'd been ravished.

She was sore below and parts of her still

quivered and throbbed in a way that might be protest, but also seemed a demand that she do it all over again.

She admired the firm muscles of his chest and a small, dark nipple. Wondering if men felt there as women did under a skilled touch. But . . .

"Did you do as you said?"

"Of course."

So arrogant that she smiled, but the arrogance made his words believable.

"You're a very practiced rake, aren't you?" she sighed.

"Practice makes perfect?"

She heard laughter in his voice.

"You are well skilled, I grant."

"Come, now," he said, raising her face to his. "Give me my due, Kat. Not just skilled, but perfect by practice. You said it yourself."

She laughed with him, and much of it came from pure happiness. She was a fool in the coils of an opportunistic rake, but for the moment she was more content and joyous than she could ever remember.

He leaned down to drop kisses on her cheek, then touched her hair.

"I've never seen a lady's hair survive a wild bout in such order."

Parades of lascivious ladies trooped through Caro's imagination.

"It's well pinned," she said.

"It must be. Why?"

"It's inclined to rebel."

"Like you."

"Me?"

"What else is this but a rebellion, Kat?" He stroked her cheek. "I hope you don't lose your head over it."

"Don't say such a thing. Why would I?"

"Your husband might find out. You must know that. But then, you seemed confident that he wouldn't resort to violence."

"I'm sure of it. You have nothing to fear."

"I don't fear him," he said, all humor gone. "Only your displeasure if I were forced to kill him."

Caro was suddenly, deeply chilled. "Why would you do that?"

"Only if he was trying to kill me."

"That scar. The hatchet. Did you kill the man who did that?"

There was no regret behind his answer. "Yes."

It swirled bleakly between them, curdling sweetness.

Caro scrambled out of the bed, down the steps to the wooden floor. Returning to earth and appalled realization of what she'd done. How could she have forgotten the harsh and violent man?

She hitched the top of her shift up and tied the lace, trying to restore decency before picking up her skirt. She glanced to see if he was a threat.

He was lying, head propped up on hand, observing her, apparently unmoved. Of course he was. He didn't care about her at all.

She turned her back, stepped into her skirt, and tied it at the waist. She heard movement and whirled.

He was rounding the bed and walking toward her, his breeches already fastened, but his chest still naked.

She snatched up her stays.

"You have no way to fasten them again," he said.

That was damnably true. "You undid them, sir, so you can put it right!"

"I see nothing right about confinement. Your sturdy jacket will hide the lack."

Slowly, he smiled, his eyes warm with it, and she felt her anger melting away like butter.

"What point to it, then?"

"I'd know," he said, "and so would you."

Caro felt heat rise into her face so she had no hope of denying her response. Horrible, outrageous man . . .

But still she melted.

"My victim had buried a hatchet in my shoulder," he said. "I had some justification."

"And he doubtless had as much for doing it!"

"All fair in love and war?"

He held out her jacket and she turned to put it on, then fastened it over her unconfined breasts. The mirror showed that he was right, that people probably wouldn't know.

But she would.

He moved behind her so she could see him in the mirror, see his naked shoulders and the ugly scar.

Self-defense.

See the way he was looking at her, the way he was smiling. She heard his husky tone when he said, "Thank you."

Then he moved away. She turned to watch as he put on his shirt and fastened the short row of buttons. It was unbearably intimate to watch a man do that.

He met her eyes. "We don't have to part now if you don't wish it."

She turned sharply back to the mirror. "Yes, we do."

Her hair was mostly in place, but untidy. She pulled out some loose hairpins and reset them, wishing she could reset her mind. She'd been educated, however, just like Eve in the Garden of Eden, taught all about good and evil, and it couldn't be undone.

She watched him in the mirror as he buttoned his waistcoat. She was changed, but for him, nothing extraordinary had happened.

Had she no pride?

Where on earth was her hat, which she'd thought such a great defense? On the table by his chair. She picked it up, but didn't even take time to put it on.

"I must go," she said, but faltered, thinking there should be something else to say.

Nothing sane. She left the room before he could attempt to stop her. By heaven's blessing the corridor was empty and she could enter her own room undetected. There, it was as if a magic spell disintegrated. She was herself again, and appalled.

What had she *done?*

If anyone ever found out, she'd be ruined beyond redemption. She had to get away. Kat Hunter had to cease to exist. She hastily gathered the few items she'd removed from the valise and stuffed them back in.

Then she froze. Heaven help her, she'd left her stays behind!

She thought for a moment of going back

for them, but only for a moment. She snapped the bag shut and went to the door.

She halted there, staggered by a new problem. She couldn't walk out of the Woolpack with her valise unless it was to take a York coach. Did any travel through the night? She had to leave this room to find out about the coach.

She put down the valise, opened the door and peered out. No sign of Grandiston.

She crept along the corridor and was halfway down the stairs when she realized that the hall was awkwardly full of people. A party of five was negotiating with the harried innkeeper, while two richly dressed men stood in the street doorway loudly demanding the attention of servants rushing this way and that. She was tempted to return to hiding, but she made herself go on.

But then one of the men looked up and raised a quizzing glass the better to study her, the impudent rascal. That didn't distress her too much, but she hurried down to floor level, her heart pattering with a new fear. She didn't know those men, but there might be other travelers whom she'd met at Harrogate or York.

Why hadn't she thought of that? She'd believed herself safe because only Phyllis and Fred knew her here, but she'd forgotten travelers. This was the Great North Road. Anyone could pass through.

She needed the ticket office in the coach yard. She turned toward the dining room. That had a door into the coach yard. But the dining room, too, was busy. Caro lurked by the door, checking to be sure she knew no one in the room. No, only the Silcocks taking tea at a small table by the fireplace. Their day must have gone as badly as hers, for they looked even grimmer.

Servants were rushing in and out of the kitchen door to her right, so Caro had to go around the long table on the left, where she'd pass close to the American couple. She prayed they not delay her.

Mistress Silcock put down her cup and used some butter from her crumpet to grease her fingers so she could remove her four rings. Each left an indentation in puffy flesh and she massaged the spots as if they hurt. Poor woman. It was a bad sign to swell like that.

In her moment of distraction, she heard a voice from outside call, "All aboard. All aboard for the Edinburgh Flyer! All aboard!"

That would go to York, wouldn't it?

People rose hurriedly, and one man's chair

knocked into Caro, staggering her toward the Silcocks' table. That saved her from a tumble to the floor, but the crockery rattled. The traveler apologized, but then rushed off to his coach.

Caro steadied the table, catching her breath. "I'm sorry. I . . ."

"Not your fault, ma'am, and no harm done." Silcock spoke without a smile, but his words were fair.

Caro smiled at him and turned to apologize to his wife — to receive a flash of malevolent fury from the woman's eyes.

Was she insane?

Caro certainly had no time for new trouble. She hurried toward the coach yard, fearing there wouldn't be time to purchase a ticket. She glanced back. It felt as if fiery arrows were hurtling toward her back. Yes, the woman was still glaring.

When she turned back, she saw the doors slamming on the coach. A moment later it was rolling out. All the energy drained out of her, but she braced herself. There would be others.

She paused to let two servants carry a box inside and stole another glance at the Silcocks. The woman had given up her rage and was talking to her husband. All the same, she was unbalanced in some way.

Caro was about to turn again, but was staggered by another collision. She gained her balance again, catching the careening child who'd run into her.

But then she heard the cry of, "Stop, thief!"

It came from Mistress Silcock, who was on her feet, color high, swollen finger pointing.

Everyone in the dining room turned to stare. A male inn servant ran into the dining room from the hall. "That weasel! Saw her creeping around the hall, I did."

"I didn't do nuthin'!" the girl screeched, clutching on to Caro as if her life depended on it. It well might.

"She stole my rings!" shrieked Mistress Silcock. "Search her, search her!"

Caro was frozen, but the rings were certainly no longer on the table. She looked down at the child, who looked back up at her, showing a thin, sharp-angled face and eyes that pleaded for protection.

She wasn't as young as Caro had thought. Caro had thought her about ten, but she was probably a scrawny fourteen or more. If she'd stolen valuable rings, at that age, she'd hang.

And she wasn't local. Her shrill, nasal accent was nothing from the north, which meant everyone in the room was thinking, a ragamuffin, far from home. Vagrant and petty thief. It was probably true, but Caro couldn't toss her to the wolves. She knew from her charity work how often dire necessity lay behind crime.

She gripped the girl's bony wrists. "Let go and I'll do what I can for you."

Crafty satisfaction flickered across the narrow face. Caro didn't let that sway her. Criminals must be crafty to survive. That didn't mean a child should hang.

Caro addressed Mistress Silcock as soothingly as she could. "You're certain the rings didn't fall to the floor, ma'am?"

"Absolutely!" The fiery arrows were flying again. How could Mistress Silcock think she had anything to do with this?

But then the woman staggered back and sank into her chair. "My rings, my rings. The one from my dear brother!"

She truly wasn't well. She might even have a seizure.

Caro wanted only to escape, but she wouldn't get out of the increasingly crowded room until this was settled. The door to the hall was packed with an audience now, and the one behind Caro was filling with gawkers from the coach yard.

And if anyone recognized her . . .

She'd rather like to collapse into a chair herself.

"Perhaps someone could look if the rings are on the floor there," Caro suggested, but the mood of the room was against her.

Those who weren't watching in hope that Mistress Silcock would expire on the spot were eyeing the vagrant child like hungry dogs. They kept their eyes fixed on their quarry even though the girl had no chance of escape. They'd hang the child right now if the law allowed, or at least whip her around town, tied staggering behind a slow cart.

"I did nuthin'!" the girl cried again in that metal-grating accent. "Search me if you want." She challenged the room with startling confidence. "Go on. Search me! But mind where your 'ands go."

"Well, go on," Silcock growled to the nearest servants. "Search the wretch, and make it thorough."

"I'll search her," Caro said, and set to work.

She felt the girl's rough-spun skirts for the slits into her pockets. She was very thin, only skin and bone really, but Caro didn't think she was starving. There was heat and energy, and she could probably run like the wind. The pockets produced three

192

ha'pennies and a sprig of limp mint.

"There, see!" the girl declared, looking around.

"She'll have put 'em down her bodice," a maid shouted.

"I'll look there," said one of the menservants with a snigger.

Caro gave him an icy look, turned the girl toward her, and probed around that area. She was almost flat-chested, however, and wore no boned stays, so it was clear no rings were hidden there. Having some knowledge of thieves' tricks, she knelt to feel down her legs for secret pouches. She found nothing, but to settle the matter, she said, "Shoes."

With a cheeky smirk, the girl stepped out of the battered pair. Caro picked them up and checked them but, as she expected, found nothing. Feeling increasingly that the girl was mocking her, she grasped the grubby mobcap and removed it. She checked inside and then made herself search through the greasy hair.

Nothing.

Clearly the girl was completely innocent, or guilty of no more than trying to steal a heel of bread.

Caro put her hands on the girl's shoulders as a sign of support. "The rings aren't on her. I suggest a thorough search of the floor.

Such items can roll."

"She took them," said Silcock. "Perhaps she threw them on the floor when detected, but she took them. She bumped into the table just as you did."

Mistress Silcock sat bolt upright. "As you did!" she cried. "There's the thief. Search her!"

"Me?" Caro gasped. "I didn't steal your rings! You must have seen them there after I parted from you."

"I didn't," the woman said.

The lunatic had found an arrow after all.

"This is ridiculous," Caro said, striving for calm, but she could sense the hostile mood shifting toward her. She heard murmurs all around.

Mistress Silcock might even have smiled. "Can anyone vouch for you?" she demanded.

"I'm from York," she said. "You know that. My husband. The accident."

"We know the story you told us," Silcock said. "Can anyone support it?"

Dry-mouthed, Caro realized just how perilous her situation was.

Here, she was not Mistress Hill of Froggatt's and Luttrell House, bulwarked by fortune and respectability. Instead, she was as much a stranger as the vagrant child, and a woman oddly unaccompanied. She'd covered that with a story, but that story would unravel in a moment if investigated. Then she'd be revealed as a liar, which would be seen as proof positive that she was up to no good.

If she gave her true name, there was no one to vouch for her, and possibly even worse, Grandiston would know who she was and be able to do whatever he had come north to do.

As if to seal her lips, she saw him appear behind the crowd staring in from the hall. Their eyes met, but she saw no concern, no offer of help. He turned and walked away.

# CHAPTER 10

What had she expected? A gallant knight?

"Look at her," bellowed Silcock, pointing. "Have you ever seen a clearer picture of guilt?"

Rough hands grasped her from behind.

"No!" Caro protested. "This is outrageous. I'm a respectable woman. Wife to a solicitor from York. I told you. . . ."

But hands were delving into her pockets while others poked and prodded. Then one of the searchers, a woman, cried, "Here they be! Look!"

The stocky, hard-faced woman stepped forward, work-worn hand outstretched, cupping the four rings.

Silcock strode forward to snatch them.

Caro struggled against her captors. "The girl. The girl must have put them there!"

Where was the girl? Gone, of course, at the first opportunity, snake-thin body somehow wriggling through the crowd, whose avid attention had been fixed on new prey.

"Shame on you!" cried the woman who'd held the rings. "Tryin' to push it off on a poor waif."

"Poor waif?" Caro protested.

But the whole room took it up. "Shame! Shame!" It rang like the baying of mastiffs after a felon.

"And as for respectable," an inn maid said, pushing forward through the hall door, "what was a respectable solicitor's wife doing in that fancy gentleman's room? I ask."

It was the one who'd brought the wine.

"In this with thee, no doubt," the maid went on, enjoying her central role. "Doubtless an 'ighwayman, 'im, so big and bold, and with sword and pistols. 'E and t'other man who just arrived. The one with the evil black patch over 'is eye."

Caro swayed, almost faint with shock. If her true name was revealed, soon all of Yorkshire would know her shame. Eyam would be lost to her. She'd never again attend any gracious event. Even the cutlers and worthy folk of Sheffield would look at her askance.

She'd rather die.

Except, she realized, that wasn't a figure of speech. If she didn't reveal the truth, she might hang or be transported. She, not the girl, could be whipped at the cart tail, or branded on the hand as warning to all that she was a thief.

Battered by gleeful suspicion all around, she was sucked back to the Tup inn, when young Jack Hill had unjustly faced a similar mob, been cruelly seized and abused, and been forced to wed her to escape.

She'd hidden under the bed, she remembered.

She wished there was a bed to hide under now.

"Someone summon the constable!"

"Let's take 'er to the jail!"

"Or to t'stocks."

"Aye, that's it. The stocks."

"The stocks!"

Hands tugged her backward so violently she was almost dragged off her feet.

"No, please! I'm innocent!"

"Thee be willin' to prosecute, sir?" someone asked Silcock.

Caro had a moment of hope. In cases of theft, the victim had to initiate the prosecution. But Silcock looked at her with a malevolence to match his wife's. "To the full extent of the law."

"No!" Caro protested again, but she was dragged across the coach yard, beneath the arch, and out into the street, where it seemed that the whole of Doncaster had gathered to gawk. Tears poured down her face now and she had no way to wipe them. Hands bruised her arms. A child threw a stone. It was a small stone and a weak throw, so she hardly felt it, but she stared in horror at the fresh-faced lad who'd done such a thing.

If they put her in the stocks, the good people of Doncaster would feel entitled to throw anything to hand at her — rotten fruit, filth, and, yes, even stones.

She no longer cared about reputation, Eyam, Grandiston, anything.

"Stop!" she screamed. "I do know people here. Fred . . . Phyllis . . ." She produced the most powerful name she knew. "Diana!"

Last names.

Titles.

Her brain was scrambled.

"Arradale!" she screamed. "Ossington."

She was drowned out by a bellow from her left. When she twisted, she saw a monstrous scarecrow racing toward her, black coat flapping, white eyes glaring in a dirt-dark face under a battered, wide-brimmed hat. A huge fist sent one of the men holding her flying, then the other. Caro was snatched, thrown over a shoulder, and carried away.

Idiotically, she screamed, "Save me! Someone save me!"

Bouncing so she couldn't breathe, with bile stinging her throat, she futilely beat at her captor's back, weeping, choking, as they careened into an alley, the mob howling in pursuit.

She heard a rattling roar behind them.

What was that?

The howls of the mob turned to frustration, but they shrank into the distance. He pounded onward, kicking and elbowing gates. One gave and he turned into a yard of some kind. A stinking yard. He ran across it. Into some sort of shed.

Caro was let down onto her feet, but would have collapsed in a heap if not for strong arms. The sudden stillness and quiet was shocking.

"Hush, my dear. Hush."

A gentleman's voice? Caro looked up through blurry eyes and saw green and gold. "You?"

A wide smile showed healthy teeth. "Me. I don't know how you fell into that boiling broth, but I thought you'd like to be out of it."

Caro gaped for something to say, but then she heard the animal cries of the mob once and clutched him. "We're trapped here!"

"Someone's decoying. Lean here." He

propped her against a rough stone wall and went to the door to listen.

Caro raised shaking hands to her grimy face, then dug into a pocket for a handkerchief. She let out a choked laugh. When he turned his head, she said, "Someone stole my handkerchief. And my purse!"

"It's a perilous world," he said, but with a grin that implied this was a game.

He was mad, too.

She should be in tears, but she seemed far beyond that, light-headed, almost as if drunk.

"What was that noise behind us? Like a rumble of thunder."

"My man dropping some barrels to block the alley."

Caro's legs gave way and she slithered down to sit on the floor, back to a wall, shaking down to her toes.

"I'm a fugitive from the law," she whispered. "I'll hang if I'm caught. I'll never be able to show my face in respectable society again."

"Especially after being hanged," he said unsympathetically. He came over to hunker down beside her. "Buck up, Kat. I won't let any harm come to you."

"How?" she demanded. "A miracle worker, are you?"

"I've brought us this far."

Caro looked around at the hovel. "To a rattrap."

"But our rattrap."

She closed her eyes and shook her head. But she opened them again to look him over. "How did you do it? Disguise yourself. Rescue me?"

"Vagrant's clothes, soot, and surprise."

"In mere moments?"

"It was longer than it seemed to you, but I'm good at thinking and acting fast."

He stood and Caro realized his legs were bare from the breeches down. "Your feet!"

"Will survive. My boots hardly matched the disguise."

He returned to the door. She heard it, too. The clatter of boots in the nearby alley. Voices calling back and forth.

"No organized search," he said softly. "All hubbub and mayhem."

"But they're bound to find us eventually. Someone will organize a search."

And if she survived their rough revenge, she'd be put on trial for theft. Even her true identity might not save her. They'd found the rings in her pocket. That wretched, wretched ragamuffin!

Caro closed her eyes and hugged herself, rocking. This had to be a nightmare. This whole day.

No letter from the Horse Guards.

No Grandiston.

No flight to Doncaster.

No Kat Hunter . . .

"Time to change."

No ragamuffin.

No mob —

"Kat!"

Her eyes flew open and she began to babble. "They'll hang me, or transport me! Whip me bloody. I can't leave here. I can't!"

He gripped her shoulders. "Yes, you can. As you said, they'll organize a search, but if you're brave, I'll get you away."

"I'm not brave. I've never been brave!"

He kissed her, quick and hard, and pulled her to her feet. "I am. Trust me. The mob's run on. We can slip out —"

"No, no!" she whispered. "We'll be caught in a moment. Everyone knows what we look like."

"So we change our appearance. Let's start with your hat." He unpinned it, crushed it, and shoved it into a coat pocket, then began to pull pins from her hair.

"Ouch!" Caro pushed his hands away.

"You need to be as disreputable as I am. Come on, Kat. You're better than this."

The challenge somehow reached her. She

sucked in a breath and tried to think. Change appearance. She could do that.

Hair.

She pulled out hairpins and fingered loose the plaits as he stripped off his coat and hid it beneath some stones and wood in one corner.

He turned back and stared at her.

"I know. It's appalling," she said, struggling with the tangle of curls that she knew was frothing around her head and down to her shoulder blades.

"It's remarkable, like a conjurer producing a bouquet of flowers out of a shoe. How do mere pins confine it?"

"By force of numbers." She shoved the pins into one of her pockets. "It was merely wavy once, but . . ." She remembered in time that she mustn't mention the Moore affair to Grandiston. "I fell ill and the doctor shaved my hair to ease the pressure on my mind. My mind recovered, but my hair grew demented."

"It fits your rough part," he said, scrubbing his face clean with his shirt, improving both. His face now looked merely grimy and his shirt was no longer too clean for the rest of him. "You look nothing like Mistress Hunter. But the jacket has to go."

Caro wanted to protest. She loved the rich

design, but he was right. Except . . .

No stays.

"The jacket, Kat."

"No."

He frowned. "Don't be a fool. It marks you like a beacon."

"And this won't?" She unfastened it and spread the front. "Remember your brilliant idea?"

"Ah, yes."

And he smiled.

Caro swung to hit him, but laughing, he caught her hand and disarmed her by kissing her knuckles. "Alas for the night that might have been." While she was still dazed, he pushed the jacket off her shoulders and pulled it off.

Caro covered herself with her hands. "I can't! Not even to save my life . . ."

Her voice trailed off.

He refrained from saying the obvious.

"Even the simplest woman wears some sort of stays," she protested.

"You're right," he said, and reversed the jacket to its snuff brown lining. "Wear it this way."

"Oh, thank you."

But then he produced a knife, and hacked off the sleeves.

"Oh, no!"

Caro knew her protest was ridiculous, but it had been her favorite. When he wiped the floor with what remained, she managed to only bite her lip. When he passed it back, she grabbed it and scrambled back into it with gratitude, dirt, mutilation, and all.

The hooks were awkward to fasten inside out, but she managed. Looking down, she supposed it did look like a simple country bodice now, with her shift sleeves covering her arms to the elbows. A good thing she'd put on a plain one this morning — one without frill or lace.

This morning.

The sunny breakfast room at Luttrell House.

Tears threatened, but she fought them back and even tried to smile. He had rescued her.

"Thank you. For everything."

"Knight-errant at your service." He looked her over. "Take off the wedding ring — it's too fine. And get dirtier. Your skirt's plain enough but much too clean."

Caro wasn't clear on the long plan, but she clung to his crisp confidence. She twisted off her ring and put it in her pocket, then dropped to the dirt floor and rolled. When she stood again, she rubbed her dirty hands all over her face.

He was scrubbing dirt through his blond hair, turning it a muddy color. He looked her over again. "Better. Can you go barefoot?"

Caro wanted to say no.

She wanted so many things she couldn't have.

"Better than hanging," she said, kicking off her brown leather shoes. Immediately she hated the feel of the rough, dirty floor beneath her stockinged feet. She supposed the stockings would have to go, too. Poor people often went barefoot, but not in stockinged feet.

She wanted to shout to someone, anyone, that this all wasn't fair. That it was intolerable and wrong, and must stop.

"Wait," he said, almost as if he'd heard. He picked up a shoe and rubbed it hard against the stone wall. He handed it back to her. "That'll probably pass for poverty."

Caro grabbed it. "Thank you, thank you!" She cleaned her foot as much as possible before putting the shoe back on while he scuffed up the other one.

"You could have done that with your boots," she said.

"No time, and boots like mine would attract attention, no matter how scruffy." He handed over the second shoe. "Anyway, I can't afford to ruin my best pair."

"Perhaps I can't afford to ruin my best shoes."

"They're worth more than your life?"

She pulled an apologetic face. "No. Why are you doing this for me?"

"Bad form to let a lover hang."

He turned to peer through the knothole, leaving Caro staring gape-mouthed at his back.

*Lover?*

But that's what they'd been. Briefly but thoroughly. Despite her situation, warm spirals of memory uncoiled to be blown into flame by his bold rescue, his crisp decisions, and, yes, even his unkempt state. She'd always favored an elegant man, but rough hair and tattered clothing had a strange appeal.

His shirt was finest cotton — she remembered the silky feel of it — but it was so dirty now no one would know. There'd been lace at the wrists. He must have ripped that off. Such strong thighs and equally strong calves.

"All's clear. Come." He opened the door and glanced back. "Now."

Caro pushed away foolish thoughts and hurried to join him. They slipped through the small yard, hissed at by a mangy cat from the top of a wall, then passing a stinking privy. As they approached the gate, it was as if ropes held her back. Beyond lay enemies who wanted her blood.

She stretched for every sound, as any hunted creature must — for the yells of the mob, or the scrape of a nearby footstep. Dogs barked. Had they been brought in to hunt? In various places householders called from windows to know what was amiss.

Thank God none of those windows overlooked this grim corner.

Grandiston forced open the sagging gate to the alley, checked, then pulled her through.

No one in sight.

He grasped her wrist and set off at a run. Caro stumbled along as best she could on the slimy, muddy ground, desperate to get away. But then she dug in her heels.

"This is the wrong way! We'll run into the hunt."

"I know." He yanked, and she had to run again, breath catching, legs aching. Soon, as she feared, they caught up with the straggling end of the hue and cry.

"Have we got 'im yet?" Grandiston shouted in a terrible attempt at a Northern accent.

*Oh God, oh God,* but Caro did her best to

help. "What a wicked woman," she gasped, deepening and coarsening her voice as she applied the accent thick and hard. "I want t'see 'er 'ang."

"Aye," wheezed an older man. "But I can't keep up, so I'm off back to be ready when they drag 'er down t'igh street." His rheumy eyes narrowed. "What're thee young-uns doing so far behind?"

"Took a wrong turn," Grandiston said, still gamely trying to sound local.

"And got us lost," Caro complained. She yanked him as he'd yanked her. "Come on, y'booby." She took the lead and stumbled onward, boggling at the daring of his plan.

Pretend to be part of the mob?

The audacity would steal her breath away if she had any, but before she could decide whether he was sane, they were among the rear guard.

This time she did the talking, asking if the thief was taken, and Grandiston was wise enough to permit it. She played her part as brashly as she could, but inside she was a jelly of fear. It would take only one person who recognized him or her. . . .

Grandiston pulled her to his side and nuzzled her ear. Caro didn't have to act to push at him, saying, "Give over!"

She had no chance of budging him of

course, but he was whispering rather than trying to steal a kiss. "Don't worry. This lot probably never saw the original incident. They tagged along for the fun of the hunt."

He was right. Relief made her sag against him, and he took the chance to steal a kiss, his mouth so sweet and hot that she kissed him back. Catcalls and scolding had her twisting free, but he was laughing and so was most of the mob.

But, Lord above, now they were the center of attention!

It didn't matter. A distant shout of excitement swirled the group and gave them a new target. They raced off and Caro and Grandiston went with them.

But then he yelled, "I saw sommat down 'ere, Pol!" and turned her into a narrow ginnel. Beyond, at the end, she saw open countryside.

Escape. She raced eagerly in that direction.

But then a shrill voice behind them cried, "What's down 'ere, then?"

"Plague take it," he muttered, and they stopped to look back.

Three bright-eyed youths had chosen to follow them.

"Saw somethin'," Grandiston said. "Right about 'ere." He turned to peer over a wall.

A good try, but the lads weren't convinced. Caro didn't think they'd guessed she and Grandiston were the fugitives, but they suspected something and would be like limpets. There was only one way to deal with that.

She faced them, hands on hips. "Shove off. Can't th'see we've better things t'do than search for a perishing pickpocket?"

Grandiston joined her and raised a fist at the lads. They turned and ran.

He grinned down at her. "You're a wicked wench, my splendid Kat, but having shed them, let's get you out of the soup entirely."

"Oh, yes, please."

They went quickly down the narrow passage and emerged onto a well-trodden footpath that ran between hedges toward the roofs of a hamlet. Caro went forward, but Grandiston grabbed the back of her jacket and pulled her sideways so they stood pressed back against the rough stone wall of the last house.

"What are you doing?" she whispered. "We have to get away."

"Some windows look out this way. If someone spots two disreputable creatures fleeing, they'll cry the alarm."

Caro collapsed back, her knees weakening. "We're trapped here, then! It's hopeless."

He pulled her close — grinning, the insane idiot — and kissed her. "You're in the care of Pagan the Pirate, my fine, splendid Kat. There's not just hope — there's the promise of victory."

"Oh, God. No wonder someone drove a hatchet into your shoulder. It was probably in a moment like this."

# CHAPTER 11

"Perhaps we should go back," she said.

"Back to the mob?"

Back to Silver Street, she was thinking, but she couldn't go there with him. "No," she sighed. "But we can't stay here, either." Caro was listening for pursuit down the alley. Perhaps those lads had gone back and cast suspicion on them.

"Trust me," he said with another quick kiss. "We can stay here until dark and then make our escape. Come. We should get farther from the path."

Caro hesitated, torn between the perils of the town and the perils of this weedy, exposed spot. Memory of hard hands and cruel faces, of thrown stones and spit, had her sidling with him along the walls of houses and gardens that made up the edge of town. The ground here was wild, and thick with dock and dandelion. There were often nettles to avoid. Once, she stumbled

214

and put out her hand to the wall, brushing a nettle and hissing at the sting.

She sucked it, hating everything about this situation. And it all came about because Grandiston had invaded her house in Froggatt Lane.

He turned back. "What's the matter?"

"Nettle."

He picked a dock leaf, took her hand, and rubbed on the antidote. It helped, but she must have glowered, for he said, "I refuse to apologize for nettles."

"I wouldn't be here if not for you."

"You'd rather be in the tender hands of the mob?" he asked, obviously wondering if she were demented.

"No, no, of course not. I'm sorry. It's only that this has been the worst day of my life." Except for one . . . but she wouldn't think about her marriage day, the true root of all her problems and caused by her own folly, as perhaps this one was. She felt tears gather and covered her mouth to fight them.

He pulled down her hand and took her into his arms. "I forget that it started with a carriage accident and your husband's injury and thus spun into terror. But you're safe now."

Safe! But he was big and warm, and despite everything, she couldn't help feeling cherished. He was cherishing Kat Hunter, however, and would do his best to save her. If he discovered she was Caro Hill, he'd see only Jack Hill's widow, his quarry in coming north.

He moved apart and guided her gently to a nettle-free spot behind some low, weedy bushes. "This should do."

He helped her to sit, but her back was to cold, rough stone and open countryside spread in front. Caro hugged her knees, chilled and feeling pinned for all to see. "There are people in that field over there, and someone could come down that alley at any moment."

He cupped her head, turning her to him. "Then we'd better make good on your excuse."

"What?"

"To the lads. You implied . . ."

She pushed him away. "No!"

"Truly?" he said, unmoved in all ways. He licked around her ear.

"Yes, truly." But her push was feeble now. "We can't. I can't. . . ."

He kissed her cheek, the corner of her mouth.

"Not here, at least . . ."

He kissed her lips. "A promise for elsewhere. But for the moment, here we are,

216

and here we must remain. With a reason for anyone who sees us . . ."

Caro opened her mouth to argue, but was silenced by a skillful kiss, and most of her didn't want to fight. All of her wanted to forget.

She tumbled into the comfort of his body, the sweetness of his kiss, the protection of his strong arms. She moaned — and that gave her strength to struggle free. Anyone could be watching.

"Stop. This is wrong."

"Wrong? Nothing so delightful can be wrong."

"You have no sense of right and wrong."

He abruptly let her go, and she saw that had stung.

She wanted to apologize, but instead she inched away.

"I know honesty from dishonesty," he said. "Did you steal those rings?"

Caro gaped at him. "What? Of course I didn't. How could you think that? And if you did think that, why —"

He silenced her with a finger. "If we're having a lovers' quarrel, my sweet, it'd better be in the local dialect."

"Which you're atrocious at," she hissed.

"I can do a good Cockney, and rural Oxfordshire."

She ignored his whimsy. "You don't truly think I'm a thief, do you?"

"You're not what you seem to be. That I know." And these words suddenly seemed more honest than anything else he'd said to her.

He was right, but must never know it.

"That wretched girl put those rings in my pocket. And after I'd tried to be kind to her."

"I missed the wretched girl. Tell me what happened. All of it." When she hesitated, he said, "But if it's going to be another bouquet of lies, spare me."

The only possible reaction was outrage. "Why assume that? Because I fell into a stupid tangle from wanting to help a waif? Because I let a . . . a philanderer wanton me into bed?"

Her harsh words made no impression. "I don't know why you lie, Kat, but you do."

Caro opened her mouth, but again was wordless. She'd told more lies today than in her whole life.

"This will be true," she said at last, and explained how she'd come to be arrested. "I saw you watching," she concluded, "but then you disappeared. I thought you'd abandoned me."

He'd pulled a stalk of grass and chewed

the tip. Barefoot and in his tattered, dirty shirt, his hair tangled, he might almost be a rough country swain.

But only almost.

"Perhaps I should have abandoned you," he said. "You'd only have had to get word to your husband's legal associates to be removed from custody. Instead, here you are, a ragged outlaw, and Mistress Kat Hunter is a wanted criminal."

What could she say to that?

He tossed the grass aside. "Shall we attempt a return to town to seek out your husband's friends?"

Disaster! "They aren't friends. I'm not sure my husband had even met them. Why would they snatch me from the teeth of the law when half the town saw me caught red-handed?"

"I'd think they'd ensure good treatment, at least."

"I dare not put it to the test." When he raised a doubting brow, she said, "I don't know why you constantly question my veracity. You're clearly not what you appear to be yourself."

"I'm certainly not a shoeless vagrant," he agreed.

"But you became one with speed and skill. A fine gentlemanly skill, I'm sure."

"I enjoy adventures and have had many. Remember Pagan?"

She remembered it all too well, and he knew it. But at least they were off the subject of her imaginary husband's associates.

"Are you claiming to truly be a pirate?" she scoffed. "What would you be doing this far inland?"

"Even a pirate may leave the coast now and then."

"I don't think there are pirates anywhere near Britain anymore."

"Smuggler, then," he said.

"Now, that is all too believable. I knew you were gibbet meat. What is to become of me?"

He rolled and put a leg over hers, trying to nuzzle her neck. "What do you want to become of you, sweet Kat?"

Caro pushed him off. "Not what you have in mind. I want my ordinary life back."

"And what is that?"

She met his doubting eyes. "Highly respectable."

"Truly?"

"Are you accusing me of lying again?"

"If I end up with a noose around my neck, I'd like to know why."

"On my honor, I've done nothing wrong,"

Caro said wearily, "except sin with you."

After a moment he said, "Very well. So once we're away from Doncaster, I deliver you to your husband in York?"

Caro was about to seek another escape when she wondered, could she do that? Have her enemy take her to her refuge? Not to Hambledon himself, but to York?

She shuddered at the thought of arriving at the legal establishment looking like this, but Hambledon was impeccably discreet and extremely competent. He'd enable her to become Caro Hill again, and then sort out her marital state, and she'd have her life back.

"That would be very kind," she said sincerely, "for I have no money for a coach."

He laughed. "Neither have I. I left it all in my jacket pocket."

Caro slumped against the wall. "It's hopeless, then."

"Never say never. We've done well so far."

"You have, I grant. Do you snatch ladies in distress from monstrous mobs often?"

"My first attempt. I'm rather proud of it. . . . Hush."

She heard it, too. Voices coming down the alley.

She twisted to look that way.

"Not the hue and cry," he murmured by

her ear. "Simply people leaving town after their day's work."

"But they might see us," she breathed. "All Doncaster must know about us by now."

"Then it's time to act our parts."

Caro landed flat on her back, Grandiston's big body squashing her, his mouth blocking her cry. Immediately she understood and tried to cooperate. Illicit lovers . . .

But when he pulled up her skirt to expose her leg, when he pulled her leg up at the knee and pressed his hardness deep against her, buried memories struck like a spear. The Tup's Byre. Moore's brief, painful assault.

She made a sound. He stifled her with his hand.

Tossed back into that buried horror, Caro panicked. She tried to scream, tried to fight, but she was trapped and powerless as she had been then, her head roiling with disgust as he pounded at her.

Gargling sounds came from deep in her throat.

He rolled off her, but kept his hand clamped over her mouth. Before she could hit or scratch, he crushed her tight against him again, her face mashed into his chest so she could hardly breathe.

"Scream and they'll hear, damn you."

Caro would have screamed anyway, shrieked her cause to the heavens if she'd had breath. She tried to bite his chest, but was mashed too tightly there. When he finally relaxed his hold, she was past doing anything but sucking in breaths and choking in despair.

Again. It had happened again.

She tried to stifle her sobs with a fist, but little sounds escaped from the pit of pain, mewling sounds that wanted to rise to wails that would rip through the firmament.

"Kat, Kat, stop it. What on earth . . . ?" He pulled her against him again and she was too overcome to resist. "Someone will hear. Dammit, woman —"

He was rocking her, but also half-smothering her again. Anguish ripped her apart. "Dammit?" It was a whisper only because her throat was so tight. She wrenched far enough apart to pour her hate at him. "Does a bit of lovemaking give you a husband's rights, you monster?"

He clamped his hand over her mouth again.

She tried to bite him again, and failed.

"I did nothing but playact, you demented woman, and damned painful it was, too. I'm probably ruined for weeks."

"Good," she mumbled.

"Struth, I had to do something. To explain why we were skulking out here, remember?"

His honest impatience somehow broke through the madness.

She did remember.

And she knew he was telling the truth about not actually raping her. She was sore below, but in a bruising way, not the deep tearing way she now remembered.

He cautiously freed her mouth. When she didn't scream, he relaxed his hold.

Caro struggled free and wiped her lips. He'd probably take it as disgust, but she was getting rid of bits of grit from his dirty hand.

Mostly.

She hadn't known that memories of Moore's brutality lurked so dark and deep, ready to leap up and savage her like that. She wrapped her arms around her knees and hugged herself, rocked herself, fighting to bury them again. Deep, deep.

He kept his warm hand on her back, rubbing, circling, trying to calm her. Finally, she unlocked her arms and rested her head on her knees. "I'm sorry. I'm not usually so . . ."

"You're not usually taken up as a thief and

hunted through town." But then he added, "I assume."

"I tell you again," she said with a deep and weary sigh, "before I met you, I was a respectable lady."

"But one who's been raped, I think?"

Caro tensed, shocked by that word. She'd never thought that. She'd gone eagerly with Moore to marry him. Her resistance had been entirely because they weren't yet married. He'd been coarse and rough, but it was only much later, perhaps only this afternoon, that she'd learned how very different that business could be.

After her strange behavior now, what did she say?

"Taken by force," she whispered.

"Your husband?" Christian asked, trying to keep his voice calm when fury surged hot through his veins.

A hesitation, but then she said, "No."

"Then whom should I kill?"

She stared at him. "What? Why should you?"

"Because he violated you."

"It was some time ago," she said wearily, "and in any case, he's already dead."

"Who had the honor? Your husband?"

After a moment, she said, "Yes. Are you

truly saying you'd commit cold-blooded murder for me?"

"My blood," he said, "would not be cold."

Her eyes went wide, but then she closed them. "Death again. How many men have you killed, Pagan Grandiston?"

Many, he could have said. He could tell her he was a soldier, that the hatchet incident had been part of war, but he didn't think it would make any difference in her present mood. He'd found ladies, and many gentlemen, approved of war, but didn't care to hear the gory details.

"Never mind. I've never killed a woman, so you're safe from my violence."

For some reason, that made her laugh in a despairing way.

"Truly, Kat. I've never even hurt a woman, and I've had reason a time or two. I have no reason to hurt you."

He drew her into his arms and she didn't object. Perhaps she even snuggled closer, but she said, "You're a harsh man."

"It's a harsh world."

She tensed and moved her head. "I hear more people."

"Stay as you are. It'll do."

They sat entwined as a party of five strolled by.

A man said, "Wish I could get that reward,

but they're long gone by now, I reckon."

There was a rumble of assent and then the people were too far away to hear.

"Reward?" she asked, looking up at him.

"The Silcocks, I assume."

"They have their rings back. Why?"

"Some people are vengeful, but it is strange."

Kat straightened, frowning. "That woman's mad. The way she looked at me, with such fury, and just for knocking her table. Then later, it was as if she wanted to put a noose over my head with her own hands."

He rubbed the back of her neck, kissed her brow. "She'll never lay hands on you. But I think I should go back into the town."

She jerked away. "No, I can't!"

"Not you, just me." He put a finger to her lips. "Listen. You could easily be recognized as Mistress Hunter, but no one will recognize me as your ragged rescuer. My man will have hidden my clothes in my horse's stall. Once I'm restored, I'll be able to establish my blameless presence and discover what's going on. I can also get money and some decent clothing for you."

"But I'll be out here alone," she whispered, eyes flickering around like a raw ensign in enemy territory for the first time.

"There's nothing to harm you."

"Foxes. Badgers."

"More frightened of you than you of them."

"People," she said.

"Men, you mean. Did your . . . attacker strike in the dark, or did you know him?"

"I knew him. Very well, I thought."

He touched her shoulder, torn between necessities. "I wouldn't leave you if I thought there was any danger. Clearly no one comes here, and it's dark enough already to hide you from view."

She hugged her knees, making a small target. "I've never been out in the dark alone before."

It surprised him, but why? Ladies didn't go out at night unescorted.

It surprised him because Kat Hunter sometimes showed an unusually independent manner, as if she expected to make her own decisions and control her own destiny. There was also that streak of wildness. It made him doubt her claim of complete respectability, especially when it tumbled her into bed with him, but here she was, behaving as most respectable women would.

"There's nothing to fear," he said again.

"Rats. You can't deny rats."

"Busy in cellars and storehouses. Give me

leave to go, Kat, and you'll be in York tomorrow."

She looked up at him, searching his features in the gloom. "You will return?"

He kissed her. "On my honor."

"What is a pagan's honor worth?"

"Heaven and earth in my case."

"Then go." She suddenly clutched his hands. "But take care. You may think you look like a servingman, but you don't. There's a gloss to you, even in rags, and your accent is ridiculous."

He laughed softly. "That's my Kat."

"What?"

"Whoever you are, you could command armies if you chose."

"No. I couldn't."

"Permit me to know better." He kissed her hands and freed himself. "I'll not be gone long and soon this day will only be a bad memory."

He realized he was waiting for her to say "Not all bad" or something similar, but she only nodded and settled, her back to the wall, arms around her knees again.

"I wish I had a coat to leave you," he said.

"Then bring me back a shawl."

"Aye, aye, ma'am," he said, and worked his way back down the wall.

Caro was left alone in the dark.

# CHAPTER 12

It wasn't truly dark. The sky was gray and a three-quarter moon was rising, but that was made ominous by drifting dark clouds that played macabre games with the light. There were scattered lights ahead from cottage windows, but they, too, flickered fitfully behind trees jiggling in a rising wind.

She hugged herself against the cooling, wishing Grandiston would hurry back with that shawl. Wishing he would hurry back.

She knew any wild animals would be more wary of her than she was of them, but a rustle to her right made her flinch. Whatever creature it was, it slipped away. Very wise. She could probably kill it. At least, she knew that logically, but she'd never killed anything bigger than a cockroach, and that by stamping on it with a sturdy shoe.

Nothing out here truly threatened her, but she held herself still and listened, peering into the shadows all around.

Her back was to the wall, and to the sounds of the town. Somewhere nearby a baby wailed. Farther away, a dog barked. A rhythmic clang was probably a smithy working late, mending a tool or wheel band.

A couple started yelling at each other — the same old tale of promises made, promises broken, promises denied. They stopped. Had they parted in acrimony or reconciled with a kiss?

Life went on, but not for her. She felt she might linger here in this fearful dark until she moldered away.

She looked again at the lights that spoke of cottages and people — ordinary people going about their ordinary lives. In normal circumstances she could go to one of those houses, knock, and obtain aid. If she tried that now, the best she could expect would be to be driven away as a vagrant. The worst was to be seized and dragged to the constables as that woman who'd stolen the rings.

For the reward.

There was a price on her head! She was an outlaw, vulnerable to any cruelty anyone wished to visit upon her. Caro fell into a daze of worry and useless thoughts, vaguely aware of darkness settling completely all around her.

Where was Grandiston? What if he'd

abandoned her?

*Oh, Aunt Abigail, you'd be so disgusted with me.*

Perhaps not over her foray as Kat Hunter — Aunt Abigail generally approved of going on the attack. Perhaps not for the affair with the little thief, though she'd have scoffed at Caro's gullibility.

*"Scoundrels are scoundrels and thieves are thieves, Dorcas, not poor put-upons to be made honest with a kind word and a loaf of bread."*

But she'd not like Caro waiting for a man to rescue her.

*I can't do anything else,* she thought to her aunt's spirit. *I've no money, I look like a vagrant, and there's a reward on my head. Where could I go?*

That seemed to silence Aunt Abigail, but it did no good for Caro's spirits.

A strange squawk made her eyes fly open.

Something was out there! Shaking, she searched the dark shadows cast by the bushes, then gasped at two lights.

*Ow-ah-ooh-ah?*

It sounded like a wailed "How are you?" Was it some strange creature of the night? A boggle or a troll . . . ?

Caro edged back, fumbling on the ground for a stick, a rock, anything.

A dark shadow moved. She fixed her eyes on that, bracing to defend herself.

It came closer, the lights flashed again — and then it was a cat. Clearly a cat. Merely a cat, though dark as night itself. All Caro's tension released in a whimper.

*Ah-ooh.*

"Be quiet," she whispered, then put a hand to her head. What was she doing? Cats didn't speak. They did scratch, however, especially if feral.

"Shoo!"

It sat in the neat way cats have and looked at her.

And now, perhaps triggered by fright and relief, she desperately needed to relieve herself. She tried to will the sensation away, but once thought of, the need became more urgent by the moment. She peered into the surrounding dark, hoping for the miraculous appearance of a privy, or even some bushes that would provide concealment. She saw nothing but rough ground and low shrubs.

And the cat was watching her.

"Shoo!" she tried again, with exactly the same result.

Muttering at it, she sidled farther along the wall, At least it didn't follow, and anyway, she needed to do this far from where Grandiston would expect to find her.

Praying there were no nettles, she squatted, bunching up her skirts so they'd be out of harm's way.

As her urine hissed onto the ground, she decided this was the depths of degradation. The complete depths. She'd lost her home, her decent appearance, and perhaps her reputation. But this base act flung her beyond decent society.

When she was finished, she stood and worked her way miserably back to her starting point, marked now by the gleaming eyes of the stationary cat.

"Shoo," she said as she sat again, but mostly for the form of it. Who was she to reject any sort of companionship?

Perhaps she'd never regain her home and reputation, never marry Eyam, never return to decent society. Perhaps she'd end up in jail, where relieving herself in the open air would seem like a luxury.

*"Dorcas Froggatt, show some spine!"*

Caro stared at the cat. No, it hadn't spoken clear English, especially not in Aunt Abigail's voice. That had been her mind telling her what her aunt would say. But before that, Aunt Abigail would say, *This'd never 'ave 'appened under my management.*

Except it had. It had been her aunt's managing ways that had created the mess.

If she'd come back to try to help, it would be only justice.

The cat butted her hand with its head, so she gave it the stroke it seemed to be asking for. Living warmth was soothing, even though its fur seemed rough, and matted in places.

"You probably have fleas, but who am I to be particular? I probably have fleas by now, too."

The cat said *ee-ow* and stepped delicately onto her lap to circle and settle. Caro had never had a parlor cat, but she tried stroking down its back. "Were you, too, chased from your home, unjustly accused of crimes? Are you hunted?"

It was foolishness, but when the cat said *ah-ooh* as if in response, Caro whispered, "Aunt Abigail?" She shook her head. "I'm going mad. You're a cat. A stray. I have nothing for you, you know. No food. No milk."

It tucked its head on its paws.

"I might as well give you a name," she said, finding comfort in her own voice. "Tabby. My father called Aunt Abigail 'Abby,' though I'm sure she never curled up in anyone's lap. Oh, stop it, Caro. Talking to yourself is a sure sign of madness."

She did stop, but perhaps that would be her fate — an asylum for the insane. That would suit Grandiston and the Hill family. It would probably give them the means to take control of all her money.

So she needed to do something.

She was a Froggatt, after all.

Froggatt strength had run strong in her grandfather, who'd begun the rise from tradesman to business owner. It had been weak in her father, but strong in Aunt Abigail.

Caro had realized only in her later years that Aunt Abigail had run Froggatt's for most of her life, but from her brother's shadow. She'd been the one to press for the use of crucible steel ahead of most, thus making their fortunes.

After Daniel Froggatt's death, Abigail Froggatt had come into her own. She'd seen the profitability of the fine steel springs for which the firm was now famous. Some had scoffed, for blades were the cutler's main trade, and war demanded more than they could produce. But now, with the war over, the springs were bringing in profit while other firms struggled.

It was time to be more like Aunt Abigail, and she would never have sat cowering, waiting for a man to come and rescue her. This was the perfect opportunity to get away from Grandiston.

And do what?

"This would be a good time for a practical suggestion," she muttered to her aunt's spirit.

"Talking to yourself?"

Caro jumped, and actually let out a mouselike squeak, but it was Grandiston, almost at her side.

"My apologies. I took longer than I expected." He hunkered down and took her hand. "You're icy. Were you frightened?"

"No," she denied, though he'd not be deceived.

"No ferocious animals?" he teased.

"Only the cat."

"Cat?"

Caro realized that it had leapt away at his voice. She peered at the shadows. "There was a cat. That's who I was talking to."

"Talking to?"

She frowned at him. "Anyone can talk to a cat."

"As long as it doesn't talk back."

It was as if he knew.

"I did not imagine it," she protested.

"No, of course not. In any case, it's gone, and we should imitate it." He rose, drawing her to her feet.

"Leave here? Oh, thank God."

She'd grabbed his jacket and was looking

up at him. She thought he might kiss her. Instead, he gathered her into a hug.

After the first startled moment, Caro realized she hadn't been hugged like this since her father died. Aunt Abigail hadn't been a hugger, and Ellen certainly wasn't. She felt like a safe child again in big, warm arms. Tears started to ache around her eyes. She fought them, but then began to cry.

She expected him to push her away, but he rubbed her back and made vague soothing sounds. She strove for control, and eventually she won. "I'm so sorry," she sniffed. "But I was afraid." She separated enough to look up at him. "I'm glad you're safe."

He moved away even more to offer a handkerchief. "You thought I wouldn't be."

She wiped her eyes and blew her nose. "You could have been captured." She suddenly realized something. "You have your coat back."

"And my boots, and money in my pocket." He picked up something and put it around her shoulders. "You requested a shawl, I believe, ma'am."

Caro gathered it around her, even if it scratched slightly at her nape. It was a country shawl knit from a coarse yarn, but large and wonderfully warm. "Thank you.

For everything."

"Your wish is my command, and I believe your next is to be on your way to York. Come along." He took her hand and led the way along the wall toward the path.

"What's our plan?" she whispered.

"There's no safe way to bring horses here, so we'll have to walk across country for about a mile. Barleyman will meet us there."

"What's the situation in Doncaster?"

"There is a reward posted."

"Heaven help me. How much?"

"Five guineas gold."

"But that's a fortune to most! Why would the Silcocks do that?"

"I don't know, but don't worry. The larcenous Mistress Hunter is in the past, and even her vagrant remnant, Pol, is about to disappear."

"You retrieved my valise?"

"Alas, the innkeeper seized it to pay your bill."

"A rather grand payment when I'd not even spent the night."

"I doubt you want to challenge him about it now. Barleyman's to get you something."

They reached the path then, and both peered into the alley to be sure no one was coming.

"Coast's clear," he said, taking her hand.

"Onward."

But Caro hesitated. Doncaster was hostile to her, but it represented respectability, safety, and security, all things fate had stolen from her this day. Ahead lay only darkness and the unknown.

He tugged, and she turned to go on with her enemy into the nighttime wild.

# CHAPTER 13

The path was darker than she'd expected. She knew it was wide and smooth from frequent use, but she couldn't make it out and felt as if she might step into a hole at any time.

"I wish we had a lantern," she said.

"We're fugitives, remember."

"And if we meet anyone, we'll look it, groping around in the dark."

"Not if we actually grope," he said, grin audible, and he turned and kissed her again.

She pushed him away. He didn't seem to mind, which pained her. Then he took her hand as they walked on and Caro felt better. She remembered the cat and twisted to look back.

"What is it?" he asked, suddenly alert.

"The cat. I wondered if it might follow."

"If there is one, it's probably looking for someone more likely to offer food and milk."

Caro felt strangely abandoned, and in her

distraction, she stumbled off the path. He caught her. "With a name like Kat, you should be able to see better in the dark."

"Can you?" she asked as they walked on.

"I just trust to fate."

"Why assume fate will be kind?" she said sadly.

"Fate, sweet Kat, has brought us together."

"I'd think you'd be regretting the moment you first spoke to me."

"Not at all. You've brought me amusement, delight, action, and adventure, and here we are, alive and free beneath a moonlit sky. Look," he said, pointing up, "that's Venus, doubtless transiting something."

"You're mad as Mistress Silcock."

"But much more amiably."

Christian put his arm around Kat Hunter again, liking the feeling. She was still an odd one, but her recent behavior indicated that she was exactly what she claimed to be — a respectable woman accustomed to an ordinary life.

In that case, she'd shown extraordinary courage and resource.

But then, an ordinary life didn't include rape. It could, perhaps, make a woman cling more desperately to respectable society.

Why, then, had she flirted with a stranger, come to his room, and ended up in his bed?

No. He'd like her to be just what she claimed, but she wasn't.

He glanced at her, but the moon was behind the clouds again and she was looking down, attempting to make out the path. He could see the mass of her astonishing hair. He supposed the most respectably ordinary woman in England could have hair like that, but it didn't seem so. It should go with a bold rebel and a soaring spirit.

She caged it with plaiting and a hundred pins. Did she also imprison her true nature?

An impulse stirred to set her free. He squashed it. He had one woman too many already.

Barleyman had checked out Silver Street but learned little. The servants were too tight-lipped to be natural, however, so they were keeping quiet about something. He'd learned that the lady of the house was called Phyllis, not Dorcas, and though she came from Sheffield, she was the daughter of a solicitor, not a master cutler.

Suddenly some sixth sense made him turn back. He saw bright eyes. "Struth."

Kat whirled. "What?" But then she said, "I told you there was a cat."

"A cat," he repeated. "And an invisible

one, to boot."

She waved a hand. "Shoo, Tabby."

"Shoetabby? Is that some local incantation?"

She turned to him. "Shoo as in go away. Tabby is its name."

"It's an old friend? Now, that doesn't match your story."

She put her hands on her hips. "What new madness is this? I had a cat all along? Hidden in my bodice, perhaps? You would know better."

"So I would." He couldn't restrain a smile. She must have heard it because she hissed like a cat.

"It found me in the dark. I tried to get rid of it."

"By naming it."

"I was alone. I was grateful for company."

He put an arm around her. "Come on."

She didn't move. "Its coat's rough. I think it has a wound on its side. I don't want to abandon it."

"You don't have to," he said, forcing her onward. "A cat will come or not as it chooses. Barleyman's probably already waiting, and it might take a little time to find the exact spot."

"You mean we're lost," she said, but she walked on with him.

"Not yet. But if you continue to hiss and claw, I might lose you."

There might have been another little hiss, but she said, "I apologize. I'm fully aware of the debts I owe you, Mr. Grandiston."

Christian assumed he was supposed to be abashed, but he said, "Good."

She twisted to glance behind.

He forced her onward. "Stray cats are designed to tug at heartstrings, you know."

"A cat doesn't design to be wounded and bedraggled."

"No? My mother says cats are often sent out to find those who need them. Stirring pity must be the easiest way to get a paw in the door."

"An old wives' tale."

"My mother's not so old as that."

She looked up at him. "Oh, I'm sorry. I didn't mean —" But then she hissed again. "You are impossible!"

"I assure you, my mother is old enough to have borne me."

"You know I didn't . . . I'm simply astonished you have a mother at all."

"Now, that," he said, "is ridiculous."

"Oh, very well. Everyone has a mother, but some seem unlikely to have spent much time under a mother's care."

Christian felt inclined to hiss himself, for

that stung. It had been to everyone's benefit that he leave home. He had lacked a mother's care, however, his own or another's. Thorn's household had been short on females. Even his childhood nurse had died when he was eleven.

"I'm very fond of my mother," he said, for that was true.

"Tell me something about her, then." She tossed it like a challenge.

"She's plump, loving, and enjoys her garden and her bees."

"In a cottage, perhaps?" she said, disbelief audible.

"Sheathe your claws, Kat. Something a little larger, yes, but still a simple place." He wasn't lying. He was talking about Raisby Manor, his boyhood home.

"I imagine such a mother must be distressed by your choice of occupation."

"True," Christian said, realizing his teeth were clenched again. His mother hated him being a soldier.

They'd come to a gate, which gave him an excuse to abandon the conversation. He groped for the rope holding it closed. As he reached it, the cat slipped through the bars with a strange *ow-oo* of scorn.

"A point to you," Christian agreed, wondering if he'd stay sane. He lifted the rope, trying to make out any shadows in the field ahead. "Play scout," he said to the cat, "and tell me if there's a bull."

"Talking to a cat?" the human Kat asked sweetly.

"Perhaps the trees will start a conversation next. A tied gate usually means animals. Cows and sheep would present no problem, but a bull would be a different matter."

"We could go another way."

"And end up truly lost. The cat remains silent." He heaved the sagging gate open about two feet. "Come along."

She picked her way cautiously, obviously knowing enough of the countryside to expect ground trodden to mud in such a gateway. Christian followed and was struggling to get the gate closed again when a wild screech made him whirl.

A cudgel whistled by his ear. He dropped to the ground to roll out of danger, knowing the cat had sounded the alarm. The cudgel came down again. What in Hades . . . ?

Christian rolled, surging to his feet and launching himself at the man. But now there were two of them and moonlight gleamed off a blade. He twisted the cudgel from the one man and swung it hard at the other, knocking the knife out of his hand. Mere amateurs. Poachers or sheep stealers, thinking they'd found better prey. But were there more?

"Kat!" he yelled. "Where are you?"

The feline screeched again.

Christian shouted, "Not *you* —" but big hands choked off his words.

Instead of clawing at them, Christian buffeted his attacker's head with both fists. The man bellowed and let go. Christian got on top and beat him senseless. He took a moment to breathe, then struggled to his feet, looking for the other man and Kat.

At first he didn't know what he was seeing, but then he put together a strange dance. In the dim light two people were twirling around and around and somewhere nearby the cat was yowling and hissing.

Ah. Kat was turning behind a man, her hair flailing, tied to him in some way. It made no sense, but Christian moved forward, chose his moment, and drove his fist into the man's belly. The man buckled forward, but Kat tumbled on top of him with a cry.

Christian grabbed the back of her jacket and lifted her off. "Are you hurt?"

She struggled free, wheezing for breath. "Is he dead?"

The man was ominously silent, but then

he started to choke. Christian put a boot on his back and twisted to look at the other one. Still down and silent. He took his boot off the man and grabbed his hair — to encounter rough wool. By feel, he discovered that the man was half-strangled by a woolen shawl.

"An interesting way of killing," he said.

"Killing? I was trying to confuse him."

"Death will do that, I suppose."

"He's *dead?*"

"Dead men don't choke."

Christian unwound the knit shawl from the man's head and used the man's own rough neckcloth to tie his hands behind his back. It wouldn't hold for long, but long enough.

He took off his own cravat and approached the other man, picking up the fallen knife. It was old and worn, but sharp. A gleam of eyes told him the man was conscious.

"It would be very unwise to try anything," Christian said softly. "Because I have other business, you're going to get off — unless you encourage me to kill you."

"Thee wouldn't," the man sneered, a nasal tone suggesting a broken nose.

"Test that and see. Put your hands out together in front."

The man did so. He was sturdily built and

doubtless used to being the one giving out threats. He'd be burning to try something. Christian hoped he wouldn't. He tied the thick wrists as tightly as he could.

"Thee's no better than we," the man said, "creepin' around in t'dark. Runnin' off with someone else's wife?" Clouds cleared from the moon, showing a square, vicious face.

"Precisely." Christian stood and tossed the knife deep into the hedge. "I doubt you'll get free in time to follow us, but if you do, I highly advise against. Stick to rabbits."

Rubbing his bruised knuckles, he turned back to Kat, who was standing holding the big cat. He wondered who was comforting whom.

"You did call out for help," she said, as if expecting reproof.

Christian smiled. "So I did. What exactly did you do?"

"Flung my shawl over his head. And Tabby scratched him."

"My two magnificent felines."

"But it went too far. The shawl, I mean. It fell around his neck. Then it twisted when he turned and I tried to avoid him. So I held on as best I could so he couldn't get to me. Are you all right?"

"Completely," Christian said, capturing one hand and kissing it. The cat gave a squawk and leapt down. "Feel free to nibble parts of them," Christian said to it. "You are not a naturally intrepid woman, but you flung yourself into the fray."

"I was terrified. I still am. Who were they?"

"Poachers, I suspect, but not above attack and thievery if the occasion presents. I'd like to see them in jail, but your safety comes first."

"I'm shaking."

He drew her into a hug again. She was a very huggable woman. "Most of us shake after extreme excitement. It was exciting, wasn't it?"

She choked on laughter. "Oh, extremely."

He separated so he had only an arm around her. "Come, magnificent Kat. Barleyman should be just beyond the next hedge."

Caro went, but she didn't feel magnificent at all.

She was shaking from the violence, and appalled by what had just happened. He'd taken her laughter as enjoyment, but it had been more of a gibber. Her life had been nothing but mayhem and violence since he'd invaded it, but he thought it wonderful.

She'd thought his casual talk of killing mere bluster, but not now.

He had killed whoever had wounded him with the hatchet.

He would have killed her rapist, given the chance, in hot or cold blood.

He had just trounced two big, armed men.

He had rescued her, twice, but she was fearful now. The sooner she was free of him, the better.

They arrived at a new hedge, but there was no gate, only a stile. It tilted and looked in poor repair. The cat leapt onto it, peering ahead. Caro stepped away from Grandiston to stroke it.

"It was violent, too," Grandiston pointed out. He read her too well.

"It's a cat," she said.

"And I'm a man."

"Not all men are violent."

"They should be if needed."

Caro wondered what Eyam would do if attacked in the dark. Of course, he'd never be in that situation, but presumably some male instinct would surface. He wore a sword and took fencing lessons. She assumed he could fire a pistol. He hunted hare and shot pheasant and such.

"Do you need help over the stile?" Grandiston asked.

Definitely not. Caro gathered her skirts in one hand, wishing she had pins to kirtle them up, leaving both hands free. She raised one foot, testing the wood. It felt solid. . . .

Grandiston picked her up. Before she could protest, he was over the rickety steps and setting her down in the road on the other side.

"You madman," she said, pushing him away. "That could have crumbled under us."

"Are we not safe?"

Caro stared at him. "We, sir, are in the middle of nowhere, in the dark, fleeing the law, having just fought off murderous assassins —"

"Assassins?"

"Very well, poachers. But we are not *safe!*"

She was pulled into his arms and kissed. She fought him, but then the madness returned and she was kissing him back.

"How do you do this?" she asked, leaning against his chest. "You turn me upside down."

"I haven't quite done that yet. But if you wish . . ."

She looked up. "Are you ever serious?"

"I was very serious when I was fighting for my life, Kat. Especially when I didn't know what was happening to you."

Caro remembered that he didn't know he was the cause of all her problems. He was rescuing a chance-met woman whose recent predicaments were nothing to do with him.

"I'm sorry."

"Don't be. You've given me the chance to play knight-errant."

"Errant?" Caro said, looking up and down a deserted road. "Meaning in the wrong, erring in judgment? I see neither man nor horses."

He looked around. "By gad, you're right." But then he smiled. "Shall I perform magic?"

Caro eyed him. "A knight wizardly?"

"Abracadabra." He whistled a strong high sound. For a moment nothing happened, but then a horse appeared around the turn. A trick of the moonlight made it seem misty, as if it might truly have been conjured. But then it trotted forward, hooves hitting solid ground, metal jingling, and she saw it was real, and both saddled and bridled, but gray, explaining the ghostly effect.

Grandiston walked to meet it, to praise it, rubbing its head. The horse seemed excessively pleased at the attention.

Caro looked around for the cat, and found it sitting patiently. "Any comment on recent events, Tabby?"

The cat cocked its leg and turned its head to lick at a most inappropriate place.

"Well," Caro muttered, looking away. "I don't know what to make of that."

Grandiston brought the horse over. "Meet Buck. Short for 'Buccaneer.'"

"He's very well trained."

"There are times when it's useful to have a horse come at a whistle. Barleyman must be just around the bend with food, drink, and clothing for you."

He took her hand and led her there. It took Caro a moment to realize that the horse was following without guidance. She knew little of riding horses, but that seemed extraordinary, especially as the cat was walking alongside as if they might be enjoying a chat.

Perhaps she really had tumbled into another realm, where none of the ordinary rules of the world held. At least she soon saw the promised Barleyman, alongside another horse.

"There's an open gate here," said the man in a voice that came close to being gentlemanly.

"But I wasn't to know that, was I?" Grandiston replied.

They were close enough now for Caro to see that Grandiston's man was stocky, and wore a patch over his left eye. Good heavens. She remembered the maid mentioning that it made him look a villain. It did.

"Heard some noise, sir, but it seemed over before I could get to you."

"Two poachers with ambitions to be foot-pads. Easily overcome with the help of two cats."

"Two cats, sir?"

"One feline, one feminine. Mistress Hunter, this is my man, Barleyman. A rogue, but an honest one. Her name," he added to the man, "is Kat."

"And the feline, sir?" He looked around, but the damned cat had slunk into a shadow somewhere. "Fierce, is it?"

"Both of them. Mistress Hunter's lethal with a shawl, I assure you."

"A shawl, sir?"

"The very one you found for her."

The manservant turned back to Caro. "I see he's in one of his funny moods, ma'am. We'll ignore him. It's good to see you safe."

Safe, Caro thought. They were as mad as each other. This had been their precious destination, but she was on a deserted road in the dark, still looking like a vagrant, and with two insane rascals now instead of just one.

She didn't think she'd ever feel safe again.

# CHAPTER 14

Christian took the wineskin from his saddle and squirted some into his mouth. For poor wine, it tasted remarkably good. He offered some to Kat. She looked at it and he realized she'd never seen such a thing before. He was about to demonstrate, but Barleyman produced a tin cup.

"Allow me, ma'am." He squirted wine into the cup and handed it to her.

"Thank you."

Christian would need to find some very unpleasant duty for Barleyman.

As she drank, moonlight played on her wild hair, and on her arms, bare except for the elbow-length linen of her shift. She looked so natural a gypsy that he could hardly believe she was the neat and fashionable Mistress Hunter who'd entered the dining room of the Woolpack not many hours ago.

The light caressed the swell of her breasts,

so much more arousing when he knew they were unarmored by stays. Her skirts hid more, but he'd fondled her high, round behind and shapely legs.

She drained the cup and turned to him. "What next?"

He couldn't hold back a grin. If they were alone, if she were what she seemed at this moment, he knew what would be next. Him sitting on the stile and her riding him. Or her up against a tree, those legs up around him.

He pulled himself together. "Next, the thief of the Silcocks' rings disappears. Where are the clothes, Barleyman?" He took the wineskin and drank again. "While you change, I'll restore my appearance."

He turned to explore his saddlebags, and to straighten out his mind.

Kat Hunter, or whoever she was, was trouble in ways he knew, and in ways he hadn't begun to understand and, please God, never would. He didn't think she was a criminal, but trouble trailed her like that damn cat.

She'd caused the death of one man — her rapist. Though Christian despised rapists, he had to wonder how she'd come to be vulnerable to attack. What had it cost her husband to kill the man? A soldier became calloused to it, but one-on-one, in the cool of the morning? For a lawyer?

Now the poor man lay somewhere in pain. Had she caused that by some carelessness? How many other mishaps? His rescue plan could have gone wrong in any one of a hundred ways.

She was a female Jonah on dry land, but he'd pledged to see her to York, and so he would. But then he'd turn back to Doncaster and his other disastrous female. If Dorcas Froggatt hadn't turned moonling over Moore, none of this would ever have happened. He'd be back in the south — trying to escape Psyche Jessingham's claws.

Hell. What he needed was another long war, far, far away. Perhaps he'd transfer to a regiment going to India.

Laughter?

He glanced back. Barleyman — blast his soul — had made her laugh. A short laugh and perhaps wry, but a laugh all the same.

Christian went over. "Start dressing," he told her. "We can't linger here all night."

Barleyman wisely went off to busy himself elsewhere.

Kat just stood there, clutching a dark bundle. He thought she was disobeying orders, but then realized she was exhausted. Not surprising. Today would flatten the strongest. It had made a dent in him. And exhaustion could fall down on a person suddenly like a heavy blanket.

"We'll find an inn," he said gently, "and you can sleep. But we need to look like a respectable couple, especially when turning up late at night."

"Oh, yes, I see. . . ." But she looked at the road, stretching in front and behind. "Where?"

Christian fought back impatience. "There are deep shadows near the hedge. We'll both turn our backs."

She looked at him doubtfully, but walked toward the dark patch beneath a short tree. Once Christian was sure she wouldn't collapse in a heap, he turned away and found Barleyman offering a new neckcloth.

Christian tied it loosely and moved a little farther away. "Any additional news about the hunt for her?" he asked quietly.

"No, sir. Reckon it'd all die down if not for those Silcocks. Chicken, sir?"

"Bless you." Christian took a bite of the cold meat. "Why? They have their plaguey rings back. What else do they want?"

"Blood, I reckon. Hers, and yours for rescuing her."

"God rot their guts. At least we'll see no

260

more of them. I'm never going to Doncaster again."

"They did mention moving on to Sheffield, sir."

"Where I need to return eventually to find out more about Froggatts. Are they sent to plague me?"

"You're for York tomorrow, sir. Perhaps they'll have moved on by the time you get back. I did make slight inroads with a maid at the Ossingtons', sir. Might warrant a bit more effort."

"Remember the fatal wiles of women."

"Never forget 'em, sir — myself."

Christian ignored the implied warning. "Then there's Nether Greasley to check."

"It's old news there, sir."

"A small place like that, people won't have forgotten such drama. There might even be a sniff of that clergyman."

"I could go there, too, sir."

Christian tossed away the chicken bone. "Right. Do that by the day after tomorrow. We'll meet up in Nether Greasley and go on from there."

"And if you don't turn up, sir?" Barleyman asked, in that tone he had that suggested many slips twixt cup and lip.

"Wait a week, then take a coach back to London and report to Ithorne."

"I'd rather set about finding you, sir."

"Do as you're ordered. If I'm in deep trouble, Ithorne's the man."

"Strange you didn't leave all this in His Grace's hands, sir."

"Damn your guts, don't be insolent. This is not a hazardous mission. If I am delayed, it will be because of a loose shoe or something of that sort."

"But look what she's brought you to in a matter of hours, sir. And if she's recognized, you could both be in the soup. That new reward — it's twenty guineas, sir. Many people'd sell their mother for twenty guineas."

"Struth. But I had no choice. Any man would act."

"Seem to remember that many didn't, sir."

Barleyman was right as usual.

Most men had stood watching; some had cheered on the mob. In any other circumstances, he would have been an observer, assuming the woman guilty and deserving of the consequences. He hoped he'd have intervened if the mob had turned vicious, but he'd sprung into action only because he knew Kat — particularly in the biblical sense.

"Get back to Doncaster. You'll have to walk. I need your horse for her."

"Very good, sir." Barleyman walked off down the road. He might even have been whistling. Strange man, Barleyman. He enjoyed walking. He enjoyed it so much he sometimes did it for no reason at all.

Christian glanced toward the hedge, but Kat Hunter was still engaged in shadowy dressing, so he contemplated the quiet road instead. There was no denying that his affairs had gone to hell since he'd met her.

"I need some help."

He turned, knowing she'd done her best not to admit that. He went a little closer, trying not to look. She was wearing something pale. "What is it?"

A silence. Perhaps a sigh. "There are stays."

"Ah." Christian fought to keep the grin out of his voice. "You have them on?"

"Yes, but they need lacing."

He walked toward her, seeing her turn her back, and realizing that the white he'd seen was a petticoat with her shift above and a pale corset. She seemed to have hidden her hair under a white cap. "You need to come out of the shadows a little so I can find the eyelets."

"You've never laced up stays in the dark?" she asked drily, but she did as he asked.

"Unlaced, yes. Laced, no."

That damned moonlight again. Now it slid over her neck and the bare skin of her back above the edge of her shift, leaving the channel of her spine darkly interesting. He began to thread the laces, tightening them to a snug fit as he went, constantly aware of her sweet curves, and her smell — earthy after her adventures, but with a trace of rose perfume.

"These fit quite well," he said. "You're fortunate."

"They fit," she said frostily, "because they're my own."

"Ah." Christian bit the insides of his cheeks. Where had they fallen that he'd missed them? "Barleyman is a pearl among men."

She shifted her shoulders to adjust to the stays. It made him inhale. "You've laced them too loosely."

"For easier riding."

She turned. "Riding?"

"You'd rather walk?"

After a moment she stepped back into the shadows and he courteously turned his back. It wasn't very long before she said, "I'm ready."

He turned and he saw she was entirely in black. He'd told Barleyman to find something respectable, not Quakerish.

Her gown was dark and even had full-length sleeves that met black gloves. The only lighter touches were a white fichu tucked into the bodice and the cap tied beneath her chin. She must have managed to compress her hair under it, for not a trace showed. A flat black hat with a wide brim sat on top.

"Certainly no one will recognize the wicked Mistress Hunter," he said, "though they might wonder how your mourning matches with my lack of it. Do I detect a ribbon around that hat?"

She reached up to feel. "Yes."

"You'll have to donate it to me." He took out his pocketknife and cut it free. "Any pins in your outfit?"

She took out one of the ones holding her fichu in place and he used it to fix the black band around his sleeve.

She hadn't eaten, so he brought her a piece of chicken and some bread. She took it eagerly. The cat gave a plaintive sound and she fed it some.

"See. It knew you'd feed it sooner or later."

"You would let it starve?"

"We'll never get rid of it now, and how do we explain it?"

"I'll think of something," she said.

"I'm sure you will." She glared at him.
"So," he asked, "who died?"

"What?"

"Our mourning."

"Oh." She ate another mouthful. "My maternal grandfather."

"Why?"

"Because I never knew him."

"A fair enough reason. We can be traveling to York for the funeral."

"Then why are we wandering the countryside?"

"Good question. Because I'm taking the opportunity to do business en route."

"To which I disapprove," she said with some relish, "as disrespectful to the dead."

"An excuse for us to bicker. How clever. What business am I in?"

"Millinery," she said, and took a bite of bread.

Christian grinned. She was getting her second wind. "I don't think so. Horse-trading."

"A disreputable profession. What else do you know enough about to withstand questioning?"

"In polite company?" he asked.

She let out a sound that might have been laughter or disgust.

"In a respectable inn," she said, "where

you might encounter anyone of any line of work."

"I surrender. I'll be an idle gentleman of modest means who has left the York road to visit a friend. Ready?"

She ate the last of the food. "Yes."

He gathered up her discarded clothing. "We want no hint of transformations in the area." He stuffed it all into a saddlebag and said, "Let's be off. Tomorrow you'll be safe in York."

She didn't move. "A night at an inn with *you?*"

He didn't like the emphasis. "I'm not the villain of this piece. I'm Sir Galahad."

"The pure and saintly?"

"Lancelot, then. Less perfect, but still a hero."

"The adulterer?"

"Unwise, unwise! You're the one locked in wed, Kat, as Guinevere was in the old tales. Lancelot, like I, was merely a lover, and free to be so."

But not any longer, he realized. He, too, had committed adultery this day.

"You're not free to philander with another man's wife," she said.

"That's for the wife to say."

He heard a hiss and was sure her hands were fisted, but by moonlight in plain clothing, her slightly long face took on the look of a virgin saint.

"I rescued you because my honor required it, Kat, not with an eye to payment. I'll see you to York for the same reason. Once you're safe, you'll see no more of me."

She stood even straighter. "Why not give me money and let me make my own way?"

"You who've never been out alone at night?"

"I have now, and I've survived."

"Stop this, Kat. I am no threat to your virtue." At a sound, he said, "No further threat, at least. And you were as willing as I for what happened before."

"I'd rather —"

"If you were a veritable Amazon afraid of nothing, I would still be a mere man who must play his allotted protective role."

Instead of gratitude, the infuriating woman showed signs of continuing the argument. He took her elbow and walked her over to the horses. He felt her reluctance, but then she stopped dead, staring up at Barleyman's mount.

"Is it the saddle?" he asked. "You will have to ride astride."

Most countrywomen did, and many of the aristocracy if intent on serious travel. A sidesaddle was a foolish thing for anything beyond a walk. Better roads and carriages, however, had led to an idiotic notion that riding astride was in some way indecent. Kat was just the sort of middling woman to subscribe to that.

After a moment, she said, "I'm afraid I'm unaccustomed to riding horses on any kind of saddle, Mr. Grandiston."

Her thin voice revealed true fear. Struth, why hadn't he thought of that? Many women never sat atop a horse.

"I'll lead your horse, and we'll go at a walk. All you have to do is sit."

"Up there?"

"Up there," Christian said, wishing he'd kept Barleyman here a bit longer. Could he even get a terrified woman into the saddle? If he lifted her up, she'd probably go right off the other side.

"I can walk."

"We can't arrive at an inn pretending to be doughty travelers with you on foot, or even riding pillion without the appropriate saddle." He led the horse over to the stile. "Come and mount from here."

Caro stared at man and beast. She couldn't do it. After a day of impossible things she'd managed to do, she'd arrived at one she couldn't.

That clarion call moved her toward the beast. Until it turned its huge head toward her. She stumbled backward. "It'll bite."

"It certainly will not. Truly, Kat, there's nothing to fear."

A laugh escaped that should qualify her for a madhouse, but she forced herself closer again. The horse was not only huge but pungent. She knew the smell of horses, but had never had need to be so close to one before.

"Get up on the stile, Kat."

At the command, she scrambled up. Once she was on the top step, the horse didn't look quite so mountainous, but it was very wide.

"Now mount."

"It's too far away!"

He nudged the horse a little closer — and Caro had nowhere to retreat. She'd seen men mount horses. It always looked so easy. "I don't know what to do."

"Put your left foot in the stirrup."

That was now at about knee height, so the movement was easy enough, especially when she dared to put her left hand on the saddle for balance.

"Good girl. Now get your other leg over."

For a moment Caro assumed he was talking to the horse. She stared over the saddle at him. "How?"

"Stand up in the stirrup," he said patiently, "as if on a high step, and pull on the pommel."

"Pommel?"

"The front part that you're holding," he said with such heavy patience it fired her courage. Or, at the least, inflamed the sort of irritation that can be a substitute.

Step up, pull up. She could do that. As soon as she began, however, the stirrup gave slightly and the saddle squeaked. Then the horse shifted, threatening the one foot she still had on terra firma.

Or stila firma.

Caro clung to the pommel with both hands, hopping on one foot, trying desperately to hold the horse still.

"Steady," Grandiston said, probably to the horse. The horse, at least, obeyed. Caro couldn't. Steadiness was beyond her, but she gritted her teeth and heaved.

She was up!

But only standing, one foot in a stirrup, the other in the air, stomach pressed to the saddle, which meant she'd let go of the upthrust bit of saddle with one hand, which flailed in Grandiston's face.

He was fighting a laugh.

"Bugger you!" she gasped, the appalling words coming straight out of the steelworks.

His laugh escaped, teeth white in the moonlight.

"That's my Kat!" he said, grabbing her right leg at the knee and dragging it over the saddle so she found herself astride — but horizontal, with the pommel poking at her midriff and her mouth full of horsehair. She spat that out and gathered breath to complain. With a tight grip on the back of her gown, he yanked her upright.

And, thank God, he kept his hand there. If she began to tumble right or left, he'd not let her fall. But her right foot flapped in the air.

Stars and angels, she couldn't do this!

Her legs were stretched wide over a slippery saddle. If she leaned even slightly, she'd be off, and the ground was a long, long way down.

By luck or his good management some of her skirt was between her and leather, but it was bunched uncomfortably. Gingerly, she wriggled, trying to smooth out cloth and ease the stretch, but then she froze again, suddenly shockingly aware of a similarity between the stretch now and the stretch she'd felt during that wicked afternoon so long ago.

Mere hours.

She even felt a lingering sensitivity there, along with a slight, foolish pulse of desire. She swallowed, her face blazing with heat. Thank heavens for moonlight.

Then the horse shifted and a pathetic little "Help" escaped.

He took her left hand and forced it to loose its hold on the saddle. "Grip the mane. You'll feel more secure that way."

Secure! Caro couldn't imagine ever feeling secure up here, but she gripped. With all her strength, she gripped.

"Vastly skilled at forcing unwilling women onto horseback, aren't you, sir?"

"Just be grateful you are a woman. If you were male, lad or man, I'd let you fall off until you learned to stay on."

"You are a horrible person."

"Whatever you say. Keep your grip."

With that, he let go of her gown. Caro gripped for all she was worth, still feeling as if she'd slide off. Or the horse would throw her. They did that all the time, didn't they? Or race away, out of control? Grandiston grabbed her ankle.

"What are you doing?" she yelped.

The horse jerked and Grandiston snapped, "Don't shriek, woman." He soothed the horse and looked up at her. She heard gritted teeth when he said, "I'm adjusting the stirrup. Billy won't race off with you — as long as you don't shriek like a banshee."

"Billy? A horse called Billy?"

"He's no Warrior or Caesar, that's for sure," he said, fiddling around near her ankle still. "But he's a good steady mount for distance work."

He grasped her ankle and Caro managed not to shriek as he put her foot in the stirrup. It did feel better to have both feet securely on something, even if the something was part of the Billy Beast and thus little use at all.

He did something else, something that jerked the saddle beneath her. She would not let a whimper escape, never mind a shriek. But then she realized something. Whispering as if it were a secret, she said, "You're not holding the reins."

"And Billy isn't running off with you," he whispered back, damn him.

Then he walked away toward his own horse.

Caro stared after him, appalled to be abandoned. She wouldn't say anything. She wouldn't. Then the horse moved. Only one step, but despite all her resolve, she squeaked.

Grandiston turned back and took the reins again, saying something soothing to the beast. Then he looked up at her, jaw tight in the pale light. "Kat, you're perfectly safe."

"He could rear."

"He has too much sense."

"He wants to throw me off."

"I sympathize."

He gave that whistle again and his horse raised its head from its grazing and stepped over, meek as a trained dog, to position itself for mounting.

Grandiston said, "I'm about to let go of the reins so I can tighten Buck's girth. Billy won't do anything alarming unless you alarm him first. Oh, there you are."

Was he some sort of lunatic? Whom was he talking to now?

He bent to scoop up something. "Here. Have some help." He dumped the cat in her lap.

Billy tossed its head and Tabby stood in a way that suggested it was as uncertain about the situation as she was. Caro wasn't about to let go of the mane, but she said, "There, there, we're all perfectly safe," to both animals, trying to sound as if she meant it.

Grandiston finished what he was doing, put a foot in the stirrup, and ascended into the saddle as if it were the most natural movement in the world. He sat the horse as if perfectly comfortable. Caro put that together with his comment about Billy being good for distance work, then added the fact that he and his manservant seemed to have their own horses.

"You rode here? From *London?*"

"I like riding," he said, leaning down to take her reins.

"You're mad."

"We've already established that. Let's find that inn."

Caro clutched and prayed as the horse began a swaying gait. It slid her slightly from side to side. She clutched more tightly and prayed harder. She'd give Grandiston, the dastardly, cunning, seductive criminal, no more opportunity to mock her. Aunt Abigail would require nothing less. Aunt Abigail had believed a woman was capable of anything a man could do, and often more.

She'd never been in a situation like this.

Caro called to mind all the ladies she'd seen riding with confidence, including Diana Arradale, who often rode astride, she'd heard. It couldn't be as dangerous as it felt.

"All right?" he asked.

No, Caro thought, she was not all right. She was bone tired, frightened, and uncomfortable. She was scared of the horse, and also of her knight-errant, who seemed able to force her to his will in a moment, be it in pleasure or torment.

"Perfectly," she said, and felt some support when the cat circled and lay down in her lap.

The body can hold tension for only so long, and Caro realized the horse provided some warmth. The night air was cool on her neck, ears, and nose, but she was sitting on a stove, albeit a smelly one, with a warming pan in her lap. It helped her relax.

She found the courage to loose one hand from the mane and stroke the cat. She stole a glance at Grandiston, sitting his horse with thoughtless ease, looking ahead, moonlight silvering his blond hair and skin.

He didn't look like a smuggler, but nor did he look like the easygoing gentleman she'd first met. Shades of white and gray made him harder in some way and he rode like a mounted warrior of old.

He'd been a hard man when he'd invaded the house in Froggatt Lane.

He'd been a wild man when he'd made that scarecrow assault on the mob. His fists had sent first one captor, then the other flying. Then he'd scooped her up like a child and carried her off like some wild raider of the past.

And in her memory, at least, it thrilled.

What was happening to her?

Sir Eyam Colne was her ideal man, the one she intended to marry. But when she tried to imagine Eyam's reaction to her predicament, she knew he'd still be pondering the appropriate reaction of a gentleman when the lady he was wooing was arrested for theft. If he ever heard of the event, even without the unfortunate element of her being alone in an inn under an assumed name, he'd wash his hands of her.

And why not? Would she not do the same to him? If she learned Eyam had been caught at an inn under an assumed name, trysting with some wanton, there'd be no wedding. She'd not tolerate a wandering husband.

Her eyes were still on Grandiston.

He'd definitely be a wandering husband.

Stars above, he was the last man any woman of sense would marry!

But Caro was suddenly aware of the warm cat between her thighs and the swaying of the horse's gait, which reminded her of pleasures she had never imagined. And couldn't imagine with Sir Eyam Colne.

Unfair, unfair . . .

"I think I see a light ahead," he said.

Caro inhaled and focused on the road

ahead. "A village?"

"Probably. There's a church spire amid the dark of the trees. If there's no inn, we'll try our luck at a farmhouse or such. Remember we're husband and wife."

Coming on her thoughts, it made Caro say, "That would be wrong."

He turned to her. "It's a simple subterfuge that people will believe unless you act stupidly. Are you wearing your ring again?"

"Yes. But we might have to share a bed," she protested.

"You're a restless sleeper?"

"You know what I mean."

"I know you're —" He bit off whatever insulting word would have followed. "Kat, I'm perfectly capable of sleeping beside a woman without rutting her. Of course, if you're of a mind to, I'll be pleased to oblige."

"I'm sure you would."

"Have I ever pretended otherwise?"

"Some men might wait for marriage before . . . *rutting.*"

"Really? Never met one. Come on." He tugged on the reins and her horse jerked into movement.

Caro held on, fighting tears that were mostly weariness. The thought of a bed was like heaven — but not a bed shared with this man.

Did he really expect her to leap on him in the night?

Did all men rut, as he put it, outside of marriage?

They probably did, but she didn't want to think of Eyam behaving that way. But then, she wasn't sure she wanted to think of him completely inexperienced. How tangled her thoughts were, and it was all Grandiston's fault for invading her life.

He brought the horses to a halt by the front door of what looked like a large cottage but had a sign hanging outside. He dismounted as easily as he'd mounted, and moved the reins back over her horse's neck. "Take . . ."

The door opened and a man came out. "Can I 'elp you, sir?"

". . . the reins," he completed quietly.

Caro did so, but terrified again that the horse would sense freedom and race off. It stood so still, however, head hanging. Perhaps it simply wanted to sleep, as she did.

"I'm hoping for a bed for the night," Grandiston said. "We've ridden longer than we intended."

"We're no but a simple place, sir," the man said dubiously.

"But the only one around, I think. We'll be grateful for any bed, I assure you."

"Come on in, then, sir. Thee's right that there's no true 'ostelry inside three more miles. You can 'ave a supper, if you wish, but plain stuff, mind."

"Bless you, yes."

Both men turned toward Caro and she realized she should look like something of a horsewoman. That's why Grandiston had put the reins back in place. She sat straighter in the saddle, but was she expected to dismount by herself?

She moved her feet out of the stirrups, but instantly froze. She'd never before been aware that there were so many things she simply couldn't do.

She wished she'd never learned it.

He came over and plucked the cat out of her lap to put on the ground. Then he pulled Caro off her horse so she was cradled in his arms. "There, see, safe and sound as promised, my dear."

He lowered her slowly until she was standing, but kept an arm around her. Caro needed it. She staggered, her legs protesting her weight.

The tavern keeper shouted and a lad ran out to lead the horses away. "Wait a moment," Grandiston said.

He took his support away from Caro and, once sure she could stand, went to remove the saddlebags, and also pistol holsters that Caro hadn't noticed before.

Caro didn't even want to walk, but that at least she could do. She straightened her spine and entered the tavern. It smelled heavily of ale and tobacco, and was, as the man said, a simple place where a few men sat at plain tables drinking ale.

Most of the seating was benches, but Caro was grateful even for that. She had civilized shelter — the first she'd known for so long. A fire gave warmth and cheer.

Yesterday, she'd have thought this place mean and sought some other hostelry.

She was changed.

Deeply.

Permanently?

Perhaps Caro Hill simply didn't exist any longer. Perhaps she'd never go home.

She struggled over to a bench and sat down.

Firelight and a few tallow candles didn't give much light, but she inspected her new clothing. No wonder Grandiston had mentioned mourning. She was dressed completely in black apart from the white cotton fichu, and her only ornament seemed to be some braid and pin tucks in the front of the gown.

Even her gloves were black. She stripped them off to reveal her wedding ring. It had the look of a ring worn for many years because it was. It was also made of twenty-four-karat gold, which made it gleam in the firelight. It spoke of wealth and propriety, so should support their story.

Looking at it, she remembered the base metal ring used at her wedding. She'd taken it off straight afterward, but it had still left a dark circle on her finger that had seemed like a stain of doom.

Distantly, she heard bits of conversation. Grandiston seemed to be managing to understand the local accent. This was Upper Burholme and this tavern was the Pot and Pig. The arrival of strangers from the south seemed to be the most exciting thing to happen here in a lifetime, but where was the bed . . . ?

She leaned forward on the table, tempted to put her head down and sleep. She no longer worried about propriety. She simply wanted a bed.

# CHAPTER 15

"Th'wife's asleep, sir," a rheumy-eyed old man said.

Christian turned and saw Kat, head down on the table.

"We've traveled farther today than I intended."

The innkeeper came over then, carrying two big bowls of soup or stew. He put them on the table, saying, "Ah, the poor lady. No point waking her to eat. The wife's running a warming pan through the bed now, sir, so bring her along."

Christian gathered Kat Hunter into his arms and followed the man across the sawdust-strewn floor. He expected to go upstairs, but the place extended farther than he'd thought at the back, and there was another room there containing a big, low bed. This was probably the tavern keeper's own bedchamber, but they'd be happy enough to surrender it for some coin. Christian hoped there were no fleas.

The innkeeper's wife was vigorously working a warming pan through the bed, but shot him an eagle stare. Though plump, she was as severe as her husband was genial, and clearly suspected they were up to no good.

Kat didn't look at all like a light-o'-love, however, and her wedding ring had the settled nature of one long worn. Christian added his charm to that. "I thank you wholeheartedly, ma'am. As you can see, my poor wife needs any comfort I can achieve for her."

The woman thawed. "Poor lady. What 'eartless pace have thee set to reduce 'er to such a state, sir?"

"Not the pace, ma'am, but the direction. In short, I lost our way."

She tutted and muttered something about men and their shortcuts as she drew back the covers. "Lay 'er down 'ere, sir."

Christian obeyed, slipping off Kat's battered and muddy shoes before the woman could notice them. Altered for her appearance as a gypsy, they didn't fit the new illusion of respectability.

Relaxed in sleep, Kat was yet another person. No gypsy now, and no saucy lady, either. Now she was simply an ordinary woman, the marks of the day on her face, both in dirt and weariness. It stirred a tenderness in him that seemed particularly perilous.

*Get her to York and forget about her.*

He thought about loosening her clothing, but it would be quite a business to get at her stays. Streaks of dirt marked her cheeks, but they couldn't be removed without waking her. He simply touched them gently. When he straightened and turned, he saw that his uncalculated action had completed the thaw in his hostess. She was close to beaming.

"I'm sure thee's 'ungry, sir, so go and eat your soup before it gets cold. A big man like thee need 'is food, I reckon."

"You're an angel, Mistress . . . ?"

"Barnby, sir," she said, dipping a bit of a curtsy and perhaps, just perhaps, blushing.

Nice to know all his skills hadn't entirely deserted him. After a day like today, he'd begun to wonder.

Caro awoke in darkness, not knowing where she was. Certainly not at home in Luttrell House. Everything from the lumpy mattress to stale-smelling blankets told her that. Somewhere nearby stank of beer.

And she was abed in her stays.

Then she remembered. Remembered — disbelieved! — the entire, impossible day. It had to be a dream.

But she was in a lumpy bed, amid noisome smells — and there was a man beside her.

She quickly checked her clothing. Everything seemed intact, but she'd slept so soundly that she'd not noticed him come to bed. Was it possible to sleep through . . .

Rutting?

Disgusting term, but that's what they'd done.

Rutted. In broad daylight.

Even though she lay in darkness, she flung an arm over her eyes as if that could block the images in her mind. She had to escape. She had to put an end to this and recapture her ordinary life.

Grandiston would get her to York. He was very effective, so he would do it. He was very effective, so it would be hard to escape him there. But she must, or he'd discover she was Caro Hill.

He'd expect to take her to her house. . . .

She saw her way. She wouldn't want to arrive looking so peculiar, so she would ask to pause in an inn so he could carry a note to a friend who'd provide her with something better. She'd need only a minute to disappear, and she'd soon be in Hambledon's chambers, safe forevermore.

She let out a breath and settled back to sleep.

But sleep didn't come. Her mind insisted on going round and around her plan and throwing up problems: encountering someone who knew Caro Hill on the way to York; encountering someone who'd recognize Kat Hunter and cry, "Thief!"

It wouldn't happen. She looked completely different now, but her frantic mind wouldn't stop, wouldn't stop, wouldn't stop.

Grandiston refusing to leave her. Insisting on taking her directly to her home.

He shifted and rolled closer, sending her mind spinning in another direction. If she moved just a little, she could steal some of that warmth and strength. He was so strong, so capable, so confident. Nothing terrible would happen to her as long as he was by her side.

She wriggled closer still, inhaling. Was that a manly smell, or his alone? It was unlike anything she'd smelled before. If there'd been lavender and cologne there yesterday, it had worn off during their adventures. She supposed that meant he smelled unwashed, but strangely she didn't find it unpleasant. Not unpleasant at all.

He smelled warm, earthy, perhaps even spicy. She couldn't put a name to it, but she inhaled, drawing it into herself, feeling it comfort, ease — and stir. It awoke memories, powerful sensual memories of the hot smell of his skin when she'd been locked with him, the taste of him when they'd kissed, when she'd licked.

Her body tensed in that deep and private place. It was as if she let slip a crucial secret. She couldn't remain still, however, and turned the next clenching into a wriggle, as if she were adjusting to the lumpy mattress. Deep inside, however, a hollow demanded satisfaction.

Sweet stars in heaven. She'd always thought this matter of man and wife as like other appetites — food, drink, the comforts of sunshine and good company. Something to enjoy when appropriate, but not something that demanded, that overrode civility and common sense. That growled and showed its teeth.

Man and wife.

Could a wife who woke in the night, who shared her husband's warmth and inhaled his smell, roll over against him, put her arm around him, and whisper, "Husband . . . ?"

Would he then wake and turn to her and begin the wondrous pleasure of the marriage bed?

At her request.

At her demand.

She reached out carefully and found the fine lawn of his shirt. She wished it weren't there. She wanted to touch, one last time, hot skin over hard muscles. Even the rough scar.

What else was he wearing?

Her fingers explored downward, then stopped.

That wasn't breeches or drawers.

That was bare skin.

She jerked back her hand. But then he moved, turned.

She tried to wriggle backward, but he gathered her into his arms. "My Kat is curious again?" he murmured. Clearly, he was smiling.

Caro inhaled. She drowned in his heat. The truth emerged. "Your Kat is hungry," she whispered.

He nuzzled at her neck. "You did miss your supper."

"And it's not yet breakfast time," she replied, heart thundering now.

"A gentleman should never let a lady starve."

"No?"

"Absolutely not." He turned her head and

brushed his lips over hers. She pressed closer and he kissed her fully, his hands beginning magic.

But then he went still, his hand on her bodice. "Stays," he said.

Caro sat up, unhooking the front of the gown, but when she tried to take it off, he pushed her down again on her back. "Stays can be fun."

His fingers traced the cotton fichu that went around her neck and was tucked into her stays at the front, and she shivered from that featherlight touch. One heavy leg came across hers. It could be holding her in place, but it felt as cherishing as an encircling arm.

He slowly worked the fichu free. Did he know how the ends dragged over her breasts, making her tense, making her hold her breath in the dark?

She turned her head to his, found his lips, held him to her as she kissed him. Gave the kiss for the first time.

But too soon, he pulled back. "Slowly, slowly. There's a special treasure here, Kat. Let me show you."

His fingers slid down inside the front of her corset to tease first one nipple, then the other. Caro closed her eyes and bit her lip. Such a sweet sensation, but she knew what she wanted, and she wanted it now!

He began to work her breasts up and push her stays down.

Caro pushed at his hand. "That's too tight."

He caught her hand and pressed it there. "Feel."

Her nipples jutted hard against her palm, poked just over the top of her stays. Her loosely laced stays, she remembered. For riding.

Loose or not, the stays pressed tightly on the breast below, but the borderline of pain seemed to make pleasure more intense.

"Imagine how it looks," he said softly. "Tight pink buds."

Caro could.

"Touch," he said, moving her index finger over the tip. Sweetness spread outward, through her breast, into her body and her mind. She pulled her hand away, but his mouth replaced it as he worked the other nipple free. Then his tongue and lips danced between both.

Caro moaned.

"Imagine," he murmured between torments, "that we're at a grand ball. We met less than an hour ago, first only with eyes across the room. We're both here with other partners, but we were drawn irresistibly together. We spoke, but mere commonplaces. We danced, hardly speaking at all. Except with our eyes — but our eyes were eloquent."

His hand was beneath her skirts now, but only stroking her knee.

Only.

"We slipped away. How fortunate we are to have found this small anteroom. It lacks a fire or candles. It's chilly and dark, but it's deserted, private. We've found this chaise. It's covered in velvet, which feels soft against your skin, but very little of your skin knows that. No time to disrobe. Certainly no time to remove stays . . ."

Caro was in that room with him, on that velvet chaise, but her hand found a bare thigh. "Yet you, sir, are half-naked."

He laughed, but he also nipped, making her jerk, but in a delicious way. "You're a wild, demanding lover. You've torn the clothes off me. They're scattered around the room. You know what that means. If anyone interrupts us here, candles flaring, our sin cannot be denied. They'll see my clothing, my nakedness, and your exposed breasts."

Caro tensed as if that might happen. "This is madness," she said, unsure if her words were part of the pretense, or the reality.

"Insanity, on both our parts," he agreed, and took her mouth again, sealing them together.

Caro didn't notice when he dragged up her skirts, only when he moved between her legs, which were already wide-open in welcome, her hips rising eagerly. She was burning down there, desperate, and when he began to enter her, it was too slow, too slow by far. She grabbed his buttocks and pulled him hard against her, arching her head back, stifling a cry down to hoarseness.

He went still and said hoarsely, "That's right. That's right. We mustn't make any noise." He lowered his head to whisper in her ear, hot and close. "The ball continues only yards away. Listen. Listen. You hear the music? But there are voices, too. Are they coming closer? Closer to this door . . . ?"

"Why didn't you lock it?"

"Perhaps I did." His whispering mouth traveled down to her breasts, to her high, trapped nipples. "Or" — he sucked — "perhaps I didn't."

Caro jammed a fist into her mouth to stifle cries as he tormented her breasts and began to move again down below. She arched so high only her shoulders were on the bed, collapsed, then arched up again as he thrust into her faster and faster.

She blocked most of her sounds, but the whole ball, the whole royal court, could burst in, candles blazing. All that mattered was building this, completing this, exploding the ever-increasing passion in her blood.

*Yes, yes, yes.*

*Like that. And that. And that . . .*

Her own intense responses shocked her, but with astonishing pleasure. This was beyond anything.

And then again she found that heavenly drifting place where everything is contracted down to peace and union, heat to heat, heart to heart.

In hot, sweaty silence, he laughed softly. "Ready to return to the ball, my wicked lady?"

Caro turned into his chest, smothering laughter of her own, but found something rough in her mouth. Her hair. She pushed it out of her way, remembering stuffing it into the cap. At some point, he'd taken off the cap, letting it rebel again.

"I'm sorry," she said. "I always plait it."

"Such a shame." He helped brush strands away from her face, but kept his fingers deep in it.

"It's wild, coarse. . . ."

"It's magnificent. Like you."

Caro wished she could see his face. Magnificent. "I'm ordinary. And cowardly."

"Cowardly? To face up to the mob pursuing you? To stay alone in the night? To sit on a horse."

"Don't laugh at me."

"I'm not." His hand cherished her. "I've ridden since I was an infant, but I can imagine how frightening it is to sit atop a horse for the first time. And you did your part with those footpads last night. I'm used to fighting, but you're not. You've lived a safe and ordinary life, Kat Hunter, which makes your courage all the more remarkable."

Caro glowed under his words, but she wished she could give him her true name. If only this tenderness was for her, for Caro Hill.

If only he weren't a violent man. If only he, too, lived a safe and ordinary life.

She held him closer. "I wish you weren't . . ."

"Weren't what?"

She pulled a face in the dark. "Whatever you are."

"I thought you liked what I am."

"Not when you're destined for the hangman."

He chuckled. "Kat, I assure you, the closest I've come in my life is in one day with you."

"Smuggling?" she fired back.

"Yes, well, perhaps. But I doubt they'd have hanged me."

Caro played with his shirt and the wonderful chest beneath. "So your work now isn't dangerous?"

"No more so than many other men's," he said, but a brief hesitation told her it wasn't the complete truth.

Before she could question him further, he gave her a kiss and a hug. "I'm in no immediate danger, and you are. When we have you safe in York, we'll talk more about this."

"Good," Caro said.

But then reality slammed back.

In York, Kat Hunter, wild wanton lover of Pagan Grandiston, would cease to exist. She knew that must be, but she couldn't bear the thought.

Perhaps, in the future?

"In case we have no time in York . . . ," she said, playing with a shirt button. It was loose. She wanted to fix it for him. "Is there a direction I could use to contact you later?"

He didn't speak and this whole illusion began to fade into mist. What was she thinking? Of course he wasn't interested in more than a brief liaison.

And nor was she. This was Grandiston, here to find, and possibly mistreat, Jack Hill's widow. And she was going to marry Sir Eyam Colne and have the perfect life.

"A letter to the Black Swan Inn in Stowting, Kent, will find me," he said.

"Not London?"

The light had increased to the point where she could make out his features and she peered to try to make sense of his words.

"I'm traveling. But a message there will always reach me."

"The Black Swan," she repeated, wondering if that was a coded message. A black swan was an impossibility — as was a future between them?

But she didn't leave the protection of his arms, or the glorious warmth of his body. This would be the last time, after all, before Kat Hunter died.

Christian woke to daylight, though not much of it. The small window had heavy shutters and only one thin slice cut into the room. It was enough to tell him it was full morning. He glanced to his side and found Kat, lying on her back, staring at the rough ceiling.

"Good morning."

She rolled her head to look at him without

298

a smile. "Good morning."

Ah, a classic case of guilt. The husband. He did tend to forget the damned husband.

He clearly wasn't much of a husband, though.

Would Kat abandon him for a sinful life?

*Danger, danger, danger!*

Christian rolled out of bed and pulled on his drawers and breeches. He was not going to become entangled with a respectable wife of York, especially one who carried disaster in her wake. "I'll find some washing water," he said, and escaped.

The only inhabitant of the kitchen was a girl tending to the fire. An already steaming kettle hung over it.

"Good morning."

She turned sharply to stare as if he had three heads. But then, flooding with pink, she dropped a curtsy. "G'morning, sir. What do thee need, sir? Dad said I was to get thee anything thee needed, sir!"

When she bit her lip, he knew "Dad" had probably also warned about what a fine gentleman might "need" that she wasn't to supply. Devil take it, when had he become a wicked ravisher?

Afraid even to smile, he demanded washing water, probably sounding like an emperor in a foul mood. She scurried around as if she feared a whip, finding a chipped pottery basin and a tin jug, which she hastened to fill from the kettle.

At that, Christian dashed over to help. Even though it was on a pivot, it was too large and heavy for a mere child. She backed away as if he might scald her.

When the jug was full, he asked, "Is there any chance of soap and towel?"

It was only when her eyes widened and she blushed that he realized he'd smiled, and his smile was having its usual effect. Damnation. He didn't need another set of local yokels after his blood.

Local yokels . . .

He wasn't thinking of Doncaster, but of Nether Greasley. The frightened girl reminded him of poor Dorcas Froggatt.

As she opened drawers, he noted the resemblances. Dorcas had been wearing a fashionable gown, not plain drugget, but she'd been as flat-chested as this one, with similar thin arms.

Dorcas's hair had been dressed in some pinned-up style, but strands had escaped the pins to rat-tail down her cheeks. This girl wore a mobcap, but a few straggling strands escaped, and it looked to be the same mousy blond. When the girl turned with some white cloths and a small pot, she was blushing and flickering shy glances at him. Dorcas hadn't blushed, and her eyes had been wide and steady, probably with shock.

He extended the bowl. "Perhaps you could put those in here."

The girl complied, still pink and with her eyes mostly cast down. A complete innocent, as she should be at her age, but Christian could imagine the toll it would take if she fell into the clutches of a man like Moore, not to mention being witness to a violent, bloody death.

And then Dorcas had been forced into marriage to a stranger with blood on his hands.

There had been blood on his hands. He'd realized that only when he'd arrived back at his billet in Doncaster and seen the dark crusting.

Doncaster, bloody Doncaster.

Heaven knew what expression he wore, but the girl was fearful again. He had to smile again. She blushed again, and the beginning of a smile flickered. Possibly even an inviting one.

Damn it all to Hades! He thanked her and escaped, fulminating about all the women who'd pitchforked him into this mess.

The Fearsome Froggatt, and her idiot niece.

Psyche Jessingham, who wanted to buy him.

And Kat Hunter, who might be hooking him, heart and soul, when she wasn't even free.

Poor Dorcas was the most innocent of the lot. If she'd never recovered from her shocks, it wouldn't be surprising. As he returned to the bedroom, he made a solemn vow to find the best possible solution for her, whatever the cost to himself.

Kat was up and dressed, sitting on the bed stroking the cat.

Christian had made sure it was fed last night, but then had shut the door on it, hoping it would find the tavern more to its taste than the wandering life. But here it was again, and he couldn't really care, because everything about this room reminded him of their potent passion in the dark.

That had been some of the fieriest love-making he could ever remember. And entirely initiated by her.

*Danger, danger, danger!*

"Did you feed Tabby?" she asked without looking up.

"Of course." He put jug and basin down on the rough table. "All yours. I'll wash at the well."

He left the room, repeating like an incantation — *Get her to York and have nothing more to do with her.*

He'd never met a more dangerous woman in his life.

# CHAPTER 16

Caro stared at the door. What right had he to turn cold and angry? He wouldn't be in this predicament if he'd not snatched her up in Doncaster! She'd be in a prison cell or ruined, but he'd be on his merry way.

Perhaps he was angry about the cat. She had to admit that by daylight it was a dismal sight. Its black fur was matted, and it had recently been wounded in three places. Half an ear was missing, and most of its tail. Something about its face suggested a scowl, and she could imagine that all its fights were its own fault.

It had a strange build, too, with a humped back and overlarge hind legs, poor thing.

She put it down and poured water into the bowl. She washed as much of herself as she could without removing any clothing; then she patted the bed. "Come up, Tabby, and I'll try to make you more respectable."

The cat scowled, but it leapt up to the

bed with effortless strength.

"You are a strong one," Caro said, tentatively dabbing at dirt and blood. When the cat didn't fight her off, she became a bit firmer.

"What war were you engaged in?" she asked.

*We-ah-ah-oo.*

"Whatever that was supposed to mean." The wound underneath was already healing, but the whole cat needed a wash. Cats usually cleaned themselves, she thought, but perhaps Tabby needed help. The bowl was too small. "A bucket by the well?"

Tabby scowled, extending one set of very sharp claws.

"I see. No bucket. I understand."

Caro continued her cleaning.

"Perhaps we're two of a kind," she said. "I could have stayed safe with Phyllis until morning, then slipped out to take the coach to York. But no, I had to turn the tables, to hunt my hunter. It must be my Froggatt blood, but why have I never been aware of it till now?"

Because one adventure, her first, the one with Moore, had been so disastrous it had sent her fleeing to tame safety for a decade.

"And there's nothing wrong with tame safety," Caro told the cat, tossing the washcloth into the basin.

She went to tidy the bed. The scent of what they'd done there rose to embarrass her, but it stirred hungers, too. She'd started it — she couldn't deny that — but he . . . he'd created an illusion that had built her hunger into a bonfire that should have left her charred.

She hurried to unfasten the shutters over the unglazed windows and fling them wide to let in fresh morning air.

She froze in place, for there was Christian Grandiston washing from a bucket by the well. It was a chilly morning, but he was bare-chested, his magnificent physique displayed to torment her.

Caro turned away, but Tabby leapt up onto the windowsill, and she turned back to hold it before it escaped.

"Idiot," she muttered, letting go. "If the cat wants to go, let it. It's nothing but a burden."

The cat didn't leave, and now Caro's will to escape had sunk out of sight. She moved to one side of the window so he'd be less likely to notice her if he looked this way.

"We shouldn't be doing this," she murmured to the cat.

It looked up and then turned its head to lick at the wound she'd cleaned, as if saying, *Me? I'm doing nothing.*

Pagan.

Grandiston looked that now, half-naked, his hair thick and loose.

Caro had never before been free to study a man's upper body totally without clothing. It was remarkable. Or rather, he was remarkable. Wide shoulders layered with muscle, contoured belly down to the navel, which she just glimpsed above his half-unfastened breeches.

She'd seen him before, in the Woolpack in Doncaster, but at close quarters and somewhat distracted. Now she could appreciate the whole, including the way his muscles slid beneath his skin. No wonder he was able to pick her up and carry her around as if she weighed nothing.

Another man joined him — a laborer of some sort who decently kept his shirt on. Even so, Caro could tell he was healthy and sturdily built, but that there was no comparison between the two. The farmworker was an ordinary man, but Grandiston could have modeled for an ancient statue of an athlete.

No, of Ares, god of war. He had the heavier build of a warrior's muscles, and that rough scar. Could he be a soldier? Could that be a war wound?

It was a possibility she hadn't considered before. The war with France was over, but it had lasted many years, and much of the action had been in Canada, where the native tribes sometimes used hatchets in battle. Perhaps that wound was not from a fight with a wronged husband after all.

No, no, she didn't want to think better of Grandiston!

"Eyam," she said aloud.

The cat looked up and made a short noise that sounded alarmingly like a laugh.

Caro turned away. "I'm going to marry Sir Eyam Colne and bear his children. Our life will be tranquil and orderly, and that's precisely how I want it."

The cat laughed again.

Caro bent down to glare at it. "That man is my enemy," she hissed, as much to herself as the cat. "Let him only find out who I am and he'd turn into that angry brute again."

The door opened and Grandiston came in, clothing back on again, thank heavens. He gave her a strange look, and she knew he'd heard her speaking to the cat. Pray heaven, he'd not heard what she'd said.

But all he said was, "Breakfast's ready."

When they arrived in the kitchen, Grandiston introduced her to Mr. Barnby, the innkeeper, and his wife. Barnby and two younger men were at the table, eating. One, Jim Horrocks, was the man Caro had seen at the well. The other was Adam, the son of the family. A daughter, Annie, was helping her mother at hearth and table.

All of them offered a greeting, but Caro saw the sort of flat expressions people use when they aren't sure they trust others. It would be her Spartan mourning when her husband wore only one black band, but she couldn't think how to explain it.

When they sat to share the breakfast, however, the problem turned out to be something else.

"Strange thing," said Barnby, chewing slowly, "a lady and gentleman travelin' with a cat like that. Killed a rat it did this morning, fast and sure."

Caro prayed that Grandiston would respond to the implied question. He didn't. She caught him smiling slightly, but attentive to a piece of ham.

"Oh, it would," she said. "It's a ferocious hunter."

"Still and all," said the man, "strange thing to take on a journey, a cat. On 'orseback."

Of all the causes for suspicion, why this?

"It's a rare breed," Caro said. She thought of claiming devotion to it, but it was showing no sign of devotion to her, and with its battered appearance, it was an unlikely lap cat.

The family still stared, waiting for more. "Not an English cat, of course. From" — where was far enough? — "Hesse. It's a Hessian cat. From Germany."

"Germany?" echoed Barnby, and he might as well have spat.

Caro had forgotten that many people hadn't resigned themselves to the German Hanoverians taking over the English Crown, even after fifty years. Had her careless invention turned the family against them all? Despite logic, Caro couldn't help feeling that if they turned hostile, they'd suddenly realize she was an outlaw with a reward on her head.

But Mistress Barnby bent to look more closely at the German invader. "Fancy that. And strange enough looking to be foreign, that's for sure. Do they dock cats' tails, then, in 'Esse?"

What to say, but "Yes"?

"Bit of a cripple, though, isn't it, with that 'ump in its back?"

"Looks like a rabbit," the farmhand said with a snigger.

"Why, so it does," said Mistress Barnby.

It was true, Caro thought.

"Tell the good people, dear," said Grandiston amiably, and forked a bit more ham.

"I think you should," she returned.

"No, no, dear. The cat is your special charge."

By now the family were waiting in wide-eyed anticipation.

"You have it exactly," Caro said. "The Hessian cat is half rabbit."

The stares turned to disbelief.

Barnby said, "Can't see cat nor rabbit allowing that, beggin' your pardon, ma'am."

"They do have to be restrained, sir," Grandiston said. He nicely conveyed that more details would not be suitable for family fare.

"Ah." The man chewed more bread, but then said, "Why? Why bother?"

Grandiston, plague take him, smiled an invitation to her to continue her tale.

"They are bred that way," Caro said, "the better to hunt rabbits."

"Hunt *rabbits?*" exclaimed Mistress Barnby.

In for a penny, in for a guinea. "Indeed, ma'am. The rare and vicious Hessian fanged rabbit."

"Fanged rabbits?" gasped the daughter. "Lord save us all!"

Barnby, however, kept chewing. "Not saying as you're mistaken, ma'am, but no matter 'ow vicious these rabbits be, it'd be easier to trap 'em."

Tabby raised its head from the plate and gave a trill of dispute. Caro said, "Hush" before she could stop herself.

"As you see, sir," Grandiston said, "they are very intelligent. You can almost believe it speaks." He looked at the cat with the expression of a doting father. "What it might be saying is that the fanged rabbits of Hesse are clever and cunning. No trap can catch them, and they avoid open ground. They can only be hunted down in their warrens and then defeated in single combat. You see the wounds our noble warrior wears. Alas, many Hessian cats lose the final battle."

Everyone stared at the noble warrior, who ate the last scrap of meat, then began to clean itself.

"But then why've you brought that unnatural beast 'ere?" demanded Mistress Barnby. "I'm sure we've no such nasty rabbits in England."

Grandiston smiled at Caro. "I'm sure we can trust these good people with the full truth, my dear."

Caro glared into his eyes, but she would rise to the challenge or die in the attempt. "Because," she declared, "it might be desirable to import the fanged rabbits of Hesse into England."

"Oh, no," the woman said. "No."

"No," echoed her husband, gripping his table knife in an alarming manner. "We don't need no vicious German beasts 'ere."

"I agree with you, sir," Caro said quickly, searching for a way out of this corner. "Except" — she lowered her voice almost to a whisper — "that the Hessian fanged rabbits have a very special quality." She turned to Grandiston. "Tell them, husband."

Perhaps he looked alarmed to the others, but she could tell he was choking back laughter. He coughed, then surveyed the innkeeper and his family. "It is a weighty secret. . . ." He paused. He sighed. Then he said, "The fluid of the stomach of the fanged rabbit of Hesse is reputed to cure the plague."

"Cure the plague!" gasped Mistress Barnby. "The same that blighted London only a century ago?"

"And did worse as the Black Death in the Middle Ages."

"Oh, my. Fifty died in this very area, almost 'alf as was 'ere." She spoke as if it had been a recent event. "Perhaps we do need some of those rabbits, Barnby."

"But not," interrupted Grandiston, "until we have an ample supply of the Hessian cat, ma'am. Otherwise, the beasts would over-run our island, killing not just mice, rats, and other rabbits but chickens, ducks, and even, sometimes, lambs."

"They kill *lambs?*" said Barnby.

"The fanged rabbit of Hesse is a greedy carnivore, sir. It will kill and eat anything it can. If it kills a Hessian cat in combat, it consumes its victim, including the very bones, crunched between its mighty back teeth. The cat, however, is generally the vic-tor and it brings its prize to its owner intact, as a good retriever does, so the stomach can be extracted and used."

Barnby had the set face of a man who wasn't entirely convinced, but wasn't about to make a fool of himself by saying so. The rest were won over.

"Let me get it some cream, sir!" exclaimed Mistress Barnby, and she hurried away to her dairy.

"Is the cat very vicious, sir?" asked the girl. "Can I stroke 'im?"

Grandiston considered gravely. "Move very slowly. He is normally of a tolerant disposition, but strikes out if alarmed."

"You watch yourself, Annie," warned Barnby, but the girl slowly extended a hand

and touched Tabby's head. The cat turned to her and purred.

*Explain that,* Caro thought at Grandiston.

"You have the knack!" he declared. "It is often young girls who can best handle the fierce Hessian cat. Lacking that, a woman of good heart can do so, as with my dear wife."

Mistress Barnby returned and put a dish of yellow cream on the floor. Tabby lost interest in the girl and set to lapping, but it did make an *ee-oo* noise that sounded remarkably like "Thank you."

"Well, I never," said Mistress Barnby, and even her husband was beginning to look convinced.

But then the woman leaned down and cautiously felt Tabby's stomach. "I do think this one 'as kittens inside." She looked accusingly at Grandiston. "What're you doing, dragging it around on 'orseback?"

Kittens? Caro's mind went completely blank.

But Grandiston was up to the challenge. "Would that it weren't necessary, ma'am, but the precious cat and its kittens are in danger. When you say we need some of these rabbits, Mistress Barnby, you are of the same mind as the highest in the land. The *very highest,*" he added portentously.

"But the king's German," Barnby objected.

"His Majesty is of the Hanoverian line, yes, sir, but he was born in England and loves his native land. He it was who knew the secret of the fanged rabbit and put this plan in motion. Under his instruction, some Hessian cats have been acquired and brought here for breeding. They are scattered around the country to disguise their presence, but the location of this one was discovered.

"As you see, Mr. Barnby, the story I told you when we arrived was not entirely true. We lost our way because we were avoiding those who seek to capture our precious cat and her rare offspring. Jealous agents of England's ancient enemy."

"The French," growled Barnby, and clearly they ranked lower than the Germans, for this time he really did spit.

Grandiston nodded. "We were forced to take to the side roads and lost our way in the dark. By God's blessing, we found sanctuary here. But they may come here asking questions. I hope I can rely on you, no matter what cunning tale they spin."

Everyone assured him that he could.

"And don't imagine for a moment that they will look or sound French," Grandiston said. "They might appear to be normal people — though perhaps not quite English to the clever eye. One pair claim to be from the American colonies, but you will soon detect their lies."

Lud, he was building protection against the Silcocks.

The wide-eyed family assured him again that they'd say not a word, but Caro was certain the tale would be all around Yorkshire within the week. By then, however, Caro Hill would be safe in Luttrell House with all this behind her.

Strange that the idea wasn't entirely appealing

"But what about the rabbit part?" asked Barnby. "What is it — buck or doe — to cat?"

"Either, sir," Christian said. Yes, she thought of him as Christian now. "But for a few generations cat can be bred to cat with fair results."

"We've got rabbits here!" said the daughter eagerly. "And cats."

Christian's jaw was rippling with held-back laughter, and Caro wanted to put her head down on the table and howl.

"It is a very difficult process," he told the girl, "and of course the cat must always be a Hessian cat."

All the same, the whole family was now eyeing the Hessian cat with hungry interest.

"We must be on our way, dear," Caro said, standing. She turned to the rest. "We thank you for your hospitality."

Caro protected Tabby from the excessive interest of the womenfolk while Christian discussed routes with Barnby.

Eventually he turned to her. "I'll go and prepare the horses, my dear."

Caro stared after him, a sudden sick feeling in her stomach. Surely he realized that she couldn't ride four miles, never mind forty. But she couldn't protest without exploding their story.

When he came to get her, she followed, cat at her heels, feeling like a woman walking to the gibbet. Then she saw the pillion pad behind one saddle.

"I fear Buck's showing signs of his old trouble," he said. "I've borrowed Mistress Barnby's pillion for you, but I'll not ask Billy to carry both of us all the way to York. Once we reach the next town, we'll travel on to York by coach. In company, we and Tab will be safe, by the grace of God."

"I suppose we must," Caro said, melting with relief. She'd still be up on a big horse, but she'd have Grandiston to cling to and he'd have complete control of the animal.

But then a new concern stirred.

"Will we have to go to *Doncaster* to catch a York coach?"

"But that would be backward," Christian said indulgently. "Mr. Barnby tells me we can take one from Adwick, a mere three miles north of here."

Caro sent him a silent apology.

He led his horse over to a trough that served as a mounting block, mounted, then let Mr. Barnby assist her onto the thick pad. It felt quite indecent to put her arm around Christian in public, but she must. She took a grip on the front of his waistcoat for extra security.

They'd forgotten the rare and precious cat. She was about to ask that someone pass it up when Tabby leapt to the trough and into Christian's lap in one bound. Christian must have started, for his horse sidled one step before steadying again.

"Dear Tab," Christian said, but through his teeth.

They thanked the Barnbys warmly and set out, Buck, reins tied up, walking behind.

"Why doesn't he run away?" she asked.

"He's well trained and knows where his next meal comes from. Are you comfortable back there?"

Not really, Caro thought, for sitting sideways on the horse felt very strange, as did holding him, pressing against him, but that was strange in a good way. She rested her cheek against his back. "As long as we continue at a walk."

"I've no intention of attempting anything else. Unless, of course, we're pursued by French agents attempting to seize a ferocious cat-rabbit of Hesse."

Caro chuckled. "Such a story. But is it really carrying kittens?"

"Explore if you want, but I trust Mistress Barnby."

"Indeed. Lord, what a complication."

"If she bore cat-rabbits of Hesse, our fortune would be made."

Caro chuckled again, but said, "Perhaps cat-rabbits are possible. It would explain Tabby's shape."

"I share Barnby's doubts. It would be a very strange match."

"Only consider some marriages."

He laughed and Caro felt it down to her bones. Lord above, riding like this was almost as intimate as bed!

They were both ignoring that — ignoring what had happened between them in the dark of the night. She wondered if his reason was the same as hers. Despite the game he'd played, it had been different —

deeper — than before. Dangerous.

Doncaster had been astonishing, tumultuous, intense. They had certainly been physically intimate, but it hadn't touched her . . .

She hesitated to think the word "soul," and it couldn't truly be her heart. It had been simply been different, as a rose still on its stem was different from the finest crafted rose of silk. Yes, despite the illusion he'd spun, it had been a deeply real connection at all levels of her being.

Could it have been the same for him? For the man who could make love so skillfully and casually to a stranger?

". . . your marriage?"

It took Caro a moment to return to the moment. "What?"

"Is your marriage a cat and rabbit affair?"

She couldn't possibly lie. Not now. "Don't ask me to speak of that."

They ambled on, but then he said, "Tell me something of your life, Kat. Anything."

"Tell me something of yours," she countered.

"Why are you fencing with me? Why not share more, unless you have secrets of which you're ashamed?"

"Please, don't."

"I'm sorry, but . . ." She felt him inhale. "You drive me demented, Kat. I know nothing of you. Nothing."

Caro opened her mouth to protest, but with a sigh she said, "I'll tell you about my home. It's in the countryside, not far from town. I have an orchard, a rose garden, and a conservatory for the winter."

"Your husband provides well for you."

"And you? What's your home like?"

After a moment, he said, "I have inadequate rooms in Horse Guards. I'm a major in the army."

Caro prayed she hadn't reacted. She'd been right, and so many things fit, especially his rapid physical response to threat.

"So some of your killings were honorable," she said.

"All of them, I hope."

"I'm sorry. Of course. I didn't mean to offend. The hatchet?"

"A skirmish against Pontiac, an Indian chief."

"You let me think it a vengeful husband."

"I have a mischievous sense of humor."

That was obviously true, though it didn't fit with her idea of an army major. "How old are you?" she asked.

"You think I should have outgrown it?"

"Probably, but I was thinking you young for such high rank."

"Don't forget the power of purchase," he said.

Of course. Most rank in the army was purchased. She'd heard there were schoolboys who were colonels, their work done by others. Moore had complained of the cost of his lieutenancy. Jack Hill had probably purchased his without difficulty.

"Are you rich, then?" she asked, returning to the questioning that had started all this. Now, more than ever, she needed to know if Jack Hill was dead, and the nature of Christian's interest in Mistress Hill. For so many reasons.

"Not at all," he said cheerfully.

"Your family, then."

"Merely well-to-do."

"But then who bought the rank for you?"

"My father. It was by way of an investment."

"There's profit in it?"

"I look splendid in all my braid as I mingle with the great."

"In London." An astonishing thought occurred. "Have you been to court? Have you seen the king?"

That seemed as rarefied an idea to her as Mount Olympus.

"More often than is interesting," he said.

Caro absorbed all this with difficulty. Of

course Diana Arradale had been to court, and she, too, seemed to see it as a tedious duty. Her husband, the Marquess of Rothgar, was often there, as he was a mentor to the young king. Christian Grandiston, however, seemed so — "ordinary" was not the right word, but not of that world.

"There's profit in attending court?" she asked.

"Why else would people bother? But you seem extraordinarily interested in profit. Are you sure you're not married to a merchant rather than a lawyer?"

"Quite sure," she could say with complete truth, but she was turning over worrisome information.

She'd thought Jack Hill's family both highborn and rich. Now it seemed that the Grandistons were poor. Not poor like the workers in a field they passed, but poor for Olympian circles. They would be very interested in her Froggatt money.

Christian was tender toward Kat Hunter, but the same man could be after Caro Hill's money with ruthless purpose. She didn't want to think that, but she had to try to find out more.

"Are you here on army work, then?" she asked.

"No. As I said, it is a family matter."

"And to do with a marriage." It felt so wrong to be trying to tease information from him, but at least she didn't have to face him.

"Did I say that? I'll satisfy your curiosity, Kat, but only if you use my name."

"Your name?"

"Christian. You never say it."

"Not Pagan?" she said, trying to dodge.

"Not Pagan."

After a moment, she said aloud what she'd been saying in her mind. "Christian. Perhaps it's because what we've done is so very unchristian."

"Is it?"

She had no answer to that. "Tell me your story," she said.

"Years ago, a marriage took place near Doncaster. The lady was unwilling, but her circumstances made it necessary. A gallant knight slew the villain of the piece."

Accurate enough, she supposed. What would she ask if this were new to her? "Slew? Killed?"

"On the spot."

"Poor lady," Caro said, remembering.

"Perhaps she wanted him dead."

"Even so, it must have been distressing."

"True."

"And your purpose in Doncaster?" Was

she at last to get the answers she'd sought?

"I came north to find if the lady still lived, and all about her."

"That sounds easy enough," Caro said.

"The bride is proving elusive."

Caro had to stop a laugh. "She's hiding from you?"

"Perhaps, or perhaps, as was claimed, she's simply traveling."

"Is she the Hill you seek?"

"Yes. You see, it truly is a boring story."

Caro asked the crucial question. "Why do you want to find her? What will you do then?"

"Talk to her. I might be doing that now if I hadn't been distracted." There was a smile in his voice.

"By me."

"You're much better company."

"And how do you know that?"

"A supposition. But it's hard for me to imagine better company than you, Kat."

It was an invitation — an invitation to talk of intimate matters, and perhaps even of a future. It hovered, pure temptation, but she would not be a fool. Until she was sure she and her fortune were safe, she wouldn't weaken.

"Your other horse has stopped to crop grass," she said to deflect.

He whistled and the gray raised its head and trotted after them, perhaps attempting an air of innocence.

"I've never imagined a mischievous horse."

"They have their characters like the rest of us."

The horse came up beside them and nosed Christian's leg. He patted it, but said, "I know you want me riding you, but Billy's better built for two."

Buck tossed its head and dropped back a bit. Caro watched it sadly. It could show affection for Christian without doubts or qualms.

"This marriage," she asked. "Why is it so important to you?"

She thought he sighed. "Did I say it was?"

"You rode north for it."

"I like riding. Marriages have legal implications, Kat. They can't be ignored."

"But you say this marriage has been ignored for many years."

"A mistake."

"Is there money involved?" she asked bluntly.

"Mercenary, too, Kat?"

"You fine court gentlemen might be able to sneer at money, but we simpler folk see its importance."

"I told you. I'm not awash in guineas."

"And doubtless would want more. Is that why you're here?"

"Kat, why are we arguing?"

*Because I've remembered I soon have to slip out of your life and disappear, and there's Adwick ahead.* The sooner she escaped, the better for all.

"I dislike keeping you from your Hill hunt," she said. "Why not buy me a ticket to York and return to it?"

"No."

"Why not?"

"Because I care too much."

Why was he doing this? "I'm married," she said.

"Unfortunate, but not insurmountable."

"What?" she asked, truly shocked. "You would kill my husband?"

He turned as if to face her but realized it wasn't possible. "No, of course not. I'm sorry. I'm growing addled."

She could feel it — his confusion.

"What did you mean?" she asked softly.

"I could take you south with me, Kat. I'd treat you in all ways as if you were my wife."

"But I couldn't be."

She felt his sigh. "And you could never be at ease as my mistress. I apologize."

Tears formed in Caro's eyes, and she bit

her lip, fighting them. *But if Jack Hill is dead, and my money is safe . . .*

"What if I had no husband?" she asked.

"Then I'd woo you, Kat."

"We've known each other for so little time."

"I've made lifelong friends in an hour, and enemies in less."

"That's different."

"Is it?"

It was frustrating not to be face-to-face. If she only dared tell him the truth.

She blocked that thought. She would not turn weak headed over any man. She'd have her affairs in order and the sort of legal settlements and trusts that would protect both her fortune and Froggatt and Skellow. Only then would she even think of wooing her wicked Christian.

She hated to be so calculating, but clearly she was enough of a Froggatt to have to be, and thank God for it.

Christian was glad when Kat put the matter aside. He kept forgetting that he was a married man.

It was one thing for a bachelor to persuade a woman to leave her husband and be his wife in all but name. It was another for a man with a wife to set up a mistress in competition. The situation would be fair to neither woman, but it would be particularly painful for Dorcas, knowing that he loved another.

Loved?

His heart missed a beat, but it was past denying. Hadn't he just as good as confessed it to her?

He smiled wryly at the flaring irony. The universal snare had caught him at last, just as he'd discovered he was committed to another.

He'd thought his situation was difficult. It was about to become hell. He'd vowed to treat Dorcas as well as possible and his honor would permit nothing less, but thoughts of Kat would come between them anyway.

He wanted to present Kat Hunter, not Dorcas, to the world as his wife. He wanted her to meet his friends, especially Petra, Robin's wife. They were very different, for Petra was Italian and aristocratic by birth and had a grand manner, while Kat was a down-to-earth Yorkshire woman. Even so, he thought they would like each other.

He wanted to take Kat, not Dorcas, to meet his family at Royle Chart. Kat might even survive that with grace. She had a lively spirit and could speak her mind. There might even be something of his mother in her.

He wanted Kat in his bed every night, not Dorcas Froggatt.

Good thing Adwick lay just ahead, promising the end of this too-intimate journey.

He had to get Kat safely to York and then find his wife. He'd like to believe that the decade-old ceremony was invalid, or there was a legal loophole that would free him, but he didn't hold much hope. If he truly was married, he saw no choice but to care for Dorcas as best he could.

If she had a child, a son . . . he put that aside for now. There was nothing he could do as yet, and there'd been no sign of that in Froggatt Lane.

His best hope was that she'd want to live apart, but it wouldn't leave the way open to an honorable future with Kat. And how was that possible with a married woman? He wanted to beat his head against the wall.

If Dorcas wanted to make the marriage real — that felt like a nightmare and he could only pray she wouldn't demand too much of his heart.

He rode into the yard of the White Hart and arranged stabling for the horses. Kat went with the fierce warrior of Hesse to a bench in a sunny spot against a wall.

There was no ticket booth here, and they'd have to wait for a coach to have seats, but coaches passed through fairly often. He hoped one came by soon. Kat seemed as willing as he to wait in silence, and he knew why. They both wanted what they couldn't have and were strong enough not to make matters worse.

He couldn't control his thoughts, however.

Black didn't suit her, especially when she was sad. She was made for rich colors, like that red and gold jacket she'd worn when he'd first seen her. It now lay ruined in one of his saddlebags. He'd keep it, foolish though that was.

She'd deny it, but she wasn't made to be the conventional wife of a provincial solicitor. She was made for adventure and splendid delights. He wanted to show her the excitement of London and the magnificence of Ithorne, the somnolent richness of Kent and the glorious coast of Devon. Had she ever even seen the sea?

He wanted to wake in the night to her questing touch. . . .

She looked up as if they had in fact touched, and their eyes met. They held for a moment, but she was stronger than he, and looked away.

# CHAPTER 17

Caro was glad to be apart from Christian, she on this bench, he on the far side of the coach yard. She couldn't think when he was near. She had to approach him in the end, however, to establish the plan she'd devised in the night.

"About York," she said.

"Yes?"

"You can't take me to my home. How could I explain that?"

"I could simply be a gentleman who offered you assistance."

"You don't look like a simple gentleman of any sort. I'll make my own way."

"How will you explain your arrest and rescue in Doncaster? Word might already have reached your husband."

Caro stared at him. She'd completely overlooked that.

"Your being there won't help, but alone I can . . ."

"Spin a story," he said. "Kat, I need to see you safe."

"I'll say that I escaped my insane rescuer and made my way on foot to a place that gave me a bed for the night. That I borrowed these clothes and took the coach the next morning."

"If he believes all that, tell him you rode to the moon."

Caro remembered her plan. He scrambled her wits so easily. "Whatever we do, I need to change my clothes. It will go more smoothly if I'm dressed normally."

"You have a way to do that?"

"Yes, I can borrow some from a friend. When we get to York, we'll take a room at the inn and then you can carry a message and bring back the clothes."

After a moment, he nodded. "Very well."

"Thank you."

Caro returned to her seat, knowing he still intended to follow her to her home. That would never happen, however, for as soon as he left with the message, Kat Hunter would disappear. A few minutes later, Caro Hill would be safe with Hambledon, Truscott and Bull. He'd be furious, but perhaps, once everything was in order, he'd understand.

Her dream now was to be with Christian,

husband and wife. She knew he wouldn't be the safe, reliable husband she'd always intended to choose, but she no longer cared. She'd throw her heart over the moon and risk her sanity, but she wouldn't risk the Froggatt fortune.

Instead, she'd make the arrangements she'd thought through for her marriage to Sir Eyam — part of her money would go to her husband, but the rest would be put in a trust that neither she nor he could abuse. Her Froggatt side could do no less.

But when all was settled, she'd write to the Black Swan in Kent and find Christian again, discover if he could understand and forgive her lies, and if heaven was truly within reach.

She spared a flickering thought for Eyam. She was sorry that he'd be disappointed, but what she'd had with him was skim milk as compared with cream.

She couldn't stop looking at him. He was such a beautiful man, his long body falling into graceful lines. At the same time, he looked so much the soldier that she was astonished that she'd never guessed.

That could bring another kind of heartbreak. The long war was over, but there would be others. Christian might ride off to fight again, be wounded again, and perhaps next time he would die of it.

If things went amiss and they couldn't be together, she might never know he was dead, for who would think to tell her?

That made her realize that she couldn't leave him without a word. He'd be frantic. She went to him again. "I must go into the inn for a few moments. Watch the cat."

"Of course."

He assumed that she needed the privy, but Caro went in search of writing paper. She found some in a small parlor, and an inkpot ready for use. The pen was in poor shape, but she quickly wrote the letter.

To my knight-errant,

I know it will pain you that I have disappeared, but please believe that it's for the best. I will soon be safe, I promise you. I fear there can never be anything honorable and lasting between us . . .

Having to lie, even by implication, was making tears blur her eyes. She rubbed them.

. . . but I promise that if there is a possibility, I will write to you at the address you gave. If you can forgive me for this, perhaps we can meet again.

Kat

She had hesitated over many possible final phrases, but in the end wrote simply her false name.

She folded the note and was looking for a means of sealing it when she heard the cry outside. "York! The York Fly. No delay!"

She put it in her pocket and hurried out. Christian handed her in, passing the cat up after. Some of the other passengers made disapproving noises, but as he joined her, Christian said, "It's both rare and valuable, and will give no trouble."

His commanding tone silenced everyone, and the coach swayed on its way.

Six hours later, the coach passed under the arch of the George in York. Once they had clattered into the yard and stopped, Christian climbed out and Caro prepared to repeat her request about the friend and the gown. He turned to assist her, but Tabby, who'd been restless, leapt down and raced toward the stables as if pursuing a fanged rabbit of Hesse.

Christian said, "I'll get it. Wait in the inn."

He was gone before she could say a word, but what would it be — "farewell"?

She had the perfect opportunity to escape and must take it. Caro needed all her strength to turn and enter the George without a backward look, but she did it.

"Ma'am?"

Caro turned to see a maidservant curtsying. "Can I get you something, ma'am? Will you be taking a room?"

This was the moment.

"No, but I must leave a message." She took the letter from her pocket. "This is for Mr. Grandiston."

But then Caro saw her plan in ruins.

What of Tabby?

Instantly she knew that Christian would care for the cat, even if he was angry at her. She trusted him, and if everything worked out well, they'd all soon be together.

"He's the gentleman with the cat," she added to the maid.

"Cat, ma'am?"

"Cat," Caro said, and walked out of the George.

She'd never visited York alone like this and wasn't entirely sure where she was, but she remembered that Hambledon, Truscott and Bull had their offices in an elegant modern house in Petergate, which was close to the Minster church, whose spires dominated the town. She could see them from here.

She'd assured Christian she was safe, but he would come after her — she knew he would — and she was too distinctive in her black clothing. It took all her willpower not to run through the streets toward those spires.

She paused in Petergate to gather herself, sending a prayer toward the great church, then approached the three-story brick building and used the brass knocker.

A moment later she was staring at the clerk aghast. "Away? How can Mr. Hambledon be away?"

She wasn't well-known here, for Hambledon mostly came to her, so the clerk stiffened at her outburst. "Everyone is away, ma'am, for the wedding of one of the junior partners. If you would care to leave a message . . ."

Caro opened her mouth, but nothing came out. What did she do now?

"Ma'am?" the clerk asked, showing a little concern. Caro supposed her deep mourning might be softening his heart.

"I'm Mistress Hill of Luttrell House. Mr. Hambledon has been handling my affairs for over ten years."

He clearly recognized the name, but regarded her with suspicion. "There's been a death in the family, ma'am?" She knew he was thinking that if Mistress Hill of Luttrell House had suffered a death requiring such deep mourning, the news would be known at Hambledon, Truscott and Bull.

"I . . ." Caro had clearly exhausted her inventiveness, for no story came to mind. "When will Mr. Hambledon be back?" she asked.

"Tomorrow, ma'am," the clerk said with frigid courtesy, easing her toward the door. "I'm sure if you return then, he will be happy to assist you."

Tomorrow. Not so many hours, but too many. Whom did she know in York? Know well enough to entrust with this strange situation?

No one. And she was penniless.

Could she beg some money from the clerk? His face provided the answer.

The man opened the door and propelled her through.

Caro was outside again with no idea what to do next.

Christian masked his reaction as he read the infuriating note.

He wanted to race out in search of her, but he needed a place to put the damned cat, which had scratched him.

"A room," he said.

The innkeeper obliged, but it took an unreasonably long time to arrive at it. He tried to tell himself he was glad to see the

340

back of Kat Hunter, who had clearly run lying rings around him for days, but he was sick inside.

He'd come to trust her, to believe her to be all she pretended. He'd as good as confessed that he loved her, and she'd shaken him off like a leaf stuck to her shoe. By gad, she wouldn't get away with it. He'd find her and wring the full truth out of her.

He closed the door on the complaining cat and left the inn to search. A coach rolled down the street, packed with people inside and more on the top. He searched it for a woman in black.

He invaded shops and stalked straight out again, people pressing back to get out of his way.

He stopped to stare at the Black Swan Inn, stung by the memory of giving her that address in Kent — the Black Swan Inn in Stowting. The lowly tavern where Thorn pursued his fiction of Captain Rose was nothing like this grand coaching inn, but it had carried his hopes. Hopes that she'd leave her home and husband and come to him.

Lying, cheating jade. Did she even have a husband, injured or not? She'd doubtless told the truth about one thing — she had friends in York and was safe with them, laughing at him. But she wouldn't get away with it.

He continued his hunt, even prowling through the Minster. Eventually he came to his senses, and simply stood, rubbing the inflamed scratches on his hand, steaming with anger at felines of all varieties.

Kat had made her escape, just as she must have planned to do all along.

He turned and walked back to the George. To hell with the woman. He'd meet up with Barleyman in Nether Greasley and complete the work he'd come north to do.

Caro was in the Black Swan Inn.

She'd stood in the street for far too long. People had stared. One man had asked if she was all right. He'd probably had kindly intentions, but he might not have. She'd made herself move, walk on as if she had a purpose. She'd stepped into a narrow alley to be out of sight, trying to come up with a new plan.

And from there she'd seen a tall, dark-haired man walking down the street. He'd been talking to another, somewhat older man. Both were dressed in plain clothing, but people gave the dark-haired man a second glance. Some even made way. Caro doubted they knew who he was; they simply recognized wealth and power. But she knew him.

He was the Marquess of Rothgar, husband to Diana, Countess of Arradale, Caro's friend. Well, not quite that, but warm acquaintance, even colleague in some benevolent work. The marquess and Diana were unfashionably devoted, so where Rothgar was, there would be Diana, too. And Diana would help her.

After a cautious look around, she'd crossed the street to follow the marquess into the inn. A male servant asked her business.

"I wish to speak to Lady Arradale."

"There's no one of that name staying 'ere, ma'am."

"Lady Rothgar, then," Caro said impatiently.

"Nor 'er, either."

Caro looked sharply at him, wondering if he was being impertinent, but he seemed truly unaware that the same woman was both. He was beginning to grow suspicious, however. She tried to look calm, but inside she was a tangle of uncertainty.

Diana wasn't here? She should leave, but what hope was there in that? Dare she approach the great marquess himself?

She had been introduced to him by Diana, but he was unlikely to remember it. It had been at a crowded York assembly with the whole of Yorkshire intent on a word with one the great lords of the land.

The servant was frowning now, perhaps even considering throwing her out.

Caro straightened and gave him a look. "So the marquess travels without his lady. Please find me some writing paper. I will send up a note."

The man pursed his lips and didn't move. Caro tried to give him a commanding stare, but she was worn to shreds by all this and she had no money to bribe him.

Then the marquess and his companion walked into the hall from the back.

The manservant looked at her with a sneer, certain she wouldn't dare approach.

She stepped forward and curtsied. "My lord Rothgar."

Caro sensed a raised guard and clenched inside. He must be accosted all the time by people wanting his assistance. He no doubt just ordered them to be removed.

But then he bowed in return. "Mistress Hill, is it not?"

Relief washed over her, bringing tears to her eyes. "Yes, my lord. I hoped Lady Arradale was with you, but the inn servant said not."

"She has remained south and allowed me to execute business for her in Yorkshire. Do you require assistance in some way?"

That seemed uncannily perceptive, but then Caro realized her agitation must be obvious. He might even think there cause for her mourning clothes. She was tempted to pour out everything then and there, but said, "I do need advice, my lord. Are you about to leave, or may I beg a moment of your time?"

"Quite a few moments," he said, "as long as you will permit me to eat as we talk." He gestured toward the stairs. "Please come up."

Caro hesitated. This wasn't Diana but a man she'd met only briefly. He was a stranger, and what's more, he had a somewhat dark reputation for ruthlessness and even violence. She'd heard he'd killed a man in a duel not long ago, merely for insulting his sister.

Her recent adventures should have taught her more sense. Yet what choice did she have? If Christian captured her now, he'd keep a close eye on her, and though she wasn't well-known in York, there were too many people here who knew her. One would be bound to say, "Why, Mistress Hill, who has died?"

She went with him to an upstairs parlor, surprised to find it in no way out of the ordinary. What, she expected a gilded chamber reserved for such as him? No, but she was still surprised to see only one liveried footman, standing by a laden table, ready to serve in any way that might be required.

There were only two chairs at the table and the marquess led Caro to one. She glanced apologetically at his companion, but the footman was already putting another in place. Then he hurried away, presumably to order another setting and more food.

It was all very efficient, but Caro felt more awkward by the moment. Was she going to have to tell her whole story in front of a servant? Or two? She had no idea who the second gentleman was.

Lord Rothgar settled in his own chair, saying, "Allow me to introduce my secretary, Mr. Carruthers. Carruthers, this is my wife's acquaintance Mistress Hill — of Sheffield, I believe?"

His remembering her from one brief encounter had been impressive, but his also remembering her hometown reminded her that he had a reputation for uncanny omniscience. Could he detect her recent, ruinous adventures?

The secretary greeted her, smiling in a perfectly ordinary and kindly manner, but Caro gave thanks for the arrival of a steaming soup tureen along with the extra cutlery and dishes.

Other servants left, but the footman remained. She picked up her spoon, knowing she should launch into her request for advice, but tongue-tied by uneasiness.

The marquess spoke. "If your concerns are private, Mistress Hill, Carruthers and Thomas can take themselves next door to eat with my other attendants. But Thomas is the epitome of discretion, and Carruthers is my other self."

So he did travel with an entourage. They were simply elsewhere, eating their own meal in relaxed comfort. For some reason, that brought Caro back to earth.

"It's not private in that way, my lord, and I'm sure your people can be trusted. It's merely complicated. . . ." She forced herself to stop babbling and plunged into her story, all of it, beginning with Moore and his sister and Jack Hill.

She was so nervous that she made a mishmash of it, confusing or forgetting details and going backward and forward in attempts to clarify, but the two men were attentive and patient, and the footman almost managed to make himself invisible except when removing used plates.

She trailed to a halt after Christian's invasion in Sheffield. She couldn't bear to reveal the rest. "So I felt I needed to conceal myself and seek counsel. I donned these clothes and came here to York to consult with my solicitor, but I have arrived only to discover he is away. And I saw Mr. Grandiston here. I don't know how he tracked me, but now I don't know what to do."

Lord Rothgar considered her for a moment and she felt sure he'd detected her evasions and inventions, but then he smiled. "How delightful. A lady in distress and puzzles to be solved."

His secretary groaned, but with a smile. "He delights in puzzles, ma'am, though this one seems simple enough, sir. The only question is whether Mistress Hill is wife or widow."

"Or if she was ever married at all," Lord Rothgar pointed out. "A most irregular affair. Do have some lemon cake, Mistress Hill."

Caro thanked him and took a little, but asked, "You think the wedding service invalid, my lord?"

"Quite possibly."

"I disagree, sir," Carruthers said, cutting a

slice of cheese. "Vows before witnesses, after all, and before the Hardwicke Act. Also, I regret to say, ma'am, but your use of the name 'Mistress Hill' for so many years carries a certain legal force."

Caro looked at him in dismay. "But it seemed the right thing to do."

"Things often do," said Rothgar. "What a pleasantly many-layered mystery. Tea, Thomas, if you please." As the footman left, the marquess turned to Caro. "Grandiston, you said? Mr. Grandiston?"

Caro blushed at the very name — she couldn't help it — but agreed. Only then did she think that he'd phrased the question oddly. In what way? Before she could pin that down, he asked another question.

"And he implied he is attempting to settle a legal matter concerning a cousin?"

"Yes, my lord," she said, for that was what he'd told Ellen. Should she tell the marquess about the details Christian had added earlier today? How? And it didn't matter.

"An attractive man, I assume?" Carruthers asked with a twinkle in his eye. Lud, had she blushed?

"To some tastes," Caro said as lightly as she could manage.

"But not to yours," the marquess said. Fortunately, before she was required to speak an absolute lie, he went on. "If we assume you did marry this Jack Hill, then the salient question is whether he is present on this earthly plane or gone to his heavenly reward."

"I feel sure he's dead, my lord, but as long as there's any uncertainty, I must safeguard myself and my fortune."

"Very wise, for the balance of power is generally with the husband."

"I know it."

Carruthers said, "Even if you are a widow, ma'am, I fear there might be lingering implications."

"An inherited interest," Caro said, putting down her fork. "That's what alarms me most. I feel sure that Hill's dead, but if he died possessed of a husband's rights to my property, that could be inherited, couldn't it? Quite possibly by Mr. Grandiston."

"You have an excellent understanding of the law," Rothgar said.

"I own a business, my lord. I was raised to understand it."

"No wonder my wife admires you."

Caro was startled to think she might have been discussed, but said, "I admire her, too, my lord. It isn't easy for a woman to hold her independence in the face of the world. I wish I'd been stronger when young. There was a document Hill signed. It was supposed to protect my property, but I don't know what it said, and I confess, I've never tried to find out. It might help."

"Do you know where it is?"

"No, and my search for the letter didn't reveal it. But my hope was that my solicitor had both documents in his trust."

"Carruthers," said the marquess, "we must ascertain that."

"Certainly, sir, but of course such a document would be unlikely to cover income earned after the marriage. What proportion would that be of the whole, ma'am?"

Caro inhaled. "Most of it. The war brought great prosperity, and my aunt's work bore fruit. It isn't fair that his family would get all that!" She looked to Lord Rothgar. "Please advise me. I'm of simple origins and Mr. Grandiston seems to be of high rank. So, probably, was Lieutenant Hill. This case may be decided in London and at a level of society where my Yorkshire friends will be of little use."

"I hope you aren't discounting the usefulness of my wife, Mistress Hill."

Caro went hot. "No! No, of course not. I meant to appeal to her."

"I believe I, too, can be useful at times."

Caro felt embarrassment was now her

perpetual state, but wariness rose over it. "You, my lord?"

A twinkle showed in his eyes. "Definitely wise to beware of tigers bearing gifts, but I mean you no harm. My wife will wish to support you in this, both for the sake of principle and friendship, and I look forward to working through the puzzles. You're correct that practical answers are likely to be in London — in the offices of the archbishop of Canterbury, at the Horse Guards, and with the sort of lawyers used to such tricky cases. I believe I can encourage the Horse Guards to rapidly find any records of Jack Hill. You did say Jack, did you not?"

"Yes. Though his name was probably John."

Rothgar nodded. "Once there, we'll soon establish the truth of your marriage and your legal rights."

Caro blew out a relieved breath. "You are most generous, my lord. I thank you. But what should I do in the meantime? I don't . . . it would be unwise to fall into Grandiston's hands, I think."

Those hands. Those strong and clever hands . . .

"Most unwise. Do you have need to remain in the north?"

"You think I should travel, as I claimed?"

"I think you should travel south. With me."

Caro stared at him. "South? To London? Now? I can't do that."

"Why not?"

She inhaled thin air. "I have a business, a house here. My companion will be worried. I have only the clothes I'm wearing!"

His lips twitched. "Distressing, I'm sure, but all these things are easily arranged. Your house and business are not solely under your management, are they? And your companion can be informed, with explanation. My wife has need of you."

"But . . ." Caro found she couldn't accuse the marquess of speaking nonsense. "Lady Arradale and I are not on intimate terms, my lord."

"All the same, she does have need of you, I promise. Diana is six months with child, which is the only reason she allowed me the honor of conducting business for her up here. She's bored and needs diversion. Your tangle should suit admirably."

Caro distrusted the tone of that, but she was already seeing what few choices she had. Sheffield and Luttrell House were barred to her because Christian would return to his search. She didn't know Phyllis's direction in Rotherham. She had other friends with whom she could seek shelter, but not without answering many awkward questions.

But London!

Christian came from London.

"You would be wise to avoid falling into Grandiston's hands until you are completely sure of your legal rights," Lord Rothgar said, "and London is the place for legal matters. If your situation is difficult, we may wish to engage the king's interest."

"The king?" Caro echoed in alarm.

"As head of church and state he can make unique adjustments to almost anything if he so chooses. He is more inclined to generosity when he sees the petitioner, so you should be presented."

"At court?" Caro gasped it. Christian attended court.

"Perhaps not in the most formal way," Lord Rothgar reassured. "But you could be made known to the king and queen at a less formal event. They are very fond of ancient music — madrigals and such. Are you an enthusiast for that, ma'am?"

"I'm afraid not."

"Perhaps we can educate you in time." He considered her again, in a way Caro was beginning to find worrisome. "Your business, Froggatt's, does it make anything the king might appreciate?"

Dazed, Caro said, "I doubt it, my lord. Swords and blades of the highest quality, but I assume the king has all the swords he needs. The only other item we make is fine steel springs. They are the best steel springs, but —"

"Ah," the marquess said.

Carruthers chuckled. "A detour to Sheffield, sir?"

"Tempting," Rothgar said, "but that would be awkward for Mistress Hill." He turned to Caro. "His Majesty and I share an interest in clockwork mechanisms, ma'am. Has the king purchased from you?"

"Not as far as I know."

"Then it will be a delightful surprise for him. Could you arrange for a selection of clockwork springs to be sent as a gift?"

Caro tried to imagine Sam Skellow's reaction to this honor, and failed. "Yes, I'm sure. . . ."

"Good. Despite the sensible warning to beware of gift horses, hardly anyone can resist a truly pleasing one. So, you will come south, ma'am?"

Caro was feeling short of breath, but she saw no choice. "If you think it wise, my lord. You will have to advise me how to go on. Oh, I'm sorry, I mean someone will. I know you are too busy. Where should I stay?

Should I hire a house . . . ?"

"Quite unnecessary. If you will honor us, I would have you stay in my house. Diana truly does need diversion, and there we can ensure your safety."

"You mean because Grandiston would not invade your house."

"Most unwise," he said. "But there might be more-serious dangers. This is a tangled matter that could work through the courts for years, consuming your fortune in the process." Before Caro had absorbed that, he added, "How much simpler if you were dead. Who would be left to object to Jack Hill's claim?"

"My death," Caro repeated. Had that been Christian's plan all along? Christian, who had killed many times. If he'd discovered her identity during their adventures, would her body now be lying beneath a hedge? She knew he was no danger to Kat Hunter, no matter how angry he might be with her at the moment, but perhaps his family had sent him north to find and remove Jack Hill's inconvenient widow.

"I'm sorry to distress you," Rothgar said, "but facts must be faced."

And one fact, Caro realized, was that the sale of her share of Froggatt and Skellow hadn't happened yet. The business was still vulnerable.

"I also recommend that you go by a different name, at least for a while."

"Why?"

"My servants are discreet, but the name of a guest can slip out. We might not want people to know that a Mistress Hill is in London."

Caro desperately longed to be herself — to be Mistress Caro Hill of Luttrell House — but it wasn't to be.

"What name do you want to use?"

" 'Grieve,' " Caro said bleakly. "At least it matches my clothing."

*And my heart, which grieves that my knight-errant could be very errant indeed.*

"Very well," Lord Rothgar said. "Now, Mistress Grieve, I have business to complete at Worksop this evening."

And heaven help any problem of road, weather, or human foible that intervened.

Caro rose, light-headed but certain of one thing: within the marquess's bastion of power, no Hill or Grandiston could touch her. What's more, if anyone could twist and squeeze the law of church and state to free her, it would be Lord Rothgar and his wife.

Whether she would contact Christian when she found herself free, she had no idea. It must depend on what she discovered about his and his family's true motives toward her.

"I must send those messages," she said.

As if by magic, Carruthers produced a small folio of paper, a pen, and a portable inkpot. He placed them in front of Caro and then stood waiting, ready to seal each letter.

The footman had already gone into the adjoining room, and voices and movement there told of people preparing to leave. The marquess showed no obvious impatience, but Caro felt urgency pressing on her. When she took the pen, however, her mind went blank — or was swamped by thoughts of Christian.

She wrote to Ellen, saying that she'd encountered the marquess in York and had been prevailed upon to go south with him. She also wrote to Phyllis along similar lines, hoping any word of Mistress Hunter's misadventures hadn't reached Rotherham already. Lastly she wrote to Sam Skellow, instructing that a selection of smaller springs be sent to the king. As she had no idea how that should happen, she asked for the marquess's direction in London.

Carruthers said, "Malloren House, Marlborough Square," and she added that before sealing the letter.

Then Carruthers said, "If you could write a note to your solicitor about that settlement paper, ma'am, to say that the details be sent to you at Malloren House?"

Caro quickly did that, too. The messages were sent off by one of Lord Rothgar's grooms, and soon Caro was off on another wild twist of fate, heading south as fast as roads and weather allowed.

# CHAPTER 18

Christian arrived at the Tup's Byre in Nether Greasley the next morning, bringing the horses. He was riding Buck, who fortunately didn't mind the basket containing not only the damned Hessian cat but two kittens. Of a litter of five, three had been born dead. Perhaps they were the result of an unnatural mating after all.

As with him and Kat. Had she been as inexperienced as she'd seemed? Had she realized that he'd lost control that night? What would she do if she found herself with child? Contact him through the Stowting address?

That he wanted that infuriated him.

He'd been tempted to abandon her damned cat, but one Kat's behavior wasn't the fault of the other. He needed to find some home for the cat and kittens soon, however. They carried memories like fleas.

He came to a halt before the solid, square inn, surprised to find that it hadn't changed except that it had been overcast before and now the sun was shining. Had there been flowering plants in front ten years ago? He remembered it as hellishly grim.

He dismounted, carrying the basket, and shouted for a groom. Barleyman came out.

"Thought it was you, sir," he said, taking charge of the horse. "All well in York?" He was staring at the basket.

"Mistress Hunter's familiar, plus offspring," Christian said. When Barleyman looked puzzled, he added, "The cat that was with us when we collected the horses."

"So there was one, was there, sir."

"It sometimes chooses to be invisible, when it's not hunting ferocious rabbits."

"If you say so, sir," Barleyman said with studious unconcern.

Amusement took the edge off Christian's unease. "Is there anything edible? We're famished, and we don't want Tab to start hunting."

"No, sir? There was a tasty rabbit pie for dinner, and some left over."

Christian looked down at the grooming cat. "Will you deign to eat prey slaughtered by another?"

The cat, however, refused to talk to him. It hadn't said a word since Kat left, and treated him with such disdain he'd found himself at one point trying to argue his case.

"I've seen a few rats in the stables here," Barleyman said.

"Rats are a mere nothing to a Hessian hunting cat, but allowance must be made for a mother in the straw."

"Right, sir. I'll just go and take care of this nag, sir, and bring in your belongings."

Christian watched him, smiling, but when he turned to enter the inn, amusement died. He'd been mad to appoint this place as their meeting spot. The last thing he wanted was to reenter it. He braced himself and strode forward, realizing only at the last moment that he needed to duck slightly to avoid the lintel. That hadn't been true last time.

He'd been so damned young.

The same innkeeper approached. Christian recognized him instantly, though the man had a bigger paunch and an extra chin. "Good evening, sir. Welcome to the Tup." He glanced at the contents of the basket.

"A highly valuable specimen. It rooms with me."

"Very good, sir. I'll take you up to your room, sir."

Christian followed him, aware of a new possibility of disaster. Let it not be that room.

"A superstitious sort, your man," said the

362

innkeeper as Christian followed him up the stairs.

"Yes?" He considered the comment bizarre. Barleyman hadn't a superstitious corner of his mind.

"Inquired about ghosts and such, sir. Of course we have no such thing at the Tup, but when I told him of a violent death in our best front room, he refused to take it for you."

Christian sent a prayer of thanks. All the same, he resented Barleyman realizing how he'd feel before he did himself. He'd better pose the expected question. "Violent death?" he asked as the innkeeper opened a door.

The man told the story with relish.

"A Lieutenant Moore — a villainous type, sir, who lies uneasy beneath the grass of this very churchyard — absconded with a schoolgirl and brought her here. Of course, I had no idea, sir, that she was so young, for he claimed she was his wife and she was cloaked, or that there was anything untoward, for she seemed happy enough on arrival. But all was not as it seemed. Fortunately another young officer burst in and slaughtered Moore, then and there. Following which, he — the other officer, sir — gallantly married the young lady to save her honor. Turned out he was the young lady's true love, sir, so I'm sure they found happiness in the end."

"Indeed," Christian said, wondering if the man believed this version of events. Very likely after ten years of telling. "Was the young lady from these parts?"

"Oh, no, sir. From Sheffield. A well-to-do cutler's family, I understand. No necessity to name names, sir, you understand."

"Completely," Christian said, "and I honor your discretion, sir."

Abigail Froggatt and her money had done their work well here, but there was probably no chance of getting the people here to recall that the wedding had been forced.

Christian was ushered into the room. He approved it. It was very like the one in which he'd been married, but not the same, and that was all that mattered. He ordered wine, which got rid of the innkeeper, who wanted to embroider the tale.

"Damnable place," he said to the cat, which was passive with its kits suckling. "Do you have no instinct for vileness and evil? Apparently not, especially as you liked her."

Tabby opened her eyes a slit, but stayed silent.

"Talk to me, damn you. You were vocal enough before."

The cat blinked.

"Come on. Curse me, at least."

"Talking to yourself, sir?" Barleyman asked as he entered, carrying Christian's saddlebags and pistols.

"To the cat. At least it's a good listener."

"In addition to being a vicious killer, sir."

"We've known some like that."

Barleyman put the bags in a corner and the pistols neatly on the table. "Indeed we have, sir. Indeed we have."

"Tell me you've news," Christian said to forestall questions about Kat, for he was damned if he knew what to say. His pride didn't want to admit that he'd been outwitted, and nothing in him wanted to admit that he didn't know where she was or if she was safe.

"A bit, sir. Doncaster first, or here?"

"Doncaster."

"The Ossingtons' maid was too discreet, but I hung around the nearby tavern and managed to strike up a conversation with a man who works for the Ossingtons. Cuddy Barraclough's the name. Just the one that does the rough work and not all that well-endowed up top, but garrulous when oiled. According to him the Ossingtons are a fine young couple with one child and another on the way. A Mistress Hill has visited the house once. He was sure of that, so no question of her being Mistress Ossington. He was sure she wasn't there then, though."

"Plague take it. What of the maid sent from the Froggatt Lane house? The one I followed. Did he know anything about her message?"

"That was the strange thing, sir. He didn't know anything about her."

Christian frowned at him. "Sure he worked at that house?"

"Quite certain, sir," Barleyman said with dignity. "I didn't like to ask anything specific, or even he might have smelled fish, but I slid in some questions about how visiting servants were treated and he said there hadn't been any for months. Mind you, sir, it was clear any part of the house beyond the basement was a foreign land to him, and as I said, he's not the sharpest pike in the batch."

Christian worked through it. "So the maid arrives by the front door, delivers her message, and leaves the same way."

"So it would seem, sir. She could have had another message to deliver elsewhere."

"Dammit, I should have waited longer. What about here? I've already heard the story of past events."

Barleyman rolled his one eye. "First thing

they talk about, sir. Though not quite the story as I've heard from you."

"Mistress Froggatt paid well. Did you get the name of the clergyman?"

"No one seems to remember, sir. Hood — he's the innkeeper, sir — did wonder if the ceremony was legal."

"As do we all," Christian sighed.

The wine arrived then, delivered by the innkeeper himself. Christian thanked him and asked if the vicar would know more details of the intriguing story.

"Reverend Bletheringhoe, sir? No, sir. Only been here three years since old Reverend Peake died."

The shifty clergyman who'd married him hadn't been known to the locals, so certainly not Peake. That line of inquiry seemed dead.

Christian dismissed Hood and poured wine. He drank some of his and pulled a face.

"As good as could be expected, sir," Barleyman said.

"True enough," Christian said, but he was remembering Doncaster, and wine, and Kat Hunter, who knew good wine from bad. He'd never heard the explanation for that. Any explanation would have been a lie. For all he knew, she rode like a trooper, too.

"What are our plans, sir?" Barleyman asked.

Christian dragged his mind to its proper business. "Have you gleaned any other gossip?"

"No, sir. Spent time in the tap with the locals. They're happy enough to tell the story, and to fall into dispute about some of the details, but I heard nothing new. One did let the name Froggatt drop, but was hushed up by the others. They do seem to have decided to protect the lady's name, both maiden and married."

Christian drained his glass and refilled it. "No point in lingering here, then. We'll go on to Sheffield and complete inquiries there. After that, it has to be Devon. Now I know Dorcas is alive, I must tell my father."

A task he dreaded. He couldn't guess his parents' reaction to the news, but he knew they'd be deeply hurt that he'd kept such a turmoil from them all these years.

"There's one other thing, sir."

"Yes?" Christian asked, glad to be distracted.

"Those Silcocks were here."

Christian stared at him. "Here in the Tup?"

"Aye, sir, though not to stay. The other day, the one when Mistress Hunter was accused of stealing their rings, they came to Nether Greasley. When I arrived and said I was from Doncaster, Hood mentioned another party from there in recent days. Didn't take so much as a pot of ale, which disgruntled him, though they did leave their gig and had their horse cared for. He only described them as a sullen pair from America, but it must have been them."

"I remember them leaving in a gig." As he and Kat were leaving the Woolpack for that fateful stroll. Which she'd engineered. "What did they do here?"

"Asked directions to the church and, as best he knows, went there."

"Is it of architectural interest?"

"Not as I could see, sir. The sexton was in the tap here when I was being regaled with the famous story, so he speaks up about the strange couple that had been prowling his churchyard. They looked respectable enough, but as they were strangers, he kept an eye on them. Very protective of his churchyard, he is. Said they seemed to find the grave they were looking for and the woman bent down close, as if she were having trouble reading the inscription. Then they stood a while, turned, and left. He didn't have to look to see which grave. It was the one belonging to the notorious victim of violent death. Whereupon all in the tap speculated that it must be a relation, and why hadn't he or she visited before?"

"By God," said Christian. "Could Mistress Silcock be Moore's sister? She'd be about the right age, and rumor said she fled the country."

"Any resemblance to Moore, sir?"

"All that face paint, and she's not well. But the hair color would be right, and perhaps the nose."

"Strange that she turn up now, sir."

"Perhaps the ten-year anniversary impelled her return. I seem to remember there was just the two of them in the family. Moore mentioned her now and then, generally because she gave him money. Her name was Janet," he remembered.

"Very natural, then, sir, to visit the grave."

"All the same, it sends a worm down my spine."

"Never a good sign, that. That worm's been a useful warning a time or two."

"And," said Christian, the worm turning icy, "they left Doncaster for Sheffield, which has no direct connection to Moore."

"But clear connection to your wife, sir."

"Janet Moore was dismissed from her teaching position after the scandal — that was the talk of the regiment — and disappeared. What are the odds Abigail Froggatt's hand was in that? Quite likely she'd have hounded her out of the country to boot."

"Meaning she might be looking for vengeance, sir?"

"Her behavior in Doncaster doesn't suggest a forgiving nature."

"No, sir, it doesn't. So, what's she going to do when she finds Mistress Froggatt's beyond her reach?"

"Go in pursuit of the only remaining Froggatt, my wife. She might even blame her in some way for her brother's death. We have to follow, but I feel a need to visit that grave. Make the preparations."

Christian grabbed his hat and gloves and left, but out in the corridor, he paused. There was the door to that room. He'd opened it so confidently ten years ago in the full, blind arrogance of youth. Now it seemed a fortress beyond a chasm, and one he didn't wish to attempt.

Losing the fight, Christian entered the room. Again, he had to duck to avoid the lintel as he hadn't in the past. It hadn't changed. The same faded green hangings on the sagging bed, the same plain chairs and table. He looked at the floor, where

Moore's corpse had lain. His first death, and the only one outside of war.

No evidence remained. Perhaps Moore hadn't bled as much as he remembered, or perhaps ten years of wear and repair had obliterated the stain.

Nothing had been able to remove the wound in the bedpost made by Moore's ferocious attempt to decapitate him. Perhaps that death hadn't been pointless after all. Christian had killed many men simply to stop them from killing him.

Time and dark polish had disguised the damage. He rubbed the spot with his thumb, considering the neat bed, trying to summon more details about his unwanted bride. He'd only glimpsed her there before having to turn all his attention on Moore. Thin legs, mousy hair pinned up in a way that had presumably been meant to show that she was a woman ready for marriage. It had begun to escape its pins, which had only emphasized her youth.

Her blue gown hadn't been disarranged on top, only her skirts up around her thighs, showing her white petticoat. A brief, rough wooing, poor child, and no wonder if she'd become a difficult woman.

Afterward? Again, his attention had been scattered.

When they'd stood to take their vows, she'd been a head shorter than he. Her hand had been as thin as the rest of her. And pale, and icy cold. The crude ring supplied had hung on her finger.

He looked around again, but nothing lingered here, not even Moore's ghost.

All it held was memories, and they were chancy at best.

He left the room and went in search of Moore's grave.

Not long afterward, he was looking down at a small but decent headstone. Who had paid for that? Doubtless the Fearsome Froggatt again, tidying up loose ends. When he read the inscription, he was sure of it.

Here lies Bartholomew Moore, an officer in His Majesty's army, 1733 to 1754. Cut down in his sins. May God have mercy on his soul.

Had the omission of the regimental details been a calculated insult? Probably, and warranted to some extent. Moore had not been a credit to the uniform, but what had Mistress Silcock thought of the omission?

Perhaps she wasn't Moore's sister, after all. Wouldn't she have left some flowers, or other sign of remembrance? Then Christian saw something dark between grass and stone. He bent to pick it up. It was a small, black silk mourning handkerchief. It was damp, but hadn't been there long.

Christian instantly thought of Kat in her black clothing, but she had no connection to this. This had been left by Mistress Silcock, who now of a certainty was Janet Moore. Poor lady. Her brother's sin was no fault of hers.

Christian was stooping to replace the handkerchief when he felt a stiff patch. He looked closely at it. The stain looked the same as the ones caused by damp, but it wasn't. He rubbed it with his thumb and it showed red.

Blood.

That put a darker twist on everything. The woman was hardly likely to have brought a stained handkerchief, or injured herself accidentally here. She'd never coughed at the Woolpack, so she wasn't consumptive. He felt sure she'd cut or pricked herself and pressed the silk to the wound, then left it concealed here on her brother's grave.

Christian was tempted to take it with him, as if it might reveal more, but he tucked it back where he'd found it. If it had been an odd but honest sign of grief, let it be, but he needed to catch up with the Silcocks.

Their anger might turn on his wife, whom he was honor-bound to protect.

# CHAPTER 19

When Christian and Barleyman rode into Froggatt Lane, hooves muffled on the muddy ground, it was its usually gloomy self. He didn't recognize the acrid smell until he was close enough to the narrow house to see it was a burned-out shell. He stared for a moment, then called out to a lad strolling along with a bundle on his back. "What happened here?"

The lad looked at the house. "Burned down, didn't it?"

Christian held on to his patience. "When?"

"Day afore yesterday, sir. That were the Froggatt 'ouse, sir. Belonged to those what own the works next door."

"Was anyone injured?" That was the crucial question.

"No, sir. Not as I heard."

That was all he'd get, so Christian thanked him with a penny.

"Silcocks?" Barleyman asked.

"Enough of a coincidence to make one wonder, isn't it? I have to find Dorcas."

"Aye, sir."

"The manufactory seems to be idle."

"Smoke damage, sir?"

"Could be. Where do we get more information?"

At that moment, a gig rattled down the lane, carrying a grizzled older man and a younger one who was driving. Both frowned at Christian and Barleyman in passing, but when they stopped in front of the house and climbed down, their attention was all on it.

Christian dismounted and went over. "Beg pardon, sirs, do you know what happened here?" Both turned to look at him. Before they could say it, he said, "Clearly the house burned down. What was the cause?"

"Now, that," said the older man in the local accent, "is the question, sir. Fires can 'appen, but there was no cause we know of, and it burned remarkably fast."

"Arson? Who would do such a thing?"

The younger man was studying Christian. He was fashionably dressed and had a certain air the older man lacked. Now he spoke with crisp authority. "You, sir, could be the Mr. Grandiston who came here not many days ago and left in anger."

Christian's hand went to his sword, but

then he saw the other man was unarmed, and in any case, it was a reasonable observation.

"I am," he said shortly. "I came in search of Mistress Hill, who was once Dorcas Froggatt, and was informed she wasn't in residence. The lady I spoke to, Mistress Spencer, seemed unhelpful and I confess I did grow angry. I regret it. I certainly didn't return to wreak havoc. If you seek assurance, yesterday I was traveling back from York to Doncaster and can doubtless find someone to support that."

The younger man turned narrow eyes on Barleyman, but the older man said, "Enough of that, 'Enry. I'm Samuel Skellow, sir, and this is m'son. We're part owners of the cutlery company 'ere, along with Mistress 'Ill. May I ask what business you 'ave with her?"

"I needed, still need, to clarify some details of the lady's marriage ten years ago. Legal matters."

"Ah," said the younger man, but both he and his father made no further comment.

"Do you know where Mistress Hill is at the moment?" Christian asked. "It would be to her advantage to meet with me."

"A will, is it?" the older Skellow asked, measuring Christian shrewdly. "She's no great need of money, Mr. Grandiston, but in any case, we don't know where she is. Your best road is to leave a message with me. I assure you I'll give it to 'er at first opportunity."

"You haven't informed her that her house has burned down?" Christian inquired politely.

"As I said, sir, we're not exactly sure where she's at."

Was she truly traveling on an unplanned path, or were the Skellows being as deliberately unhelpful as Mistress Spencer?

Why?

What was wrong with Dorcas?

"You're sure she didn't die in the fire?" Christian asked, eyeing the blackened building with the gaping holes where windows had once sat. The smell of smoke and charring lay heavy in the air.

"Quite sure, sir," said the younger Skellow. "By God's grace, no one did."

"Including Mistress Spencer?"

"She wasn't here."

Had he backed the wrong horse? Had the Spencer woman rushed off to Dorcas while he'd followed Carrie the maid to Doncaster? Had that been the plan? It seemed far-far-fetched, but this whole situation was tangling his mind.

"Where is Mistress Spencer?" he asked. "Perhaps she can help me."

"Not rightly sure, sir," Sam Skellow said with a blandness Christian recognized from the army. He'd get nothing more without threatening a flogging.

It wasn't surprising that the Skellows didn't intend to give him information when he'd behaved so badly. Probably Mistress Spencer had run to them in tears. He wasn't sure why he'd lost his sense and balance here that day.

Yes, he was. It had been the shock of learning that Dorcas was alive. He'd not expected it, and it had overset him.

He looked at the house again, wondering if telling these men that Dorcas Hill was his wife would help matters, but he'd already given them what would seem to be a different name. Proving it was a title would take forever, and it was more urgent than ever that he find the Silcocks.

"Thank you, sirs. I will leave the message." He went back to his horse and found his tablet and pencil. This would hardly be elegant, but it would do. He simply wrote that it was urgent that Mistress Hill communicate with the Hill family solicitor, and gave the address of Thorn's principal London lawyer.

He folded it and gave it to the older man. Then he remembered the Silcocks. "There was no suspicious activity here? No one lurking?"

"Well, now, sir," said Skellow Senior. "There was one thing. Becky, the young maid in training 'ere, said she saw a couple in the street just looking at the 'ouse. She was dusting upstairs, so she saw them, sir, but they didn't see 'er. A respectable-looking couple, she said, but we don't get people just standing to look, sir. It's not as if Froggatt and Skellow's is a handsome church or anything like that."

"No," said Christian.

The Silcocks had come here

They'd not asked for Abigail or Dorcas Froggatt. They'd come here, made their plan, and returned in the night to burn down the house, not caring who died. It seemed unreal, but was in keeping with the secretive menace of that bloodstained silk.

The fierceness of his inner rage startled him, but Dorcas was his wife. Any affront to her was an affront to him. All the same, this churned in his gut, not his head. It felt —

As if the intended victim was Kat Hunter.

Ah. He was remembering the Silcocks' furious hounding of her, the large reward offered, but Dorcas and Kat were two different women, who had offended the Silcocks in two different ways at a time separated by ten years.

Skellow Junior broke the silence. "You think that couple might have something to do with this, sir? But why?"

Christian had no explanation that would make sense, but in addition, he didn't want the Skellows or the law after these villains. They were his now. His personal enemies, and he'd personally see them to hell.

"Could it be the work of a business rival?" he asked, to deflect.

The response came from Samuel Skellow, in flat certainty, but, strangely, in badly pronounced French. *"Pour y parvenir à bonne foi." To succeed through honest endeavor.*

Christian instinctively looked to the younger man for explanation.

Henry Skellow smiled slightly. "The motto of the Company of Cutlers in Hallamshire, sir. Our guild. Hallamshire is the ancient designation for this part of Yorkshire." Despite the smile, he showed an admirable lack of embarrassment. It wouldn't be easy to be so clearly moving out of his parents' sphere. Many tried to smooth their way by disdaining their roots.

Christian liked the man, but he probably knew more about Dorcas than he was saying and that infuriated him. He wanted to put a hand to both Skellow throats and force information out of them.

He didn't need another Yorkshire town in pursuit of him, however, especially not one whose trade was sharp knives. He took farewell of the men and rode off with Barleyman.

"Nasty business, sir."

"Very. I need to find those Silcocks with all speed."

They went first to the Angel, but the colonials weren't known there, so Christian and Barleyman worked separately through the town's hostelries.

Barleyman picked up the trail at the Boar's Head, and reported back to Christian. "Stayed the two nights, sir, and left yesterday morning on a coach to London."

"London? Could they have discovered that Dorcas is there? She'd be a frog among roses at court."

"Plenty of places in London away from St. James, sir."

"True enough. She might have relatives in the City. Devil take it, though, it's going to be damned annoying to find she's been there all along."

Barleyman wisely didn't comment on that. "Follow the Silcocks, sir, or make more inquiries here about your wife?"

"Both," Christian said. "I'm for London on the Silcocks' trail. You find out all you can here, in particular any connections Dorcas might have in London. Send any useful information after me at all speed, care of Ithorne. Return south with the horses within three days at the most."

"Watch your temper, sir. You can't go killing them out of hand."

"I have to wait until they murder my wife?" Christian demanded, and went downstairs to buy a ticket on the first coach south.

It was the same ticket booth that the maid had approached only days ago, sending him to Doncaster, to another frustrating blind alley, but to Kat. Kat Hunter, with the revealing dimples at the corners of her lips, and the jaunty red feather on her hat.

The hat he'd crushed and left under a pile of rotting wood.

The dimples he'd not seen again once she'd been plunged into terrifying danger.

Except when they'd been spinning the story of the fanged rabbits of Hesse.

"Sir?"

He came to himself and saw the ticket clerk waiting. Above all, he wanted to buy a ticket north and comb York until he found her. Until he was at least sure she was safe.

"The speediest coach to London," he said curtly.

He'd never been besotted out of his duty by a woman before, and he wouldn't start now. He'd go south to London and give all the information to Thorn, who was better able than he to deal with the Silcocks. Then he'd carry on to Devon to face his father.

# CHAPTER 20

The marquess traveled fast, but it still took
two full days to reach his London house,
especially as he rested the night at the home
of the Earl of Huntersdown, which required
stopping earlier than usual so that he could
attend a meeting of local gentlemen and
discuss some political matters.

Caro was startled to find that Lady
Huntersdown was not only Italian but the
marquess's illegitimate daughter. He must
have been very young when she was con-
ceived, but no younger, she supposed, than
poor Jack Hill. She was three months named
and with child.

They had taken supper in Petra's boudoir,
leaving the gentlemen to their business, and
had fallen into an easy friendship. Not an
honest one, however. Caro felt there were
holes in Petra's account of coming to
England from Italy to join her father. Her
own account of recent events was similarly

inexact. In any case, her life was unlikely to weave with that of the Countess of Huntersdown, whose country home was in Huntingdonshire, far to the south. Even without Sir Eyam, her own milieu was Yorkshire.

Lord Rothgar had given only the scantiest explanation for Caro's presence in his party, for which she was grateful. He'd said she was traveling to London to visit Diana and to untangle some matters to do with her first marriage that were delaying a new marriage. Her black clothes had been explained as the result of an unfortunate collision between her traveling chest and a manure cart.

Lord and Lady Huntersdown had looked skeptical, but hadn't questioned it. Probably few people questioned the Marquess of Rothgar, not even his family.

Petra had willingly provided some replacements, and after some hasty hemming by her needlewoman, Caro was wearing a forget-me-not blue sacque with pretty embroidered detail. She was relieved she wouldn't have to arrive in London looking like a dowdy widow.

"My baby will be born only months after Diana's," Petra said in her lovely accent as she poured aromatic coffee, "which will give society something else to cluck over."

"You won't mind?" Caro asked.

"Oh, no. I find it quite amusing!"

Caro definitely felt she was moving into the wicked world of the south. She sipped her coffee and found it tasted as good as it smelled. "This is wonderful."

"But of course. It is something I share with my husband and my father, a love of excellent coffee. Of course that horrible Fowler woman is determined to be unpleasant."

"About coffee? I wasn't aware she disapproved of that, too."

With an eloquent foreign gesture, Petra said, "She disapproves of *everything!* She's using my existence as an example of the unnatural wickedness among the aristocracy. Robin wished to murder her, but my father says it would do more damage than good and she must be dealt with in some other way."

Caro felt slightly sorry for Lady Fowler, but as for the earlier part, had she misunderstood Italian levity?

"Surely your husband wouldn't really have killed the woman?"

"Probably not. But I ask, would he not kill a man who said the same thing? If I were not with child, *I* would challenge the woman. I was enraged that he gave her a thousand guineas."

Caro was definitely misunderstanding. "Your husband gave a thousand guineas to Lady Fowler's Fund for the Moral Reform of Society — to the woman he'd like to kill?"

"But *then* she hadn't begun her slanders, so he didn't want to kill her. He gave her the money because of a most foolish wager. Well, no, not exactly a wager. A foolish vow not to marry before they turned thirty. He and two friends. They felt so strongly about it that they made the penalty a thousand guineas to be paid to the most unworthy cause they could think of. Poor Robin was so distressed to have to do it that the others allowed him to do it anonymously."

"How . . . odd," Caro said, completely at a loss. "But surely Lady Fowler's Fund isn't the *most* unworthy cause possible?"

"To three young rakes it was."

Caro had to ask. "Don't you mind — your husband being a rake?"

"He isn't one *now*," Petra said with mild surprise.

Caro wanted to ask how she could be sure, but she'd seen the couple together and there had been a palpable connection.

"Do many rakes cease to be so when they marry?" she asked.

"If they marry for love, yes," Petra said

with great certainty.

"I hope that's true," Caro said, then to hide her own interest said, "For your sake."

Petra's dark eyes flashed. "You will not imply that Robin is unfaithful to me!"

"No, no, of course not."

Petra continued to frown for a moment and then smiled. "I have a temper. So who is your beloved?"

"I don't know," Caro said, meaning it on many levels.

"You don't know if you're in love?"

"Yes, perhaps that's it."

Petra chuckled. "You are. I know. Tell me about him."

Caro was trapped, but she also wanted to talk of Christian, in vague terms at least. "He's very strong, brave, and bold, but I'm not sure I can trust him with my heart."

"If not love, what do you feel?" Petra asked.

"He's turned my life upside down."

"Oh, that is excellent! It was just the same with Robin. But then, I turned his life upside down, too. Have you done that?"

"Yes, definitely."

"Excellent. I approve. You must at least experience more of your unsettling gentleman until you're sure."

She'd experienced more than enough,

Caro thought, then wondered if her thoughts were visible, for Petra's brows flickered and her lips twitched.

"There are times when it's wiser not," Caro said firmly.

"And some who think themselves wise go to very unhappy graves."

Talk moved to other subjects and Petra proved truly interested in Caro's Yorkshire life. Still, the next morning, as Lord Rothgar's party prepared to leave at first light, she repeated her insistence that Caro experience more of her unsettling man.

"And you must write!" she insisted. "I wish to know everything that happens in London. Everything."

"Very well," Caro said, smiling, "but I fear it will be dull reading."

"As I do not. I sense drama around you."

"Please don't," Caro protested, but Petra laughed.

Foreigners, Caro thought as they rolled off on the last day of the journey, but she suddenly remembered Christian saying that true friendships could be forged in a moment, as could true loves. That felt like it had been the case between her and Petra. But when would she encounter the Countess of Huntersdown again? Alas, their friendship was as unlikely to thrive as hers and Christian's.

Yes, for a brief moment she and he had almost been friends, something she'd never expected with a man, not even a husband. Not in that way. But the promise of that friendship had been wrecked on secrets. Her friendship with Petra would founder on other rocks — distance in geography and the separation of social rank.

Petra did have friendship with her husband, however. Caro had noted it in little ways, even amid their obvious love and passion. She would like the same.

With Christian?

That was her first thought, but she blocked the thought. She had to learn more about him before she allowed that sort of yearning or she knew where it would lead. If she met him again, she'd fall into his open arms.

Well, no, because they wouldn't be open. He must be furious at the way she'd left, and when they finally met again, he'd know how she'd deceived him all along.

Yet still she hoped. There had been something precious between them, like true gold among pinchbeck, something she could never entirely forget. She sighed at the misty dawn, adrift in equally misty uncertainties, and prayed that in London everything would finally be made clear.

Her first glimpse of the city wasn't promising.

"There's a dark haze ahead. Is something afire?"

The marquess looked up. "Many coal fires," he said. "A convenient fuel, but dirty. I fear in time England will turn black with soot."

Carruthers was putting away papers and Lord Rothgar seemed available for conversation.

"London is a monster," he said, "and new people pour in every day. If London had to be fueled with wood, England would soon be treeless. As it is, an ever-expanding circle of countryside is devoted to its maintenance — grain, fruits, vegetables, and meat sent in daily from places like these we are passing. Soon the distances could become too great for some foods to be wholesome. Animals are sent in on the hoof, but then their slaughter creates noisome shambles. The city is an unnatural beast, choking on itself."

"Then why do people pour in?" Caro asked, pressed to the window to look ahead.

"For employment and the opportunity to rise."

"But why do the rich live there?"

"Because it's the most exciting place in the world. The king and government are there, which means power and opportunity. There's opportunity for gain, but also to effect change. Foreign governments from all over the world keep embassies and consulates here; artists and scientists gather in unsurpassed numbers. Anyone who is anyone passes through. Take time to enjoy it, Mistress Hill, and you will be rewarded. But for sanity, live elsewhere."

"Do you?" she dared to ask.

"Not as much as I would like, but as much as I can."

"It's fortunate I have no interest in living in the south, never mind London."

"There is the danger that you will meet a Pluto to your Persephone."

"A man who will snatch me away to his dark domain?"

"A man who will tempt you to remain in sooty London."

"I don't think Pluto tempted, my lord."

"He tempted Persephone to eat a bite of pomegranate."

"Thus creating winter." Caro smiled. "Is that why the rich and powerful return to London for the winter months and return to the countryside for summer?"

"Ah, you have our secret. We are all pomegranate eaters."

"I shall be very careful what I eat."

"And what gentlemen you dally with."

"I have no intention to dally at all," Caro said.

"Nor, I suspect, did Persephone. You have not the slightest temptation to win a great lord?"

"I try not to be tempted by the impossible, my lord."

"How very limiting. I gather you are rich."

"By Yorkshire standards."

"I doubt the standards are so different. But if we look to the north, there's the Duke of Bridgewater, unmarried and constantly seeking money to continue his canals and aqueducts."

An unpleasant suspicion rose in Caro. Could the marquess plan a marriage between herself and her money and some friend? "I believe I will be happier married to my own kind, sir."

"To a cutler of Hallamshire?"

It startled that he knew the old name for her part of Yorkshire.

"Simply to someone from Hallamshire."

"We shall see."

That did not reassure. Caro returned to watching the great city unfurl around them, wondering if she was hastening into a trap.

Soon they were traveling through streets lined with long, tall terraces, street after street, more streets than she could ever have dreamed, more people than she could have imagined in one place.

They rattled into a vast square surrounded by tall, grand houses and followed the road around a central garden to a mansion. It was detached on both sides from its neighbors and surrounded at the front by tall iron railings. Grand gates swung open to greet them.

The coaches drew up before porticoed doors from which servants poured to assist. Caro was swept inside the largest house she'd ever entered — and this was Lord Rothgar's town house, not his country seat. She tried very hard not to gawk.

The entrance hall was paneled in gleaming dark wood, indicating age when she knew much of London was of newer construction. A grand staircase rose to upper floors and Diana Arradale was coming down, her belly showing her growing child.

She had no eyes for anyone but her husband as she gave him her hands and welcomed him home. For a moment he, too, had no attention for anyone else, but then he said, "I've brought a guest, my dear, and some diversion."

Diana turned, astonished. "Caro! How lovely, but why? How?"

"All will be explained," Rothgar said, "but we must make Mistress Grieve comfortable. I snatched her away and rushed her here."

Diana's brows rose at the name, but she didn't question it. "So you've been caught in one of my husband's coils, Caro."

"I fear he's been caught in mine."

"Which makes you double welcome." She turned to a servant and gave rapid orders, then back to Caro. "Come and I'll show you to your room."

Caro went, knowing the couple would prefer to be alone together but that Diana would refuse to hand her over to a servant. "You must wonder. . . ."

"Not now," Diana said lightly. "Our people are trustworthy, but words spoken in the hall and on the stairs are audible in many places."

She took Caro along a corridor to a grand room with yellow and white striped hangings on the windows and bed. There were also upholstered chairs and a settee, a small wooden table and chairs, and a writing desk.

Diana opened a door to reveal a small dressing room with chests and clothes-presses, plus a tented bathtub waiting close to the hearth. There was everything a guest could need. Perhaps that was the idea. Caro would not need to intrude on the great lord and lady's life.

"This is the bellpull," Diana said, going to the fireplace in the bedchamber and indicating a pretty porcelain knob beside it. "If you tug it, someone will come to assist you. So much more pleasant than bellowing, or always having an attendant hovering."

"Of course," Caro said, never having lived in a place so large that summoning a servant was a trial.

"Request whatever you want, but for now, what first? A supper? I'm sure Rothgar didn't pause in the last stretch."

Caro smiled. "He did seem anxious to be home."

Diana blushed.

"You must go to him, Diana, but thank you for your warm welcome."

"I'm delighted you're here," Diana assured her, "but is the coil serious?"

Caro didn't want to delay her. "Merely an inconvenience."

"But something to be straightened out. Lovely. Town is quiet now apart from the routines of court. Rothgar must often be in attendance on the king, but my condition excuses me." She put a hand happily on her front. She suddenly laughed. "It kicked. It's so lively. I dread to think what he or she will be like as a toddler."

Caro smiled. "I'm very happy for you."

"It is delightful." A slightly distant look was probably as much about her husband as her baby.

"Please, go to him, Diana."

Diana laughed, eyes bright. "Ah, you understand! You must tell me all about the man you long to be with. A servant will be here shortly. Ask for anything you require."

Then she was gone.

*The man you long to be with.*

Caro went to the window and looked out over a complex garden that ended at a high wall. The courtyard in front was enclosed by railings and guarded. It reminded her that the Marquess of Rothgar was a great man and a great man had enemies. There was also the mob, the common people gathered together in mayhem. They could be dangerous anywhere, as she'd found in Doncaster. In London they could form a small army, storm the houses of the unpopular great, break windows, do other damage.

London — place of wonder, place of danger.

The place that Christian had claimed as home.

He probably wasn't here yet, for Lord Rothgar had traveled quickly with frequent changes of horses, and Christian would be riding Buck, who would need to stop to drink, feed, and rest. But eventually he would be somewhere in this great city.

More than that, he would be part of the smaller aristocratic circle in which she now lived. There was a title on the Grandiston family tree. He spent more time at court than he wished. He was an officer in the Guards, which she thought were the elite troops that formed the monarch's personal guards.

One day soon they might meet again.

Despite her rational wariness and vague fears, Caro couldn't help but pray that by then there could be truth between them and they could find again the friendship and the passion that had briefly been theirs.

# CHAPTER 21

Christian had to identify himself at the gates of his family's home at Royle Chart, which embarrassed the gatekeeper and disturbed himself. It was mostly because he was out of uniform, but he'd been here only twice before, and not for long visits. He had his duties in London, and his pleasures, too, but guilt nibbled that he hadn't come more often.

He'd delayed in London only long enough to give Thorn a complete account of his investigations and ask him to house the cat and kittens. Thorn had seemed slightly pained, so it was as well Barleyman had arrived and could remain as cat groom.

Christian had no choice but to include Kat in order to explain the strange interaction with the Silcocks in Doncaster, but it was their threat to Dorcas that most concerned him. Thorn's people would track down the Silcocks, and Dorcas, too, if she was in London.

He'd learned some things from Thorn. The Froggatt business was well-known and respected among those who dealt in swords and other blades, but also for their fine springs, which were increasingly in demand for clockwork mechanisms and such. The company was now Froggatt and Skellow and run by the Skellows, as Christian had learned. Those who knew about such things speculated that it should create a healthy income for the owners. Thorn had also discovered that Mistress Hill of Froggatt and Skellow lived, not in that house in Froggatt Lane, but in the country at a place called Luttrell House.

"Something you could have discovered with very little investigation," Thorn had pointed out.

Christian hadn't taken that well, for he knew he'd leapt into action instead of gathering intelligence. It was probably as well he'd had to leave it all in Thorn's calm and capable hands and come down to Devon.

Riding up the winding drive for the third time, he tried to recall details of the house. Royle Chart was much larger than Raisby Manor, so it held the family with ease, but it was also a Jacobean tangle of chambers and corridors, and on previous visits he'd frequently been lost and rescued only by one fledgling brother or another.

Damned embarrassing, especially when he often didn't know which was which. The six oldest in the family were female except for Tom, who was sailing southern seas with the navy. Christian never confused the girls, perhaps because he'd grown up with them, but it did seem a man should recognize his own brothers.

When he'd set sail for Canada, Kit, Matt, and Mark had been infants and Luke, Jack, and Ben had yet to be born. Matt and Mark, now twelve and eleven, were inconveniently alike, and their similar names didn't help. He could tell them apart as long as he had a clear look at their eyes, for Mark had the same hazel eyes as himself, while Matt's were a plain blue. Luke and Jack were distinct at nine and seven, and Ben was an infant. If there was any sanity in the world, he'd be the last.

Christian came alert when his horse veered to the left. Only a rut in the drive, so he praised Buck for his initiative. The drive was in no better state than when he'd last visited, and there'd been no improvements to the rugged landscape. No stands of choice trees, no lake, no Grecian temple.

His father could simply be managing Royle Chart the way he managed everything — by letting nature take its course. But perhaps the family was draining even an earl's income.

A turn in the drive brought Christian his first clear view of the house, built of honey-colored stone that looked warm even on a cloudy day. He remembered the gray stone of Yorkshire and the heavy skies, and shuddered.

*Dorcas, Dorcas, would that I'd never known you.*

*But then, would I be facing a future of La Jessingham?*

And what of Kat Hunter, whom he couldn't get out of his mind?

Dammit, how could a battle-hardened man be so adrift in a tangle of women? And now he had his mother to face.

No, he wouldn't link her with the others. His mother was a queen among women, lovingly, generously cherishing her family, even the least worthy of them. He was probably going to break her heart.

Wild yells and pounding hooves fired army instincts into action. He tightened his leg grip and reached to draw his sword.

Which he wasn't wearing.

He was fumbling at the saddle holster

when he came back to reality and saw that the attacking force was four youngsters on ponies hurtling toward him in a mock cavalry charge, complete with flailing wooden swords.

"Halt!" the leader yelled, hauling to a stop. "And state your business!"

"Tanning your hides," Christian said with a grin, but trying frantically to decide who was who.

Matt was in the lead because the second lad had hazel eyes, so he must be Mark. Matt was always in the lead anyway. Luke came third, and the small lad panting up last, legs stretched wide over a shaggy little mount, had to be seven-year-old Jack.

Jack Hill in the flesh, hale and hearty.

"Christian!" Mark cried. "Why're you not in uniform?"

"On furlough."

"Are you staying long?" Jack asked, wide-eyed and rosy cheeked, nudging his pony right up to Buck, who turned his head to stare.

"Not very long," Christian answered, feeling yet more guilt and resenting it.

"We wish you would stay," Matt said. "The parents do, you know."

Christian almost began excuses about military duty and the honor of serving the king, but now wasn't the time or place.

The awkward moment was broken by Mark declaring, "We'll ride ahead and announce you!" and the lad turned, suiting action to the words.

Matt wheeled to pursue and end this challenge to his leadership. Luke followed, sword again aloft.

Jack remained, looking up.

"Escort duty?" Christian asked.

The boy nodded.

"You'll get a crick in your neck down there. Would you like to ride up here?"

The boy's eyes lit with excitement and he leapt off his pony.

"Tie the reins safely, so they can't trip him," Christian reminded him, then hoisted the lad up in front. "Shall we, too, charge the fortress?"

Jack nodded, so Christian kicked his horse up to speed and galloped toward the house on the safer grass, letting out a ferocious battle cry. Jack warbled one at his own pitch until they arrived at the opening front doors, where his parents and assorted others poured out.

Christian brought Buck up into a showy, dramatic rear. "All hail the fair and bounteous Hills!" he declared, waving an imaginary sword, before bringing the horse down and swinging a laughing Jack to the ground.

"Christian Hill, you could have killed the child!" his mother declared, but her eyes were like stars and her smile almost split her round face.

It hurt to be so loved.

He swung off, surrendering the horse to a groom, and went to sweep her off her feet. "He was the ringleader," he protested.

"Oh, you," she declared, giving him a buffet. "You give the boys fanciful ideas about the army."

She was a good foot shorter than he, and very round. He couldn't help checking for evidence of fertility, but it was hard to tell. He could see her eyeing him in turn, taking in his civilian dress and hoping.

"Just on furlough. It can be a good career, Mama, and the boys will need to do something."

"Then I pray for peace."

"Amen." Christian turned to embrace his father, who was only six inches shorter than he, but equally round, though the weight was so much in his belly that he could be about to produce another little Hill himself. He looked as delighted to see Christian as his wife, but his color was high. Not a good sign if Christian wanted to be free of all this for another forty years or so.

As they all turned toward the house, Christian said to his father, "All seems well."

"We are abundantly blessed."

Christian's father often made this simple statement without any sign of reservation. It was mostly true. Thirteen children, all still alive, and an earldom his father hadn't expected to inherit. Even Christian had survived the war with but one, fairly minor wound. He knew other people, other families, who seemed dogged by misfortune, equally capriciously. He had no way to explain the phenomenon, but was grateful to be among the blessed.

All the same, as he entered the darkly paneled hall, surrounded by youngsters demanding attention, to see a gaggle of smiling servants anxious to welcome home the heir, he flinched from the crush. He'd lived in impossibly crowded army billets, and endured long sea voyages on ships crammed with hundreds of men, but as always, his home overwhelmed him.

Men crammed together in billets and on ships were careful to respect one another's privacy as much as possible. In his family, privacy didn't exist.

His father was talking about some intriguing find on the family tree; his mother was declaring to servants that here was Grandiston, and his room must be freshened; an assortment of boys were fighting for proximity and attention; and three young women held back. Jack had somehow captured Christian's hand and was holding on tight.

Christian supposed he should be grateful that his two eldest sisters were married and had homes elsewhere, but they were producing offshoots of the Hill family tree.

He gently broke the connection with Jack. He ruffled the lad's hair, tossed a general greeting at his sisters, called, "Must clean up to be fit for company," and ran for cover.

He managed to find his room without help, thank God. Ridiculous to have a permanent room here at all, especially as it was the next largest after his parents'. They'd hear of nothing else, however, for the heir.

The windows looked out over the orchards to cow pastures and then down to the stream beyond. A good fishing stream, he was told. He hadn't tried it yet. Perhaps he would — tagged by boys, he was sure.

If, that was, his father didn't order him from the door when he heard the mixed-up story of the impossible wedding. Hard to imagine such a harsh reaction, but the news was bound to be a shock if only because he'd kept such a thing secret for so long.

Leaning against the window frame, Christian accepted the charms of Royle Chart and tried to imagine being born and raised here rather than Raisby. He might have become very fond of it.

He might even like living here now — if not for the family. He flinched from that thought, but it wasn't as dreadful as it would sound if voiced. He liked the house. He loved his family. For whatever reason, he could not abide the press of devotion and attention.

Perhaps he was like a cat, with a strong instinct to independence. He'd told Thorn he and Tab were kindred spirits. Certainly Thorn could be a true and deep friend while keeping privacy around him like silken armor.

Unlike Robin, who sought company and gathered friends as a bee gathers pollen. He even, God help him, enjoyed court — both in England and Versailles. Robin had recently married. Would he fill his house with children? Christian thought not, but mainly out of consideration for his wife. There were ways of limiting the likelihood of procreation.

Once he'd learned of them, Christian had wondered if his parents needed a hint. If so, it was beyond him now, never mind as a lad, and he suspected they wouldn't have been interested. Children were part of their abundant blessings, and now they had the joy of grandchildren from his sisters. England would soon have so many Hilly offshoots it would rival Switzerland, but not from him.

Kat Hunter invaded his mind again. Had he already created another little Hill? The ways to avoid conception weren't inevitably effective and that last time, he'd lost control.

Thank God he'd given her the Stowting address.

But hell, he was actually longing to hear from her even with disastrous news, longing to hear that they were bound together by a child. He'd never felt this way about any other chance-met woman, and she was married! So, he remembered, was he. If Kat bore him a child, it would be a bastard, and there'd be nothing he could do about that.

He reminded himself that Kat, or whoever she really was, had abandoned him, not the other way around. She had her own schemes and had all along, and she'd discarded him as soon as he was no further use.

To hell with her. Hell, Hades, and the darkest depths of the Styx.

A servant brought washing water and he used it. With no further excuse to lurk, he

left the room. There were worse things —
many, many worse things — than belonging
to a loving family blessed with good health
and good fortune.

Pray God he'd be allowed to remain part
of it.

# CHAPTER 22

Two hours after she'd arrived at Malloren House, Caro was summoned to take supper with her hosts.

The marquess and Diana awaited her in a small room with a table that could seat only eight at the most and was set for three. Caro relaxed a little, but Lord Rothgar still made her wary. She assessed Diana's warm smile and tried to believe that she wouldn't allow female oppession.

Diana rang a bell, and servants brought dishes to the table and served the soup, but then they left and Caro and her hosts took their seats.

Lord Rothgar said, "I think it would be best if you told Diana your story in your own words."

Caro obliged, interrupted only by pertinent questions from both her hosts. Diana seemed merely attentive, but at one point shot a puzzled glance at her husband. Was she detecting the omissions?

In the end, Rothgar said, "Your interpretation, my dear?"

"An unpleasant predicament," Diana said. "We must first discover if this Hill is alive. If he is, if the marriage was legal. If so, how to end it."

"I agree. However, the first is likely to be a great deal easier than the third."

All very well for them to speak as if this were an intriguing puzzle. "Hill is not alive," Caro said.

"You can't be sure, Caro," Diana said. "It's never wise to self-deceive."

Caro was about to protest, but Diana rang a small bell and servants returned to take away the soup dishes and substitute plates. They were in and out with almost magical swiftness.

As soon as they were gone, Caro exploded, "I will not be forced into a marriage against my will! I will *not.*"

Lord Rothgar served ham. "You already were so forced. Therein lies your problem. But at the least, we should be able to obtain a separation *a mensa et thoro.*"

Irritated but without a retort, Caro said, "What does that mean, my lord?"

"Separation from bed and board. Your husband couldn't force you to live with him,

414

and his powers over you and your property would be limited. It is as far as the church courts are usually willing to go in breaking sacred bonds."

"There was nothing sacred about my marriage."

Her hosts made no response, and indeed, what was there to say? Railing against facts, no matter how unfair, was as pointless as self-deception.

Caro steadied herself and took some braised celery. "But I'd still be married," she said.

"Yes."

"And thus unable to marry another."

"Yes."

"Then I will seek a divorce."

Rothgar refilled Caro's wineglass. "A rare and expensive undertaking . . ."

"I have money."

". . . and difficult to achieve, especially for a woman. It is usually the man that gains the divorce on the grounds of adultery."

"His adultery not being a sin at all," Caro snapped. But she closed her eyes. "I'm sorry. You are not the cause of my predicament." She ate some ham, memories of beds and Christian weaving through her mind. "So if I were to commit adultery . . . ?"

Her hosts looked surprised, but not

shocked.

"Your husband would still have to bring the suit," Rothgar said. "Moreover, being divorced for infidelity would ruin your reputation. Many men would balk at marrying you."

But perhaps not the one she'd sinned with. One advantage of a rake, she supposed, was that he'd be less shocked by such a situation. Sir Eyam, on the other hand . . . he might actually faint.

"Then let us assume that Jack Hill died as reported," she said. "I hate to want that, for he did nothing wrong, but that is the easiest portal to freedom."

Diana reached out to touch Caro's hand. "We'll find out tomorrow, and then we'll know what to do for the best."

"With a Malloren, all things are possible," said the marquess with a slight smile, "but on the morrow I can only promise to discover if Hill died in the service of the Crown and, if not, if he is still in the army. If he left the army alive, it could take a great deal longer to find out his present situation and whereabouts."

"I can't continue on like this, not knowing," Caro protested.

"No," he agreed.

Caro looked between her hosts. It took effort to say the name. "Grandiston. He must know."

Lord Rothgar smiled. It seemed oddly . . . savoring. "Yes, one assumes he must."

"Can you find him?" Caro remembered that she'd not revealed that he was in the Guards. Could she do that, without Lord Rothgar guessing there was more to her story? In her telling, her only acquaintance with Grandiston had been that that brief encounter in Froggatt Lane, with her playing the maidservant.

"I believe I can," he said, and she let that quiet her conscience.

"But you'll probably be here for a few days at least, Caro," Diana said, "and I admit that I'm selfishly delighted. I will enjoy showing you some of London's delights."

"I must be careful not to meet anyone I know, or Mistress Grieve will be unmasked."

"There are not a great many people in Town at this time of year," Diana assured her. "Only those closely connected to court and the ministry. Unless you know any such . . . ?"

"Only you," said Caro.

"Then all will be well," Diana said with disconcerting cheerfulness.

Well?

Not if Jack Hill was alive. The marquess might say that with a Malloren all things are possible, but bonds of church and law could be severed by no man, not even a Malloren.

Later, in their bed, curtains drawn, Diana asked, "This Grandiston, surely he must be Lord Grandiston, and thus a Hill?"

"It would be extraordinary if he wasn't," Bey agreed, brushing his lips over hers.

"*The* Hill?"

"I believe the name is Christian, not Jack, but he's in the army and served in the colonies."

"But if he married Caro, why has he ignored the matter all these years?"

"Why has she?"

"Because she believed him dead."

"Perhaps he believed the same. I, on the other hand, am not dead."

"So I perceive," said Diana. "You see how invigorating a journey to Yorkshire can be?"

"Hush, or the whole of the south will stampede north. The infant is active."

"So am I," Diana said, moving with delight. "Grandiston must know his wife's alive. It's a tangle."

"Especially," said Bey, settling deep inside her once again, "as he is reputed to be courting Psyche Jessingham."

"Oh!" It did double duty.

"Precisely," he said, smiling and paying due attention to her breasts.

Much later he said, "One can't help thinking that Mistress Hill would be a more congenial wife."

"Than me?" Diana asked in disbelief.

He chuckled. "You lose the thread of a conversation so easily, my love. Than Lady Jessingham."

"Almost anyone would be. But Lady Jessingham is beautiful. Many men appreciate that."

"Many men," he said delicately, "have."

"Indeed!"

"Including Ithorne until recently."

"Grandiston's close friend," Diana said, looking up at the shadowy canopy, her right hand exploring his beloved, familiar body.

"Foster brother. He went to live with Ithorne at age ten."

"Worse still. Of course you've mined every detail about Ithorne since Petra married Robin."

"Robin being Ithorne's cousin and the third in that merry band of revelers," he agreed. "Ithorne, Grandiston, Huntersdown."

"Heaven help us all," she said. "Caro's

marriage has become a family affair."

"It was from the beginning," he said, "because it was something that would concern you, and any care of yours is one of mine."

"And any enemy." She rolled toward him. "If Grandiston wishes Caro ill, he is my enemy."

"And any enemy of Grandiston's is foe to Ithorne and Robin."

"Which puts Petra between her husband and her father."

"Which cannot be allowed."

"But what can we do?" Diana asked. "Don't you think we should tell Caro our suspicions?"

"I would like to know the truth about their relationship first."

"There is none beyond that brief encounter in Sheffield."

"Perhaps."

"Why suspect otherwise?" she asked.

"I've spent more time with her than you, my love, and a few things suggest a more complicated involvement. The sequence of events she presents isn't entirely convincing."

Diana frowned into the dark. "Do you want me to compel the truth from her?"

"Not yet. With most people truth has a

way of leaking out over ordinary days."

Diana nodded, but she was still frowning. "If they're legally married, there's no way to free her."

"Grandiston is one of the most alluring men in London."

"And enjoys it far too much."

"You have something against enjoyment?" he asked, kissing her.

She enjoyed that, then pushed him away. "In moderation."

"Really?"

"I have to be able to walk tomorrow, and I'm worried about Caro. I'm not sure it's right to keep this from her."

"Trust me, my love."

"Always, you know that. But Caro deserves happiness. I've always felt that she lives constrained, and now I know more of her marriage, I can see why. She's a strong, kind, generous woman and deserves the perfect husband, not one like Grandiston."

"He's a military hero, handsome, skilled at pleasing women, and overall a good and honorable man."

"But an inveterate rake," Diana said. "Which makes his enticing charms particularly dangerous. If Caro's compelled to keep to the marriage, she might well fall in love with him, but eventually he'll break her heart, I know he will."

"Divorce would be better?" he asked.

"No, but . . . I want happiness for her, Bey. Perfect, complete happiness."

"You're an incurable romantic," he said.

"Why not," Diana said, "when we have us?"

# CHAPTER 23

Christian left his room and found Jack sitting cross-legged in the corridor. The lad's face shone as he rose with that agility that comes naturally only to a healthy child. "I thought you might need a guide to the dining room."

Christian fought a smile. "How very thoughtful of you. Thank you."

The lad shone even more. A part of Christian wanted to fight this, to back away, but the lad was irresistible. He'd be trouble when he grew up.

"This is a grand house!" Jack declared, going downstairs half backward at an alarming speed. Having the lad break an arm or worse when in his custody would not start this evening out well. "We can play hide-and-go-seek and sometimes not be found for ages! And chicks-in-a-box, because there are some really good hiding places. We haven't even found all the ones here yet."

"The family's fortunate," Christian said, grateful when he and Jack reached the level surface of the hall unharmed.

"Aren't we just! I bet Kit's green at being away at school so much when he could be here. I don't know why you don't live here, Christian. You're the heir, so you could."

Before Christian could come up with a response, he was smothered. Brothers thumped downstairs — or in one case slid the long banister to land with practiced acrobatic ease on his feet. That did look like fun. Margaret came down behind, Ben by the hand, faintly protesting at such wild behavior. Did she have governess duty? That didn't seem fair. The other sisters had appeared from somewhere, and his parents came out of his father's study and sanctum.

Oh-ho. His parents together in there meant serious matters to be discussed.

Him?

Undoubtedly.

Like a strong tide, they all swept him into the dining room for supper. The grand room could actually cope with the numbers, though it had surely never been intended for such a rambunctious gathering.

His father sat at one end of the table and his mother at the other with Ben on her right, perched on a padded box set on the seat of his chair. Christian knew his place — on his father's left. The seat on his father's right hand rotated through the children and this evening Luke took it with a mixture of pride and trepidation.

That custom had been in place when Christian had left home, when there had been only five others and the youngest had been toddlers and babes. His turn had come frequently. When he'd brought Thorn here, the system had absorbed them so that Thorn, too, had occasionally found himself on then Sir James Hill's right, drawn out to talk about his recent adventures and gently advised.

Servants came in to serve soup, but before they could eat, Luke had the job of saying grace. He dutifully thanked God for their food and many blessings, for his parents and family, then added, "And that Christian's home."

All said, "Amen."

Christian found himself ridiculously close to tears and had no idea whether it was because he was touched by affection or exasperated by it.

As they ate, his father turned to Luke, so Christian gave his attention to nineteen-year-old Anne, who was bouncy and inclined to silliness simply through high

425

spirits. She expressed pure ecstasy at his visiting, then added, "I do wish you'd bring Ithorne, though. He must be looking for a bride."

Stopping his eyes from rolling, Christian said, "Must he? Why?"

Anne did roll her eyes. "The succession, you booby."

"And if the Ithorne dukedom died out, the world would come to an end?"

"Yes!" Anne declared, then appealed to the table. "Ithorne must marry and get an heir, mustn't he?"

The lads looked blank, but the females all agreed.

"He certainly needs a wife," said Christian's mother, "but don't pester Christian, dear. I'm sure he'll think to bring Ithorne here soon. He must be miserable, living alone."

*Et tu,* Mama? But he knew her main concern was probably precisely as stated — that Thorn moped in misery, rattling around in big empty houses without family to nourish his soul. Strangely, he now wondered if there might be some truth to it. He shook himself and deflected Anne to talk of local gentlemen who might be of interest. He knew why there was such general interest in Thorn's marriage plans. Despite the earldom, the girls' portions would still be small, limiting their chances, and he was the most glorious chance in England.

A large rabbit pie was served, distracting Christian to another meal, fanged rabbits, and the Hessian cat.

Eventually Christian's father directed his attention at him. "Well, my boy, and how is life treating you?" Christian almost spilled the whole story, but brought his wits to order. This wasn't the place for grand revelations. "At least it's not boring me, sir."

"Tranquillity is generally considered a blessing."

"But it's not common in the army or at court."

"Court? These days that's boring by my lights. Now, back when I was young, court was lively."

This was an aspect of his father's life Christian had never considered. "Really, sir?"

His father obliged with some stories that hinted at a surprisingly wild career in his younger years, when George II had been king and enjoyed a court almost as wild as that of the Restoration. The picture painted was somewhat unsettling, especially when his mother chuckled as if remembering some of the wild adventures, but the stories sped the meal along more smoothly than Christian had hoped.

In due course, however, his mother shepherded everyone away, leaving Christian alone with his father. The exodus was the norm, but his stomach knotted and he rather wished he hadn't enjoyed the meal so heartily. Now his father would retreat to his study, and apparently Christian was to go with him.

Christian followed, grateful that this room carried no memories of his boyhood. His father's study at Raisby had been the place for discussion of misdoings, and for the occasional, sadly administered riding crop to the rear.

Christian remembered the one time Thorn had received six stingers from his father. That had been after an adventure with some sheep had spun out of control and caused a farmer's gig to end up in the ditch with hazard to life and limb. Christian had known he warranted punishment, but had been mortified that his father thought he had the right to beat Thorn as well. Thorn, however — who Christian was pretty sure had never been flogged before — had been quite cheerful about it, saying it made him feel like one of the family.

Thorn had become one of the family, for

Christian's parents had treated the fostering as going both ways. They'd visited frequently and Thorn had been treated as another of the Hills. Christian hadn't realized that Thorn hadn't visited the family without him. He would be welcome at any time, but he might not believe that. Christian decided to bring him soon.

If he was still welcome here himself.

"Brandy?" his father asked, pausing at the decanter and glasses set out on a table.

"Yes, thank you."

His father poured two glasses, passed one over, and then sat in one of the two upholstered chairs by the fire. Christian almost felt that standing like a naughty child would be more appropriate, but he took the other seat and a sip of brandy. As always, it was excellent. His parents weren't extravagant but they knew how to enjoy the little luxuries.

Such sensible people apart from the one thing. But then, perhaps to them, children were luxuries worth the cost.

"Well, Christian?" his father asked. "You visit us so rarely that you must have a purpose."

That stung and delayed Christian's response long enough for his father to say, "Mistress Jessingham?" with what looked like a hopeful smile.

"No," Christian said, and then some disastrous impulse had him adding, "Dorcas Froggatt."

His father stared. "Dorcas Froggatt? My son, what have you done?"

"Nothing. Not recently, at least. Hell . . ." He hadn't been so tongue-tied in a decade.

"Nine months ago, perhaps?" his father asked, a seriousness settling on his face that was terribly familiar from the past.

"No," Christian said, getting a grip. "Father, I need to tell you this story from beginning to end, but it starts a long time ago. Ten years ago, to be precise."

"The year you went abroad?"

"How can you remember that amid so many other details?"

"I may sometimes address one of my children by another's name, Christian, but I never forget the important details. We prayed for your safety every evening."

And he had hardly given home a thought. "I'm not the heir you deserve."

"Nonsense. Your mother and I know you will always do what is right."

"But I'm hardly ever here."

"As I intend to live a long life, it would be ridiculous for you to be so, as I deplore idleness. Now, tell me about Dorcas Froggatt."

Christian had planned to make a saga of it, hoping it would go down better, but now he said, "It appears she's my wife. From ten years ago."

Silence settled. His father drank more brandy. In the end, he said, "And you never said a word. My boy, that will pain your mother deeply."

Dammit, he was coloring with mortification. "I know, sir. I . . . I didn't think it was real. Let me tell you what happened." He plunged desperately into the story, but in his ears it sounded like twaddle. He finished with his recent search, then waited for judgment.

His father shook his head, but more in bemusement. "A very strange story. Your wife is possibly well raised, you say, even if not well-bred?"

"Yes, sir. But I hope to dissolve the marriage. She clearly wants it no more than I."

"How can you know if you haven't spoken to her? She might truly be visiting London, and you have qualities that appeal to women."

"The title," Christian said with a grimace.

"And other things," his father said drily, "unless you wish to convince me you were celibate until you became a viscount."

Ridiculous to be embarrassed, but Christian was, and tempted to retaliate with a cynical remark about any man being able to get a woman for money. But images of a sweaty room in Doncaster rose up to swamp and disconcert him even more. Neither title nor money had played a part there. Just healthy, shared lust.

"Perhaps your wife is rich," said his father. "An orphan and her father's only child? A cutlery company, you said?"

Christian grasped the businesslike topic with relief. "There has to be some money, yes, but," Christian confessed, "I believe I signed a document that gives her complete control over her property."

"Well-done, my boy."

Christian must have shown his surprise, for his father said, "Despite the problems your noble act caused, I am gratified that you could not turn a blind eye to this abuse when you heard of it, and that you were unwilling to gain by it."

"Thank you, sir. But I'm sure I should have been able to avoid the marriage."

"You were young. Lord above, not much older than Kit is now, and he plunges into every kind of mayhem out of enthusiasm and good intentions. I'm sure he would do exactly as you did."

"But promptly confess his folly to you, sir."

"Yes indeed," his father said. "He is more completely our child."

That cut deep, but Christian concealed it. His father did not mean to hurt, but the statement was true.

Of course, his father noticed.

"I did not mean that, Christian. Not as it sounded." He sighed. "It was a grand opportunity as we all acknowledged, and back then I was a little perplexed as to how to provide for all God's bounty. As well, young Ithorne was alone in the world. You probably didn't realize at the time how much discussion and thought went into it, but your mother and I agreed that Ithorne needed a gentleman companion with a merry heart, but also one with sound principles and moral sense."

"Sound principles and moral sense?" Christian echoed, remembering some of his boyhood follies.

His father waved a hand. "I speak of behaving well and with a care for others. Rules and sins? They are for petty minds."

"How do you sit through the weekly sermons?" Christian asked, astonished.

"With tolerance, my boy — and a firm hand with intolerant vicars."

Christian laughed aloud, and his father's eyes twinkled.

He sobered as he said, "Your mother and I agreed to let you go to Ithorne not only because it would do you good but because we hoped you could do good there. We were proved right, but we paid a price, as we always knew we would. We have always prayed you not suffer from that separation from your family."

It was a tricky question, but Christian could only speak the truth. "I don't believe I have." After a moment he added, "But sometimes I feel I should."

"Now, now, none of that! We want your happiness. Above all, that is any parent's prayer. Now you have this little problem and we must deal with it. It is unfortunate that you didn't inform us immediately, as I'm sure it could have been tidied up."

"I'm sorry about Lady Jessingham, Father."

His father pinned him with a look. "Are you?"

Damnation. "No."

His father surprised him by nodding. "I have begun to hear some stories. I might have acted impulsively in considering her a suitable wife for you, but I saw a beautiful woman, so eager to marry a title, so inclined to be generous. . . ."

There seemed nothing to say.

"Quite," his father said, sipping his neglected brandy. "I even gather that she and Ithorne . . ." Christian retained a bland expression. "Quite. Thus I am served for greed — or not quite, as your situation has rescued us all, God be praised. You do see how he watches over us, even in our folly?"

Christian struggled with the idea that his mayhem marriage ten years earlier had been designed as defense against Psyche Jessingham now, but he said, "Yes, sir."

"Then all is for the best, and now you must find your wife and bring her into the bosom of her new family."

Christian was beginning to get a familiar pounding in his head. "She may not want that."

"An only child, orphaned young, left in the care of an unpleasant aunt. She will welcome the embrace of a large and happy family." He rose. "Speaking of which, we should join the others. I'll break the news to your mother later, and to the rest of the family tomorrow."

Christian followed his father out of the room feeling a strong desire to get very, very drunk.

The large and happy family was in the

drawing room — those in residence, that was — and despite fine paintings and a gilded ceiling, it looked as crowded and disordered as the smaller room at Raisby. Heaven alone knew what his parents did if they had guests to entertain.

Margaret was playing the harpsichord and Elizabeth and Anne were dancing with Matt and Mark. What form of brutality had been necessary to bring that about?

Luke and Jack ran over to beg Christian to join in a game of spillikins. He went — anything was preferable to talking to his mother right then — but almost tumbled as something grabbed on to his leg. He looked down to see little Ben laughing up at him, cinched like a shackle. He remembered the game and continued onward, swinging his leg, giggling child attached.

At the small table, he sat and took the lad on his knee, finding he didn't mind too much, but he couldn't imagine how a stranger, someone raised by the Fearsome Froggatt herself, would take to this.

He took his turn at trying to extract a delicate ivory spillikin from the pile without moving any other, handicapped by big hands. Jack was winning when the music ended and Mark and Matt rushed over to try to eject the young boys from their chairs.

A word from Christian ended hostilities — would that his men were as easily cowed — and they set to deciding on some other game. The boys enthusiastically introduced him to a version of marbles they'd come up with to exploit the design of the Turkey carpet. The Earl of Royland acted as umpire, but the countess insisted on playing, down on her knees and showing deadly skill at finger-flipping the glass balls into winning spots.

As always, the youngsters were dispatched off to bed in waves. Ben went first; then two maids came for Luke and Jack, who kissed their parents and departed, but not until Christian promised he'd still be here in the morning. Half an hour later, Matt and Mark were collected by the aged manservant who was their personal attendant. They, too, kissed their mother, but bowed to their father and received a hand on the head as blessing.

Christian remembered that transition. It happened at the eleventh birthday, and felt like an elevation to manhood.

Now his parents demanded whist. Clearly two of the girls normally made up the four, but Margaret returned to music and Elizabeth insisted that Christian take her place at the whist table so she could sketch him.

He obliged, because he knew she was a reluctant player, unlike Anne, who enjoyed the game but was chaotic in her strategy. As his parents were both excellent players, he and Anne were soundly beaten, but everything was in good humor.

As the clocks struck ten, there was a general move to bed, but Elizabeth came to show him the picture. He was prepared and so could make kindly comments about the rather strangely featured man who for some reason was straight in the body from shoulder to knees instead of bent at the hips to sit. Elizabeth could execute charming pictures of flowers and trees, but for some reason the human body eluded her.

Christian went up to his room, emotionally drained but smiling, even though he had his mother to face. He drank a little of the brandy set out for him and waited.

She came in and gave him a thorough hug. "You silly boy! Not to say a word about such a thing. You must have worried."

"Not really," he confessed.

She shook her head, laughing. "No, of course not. I suppose you were having too much jollity playing war."

"Not playing, Mama."

She sobered. "No. I'm sorry to be so thoughtless. But can you deny you enjoyed it? That was certainly the impression I had when you were home on furlough. Not only were you burning to get back to your regiment, but you went off on that smuggling business with Thorn and Huntersdown, dodging the French navy all the way across the Channel and back."

He laughed. "You're right as always, Mama. I'm sorry for keeping the marriage secret, but at first I was ashamed of being caught in such a predicament, and then I truly did almost forget about it. Once it seemed my bride was dead, it all seemed over."

She nodded as she sat in the chair by the fire. "Selective memories are key to contentment, you know."

Christian contemplated that with amazement. "They are?"

"Only think, dear, don't we naturally forget the worst — like having a tooth pulled or a broken arm set? God has provided that for our ease of mind. Why should we not choose to do the same with other hurts? Generally it does no good at all to dwell on painful mementos of our lives, and I am most pleased about the Jessingham woman."

"You are?"

"Oh, yes. I was praying you'd refuse, and

trying to decide how to hint you off if you seemed likely not to. It's had me in a bit of a twitch, in fact, that you might plunge in without warning, for though that woman seemed warm, she avoided the children, especially Ben."

"When was that?" he asked.

"She came here. A casual visit while traveling, or so it was presented, but it was an assessment on both sides. There was much to recommend her, but I had my concerns."

He smiled. "You're very wise, Mama. I look forward to your impressions of Dorcas if I ever get my hands on her."

"Now, now," she said severely, "I'll hear no talk of force!"

"Of course not, Mama. But Father wants me to bring her here. I can't promise she'll come, but as we're married, we might as well try to make something of it."

"Make sure you do, dear," she said, baffling him again. "Use your wiles on her, as you're married, perhaps in bed." She rose, gave him another hug and kiss, and left, leaving him as usual feeling as if he'd been whirled around on the end of a string — and slammed into a wall a time or two.

Coax Dorcas Froggatt into the marriage bed? Once he might have shrugged at that, but now his desires would turn constantly toward a damned, dementing Kat. What sort of union could that be for a woman already treated heartlessly by a man?

There was nothing to do about that until he found his wife, talked to her, and learned her wishes. Again he resolved that despite the pressure upon him and his ridiculous authority as her husband, he'd do nothing to make poor Dorcas's life worse.

He prepared for bed, realizing that he'd come through this bit of rough terrain intact, which was something. It was a great deal, and he appreciated his loving, tolerant parents even more.

He settled into bed, feeling all in all at peace. Then he heard a rhythmic squeak of a creaky bed.

What?

His room, he realized, was next door to his mother's bedroom.

Oh, struth. He pulled the pillow over his head and tried to block all thought of what was happening.

# CHAPTER 24

On Caro's second full day in London, a carefully packed trunk arrived, sent by the fastest coach at considerable expense. Caro was delighted to have her own clothes and didn't mind the cost, but was dismayed by the accompanying letter.

Ellen was following at a more decorous pace, escorted by Eyam.

A moment's thought told her there was no possibility of stopping them. She was going to have to face Eyam and tell him she couldn't marry him. Part of her hoped that Jack Hill was alive and would provide escape — but that would truly be a case of leaping out of a pan into the fire.

As for Ellen, Caro realized she didn't want her here, either. She would disapprove of everything, probably with quotations from Lady Fowler. Ellen had said in her letter that she hoped to meet the lady and attend some of her "worthy gatherings."

Caro sought Diana and explained the situation.

Diana said, "Of course, your friend must stay here."

"She's not exactly a friend," Caro said. "She was my governess and is now my companion."

Diana cocked her head. "I have wondered if you were congenial. Perhaps it's time to dismiss her, with a generous annuity, if you see the need."

"Oh, certainly, but even a generous one won't allow her to live as she does at Luttrell House."

"But what did you plan when you married?"

Caro had to think about that. "I think we assumed Ellen would come with me. . . ." *To Colne Hall,* she added, but silently. Diana didn't know anything about that. "Truly, I've been drifting on the stream until recently. It hasn't been unpleasant, but . . ."

"But?" Diana seemed to be watching Caro closely.

"But now I've struck a rock. Whatever I do, nothing will ever be quite the same. I was happy," she said fiercely, "before this happened."

"Were you?"

Caro found she couldn't say yes. "Con-

443

tent, at least."

"Content is not enough. You must be brave, Caro."

"Brave? What do you mean?"

"Sometimes the most frightening challenge is to accept the truth."

"What truth?"

But Diana only said, "That is for you to discover, but . . . is there no man you are drawn to? I had thought Sir Eyam Colne might please you, and now he comes south."

Caro supposed it couldn't be concealed. "He is a suitor," she confessed. "And I have even encouraged him, but now I realize it will not do."

"Why not?"

"I don't love him. Foolish, I know. Love isn't necessary. It's probably an illusion. . . ."

"You know better than that."

"Yes, but perhaps it isn't for everyone. Or perhaps love can carry a person to disaster."

Diana surprised her by nodding. "Sometimes it is so, but a love that includes trust and honesty can never lead us amiss."

"Trust and honesty," Caro repeated. She came to one decision. "In that spirit, I'm finished with Mistress Grieve and shall be myself, Mistress Hill, again."

"Are you sure?"

"Yes. I need to be me. In any case, that

trunk came addressed to Mistress Hill, and I don't want to have to explain to Ellen and Sir Eyam why I've been hiding under a false name. Is there no news about Hill? Lord Rothgar implied his being dead or alive in the army would be easily settled. Do you know if he's learned anything yet?"

"It's proving a little more difficult than we thought," Diana said. " 'Hill' is such a common name, and some colonial records were apparently lost in a shipwreck. Would Mistress Spencer like the bedchamber next to yours, do you think?"

Caro accepted the new topic of discussion, but she had an uneasy feeling that Diana was not being entirely honest with her. Were Diana and Lord Rothgar hoping to present her and her fortune to one of their friends if she was free to marry? She'd already begun to learn how much of life in London was based on the trading of influence and favors.

If the Duke of Bridgewater was presented to her soon, she wouldn't be surprised, but murder might be done.

Ellen arrived the next afternoon in a flutter of excitement and disapproval. Such an excellent carriage. Such poor weather in places. So large a city. Such dirty air. Such buildings. The dome of St. Paul's! How kind Sir Eyam had been. How scandalous the clothing of one woman in the street.

Eyam had escorted her here and waited, the very picture of expectation.

He was also preening, Caro noticed, to be in Malloren House, greeted warmly by Lady Arradale.

Diana carried Ellen off to her room, leaving Caro alone with her suitor. He would have taken her hand, but she waved him to a chair, taking one herself. She felt she should stand like a guilty child, but she would not. She would be dignified, but above all firm.

"I have some things to tell you, Eyam," she said.

"If it's the truth of your marriage, Caro, Ellen told me."

Caro wanted to wring her companion's neck. "Did she also tell you my husband might still be alive?"

He leaned back slightly. "No. How could that be?"

"I believe my aunt fabricated the news of his death. Lord Rothgar is trying to establish the truth."

He rose and paced the room, ending up considerably farther away from her. "How long have you known this, Caro?"

"Known? I still don't know."

"That there was doubt."

Caro saw very clearly that she was supposed to look down and be repentant. Very deliberately, she met his eyes. "As soon as I thought seriously of marrying again, a little doubt worried me. It grew."

"And you said nothing to me."

"I hoped it wasn't true." Immediately she recognized a mistake. "Eyam —"

But he'd rushed over to her, gone to one knee. "So you do love me, Caro."

*Oh, God.* "Eyam, no. I have to tell you that I do not."

He remained there on his knee, looking as if she'd presented him with a conundrum. "You don't love me?"

"No. I'm very sorry. . . ."

He got to his feet, more awkwardly than he'd gone to his knee. "Have you ever loved me?"

This was so painful. "I thought I did."

"You've fallen in love with another," he said.

Caro hated to lie, but for his pride's sake, she said, "There is no other at the moment, Eyam, and perhaps will never be if Jack Hill is alive."

"You will become his wife in fact?"

"No, I'll obtain a legal separation. We have

447

nothing in common other than half an hour ten years ago."

He turned away, but then turned back. "What of this Grandiston, who was so unpleasant?"

"Grandiston?" Saying his name caused a quiver. "Ellen told you of that incident, too?"

"She wanted to explain why you'd felt the need to come south. Are you in danger from him?"

He still wanted to protect her, and that touched her heart. She rose and went to him. "I'm safe here, Eyam, under Lord Rothgar's protection, but it is very kind of you to care."

"Of course I care. I'll stay in Town for a few days. I have some matters to attend to, but I will be on hand if you need me. Staying with Henry Fleece in Brook Street."

"Thank you. I'm sorry for causing you pain, but I think we both deserve true love."

"You've turned romantic, Caro?"

"Have I? It doesn't feel that way, but I hope that in the future things will improve."

He nodded and took his farewell with only a bow. He was a good man and in a fair world she would love him, but she didn't.

Caro gathered her strength and went in search of Ellen and the next painful scene.

"You've dismissed Sir Eyam?" Ellen exclaimed. "After he'd come all this way to be at your side?"

"That isn't reason enough to marry anyone," she replied. She was glad to see Ellen had been given a room equally as fine as her own, but that didn't distract her companion.

"I think you've run mad, Caro. Can you deny that before we went to Froggatt Lane that day, you were planning your wedding?"

"I've simply realized it won't do."

"But *why?*" Ellen demanded.

"I don't love him."

"Well, really! And when did you decide that?"

Ellen's questions were completely reasonable. If the situations were reversed, Caro would have asked the same. Thank heavens Ellen knew nothing of her adventures.

"With everything being tossed to sixes and sevens and then traveling here, I began to see things differently."

"In other words, you've been corrupted by the wickedness of London."

"Thus far I've visited Westminster Abbey, viewed an exhibition of pastoral drawings, and taken two walks around the park. Yesterday being Sunday, we went to service and to a meeting concerning a charity hospital. My experience of London has not matched Lady Fowler's."

"I suppose that Lady Rothgar being with child must have moderated her behavior. Of course of *him,* I will say no more."

"Ellen, I will not have you be discourteous to our hosts."

"It is every Christian's duty to denounce sin, and he sired a child out of wedlock."

Caro inhaled. "I met Lady Huntersdown on the way south. She's a delightful lady and she and her husband are very much in love."

"She's a *Papist!*"

"Ellen!" Caro gained control. "If you'd rather not stay under this roof, I'll find you a room in a respectable inn —"

"Alone?" Ellen protested.

"Then . . . oh, never mind. But do not insult Lord Rothgar or Lady Arradale or I will personally put you on a coach back to Sheffield!"

# CHAPTER 25

Christian arrived back in London and went directly to Thorn's house, where he found chaos.

Large faux-marble panels were being erected, while other workers draped ells of dark cloth from the ceiling. He fought his way through to Thorn's sanctum with difficulty. "What in Hades is going on?"

"Not Hades — Olympus," Thorn said, and gave instructions to two people who hurried away. "I'm hosting the Olympian Revels this year, so everything must be made classical."

Christian sat down. "Is the Olympian Revels as promising as it sounds?"

"No," said Thorn. He poured brandy for them both and passed over a glass.

"Not tea?" Christian said, taking a welcome sip. "You must be in a bad way."

"Likely to become a tosspot." Thorn took his seat. "The Olympian Revels is an annual autumnal masquerade for the elite. Everyone wears classical costume — Roman or Greek — and there's no unmasking."

"*Very* promising."

"Except that in such a closed circle, most people can guess who the others are. In part the event is simply an amusement for those required to be in Town by duty, but it also allows interesting interactions between those who do not normally talk. Convention says that divisions and animosity must be put aside."

"Politics," Christian said. "No vestal virgins and nubile nymphs?"

"Many, but it would be unwise to take advantage. Particularly when you have enough women in your life as it is."

Christian groaned and took a deep drink of brandy. "What news?"

"First, I haven't found Lady Grandiston. If she's in London anywhere, she's keeping well out of sight."

"I never thought it that likely. What of the Silcocks?"

"Them, I have. They're staying with a Mr. Matthews in the City. He's an American merchant."

"What have you done?"

"Nothing other than put a watch on them.

What did you expect? That I could hurl them into a ducal dungeon?"

"No, but . . . it's good you have them under surveillance. Thank you. They're doing nothing?"

"I wouldn't say that. He is obviously doing business of various kinds. They went together to a physician, Dr. Glenmore, and Mistress Silcock has returned there, so you could be right about her being unwell."

"Is he a specialist in the insane?"

"No. In wasting diseases."

Christian shrugged with frustration.

"The lady has one other interest," Thorn said. "She frequently visits Lady Fowler."

"Struth! That explains everything."

Thorn's lips twitched. "Dearly as I'd like to blame all your troubles on the Fowler woman, I doubt it's reasonable. I've pried a little there, too. It seems Mistress Silcock has been corresponding with Lady Fowler for many years and is a generous supporter of the Fund."

"Birds of a feather . . . Any news from the north?"

With a knock, a man came in to bow and ask permission to remove some portraits of previous dukes from the upper hall. Thorn gave it and waved him away. "Lose them if you can!" he called after.

When the door shut, he said, "No sign of your wife at Luttrell House, but the companion, Mistress Spencer, left. The idiot put to watch the place didn't follow her, but merely reported that she left with a gentleman in a traveling carriage. The gentleman was Sir Eyam Colne, a local baronet."

"Eloping? I wouldn't have thought it of the mouse, but good luck to her."

"More likely a very proper journey to visit relatives while your wife is away. Ah yes, there is more about Mistress Hill — as she's known up there."

"What?"

"No sign that she's a lackwit. She doesn't manage Froggatt and Skellow, but she pays regular visits to inspect the books and such. I have a general description — average height and build, light brown hair, not pretty but not ill-favored, either."

"In other words, she could be anyone."

"I'll have more in time. I have begun to wonder if she's eloped."

"Why?"

"General peculiarities. She left Luttrell House to go to Sheffield, and then went on to visit a friend while the companion, Mistress Spencer, returned alone, but sent some clothing off to Doncaster."

"Doncaster again! I'm due for insanity

myself. Doncaster's on the road north, so perhaps she did elope. After all, she's done it once. Then a couple of days later the companion sets off to join her?"

Thorn shrugged. "It's hard to piece together anything at such a distance."

"Which is why I went north."

"And lost track of the game."

Tab suddenly appeared and looked at Thorn. *Ee-ow-ah-ooh.*

"Quite. Do you want Tabitha back, by the way?"

"Why Tabitha?"

"A mother is entitled to some dignity, and we have interesting conversations."

"While she studiously ignores me. Far be it from me to tear apart two souls in harmony."

"Speaking of which, no messages have arrived at the Black Swan."

"I don't expect any," said Christian coolly, but all the same, pain stabbed. If he only knew she was safe.

"You need your spirits raised. Attend the Revels."

"Why not? Always amusing to watch the gods at play."

To Caro's relief, Ellen chose to keep to her room on her first evening, pleading exhaustion from travel. When she told Caro the next morning that she wished to visit Lady Fowler, it seemed a little rude, but Caro was glad enough to see her go. She didn't relish more battles.

The post brought a letter from Hambledon. He began with an account of a strange visitor claiming to be her, and she realized she'd not mentioned that in her letter to him. Perhaps as well. Let it remain a mystery.

He had sent a transcription of the short document. Caro read it, then took it to Mr. Carruthers for further consideration, but she felt sure it was just as he'd suspected — no protection at all for any wealth she'd accumulated after the ceremony.

Diana commiserated on that, but said, "There's nothing to be done about it, I assume, and Rothgar's not here to discover a miracle. Come with me and lose cares in a mercer's shop. There are a number of rooms needing new curtains."

They came home hours later to the news that Ellen had returned and left, taking her luggage. There was a letter from her, which Caro read with disbelief.

"She's moved to Lady Fowler's house," she said, not relaying Ellen's reasons. "Diana, I'm so sorry."

"Never mind," Diana said, taking Caro to her boudoir. Once there, she said, "We'll all be more comfortable, and it will make some plans of mine a little easier."

Caro sat down, relieved and grateful. "What plans?"

"I believe Lady Fowler is particularly opposed to masquerade events, so I assume her disciples are, too."

"Oh, yes."

"But I hope you'll attend one with me."

"Yes, of course. I love them."

"As do I, and it will be easy to hide your identity. This is a special one, though. Not scandalous, I promise. At least, no more than usual. It's called the Olympian Revels, and everyone must wear classical costumes. No concealing domino cloaks or such. The gentlemen generally choose costumes according to their occupations, so the politicians wear the toga style, while the soldiers wear ancient armor. Those who are neither sometimes attempt a minor god."

"And the clergymen?" Caro asked, amused.

"Vague priestly robes, but I have seen a druid or two waving mistletoe."

"What do we ladies wear?"

"Robes of a Greek or Roman lady or, of course, the flimsier style of goddesses, nymphs, and vestal virgins."

"It sounds delightful. When is it?"

"Tomorrow."

Caro blinked. "That gives no time for me to obtain a costume."

"But if you'll be a goddess, I have one."

"Won't you want to wear it?"

Diana laughed. "In draperies, I'd look like a billowing sail. I'll wear substantial, matronly robes. Do come."

"Yes, thank you."

"Excellent. I'll send for the costume. You go into my dressing room and take off your clothes."

Caro discovered that was literal. Diana's maid said, "Down to the skin, ma'am. At least, that's how her ladyship wore it."

"No shift, no stays?" Caro asked, tossed back into a Doncaster whirlwind.

"You keep them on, then, ma'am. I would."

When Caro put on the deceptively simple costume, however, she saw that her underclothing would have to go. The white linen gown wasn't as flimsy as it appeared, but it left one shoulder uncovered, revealing the sturdy strap of her stays and her shift beneath. Lower down, bones and buckram were obvious and ugly.

"Off they come."

When she put on the costume again, it looked perfect, and the sturdy lining was almost as decent as the jacket she'd worn in Doncaster. All the same, it seemed that she was wearing a thin layer of cloth over nothing, and the whole of her right shoulder would be exposed to public gaze.

"I'm not sure. . . ."

"It looks lovely on you," Diana said. "I wore it as Diana the Huntress, but Rothgar suggested Persephone. I'm not sure why, though I suppose you are half-married."

"No," said Caro, "I'm all one or the other. Still no news?"

"Not now," Diana said, with a glance at the servants all around.

Caro had to leave questions for later. "Lord Rothgar seemed to think I'd find a Pluto to trap me in London's underworld."

"Sometimes he's whimsical," Diana said, circling Caro. "Persephone will do very well, though. What do we need? Spring flowers," she commanded one maid, "and" — she turned to another — "a pomegranate, real or false."

She twitched a fold into place. "Some flowers can be stitched onto the gown, and in a circlet for your hair. Mr. Barilly must come to arrange it in the Grecian style." Another maid was dispatched. "No jewels, I think. Simplicity. Yes, it will do."

"Mask?" Caro asked, feeling as if a wave had broken over her.

"Ah, yes. Something simple, but full-faced. Many revelers will know each other, but you'll be a true mystery, a center of attention."

"I'm not sure I want that, Diana."

"Don't be foolish. It will be delightful. The unique feature of the Olympian Revels is that there is no unmasking. If you can remain unidentified when there, you will leave undiscovered."

"How odd."

"How delightful. Ah, the mask."

A servant entered carrying a plain white mask and Caro tied it on. It covered her face from her hairline to just below her cheeks. She turned to the mirror to see a very mysterious creature indeed. The white gown hung simply, girdled around her hips and falling to an uneven hem that in places exposed inches of ankles. Her shoulder was blatant, and the smooth, pale mask made her eerie.

"Rouge for the lips," Diana said. "So distinct against all that pallor." A maid came forward with pot and brush and applied a deep pink.

"Startling, one might say," Caro commented, but she was coming to like being a daring inconnu.

It was too long since she'd enjoyed a simple entertainment, and there was no danger of anyone recognizing Mistress Hill of Luttrell House.

# CHAPTER 26

Caro entered the carriage with Diana, both of them in concealing cloaks. Beneath, Diana wore the substantial, layered robes of a rich matron. Her brown hair had been tightly curled into the elaborate style that suited the robes, and was topped by a diadem set with rubies. Her mask was a simple one, covering only the eyes. She'd made no true attempt to be unrecognizable.

The marquess, on the other hand, had. His mask covered the upper half of his face and gave him a slightly bulbous nose and bushy eyebrows. His long hair was loose to his shoulders and dusted with gray, giving an impression of age. He wore a long robe of plain white cloth, belted at the waist with a roll of paper tucked under it. It seemed to have a diagram drawn on it.

As they moved off, Caro said, "I confess, my lord, I can't guess who you are."

"I am Daedalus, engineer and maker of mazes."

It seemed an odd choice for such a man.

"Rothgar amuses himself with mechanical matters," said Diana, "in particular clockwork mechanisms."

"Oh," Caro said, remembering. "Springs."

The marquess smiled. "Indeed. I, too, have an interest there."

"And astronomy, I think."

"Yes." The mask hid his reaction, but Caro sensed surprise, and no wonder. She'd had that information from Christian.

Grateful that her own mask concealed her face, she said, "Diana must have mentioned it."

He spoke a little of the voyages to witness the transit of Venus. Caro was glad of her concealing mask, for she could think only of Christian. Perhaps she drifted into longings, for he said, "But I think I bore you, Mistress Hill."

"Oh, no!"

"It is clear what character you play," he carried on. "You are marked by your pomegranate. Is it real?"

Caro looked at the object in her hand. "No, it's pottery, and quite heavy."

"But cleverly painted," Diana said. "I gather it came from the kitchens, though why they'd have such a thing, I have no idea."

"Anything to amuse a good cook," the marquess said.

Their carriage was slowing as they approached the Duke of Ithorne's house.

"This will be a well-ordered affair," Diana told Caro, "with the most select guests, so you needn't stay by our sides. Don't be foolish, though, and go apart with a gentleman. Unless you wish to," she added with a smile.

"I would never do that."

Instead of disapproval, Diana said, "Never?" as if Caro had said she never ate bread.

"Never," Caro repeated.

Diana's brows rose. "As you choose. I hope you won't object to some teasing and flirtation."

Caro was feeling uncomfortably odd. "Of course not."

"Alas," Diana said, "no one will tease and flirt with me, so obviously enceinte as I am."

"Except me," said Lord Rothgar.

"Except you," said Diana, with a slit-eyed smile at her husband that made Caro feel hot all over.

She quickly looked outside, wishing she were back in Yorkshire, where she understood the rules.

The Duke of Ithorne's mansion rivalled Malloren House, and every window was lit for the event. The carriage drew up and they all climbed down. The street was packed with people who'd come to see the guests arrive, held back by lines of men dressed as Roman soldiers, each holding a lance.

The lances looked real.

Could such a crowd be dangerous? The London mob was notoriously volatile. Then she saw some women holding up a banner that said something about Sodom and Gomorrah. Lud, Lady Fowler! She prayed Ellen wasn't there, but only for Ellen's sake. She felt no danger of recognition.

She was glad to get inside the house, but nervous now about shedding her cloak. She saw instantly that most of the women wore costumes like her own. Only the older ones had chosen heavier layers. It was as well the place was warm, she thought, or some of the nymphs and goddesses would contract pneumonia.

Many of the men were also lightly dressed, some in togas that left an arm and shoulder bare. Many togas were edged in gold and purple, which indicated high rank, and a few wore gilded laurel wreaths. Were those men dukes, marquesses, and earls? She saw the amusing aspect of the Marquess of

Rothgar taking on the identity of a simple engineer and rather wished she'd come as a maidservant.

Which made her think of Carrie, and Christian large and furious in Froggatt Lane. How could he have so many different aspects? Why couldn't they all be vile?

Many of the men wore ancient armor with scarlet cloaks and crested helmets. Every one an officer, she thought, but that was probably true. Lowly soldiers would never be permitted here.

As they moved farther into the hall, Caro wondered what this house looked like normally. For this occasion a classical effect had been skillfully created. Large panels and columns had been painted to look like marble, and great dark draperies swathed the ceiling, suggesting the night sky, as if they were outdoors.

There were smells, too. She identified some herbs, and when a servant offered a tray of morsels of food, the aroma of garlic rose. The duke had even contrived the smells of a foreign land. She imagined him, grand and old, large-bellied and red-nosed, planning his bacchanal. Then she laughed. He'd doubtless simply paid professionals a great deal of money and absented himself until tonight.

She realized she was hovering near Lord Rothgar and Diana like a nervous child. That wouldn't do. She stepped away and let the throng carry her through the linked reception rooms, enjoying every detail of the house and the guests.

Some had taken excessive advantage of the classical style. One buxom young lady was wearing a sleeveless, knee-length robe, a half-face mask, and a bold smile. Could she really be from a good family?

Others clung too much to the modern style. One togaed senator wore a powdered wig, and a soldier had on modern riding boots and breeches beneath his leather-skirted armor. Some took the ancient style too far. She passed a group of robed men speaking in what was probably Classical Greek. She knew they all learned to use the language fluently at school, but it seemed rude to do so here.

"You frown, fair nymph? Who has displeased you?"

Caro started, but plunged into the fun of the masquerade and played her part.

"Rude men, of course. What else?" she said, strolling along with the togaed gentleman. A purple band, but no laurel wreaths. He was one who left a shoulder bare, but it was too heavy for her taste and thick dark hair crept out from his chest almost to his shoulder bone.

"Alas, we are base creatures, every one of us. And who are you, then?"

"That is for you to guess, sir."

He looked her over, saw her pomegranate, and smiled. "Persephone! May I be your Pluto for the night?"

She smiled and considered him. "You don't seem grim enough to be the lord of the underworld."

"Too jolly?" he said, grinning. "I could show you a jolly time."

A woman appeared on his other side, distinctive for being dressed in a robe of deep dark red, part of it draped over her head. A representation of grief. Her mask suggested sadness, but her lips curved up. "You could show a widow a jolly time, Jasper."

"Psyche, you could at least pretend to be deceived."

"Why?" she asked, and drew him away from Caro without apology.

Well! Caro didn't want him, but that was excessively rude on both their parts. She noted that when Psyche walked, her gown parted at the side to reveal most of a long, slender leg. If this was the haute volee's notion of a select company, heaven help them

468

all. Perhaps she'd join forces with Lady Fowler.

But, as the saint said, not just yet.

"Persephone," growled another man, stepping to block her way. "Let me bite your pomegranate, my juicy delight."

He wasn't looking at her fruit.

Caro raised the piece of pottery, smiling. "By all means, sir, but you'll break your teeth."

He leered, showing crooked teeth. He was in toga and wreath, but he also carried a violin. The emperor Nero, she realized, and acting down to his part.

"I am Pluto," he declared, "and command you to my underworld."

"You are Nero, and have no power over me."

"I am your emperor. Obey me."

Caro felt a tremor of fear, but they were surrounded by people, all playing merry parts. She simply had the misfortune to encounter an unpleasant specimen.

"I could take you to *my* underworld," she said. As his eyes gleamed, she added, "To the kitchens, perhaps? You could fiddle as the hearth burns?"

His smile curled a little in the lip. "A spicy wench with a clever mouth. I'm sure you went willingly enough into Pluto's bed, for all your bleats."

"But he is a god," she said, "and you, though emperor, a mere man."

With that, she turned and walked away. She thought he might pursue, but it seemed he had the wit to see a lost cause. More encounters like that, however, would make this evening tiresome.

Music was playing somewhere in the house, but now the tune changed to the lively beat of a dance. With exclamations of pleasure, many turned to go up the stairs. Caro flowed with them, smiling again. She loved to dance.

But then her hand was grasped.

She looked sideways, fearing to see Nero, but this was a younger man in a simple, short tunic of what looked like dingy home-spun. She'd think him a costumed servant, but though he wore a mask contrived to look like cloth tied around his upper face and had let stubble grow on his cheeks, voice, posture, and everything else suggested he was of the elite. The whole costume had probably been skillfully made by an expert at high cost.

"A hermit?" she guessed, letting him lead her onward.

"Too melancholy. I'm a goatherd. Even our emperors and philosophers need someone to provide their food."

She chuckled, liking the contrariness of his choice and delirious that he'd not mentioned Pluto.

She raised their linked hands, however, and considered his — unblemished and with perfectly manicured nails. "You have very gentle goats."

He grinned, showing excellent teeth. "What point to a masquerade if one is one-self?"

"Will most people here know you?"

"Probably. Will most people here know you?"

"Probably not."

"Then I have captured a treasure." He kissed her knuckles.

At last, some elegant amusement. "At least until winter, when I must return to Hades."

"All the more reason to revel while we may. Come dance."

He drew her into a ballroom even more impressively transformed with pillars, marble, and drapery. Then her bare shoulder brushed against a marble half pillar and she realized that, at least, was real.

"The duke has created an excellent illusion," she said as they took their place in a dancing line.

"Or his slaves and minions have."

"Are you a Leveler, then, wanting to drag down those on high to raise up the goatherd?"

"No. I enjoy my privileges and luxuries." He looked at her pomegranate. "That's a pretty fruit, but what do you with it as we dance?"

Caro popped it into a dangling pouch on her belt. Being white, the pouch wasn't obvious until in use. As it was her own invention, she was proud of it.

"Brava," he said as the dance began. "Does it come off? If so, it'd make a handy weapon."

"Which I fear I might need tonight."

"Have you encountered a boor?" They turned one way and another. "You shouldn't be so alluring."

"Alas," she said, "how true. Especially as my charms caused Pluto to carry me down to hell."

"But would you choose ugliness?"

She laughed. "No more than you, sir, would choose poverty."

The dance carried them apart, and she saw the next woman he danced with embarrass herself with enthusiasm. He was handsome, she granted, and, despite leggins beneath the tunic, was revealing a fine, sleek body, but she suspected he was also rich and titled and many women's dream.

She paid attention to her other partners, but whenever she danced with her goatherd, she liked him best. Not to catch and wed, but simply for amusement. He certainly flirted delightfully. Caro found herself truly lighthearted for the first time since Christian had invaded the house in Froggatt Lane.

Christian.

A military officer from London.

She realized that he could just possibly be here.

She couldn't help but search all the soldiers around her. Many had discarded the heavy helmets, which helped identification. She saw large men and blond hair, but no one who combined both to make the right man.

What would she do if she saw him?

She'd have to avoid him. She still had nothing to offer. But it would be almost more than she could bear.

Caro's searching eyes saw a tall, plainly togaed young man with a round face insisting on someone else's place in the dance. She was surprised that he was given it without complaint.

"Who is mighty Caesar?" she asked her goatherd, indicating with her eyes. "He seems to command."

He glanced, but then danced her on. "The king," he said quietly. "Nearly everyone knows, of course, but it's supposed to be a secret."

Caro looked again as soon as she was able. She supposed he did resemble his image in prints and on coins. When the dance took her to the point where she partnered him, she had to work hard not to act strangely.

"And who are you?" he asked, considering her costume. "A nymph?"

Caro almost curtsied and had to catch up her step in the dance. "Persephone, sir." To prevent him making the weak joke, she added, "Poor Pluto's victim."

"Would that I had been there to defend you. And who do you think I am?" he asked.

Lord, what to say to that? Even anonymous kings probably didn't want to be thought low. Caesar seemed too obvious and didn't suit his costume.

"A philosopher," Caro said, hoping that would please.

It did. "Clever girl," he said, and it was as well they parted then, for she didn't appreciate being called a girl by a man of her own age, even if he was the king.

A glimpse of blond hair across the room fired her back to her greatest concern. No, not tall enough.

But then she wondered about Jack Hill. Lord Rothgar had failed to find a record of his death in the military records. That worried her. If he was alive, could he be here? She didn't know him any more than he would know her. They could dance and flirt in innocent ignorance.

Would she feel something? When she was dancing again with her goatherd, she assessed him with new intensity, thinking, *Taller than I'd expect, but fine-boned as he was, and he certainly has the air.*

"You think you recognize me?" he asked.

"I might. Are you a military man?"

"Wouldn't I have come in armor?"

She turned his earlier comment on him. "What point to a masquerade if one remains oneself?"

"Touché, but are you one who will only smile on Mars?"

"Perhaps," she said, abandoning her sudden folly. Jack Hill was dead, and if not, this man wasn't he.

The dance ended and her partner led her from the floor. "Come, then, let me find you a Mars to play with."

Caro would have preferred to stay with him, but courtesy required a gentleman to dance with many ladies. She was a stranger here and he was being kind.

He looked around and then said, "Ah, there's a likely one." He guided her toward a group of soldiers. The nearest one had his cloaked back to them.

Caro's steps faltered. The height, the broad shoulders, the blond hair. The goatherd was already calling. "Ho, Mars! No, not you, sir — *You.* A fair goddess commands your worship."

All three men had turned. The tall, blond one in the middle was Christian Grandiston.

Thank heaven for her own concealing, impassive mask.

The molded breastplate was no more impressive than his naked form, she knew. Beneath it he wore a white, sleeveless tunic to his knees, metal guards over his shins, and sandals, but his muscular arms were completely exposed. He looked every inch the warrior, even smiling merrily in the way she knew so well.

She was hot and cold at the same time.

Did shoulders blush?

Might she actually vomit?

He turned severe. "You accost me?" he said to the goatherd, putting a hand to the short, broad sword at his belt.

"Great sir, noble sir," groveled the goatherd unconvincingly. "I merely obey the goddess."

Christian's eyes turned on her and he smiled again. "It is every man's duty to obey a goddess. What is your command?"

Caro realized she was jealous! Jealous that he was smiling that smile, looking that look, at a stranger. Ridiculous, but she didn't want him to recognize her. It would lead to nothing but pain.

She had to get away, but as with their first encounter, to run now would reveal all. Clearly he hadn't recognized her, and he couldn't expect her to be here. She need only disguise her voice.

She pitched it higher than normal and used nervousness as an excuse to sound breathy. "Lud, sir, to have a mighty warrior such as you at my command!"

He bowed in anachronistic style. "Which goddess do I have the honor to worship? Venus, goddess of beauty, or Juno, who rules Olympus?"

"She has a pomegranate," the goatherd said with a grin. "Be wary of it."

Choosing mysterious silence, Caro took it out.

"Ah, the eternal promise of spring," Christian said. "Begone, varlet. You have no place here."

"Only if my goddess approves," said the goatherd.

Caro could tell they knew each other and were on good terms.

Christian drew his sword. "Approve, Persephone, or your lowly companion dies."

"Oh!" Caro squeaked. "I approve, I approve!"

The other two soldiers had gone and now her goatherd also abandoned her.

Christian smiled at her, but he must have seen alarm. "I'm not so terrifying, I assure you. We but playact."

"I but playact, too," she squeaked.

"Then of your pity, act enchanted."

Caro looked down in what she hoped was a nervous manner. "I am new to London, you see, and quite terrified by so many strangers."

"Then allow me to return you to your party. Do you know where they are?"

"No."

"We will go in search."

He was being kind and good-humored, and she realized she'd never had any choice in this. Despite everything, she loved him so much.

He'd extended his hand, palm up, and she had to put her hand in it. Would he know her at a touch? She was quivering at that contact, her body remembering, and her mind remembering other things.

He'd seduced Kat Hunter out of pure wickedness, but rescued her out of gallantry. And here he was, rescuing a lady made nervous by the masquerade. A lady he didn't know at all and had no hope of seducing.

"We are looking for?" he asked.

Fearful that something about Diana and Rothgar would give her away, she plucked a name out of nowhere. "Lord and Lady Bingham."

"Don't know them. How are they disguised?"

"A centurion and a Roman lady."

"Our search is likely to be long, Persephone, but I can't regret that. How long have you been in Town?"

"Only days," she breathed, willpower melting.

He talked easily of the charms of London, and of places she might want to visit. A Galahad in Grecian armor.

He paused, expecting some response, and she'd no idea what he'd just said. They were in a corner of a landing overlooking the spacious hall below. She looked down as if searching and saw the man the goatherd had said was the king.

"Oh, I'm sorry, I was distracted. According to my goatherd, that man there is the king. Is that true?"

She turned back to look at him, and froze. She'd never known his eyes could turn so cold and hawkish.

"Curious again, Kat? What, in hell's name, are you doing here?" He angled her into the corner and trapped her there.

Caro gaped, dry-mouthed with fear.

"Don't waste time denying it."

"Very well, I won't," she whispered, and this time nervousness was no pretense.

"Very wise. Now, why are you here?"

"For . . . for pleasure, pure pleasure!"

"There's nothing pure about you. Why are you here?"

"Don't, please. . . ." She had no idea what precisely she feared, but his irrational rage melted her bones.

"You're wise to be frightened, Kat, if that is your name. No? I didn't think so." But then he asked in a different voice, "Why did you flee?"

"What?"

"In York. Why?"

He was so angry because of that? She pushed at him. "Because I was afraid of a scene like this. Let me go."

"What did I ever do to warrant that?"

*You made me love you.*

Caro closed her eyes. "Let me go, please. There's no point to this."

"I took time in York to find out that there are no lawyers there by the name of Hunter."

She looked at him wearily. "Yes, I lied. The name is false. I'm sorry if you're angry —"

"And here you are, asking about the king."

Caro stared at him, trying to understand.

A group passed by, forcing him closer, pressing his breastplate against her unguarded breasts. She hissed with pain, but also with a twisted arousal.

He stepped back, with no sign he'd even noticed, but now he had a steely grip on her wrist. "Come with me."

Caro twisted against his hold, even though it hurt. "No."

"Come with me," he said softly, "or I summon assistance and take you to the Tower."

"The *Tower!*"

"As a possible threat to the king's safety."

Caro gaped, but she could see he was deadly serious. It was insane. It could be sorted out in a moment, but not here, not now. There were military men all around who would probably leap to his command. She had no idea where Diana and Lord

Rothgar were.

He dropped the grip on her wrist, but immediately put an arm around her, holding her so tightly that she had no chance to escape. He marched her away through the merry crowd, a smile on his face. To her it looked like a promise of death, but it must have fooled others.

"How did you recognize me?" she whispered.

"The scar on your jaw. But I already had a feeling I knew you. In all senses of the word."

Ridiculous to be hurt by that sneer, but Caro had to press her lips together to fight tears. "Stop this and let me explain."

"Not yet."

This tyrannical behavior reminded her of their first encounter and should kill any tender feelings, but her anguish over his anger and distrust showed she was a fool.

The farther they went from the ballroom, the thinner the crowd of revelers, the more frightened she became. She wouldn't believe he'd truly hurt her, but when he opened a door and forced her through, her legs almost gave way.

He closed the door. The ball became a distant murmur. She was alone with him in some sort of boudoir, unused, and chilly without a fire in the grate. The only light came from the moon, but that shone directly in, washing both him and the room with a pale icy light.

# CHAPTER 27

She made herself speak. "There's no need for this." Her voice was as high and breathy as when she'd tried to disguise it. "I'm sorry I left you in York —"

"You think I care about that? Our game was over, and thus, you left. Who are you working for?"

"Working for?"

"The French? The Stuarts? The Irish malcontents?"

Moonlight had turned him into a marble statue with obsidian eyes.

"No one! I'm not a traitor. Christian . . ." The name escaped, but she saw it have an effect.

More softly, he asked, "Give me one truth, then. Tell me your real name."

Such a simple thing, but that revelation was too much for her here, now, with him so furious and them enemies.

He turned cold again, grabbed her wrist

and towed her to the window.

"What are you doing?" she cried, struggling.

"Making sure you can't escape." He inspected the window and looked out. "Are you an intrepid climber of walls? I'd say no, but I don't know you at all, do I?"

"I am," she spat, "a respectable lady of Yorkshire — who had the ill fortune to encounter you! What is this evil you suspect?"

"Assassination."

"*What?* You're mad. Killing's your expertise, not mine." She remembered the comment about her pomegranate being a weapon and tried to untie the sling from her belt.

He spun her hard against the wall. "Let's see that. Take it out."

"Why? Why ever think I'd kill anyone?"

"Because you're a liar and a thief —"

"I didn't —"

"— and you're here when the king is also here."

"But I didn't know!"

"You asked me to confirm which one he was." He stepped back, but in the same movement, he drew his short sword, grabbed her pouch, and sliced it free like a knife through butter.

Caro flinched back. "That blade is real!"

"Remember it."

He was studying the pottery fruit, but she stayed pressed against the wall. She had no doubt that her slightest move would have her pinned there again, perhaps by a blade.

"I am what I say," she said as calmly as she could. "That is a piece of pottery. I don't want to kill the king. You've leapt to this wild suspicion. . . ."

He twisted the fruit with both hands and it separated into two halves, revealing small silvery balls that glinted in the moonlight.

Caro looked from them into cold, flat eyes. "I don't know what they are," she babbled. "What are they? Pistol balls? I don't know. I didn't know. No wonder it was so heavy. . . ."

"Explosive of some sort? Were you to set it alight?"

"No. I don't know. I don't know anything! You think I'd blow myself up?"

"A very dedicated assassin."

Suddenly furious, Caro dashed the pomegranate out of his hands. The two halves clunked to the floor, the balls rattling over the wooden floor.

Grandiston slammed her against the wall. Caro thrust back at him with all her strength, but then she went still, realizing

486

that he was shielding her with his body.

After three slow breaths she said, "Perhaps not explosive?"

"Yet." But he was looking down at her in a different, somber way. "Give me your name."

She could hold out no longer. "Caro," she said, praying he'd allow only that. "Are you truly 'Christian'?"

"Baptism and all," he said drily. "I was never the liar, after all. But for full truth, 'Grandiston' isn't my name. It's my title. I'm Viscount Grandiston, and you, you're the very devil in my soul."

His lips sealed hers.

The metal balls might not have been explosive, but he was; they were. Many parts of Caro screamed warnings, but the rest screamed in a different way, in a ferocious howl of need. She grabbed his hair and kissed him back. He grabbed her legs and put them around his armor-hard torso. She locked her ankles, wide-eyed at the position, but arching against him, wanting, wanting.

The one shoulder of her gown ripped and his mouth was hot and hungry on her breasts. Caro let out a long, throaty cry, her whole body going rigid. She pushed against him harder, wanting him inside her. Deep,

deep inside . . .

Light burst against her closed lids.

"My, my," said a woman's voice. "It seems the revel has become an orgy. And so early."

Grandiston went still. Caro stared over his shoulder at the widow in bloodred clothing and the leering Nero beside her, bearing a branch of candles. "I think," Caro said, "you forgot to lock the door."

A laugh escaped him, but he was sucking in breaths, as was she. Was he growing as cold with fear?

This, finally, was the complete disaster. Like a terrified rabbit, Caro would have stayed frozen in futile hope of being ignored, but he unlocked her ankles and eased her feet back to the ground. Her knees threatened to buckle and but for the wall she might have crumpled.

He turned, again concealing her with his body. Caro clutched her torn bodice over her breasts and rested her head against his broad back. But even that was wrong. The leather armor didn't feel like him, or smell like him.

Christian spoke. "Find another room, Lady Jessingham."

"But I like this one," the bloody widow said. "Perhaps we can all play. Who do you have back there, Grandiston? Come, share."

"I say," said Nero, "isn't that a pomegranate? He's got the pretty Persephone. Well, well, well. Yes, do share."

Christian snarled, "Go fiddle in hell where you belong."

But it was hopeless. Caro heard a new voice say, "What's going on?" and Nero's reply, "Grandiston's found some juicy pomegranate."

She had to look. She peered around Christian and saw three additional laughing guests. There'd be more soon, and now the widow took Nero's candles and lit another candelabrum that sat on a table, brightening the room.

How long could she hide here? Someone would remember that Persephone had arrived with Lord Rothgar, but she was still wearing her mask. Perhaps no one need know she was Caro Hill.

"Lady Jessingham, if you please?"

At the sound of Lord Rothgar's voice, Caro wanted to shrink into a ball as tiny as the ones on the floor and disappear.

The people in the doorway parted and he entered, Diana at his side. They both looked calm and even slightly amused. Diana was in full costume, but Lord Rothgar had taken off his mask.

Nero said, "Ho, Rothgar! A pretty play, is

it not? Make them carry on."

He was very drunk. Rothgar looked at him so coldly that Lady Jessingham stepped back, distancing herself.

The marquess looked past Nero as if he didn't exist, and addressed the group. "Some allowance must be made for a married couple recently reunited, don't you think? And some privacy allowed?"

He might as well have pointed. The more-distant spectators disappeared.

Lady Jessingham didn't move. "Married! But that's Grandiston."

"Married," Rothgar repeated.

Nero grabbed the widow and tried to follow. "Come on, Psyche. Best out of here. Married couple, you know."

"Grandiston is *not* married," she hissed, eyes narrowed, not moving an inch.

Christian said, "I am, you know."

Her eyes flashed with fury, and her face pinched so tight that she lost any trace of beauty. "Then you're a fool and your family will eat crusts."

She swept out, and Rothgar closed the door.

Caro knew she should step out and face her fate, but again, she couldn't make her cowardly legs move.

In front of her, Christian stood straighter.

"I thank you for removing the problem, my lord, but regret the lie you felt obliged to make. May I ask what interest you have in this?"

"The lady is under my protection."

Christian turned to Caro, blank with astonishment. "An endless conundrum, aren't you?" He turned back. "I'll meet you, of course, but her reputation should be preserved if possible."

At that, Caro rushed out of concealment, clutching her bodice over her breasts. "What? A duel? No!"

"No," said Rothgar. He raised his brows at the state of her gown, but didn't look furious. Diana was biting her lip, perhaps on a smile. Was London so wicked that even this was a mere nothing?

"It can't be swept away," Christian said angrily. "The tale will be spreading now and easily proved a lie."

"You agreed that you were married," Rothgar pointed out.

"It happens to be true, but not to this lady."

"No? Forgive me the dramatic moment, but it is quite irresistible. Allow me, sir, to introduce to you Dorcas Caroline Hill, née Froggatt, your legally wedded wife. Caro, your husband, Major Lord Grandiston."

Caro stared at Rothgar, and then at Christian, who turned to stare at her, stepping away as if repelled. . . .

Onto the metal balls.

His right foot went out from under him.

He staggered to stay upright.

Caro leapt to help.

Her bodice fell down.

He grabbed it and pulled it up, getting his footing again.

They froze like that, gaining their balance, looking into each other's eyes. Heaven knew what he was feeling, for his expression was perfectly blank.

# CHAPTER 28

His wife, Christian was thinking.

Dorcas Froggatt.

Kat, Caro. Whoever she was, his two adventures had always been one and now he had no idea how he felt or what he should do.

Then Lady Arradale stepped between them, extracting a pin from her robe. "While explanations are made, let me repair you, Caro."

"I'm sorry," she said, eyes wide with shock.

His wife.

A part of him was growling with triumph, but another growled with rage. She'd fooled him finely. With Lady Arradale's assistance? They were clearly on good terms. Both from Yorkshire, but from such different stations.

But Kat Hunter had mentioned the countess at least once.

He turned to face the Marquess of Rothgar, a man he knew by sight and reputation, but with whom he had never passed more than a commonplace remark. A man with enough power to break him, and a skilled-enough duelist to kill him.

There wouldn't be a duel. Even Rothgar couldn't kill a man for pleasuring his wife, even in a scandalous location. But he could wreak vengeance in other ways. Anger rose at the way he'd been duped, played with, run rings around. And to what end?

What had the damned woman hoped to gain?

Lord Rothgar spoke. "What did Lady Jessingham mean about your family eating crumbs?"

Christian stared at him, dragging his mind on to a new topic. Was that the marquess's threat? Though Psyche's words worried him, he said, "Hyperbole. She offered herself and her fortune in exchange for the title and is put out."

"The earldom of Royland is not a prosperous one," Rothgar said, "and your father has many children."

"But is not extravagant."

"Your brother is."

"What?" Christian wanted to beat his head against the wall. "My lord, if we could stick to the point. How do we avoid scandal

494

touching my . . . my wife." The word almost choked him.

"The story will already be the buzz of the Revels," Rothgar agreed, "but it can easily be turned romantic. A secret wedding, a long separation due to war, some misunderstandings, an unexpected reunion. So you are unaware of your family's dire financial straits?"

"There aren't any."

"Alas, there are."

Christian glared at him. "If there are, how do you know?"

"You and they recently became a matter of interest to me."

*God save him.* "You will leave my family alone, my lord."

Not surprisingly, Lord Rothgar was unimpressed. "Your wife is a friend of my wife's, Grandiston. Does that make us friends-in-law?"

Lord Rothgar playful was more terrifying than him vengeful.

And which brother was extravagant? It had to be Tom. The others were at school or home. What had he done? The navy doubtless presented many temptations.

The door opened and Thorn entered, still in his goatherd costume, but every inch the duke. He closed the door. "Am I needed?"

Christian had an ally, but that icy worm started crawling down his spine again. Though younger, Thorn outranked Rothgar, and he had the nature to try to use that in defense of a friend. Christian wouldn't place a bet on who would win, but worlds might tremble.

"I could do with a strong brandy," he said as evenly as he could. "It appears my errant wife has been under my nose all the while."

He turned. Her gown was roughly pinned together and she'd taken off that concealing mask. She was, without doubt, Kat — his lovely, frightened Kat. He wanted to pull her into his arms and keep her safe. He wanted to beat her.

"Allow me to introduce Caro — not Dorcas, you note — my wife. My dear, this is His Grace, the Duke of Ithorne."

Thorn bowed, managing not to look ridiculous. "Charmed, Lady Grandiston. Lady Jessingham is spreading doubt that you're married, Christian, and is casting the lady in a most unflattering light. I came to discover the exact nature of the poison before applying an antidote. Now I see we have a panacea. If," he added, turning directly to Rothgar, "there is no other malice."

"Be very careful," Rothgar said. "But on

this occasion, Ithorne, I believe we have a common interest."

"Only if Christian's interests are in accord with his wife's. She's done her best to avoid him."

"Because I will not be married to a stranger," she protested, stepping forward. "And here I am, without choice again." She turned on Christian, her eyes flashing with anger. "This is all your fault. You dragged me here with that ridiculous suspicion. You . . . you . . ."

"I what?" he demanded, deliberately adding, "Forced myself on you?"

She went pale, but the anger still burned. "Don't you realize what you've *done?* If I had any possibility of ending our marriage, this incident has shattered it. If we had no opportunity to consummate ten years ago, we clearly had one now!"

Christian stared, astonished and aroused by her magnificent fury.

"Was this your plan all along?" she swept on. "Did you know who I was and make sure to bind me?"

"Why on earth —"

But she'd already turned on Rothgar — Rothgar of all people. "You promised safety. Were you in league with him?"

"No," Rothgar replied.

"But you're so powerful! Omniscient, omnipotent." She was even sneering those words. "You must have known he'd be here, but you didn't warn me. You made no attempt. . . ."

Christian found he'd stepped to her side without thought. "Kat . . ."

She turned and pushed him. "Leave me alone!"

Rothgar raised a hand. "Peace. You have my apologies, Lady Grandiston, and I sincerely beg your pardon. I didn't know Grandiston would be here, but I should have guessed, because of his relationship to Ithorne. I brought you here to meet the king in an informal situation."

"Why?" she asked.

"I've discovered no likelihood that your marriage could be annulled, so I hoped to pave the way to His Majesty making some special arrangement. He is a devoted and faithful husband, but not immune to a pretty woman in distress, especially if virtuous."

He didn't have to say the obvious. A passionate encounter like the one interrupted would not count as virtuous even between a married couple, and it also exploded the idea of intolerable differences.

She put her hand to her face. Then she

seemed to notice her wedding ring for the first time. She twisted it off and hurled it in Christian's face. He put up a hand as shield and it bounced off to tinkle on one of the metal balls on the ground.

"What are those?" Thorn asked.

"Explosives," she spat. "Aren't you afraid? Just think, if there was a flame here, I could ignite them and kill us all!"

Calmly, Diana said, "I think they're glass pastry weights. The pomegranate came from the kitchen. I assume that's where they keep them."

"Pastry weights," Christian said, remembering as a boy watching the cook use beans to hold the pastry case down as it cooked. In grander houses, it seemed, they used glass marbles for the purpose.

"Having disposed of irrelevancies," said Rothgar coolly, "let us return to important matters. As I said, I had a Daedalian plan and was engineering a meeting when His Majesty demanded my attention on another matter. You disappeared, and by the time we'd tracked you down, it was too late. And thus," he said, "your hopes are dashed, and I can only beg your pardon."

She stood still, her flaming anger dead so that she seemed a pale shell.

Christian was thrown back to that room

in the Tup ten years ago. Even angry, he'd wanted to offer some comfort to the thin, pale girl. She wasn't a girl any longer, but he wanted to put his arm around her, support her, defend her.

Before he could move, she said, "I could still get the separation from bed and board, couldn't I?"

Rothgar studied her. "Only if you claim this encounter involved force. Then it might substantiate a claim of intolerable cruelty."

"There was force involved." She held out her wrist. "I have bruises. I ask you all to bear witness to them."

Damn it all to Hades, it was true.

Christian sat in Thorn's private parlor, a cloak gathered around him. He'd shed the armor, but that left him in a knee-length tunic. All Thorn had that would fit was this domino cloak of black satin. He was drinking, but Thorn wasn't refilling his glass as often as he'd like.

"We're a damned dismal couple," Christian said, indicating Thorn's black banyan robe with silver clasps.

"There are things to mourn. Your reputation, for example. If she pursues the separation and invokes force, it will not go well with you."

"A man can't force his wife."

"No one will claim it was a crime, but you'd probably be required to resign your commission in the Guards, perhaps in the army as a whole."

Christian rolled his head back to contemplate the plain ceiling. "I won't force her to cohabit." Inside, however, argument churned. If she was Kat . . .

She was not Kat.

Yet she was. He knew she was.

A lying, cheating jade, but better moments rose to torment him. The cat-rabbit of Hesse. The ride to Adwick, her close at his back, their conversation fluttering close to honesty. Had she truly not known he was her husband? Would she still have fled him if she'd known?

Yes. She wanted her freedom and still did, strongly enough to try to use what she had to know was a fundamentally dishonest accusation.

She probably wanted to marry someone else.

"I suggest you come to a private arrangement."

Christian straightened and tried to focus. "What?"

"Persuade her not to go to the courts. I can have documents drawn up that sever your connection just as effectively. She can return north. You can resume your military career. All is well."

It didn't feel well, but Christian didn't say so. "Except she wants her freedom to marry, and apparently I need to marry Psyche Jessingham's money. When Father was trying to persuade me to marry her, why didn't he tell me they truly needed more money? And what the hell has Tom been up to?"

"I have no idea. As for your father" — Thorn shrugged — "once you'd revealed that you were married, what point in revealing the true need? He's hardly the sort to heap coals of fire upon your guilty head. He's doubtless been praying that your wife is dead, however."

"I think even that degree of hardness is beyond him, but I'll have to break the bad news soon." Christian drained his glass and held it out. Thorn filled it. "I think I see how it is. In the past, with the limited income from Raisby all they could expect, my parents accepted limited futures for their children, cheerfully confident that sound values and hard work would do. Once they had the much larger income of Royland, however, their vision expanded. Substantial dowries for the girls, the Guards for me . . ."

He drank more wine. "I'm sure they

intended to live within their means, but perhaps they didn't grasp the cost of maintaining the properties, the expenses of coming to Town for court and Parliament and such. If Tom's run up debts, they'd pay them, too. Money's tight again, and there are all the youngsters still to provide for. They must have the same benefits as the older ones, so when Psyche places a bid for me, it seems heaven-sent. Now . . . ."

"You can break the entail."

"We'll have to so that we can sell some property, but that won't be enough." He grimaced. "I'm going to have to take over the management."

"Leave the army?"

Christian shrugged. "I get a quick four thousand for the commission, and it's damned boring these days anyway."

"You know nothing of estate management."

"You can teach me."

"With a stern demeanor and a whip, but will you be any more able to deny the younger ones the advantages the older have had?"

"One thing about ten years as a soldier, one learns to do what has to be done. The girls will have to have some sort of dowry, but it'll be modest. If the boys want the military, it'll be the navy, not the army. Or the engineers. No need to purchase a commission there. In the unlikely event any of them want the church, it should be possible to educate them and find a living. If not those options, I assume the earldom needs stewards and such. Or perhaps one or two will take the modern way and venture into industry and fill their own coffers."

"I could always marry one of your sisters," Thorn said. "Who's of marriageable age?"

Christian sat upright. "Struth, no."

Thorn stared.

"Nothing against you, but none of them would suit."

"I'm glad you're certain what would suit me."

"Dammit, don't pick a fight with me now. I won't have you sacrificed to the bounteous Hills."

"I might think it worth it."

"Thorn, you don't have to suffer to be part of the family. God knows why you haven't been visiting while I was away."

"No one invited me."

"No one thought you'd need an invitation."

Thorn dropped the subject. "Why do you feel the need to sacrifice yourself to the bounteous Hills?"

"Because they're my family."

"You don't think I might feel the same way?"

Christian rubbed a hand over his face. "I'm sorry, it's not the same. The family can pull together and sort this out."

"But you don't want to leave the army," Thorn protested.

Christian drank more wine. "There's a part of me that adores a blood-roaring battle, the steel-edged certainty of the moment, live or die. But I know the foulness of it, and some thrills are best denied." He put his empty glass aside and stood. "Will you act for me?"

"Persuade her to accept a private separation?"

"Yes. I'll meet with her, of course, if she wishes, and assure her that I have no desire to compel her into anything. But I don't want to impose myself upon her."

A lie. He wanted to force himself into her presence and plead his case, try to use his unworthy abilities to charm and seduce to win back his wife. But he'd always vowed to allow his wife to make the choice, and so he must.

"Just persuade her to avoid the courts," he told Thorn. "For her sake as much as mine."

# CHAPTER 29

Caro had been neatly slipped away from the ball and back to Malloren House in the care of one of Ithorne's senior maids. Diana and the marquess had remained to apply antidotes with a lavish hand. Caro was glad to have only a servant with her, to not have to attempt explanations and discussion yet. Her thoughts were so chaotic any attempt would have been nonsense.

Christian Grandiston — no, Christian Hill, Lord Grandiston — was the man she'd always thought of as Jack Hill, that slender, intense Galahad, rushing in to save her. Rushing to save ladies in distress seemed to be a fatal weakness for him.

Worse by far was the harsh reality that her husband was alive. All choice, all independence, had been torn from her. Lord Rothgar had agreed with her on that, sealing her fate.

A part of her wanted to laugh for joy that

Christian was her husband.

Most of her knew marriage to a rake would break her heart a thousand different ways. She'd marry Eyam now if it were possible. He, at least, would be safe.

Caro arrived at her room alone, for none of the servants had expected the family back so early. She'd have been happy for it to remain so, but Martha, the maid allocated to her here, came rushing in. She immediately saw the damage to the costume. Did she see the bruises blossoming on Caro's wrist?

"I had an accident. I fell. I have a terrible headache. I just need to rest."

"Yes, ma'am. Would you like a draft for the pain?"

If only there were such a thing, but Caro said, "Yes."

With the maid gone, she stripped off the costume and put on her nightgown with the long sleeves that hid her wrist. She began to unravel her hairstyle, but hadn't made much progress when Martha returned. Caro drank down the sickly-sweet brew with the bitterness of opium beneath. It would only postpone the pain, but she'd accept that sweet mercy.

Martha quickly took down her hair and braided it into a plait and then Caro crawled into bed and sank into oblivion.

When she opened her eyes to gray light and rain, the whole disaster came back to her, but she was, she thought, in a better state to face her future. She was glad, glad, glad, however, that the sun wasn't shining. This was assuredly a day for rain.

She sat up in bed but didn't ring for her maid. She wrapped her arms around her raised knees and tried to assemble facts.

She was married. It rang in her head like a tolling bell. Married, married, married, and thus subject to her husband's will. Perhaps that brief marriage settlement would safeguard something, but he owned nearly all she possessed and could do with it as he wished.

She'd felt his pain when she'd demanded witness of her bruises. Pain and anger, and in truth she'd been unfair. He'd hurt her, but at that point he'd thought her a wicked assassin. She would do anything, however, to escape the prison of this marriage.

Except that it appeared there was no true escape. Separation from bed and board did not mean she could marry again. She was condemned to eternal chastity, a particularly bitter fast when she'd feasted.

Her door began to open. She wished Martha hadn't come yet.

But it was Ellen's face that peered around the door. "Oh, you're awake at last. I rushed right over and I've been looking in every now and then. I didn't want to disturb your rest, but I knew you'd need me."

Ellen was in now and closing the door so Caro could hardly disagree. She glanced at the clock. Lud, it was nearly eleven.

Caro wished she could send Ellen away, but what was the point? If she was going to live in a nowhere place for the rest of her life, neither wife nor widow, she might as well keep Ellen as companion. At least one person would be happy.

Perhaps she'd support Lady Fowler's Fund.

Rakes had ruined her life.

"How are you, dear?" Ellen asked, true concern in her eyes.

"As well as can be expected. You've heard?"

"I heard at Lady Fowler's. We hear all such things. There are servants true to the cause."

Caro wondered just how much Ellen and Lady Fowler knew.

"Your husband truly is alive? And he's that terrible Grandiston man?"

Perhaps they didn't know too much, thank heavens.

"Yes."

"Oh dear, oh dear, oh dear. Poor Sir Eyam."

"Poor me, too."

"But he's the innocent party."

"I'd already dismissed him, Ellen. Last night didn't create that."

"But you only did that because you feared you couldn't wed. You know you're perfectly suited. Is there nothing to be done?"

"According to the marquess, no."

"Such a brute. You will have to . . . submit to him?"

Caro went hot. "No, I told you. The marquess said we can arrange to have what's called a separation *a mensa et thoro*. Which means we will live apart and he will have no power over me. But now, Ellen, please, could you tell my maid I want a bath and my breakfast?"

Ellen looked as if she'd like to continue bemoaning the situation, but she went, leaving Caro clinging to her declaration — *he will have no power over me* — but hollow inside. Beneath reason, like bad food churning, lay the memory of that room last night, and that flaring passion. Sooner or later it would make her truly, vilely miserable.

How had his anger, his belief that she could be evil, and her fury and terror over

510

that have raged into that mad passion, re-forging a bond she'd thought shattered and buried? A bond that lodged painfully in her chest, begging her to be weak, to bend, to surrender everything to him in return for scraps of his charm and bursts of wild, mindless pleasure.

She made herself face that truth. Mind-less lust. What had he said about her run-ning away in York? *You think I care about that? Our game was over and you left.*

Game. That was the truth of him, and she must never forget it. He took any woman who offered, as a dog will take a bone, and forgot them just as easily.

Oh, he helped and protected, and could be truly kind. She didn't think him vile. But he couldn't care deeply for any one woman and she couldn't entrust her heart and her property to a man like that. He'd charm her when it pleased him and neglect her when it suited. He'd spend her money on other women, and perhaps even game it away in a night.

She straightened, realizing something truly terrible.

He was a liar of the basest kind.

On that road to Adwick, he'd tried to persuade her to leave her supposed husband and be his mistress. But worse, he'd claimed that he'd woo her and wed her if he were able.

But he knew then that Dorcas Froggatt was alive, that he wasn't free to marry. He'd simply said whatever he thought would persuade her to break her marriage vows. She must remember that as armor against every trick he tried to play.

Martha came with a tray holding the chocolate pot, some bread, and some sliced fruit. "You're bath's ready, milady."

Milady. The news was around the servants' hall, too, was it? No point in hiding it, she supposed. There was a folded piece of paper on the tray. Caro picked it up and read it. It was from Diana to say that when she was ready, she should come to her boudoir.

That was an interview Caro didn't look forward to, but like everything else, it could not be avoided.

In half an hour, clean and dressed in a dark green gown that was the most sober one she owned, Caro went to Diana's private parlor.

Diana smiled at her as if it were just another day. "How are you, Caro?"

"Ready to face the lions."

"Sit, please. I'm sure it won't be quite so bad as that. Ithorne has requested an appointment."

"The duke? With me?" Caro couldn't imagine why.

"He and Grandiston are foster brothers. It's natural he'd ask Ithorne to act for him in this."

In her wildest dreams, she'd never imagined a duke would be her opponent. "Will they contest the separation?"

"I hope not, but we shall find out. May I send word that he can come to speak with you?"

Caro remembered the merry goatherd, but it would be the cool, formidable young man who'd challenged Rothgar that she'd face. "Of course. The sooner it's done, the better."

Diana wrote a letter, then rang a silver bell. When her maid came in, she gave her the letter and added, "Inform the marquess that I request his company, please."

Caro wanted to ask if that was necessary, for she'd much rather not face him, but of course it was.

She turned her mind to the one thing she might be able to control. "Will I be able to preserve my money?"

"Some, at least. Wait until Rothgar comes. Do you think Grandiston knows you are rich?"

Caro thought about it. "He knows about Froggatt and Skellow, but he may not know the extent of it."

"Good. Then we'll try for a fixed sum."

"I will have to give him something?"

"You are married. And," Diana added, "he did you a great service once."

The marquess came in and wished Caro a good morning as if he had some expectation that it might be.

Caro went straight to the point. "What do you think the duke will want, my lord?"

"The best for Grandiston. The question is, what do you want?"

*To regain my freedom of choice,* Caro could have said, but she was determined not to be petulant. "I want to be free of my husband's control, both of my person and my property. That woman implied that his family is in need. Is that true?"

Rothgar smiled slightly. "I'm glad your wits were working despite the situation. Yes. Psyche Jessingham is a widow who inherited a great deal of money from her elderly husband. She decided to use it to buy Grandiston, thinking it would be easy, given his family's need, and his family approved."

*"Buy . . . ,"* Caro said, but then masked her outrage. The bloodred widow wasn't the villain here. "So he planned to marry money,"

she said, as calmly as she could. "That means now he'll want as much of mine as he can get."

"One might assume so," the marquess said.

"He showed some true care for you last night," Diana said. "He attempted to shield you from view."

"It was his fault I needed shielding!"

"But, truly, at the end he looked as if he wished to wrap you in a cloak of protection."

Caro looked down at her hands, seeing for the first time the lack of her wedding ring. Where had that gone? It didn't matter. She'd never wear it again.

"He does have an inclination to protect," she admitted, "but he'd be likely to protect anyone. At my expense."

"This raises another matter," said the marquess, and the tone of it made Caro look up sharply. "I have thought all along that your attitude to Grandiston fit oddly with your story of a single encounter at your house in Sheffield. When, precisely, did he reveal to you this extreme inclination to protect?"

That assault took Caro unawares. "He . . . he charged in ten years ago to save a stranger."

Lord Rothgar merely raised his brows.

It was hopeless. She surrendered her story. Most of it, at least. She left out two passionate encounters, but had a sinking feeling they might guess.

"You were arrested?" Diana said. "Grandiston's rescue sounds positively heroic."

"It was impressive," Caro admitted. "He's probably an excellent soldier."

"The Silcocks interest me," the marquess said. "There have been other inquiries at Horse Guards about a Lieutenant Hill, made by a middle-aged couple, well dressed but the lady perhaps in ill health."

"That sounds like them," Caro said. "Asking about Hill? But they couldn't have known that the person who rescued me in Doncaster was Grandiston, never mind that his surname was Hill."

"How did Grandiston recognize you last night?" the marquess asked. "By your voice?"

Caro blinked at the change of subject. "No. I was disguising it. By a scar." She touched the ridge on her jaw.

He rose and came to look at it. "Ah, yes. Not easily seen at a distance, but quite distinctive. The most likely supposition is that Mistress Silcock was your teacher, Moore's sister, and that she, too, saw the scar in that inn in Doncaster."

"Miss Moore?" Caro gasped. "But that's fantastical."

"Is it? Something enraged the woman beyond reason. Recognizing a person connected to her brother's death might do that."

"But I was not to blame for it."

"No? People have a way of warping facts to suit themselves. You have doubtless become a young siren who tempted him to his doom. Don't forget, someone burned down your house in Sheffield. That indicates some powerful emotion. Now they are in London, seeking Hill, the person who struck the fatal blow."

"Christian!" It escaped before Caro could stop it.

The others didn't react, but in a very obvious way.

"I don't wish him dead," Caro said defiantly. "I simply don't want to be subjugated to him. And if Mistress Silcock is Moore's sister, why come now, after ten years?"

"Perhaps the tenth anniversary opened old wounds."

Caro thought about it. "The Silcocks did drive out somewhere. It could have been to Nether Greasley. But the wedding took place in winter. It's now September."

"Transport is difficult across the Atlantic in winter and there could have been other delays." Lord Rothgar considered the opposite wall. "Perhaps she only intended to visit the grave, but then her grief turned to anger. People find it surprisingly easy to twist past events to suit themselves. By now her brother may be the victim of injustice, murdered in cold blood. Then, quite by accident when the wound is newly raw, she sees that scar and realizes who you are — the wicked instrument of her brother's destruction."

"I was not!"

"Remember, this is in her mind. You are her enemy and she grasps the opportunity to make you suffer."

"I knew she was mad."

"Is there a resemblance?" Diana asked.

"To Mistress Moore?" Caro said, trying to take it all in. "I suppose it's possible, with ten years and ill health. The eyes, perhaps. But I was the injured party."

"As Rothgar said, the heart is not logical or determined on truth," Diana pointed out. "But as you said, Grandiston would be the chief target of her hate. Or, rather, Hill. How easy will it be for her to discover who he is now?" she asked her husband.

"She already knows. The inquiring couple

had the advantage of knowing the regiment and other details, so she received full information more quickly than we did. I have people searching for them, but they didn't give a name."

When Caro said, "He must be warned," she knew it would be misinterpreted, but said it anyway. "My concern means nothing about the marriage. I care enough to warn, but not to wife."

With a tap on the door a footman entered. "The Duke of Ithorne has arrived, my lord, my lady."

"Bring him up," Lord Rothgar said. Once the servant left, he glanced around the pretty room, which had Chinese wallpaper and flowered brocade upholstery. "We can hope a certain amount of frill and flowers will cool the manly heat."

When the duke entered, he already appeared cool, but in a formidable way. He'd come elegantly and formally dressed in brown velvet braided in gold, a sword at his hip. His heeled shoes had diamond buckles. His dark hair was powdered, or he wore a powdered wig. If a wig, it was so expertly made Caro couldn't tell.

He bowed with a completeness that created distance, every inch a high aristocrat. His portrayal of a goatherd, imperfect though it had been, had been a tour de force.

Once he was seated, upright and on guard, he said, "I come as Lord Grandiston's agent in order to make arrangements that will rouse as little social stir as possible, and which will be agreeable to Lady Grandiston."

Caro was profoundly unaccustomed to that title. Would she be obliged to use it all her life?

"Social stir will be unavoidable," Rothgar said, his manner equally formal. Caro remembered the taut atmosphere between the men last night and prayed there wasn't a new layer of trouble on her affairs.

"Of course," said the duke, "but time and a suitable story will waft it into oblivion."

*Oblivion?* Caro spoke. "Not for those living with the result, Your Grace."

He turned to her, his eyes without warmth. Foster brother, and he saw her as the cause of Christian's problems. She'd finally encountered Hill's family, she thought, wild laughter threatening, but in a form she'd never imagined.

"You wish a separation *a mensa et thoro,*" he stated.

Disastrous hesitation held her silent for a

moment, but then she got the word out. "Yes."

"Your husband is willing to grant you that of his free will, without need of courts."

That almost hurt. That he wouldn't fight. Caro turned to Lord Rothgar. "Will that have legal force?"

"Any documents will be as legally binding as can be, but I'm unaware of a prior instance, so we can't be sure what would happen if either of you attempt to overturn it later."

"I am hardly likely to."

"That might depend on the terms laid upon you. In time, they could become onerous."

Caro turned to the duke. "Terms, Your Grace?"

"None, ma'am."

"None? What of my property?"

"Your husband signed a document at your marriage waiving all claims. He will hold to that."

"Overgenerous," Rothgar said sharply. "Why? Guilty conscience?"

"Simply generous," the duke replied, the chill deepening.

"I agree, then," Caro said, anxious to prevent more discord. "How quickly can this be arranged?"

Ithorne turned to her, clearly disgusted at her enthusiasm. "As this is unusual, the lawyers need a few days to put together a document. Perhaps as much as a week."

"But what am I to do during that time?" Caro asked, turning mostly to Diana. "I'd rather not even be in London while my affairs are the latest gossip."

"Perhaps you would like to go down to Rothgar Towers for a few days," Diana said.

"Oh, yes, thank you."

But what then? Caro contemplated the bleak life that stretched ahead of her.

What would Yorkshire society make of a scandalous half marriage? Even if they accepted her back into the fold, where would she fit? A single woman was always an oddity, and one who could never marry had no place. At the same time, the title would distance her even more from her father's circles in Sheffield and even friends such as Phyllis. Was there a rule saying she had to use the title? Perhaps she could insist on being known as Mistress Hill.

And there would be no more lustful delights.

Her thoughts turned to Christian, to her husband. Last night had shown the passion was still there, on both sides, but there had to be more than passion. She didn't know him, this soldier, this viscount, this heir to an earldom, for heaven's sake. She trusted him to stay away from her now he'd promised to do so. She didn't trust herself if she allowed him back into her life.

Laws and documents were all very well, but there were many stories of wives forced or seduced into surrendering all the rights they held. If there were children, they were always, as someone had once written, hostages to fortune. In a separated couple, the husband was generally given complete control of any children. . . .

"Caro."

Diana was trying to attract her attention.

"I'm sorry."

"We're to build on the story already told in Yorkshire," Diana said. "Your romantic elopement, your husband's departure for war, the report of his death. We'll pass over everything else to come to your dramatic recognition of each other last night. The details were wrongly reported, but the discovery was a shock. You were arguing when interrupted. You have, alas, discovered that in ten years you have grown apart so completely that you cannot stand each other. Thus, you separate. Do you agree?"

Caro felt she should point out just how far their situation had been from an argument, but lacked the courage. "Yes, of course. Thank you. You're all being very kind."

She included the duke, though he didn't look kind at all.

He rose. "Your husband asked me to tell you, ma'am, that he is willing to meet with you if you need any personal assurances from him."

"No," Caro said quickly, meaning she didn't need the latter. She saw him take the rapid response as a complete rejection. His lean features hardened.

"He will do his best not to discomfort you with his presence in future." He bowed formally again and left.

"I suppose that went well," Diana said. "Shall I ring for tea?"

*Well?* Caro wanted to scream.

Then she shot to her feet. "We didn't tell the duke about the Silcocks. Grandiston must be warned."

"His death would simplify your future," the marquess pointed out.

"What? No!"

He smiled slightly. "Very well. I will correct the omission." He left the room.

"Why," asked Caro, "do I feel as if I'm in a play?"

"All the world's a stage," Diana said. "We

can only try to make sure that it's a comedy and not a tragedy. Will you want Ellen to go to the country with you?"

No one seemed to understand that this already was a tragedy. Caro sat down again. "Why not?" she said. "If she wants to come."

# CHAPTER 30

Christian left Horse Guards blistered by his commanding officer's opinion of the whole mess, but with leave to go to Devon to explain all to his family. From frying pan to fire indeed, though he expected his greatest problem at Royle Chart would be explaining the absence of his wife.

He went to Thorn's house to receive a report. The place was in a chaos of dismantling and bitter memories.

"Why is she so angry with me?" he demanded.

"She has to be angry at someone, and you triggered the situation."

"I triggered a damned disaster. I truly thought she might be there to kill the king. All I knew was that she lied and lied and lied again, and then turned up where she shouldn't be."

"What's done is done, but we need to talk about the Silcock couple."

An enemy to fight. "Yes, indeed."

"Rothgar knows of them."

"They're in his pay?"

"No. Keep your wits. He pursued your wife's cause by probing for the connection between you and Jack Hill. In the process he crossed paths with a couple making similar inquiries. I was told to warn you that they might plan to harm you."

"Not Kat . . . Caro? But then why burn down her house?"

"Passing spite, I assume. You killed Moore. Be careful."

Christian wanted to say that the Silcocks were no danger to him, but he knew better. There were underhanded ways to kill. "If I'm not immediately needed for legal matters, I need to go home for a day or two."

"I don't suppose I can persuade you to travel in my coach with outriders."

Christian just raised a brow.

Thorn sighed. "I can't compel you. I'll keep close watch on the Americans, but . . . at least stay here overnight."

"Amid all the wreckage?"

"There are still some orderly areas. Agree, damn you. You're turning me gray."

"Very well." Christian grimaced. "Watch over her, too, Thorn. My wife. They'll harm her if they can."

"Rothgar has that in hand."

"I don't trust him. You take care of her, too."

Caro wanted to hide in her room, probably under the bed, but she knew every eye in the house was on her, so she tried to pretend all was well. Unfortunately, Ellen didn't help. She'd insisted on moving back to support Caro, but seemed to see anything less than prostrated collapse as unwomanly and even immoral.

Diana kept them both busy with paperwork to do with her charities. Those to do with aid for prostitutes and bastard children had Ellen clucking her disapproval. For her there were the worthy poor and the unworthy, and anything short of sackcloth and ashes placed a sinner in the unworthy fold. How she allocated blame to children, Caro had never understood.

The hours were useful in one way to Caro — it gave her time to realize that no matter what her future, she couldn't bear Ellen Spencer any longer.

A few people attempted to call but were denied. A stream of missives arrived. Diana glanced at each, then had her secretary send rote replies. Caro didn't know if any were addressed to her, but she was glad not to have to deal with them. She felt as if she were in a beleaguered fortress.

She expected to be embarrassed by more of Ellen's criticisms of her hosts, but at least she was spared that. When Ellen received a note at two o'clock and excused herself to go to Lady Fowler's for dinner, Caro sighed with relief.

"She'll have someone who shares her outrages," she said wryly to Diana.

"And we'll be free of her disapproval."

"I'm so sorry."

"No matter. Let's take our dinner quietly. Rothgar's still out, doubtless applying more antidotes."

Perhaps it was Ellen's absence, but the meal was surprisingly relaxed. Caro and Diana even found topics that were mildly amusing. When Lord Rothgar came home, however, he and Diana went off in private and Caro's spirits sank back into gloom. She was in a bad enough state to be glad to see Ellen when she returned, even though she expected to hear Lady Fowler's vinegarish opinions on recent events.

But Ellen had her governess face on. "Caro."

"Yes?"

"I think you should speak to Lord Grandiston before you leave Town."

"What? I think not."

"So recalcitrant. Only consider — he is your husband, and he is waiving his rights. Don't you owe him simple thanks?"

"Is this Lady Fowler's advice? I'm astonished."

"It's the right thing to do."

"I'll write, then," Caro promised.

"You know that's not as it should be."

"Ellen, it would be horribly embarrassing to meet with him, especially now. Perhaps later. Much later."

"I really must insist."

Caro held on to her temper. "You aren't my governess anymore."

Ellen's lips pursed in a way that might be a struggle with tears. "But I thought you still valued my judgment."

Oh, lud! Caro gave in. "Only if you remain with me whilst he's here."

"I would not consider anything else," Ellen said.

"We are husband and wife."

"But he's a brute." Caro was about to protest that illogicality, but Ellen rose. "Send the invitation and I will arrange the refreshments. You won't want to inconvenience Lady Rothgar's household."

Providing light refreshment would hardly strain the great house, and Caro doubted the encounter would extend to tea drinking, but she had no heart for a fight over trivialities. She was both alarmed and desirous at the thought of one more meeting.

She should really ask Diana's permission for the invitation, but she couldn't possibly intrude, and, she admitted, she was afraid Diana or Lord Rothgar would forbid it. She'd see Christian in one of the reception rooms, which were not part of the private household.

Composing the simple note was torture. She'd written to him only once before — that hasty letter in York. In the end, she made it formal and terse; then having no idea whether it would be appropriate to send it to Horse Guards, she had it taken to the Duke of Ithorne's house.

She'd set the appointment for an hour hence. Perhaps he wouldn't receive it in time. She could hardly bear that thought. She couldn't give him a husband's power over her, but she dearly, deeply wanted to see him just once more.

Diana reappeared and had to be told. To Caro's relief, she approved.

"Very wise," Diana said. "I misjudged your companion."

"Why?"

"I thought she'd buckle on a sword to

keep you and Grandiston apart."

"Lady Fowler doubtless recommended it, but heaven knows why. Ellen's insisting on organizing tea. I hope she's not upsetting your people."

"I gather she's making some special cakes, but I'm sure the kitchen will survive."

Caro winced. "I'm sorry. I —" In the distance, the knocker rapped. A glance at the clock showed it wasn't yet time, but she knew she'd given away her feelings.

"Come for a walk in the garden," Diana said. "The weather's cleared a little and you've been cooped up all day." Cloaks were ordered. "As for the kitchens," Diana said as they waited, "it's no great matter and perhaps makes Mistress Spencer feel particularly useful."

Diana's cloak was of rich blue wool and didn't quite meet at the front anymore. Caro put on her own rust-colored one, and they went out through the back of the house. The day was overcast, but Diana was right. Fresh air felt calming.

"She's quite an eccentric, isn't she?" Diana said, as they followed a paved path lined with low-growing shrubs.

"Ellen? I never thought so, other than having very limited views of a woman's place in the world. She never approved of things like masquerades and most plays, but it was Lady Fowler's regular letters that made her odd."

"How did that happen? I thought the Fowl Flock was a London phenomenon."

Caro chuckled. "Is that what you call it? I do imagine them clucking."

"They do more than cluck sometimes. One hurled a pot of paint on the stage at the King's Theatre at an actress she considered immodest. Biblical quotations were scrawled on Madam Cornelys's establishment in Soho, probably because she hosts masquerades."

"They were outside the Revels last night, weren't they?" Caro paused to admire a small tree with blue flowers. "I can't imagine Ellen doing anything like that, but I've been thinking that if I provide enough for her to have rooms in London, she might like to devote herself to the cause in more-peaceful ways. Writing letters, and such. I gather there's quite a scriptorium there, turning out the letters to people all around the world."

"So much energy and efficiency to so little purpose," Diana said.

"You don't think reform is necessary?"

"Oh, probably, but our present king is saintly compared to his grandfather. Court could almost be designed by Lady Fowler herself. But of course that simply means that amusements have moved elsewhere."

Caro was wondering what time it was. She paused at a sundial, but if it told time at all, it needed sun, and today was overcast.

"Perhaps we should return to the house," she said.

Diana's lips twitched, but she didn't object. "Was her husband virtuous?" she asked."

"Ellen's? He was a clergyman."

"The two don't necessarily go together. Only think of Reverend Pruitt."

Caro laughed, for that vicar was notoriously attentive to neglected wives. "I suppose not, but at least he's unmarried. Why do you ask?"

"Because it's been my observation that the most devoted members of the Fowl Flock are those betrayed by wicked men, or wives of lecherous husbands."

Caro considered what she knew about Ellen's marriage and realized it was very little. "I don't know, other than that her marriage bed was a not intolerable duty."

Diana stared, her eyes bright with laughter. "Oh, dear. Poor woman."

"I suppose many women feel the same," Caro said as they approached the glass doors into the house. She realized that she'd like to discuss such intimate matters with Diana, but then, what was the point? That part of life was over for her. She could imagine gnawing the doorjamb.

The hall clock said five minutes to four. Diana paused at the bottom of the stairs. "Would you like me to stay with you?"

"I'll have Ellen. Anything more and he might think me afraid of him."

"He certainly won't harm you here. That would be insanity."

"I know. I mean, I'm sure he wouldn't anyway."

Diana nodded and went upstairs.

Caro surrendered her cloak to a maid and checked her appearance in a mirror. She wanted to go to her room and fuss over it, but she wouldn't. In any case, Christian had seen her in far worse state than this.

And nearly naked, too.

She hurried into the small reception room she'd chosen for this. It was elegant and pleasantly warmed by a fire, but close to the front door, so not part of the house proper. Ellen was already there, neat as a pin, with everything except the teapot spread on a small table with three chairs around it.

Caro would have preferred the greater distance of settee and chairs, but a clock chimed, telling her there was no time to alter anything. The china was fine, and a plate held about a dozen small yellow cakes with some kind of icing.

"It looks lovely, Ellen. Thank you."

Someone firmly applied the door knocker.

Caro heard voices in the hall.

She began to sweat.

Christian came in. He halted, but then bowed very formally.

Caro curtsied a little too deep. She had no idea what Ellen did except that vaguely in the distance she was ordering the tea brought up.

She should have chosen a larger room. This one was the same size as the parlor in Froggatt Lane and he was looming again. He couldn't help it, but it would upset Ellen. His presence pressed on Caro in quite another way. Everything about him filled the room and her senses.

"My lord," Caro said, her voice too high. "Please be seated."

"My lady. Mistress Spencer." He bowed again and waited until they were seated before taking the vacant chair between them. Caro's hands were clasped in her lap, and poor Ellen had obviously strained all her instincts in recommending this meeting.

Her lips were tight and she seemed a little pale.

Caro launched into a prepared statement of her gratitude for his understanding. He replied that it was simple justice and he wished her well.

It might have ended there, and perhaps should have done, but the footman carried in the tray with a china teapot and water jug, and arranged things on the table. Caro supposed she should be the one to serve, and did so, wondering if he'd take it amiss if she gave him freedom to leave.

Foolish though it was, she wanted him to stay a little longer. There were other things to say — simpler ones to do with their better moments, and perhaps indirectly about the intimate ones. But Ellen kept her silent.

As she passed him a cup, their eyes met and she thought she saw a similar desire. Their fingers brushed. When she offered the cakes, her hand trembled. He took one. So did she. So did Ellen.

Someone had to say something. "I'll be traveling to Rothgar Towers tomorrow. A few days away will be pleasant. Do you stay in Town, my lord?" She picked up her cake.

"No. I intend to visit my family in Devon." He did the same.

"That will be nice."

"I doubt it."

That came too close to the personal. Caro took a bite of cake. Her nose warned her before her teeth sank in. Caraway seeds. She disliked them. She turned her bite into the tiniest nibble, seeking another subject.

She wanted to ask about Lady Jessingham.

"How did you get from York to London?" he asked, cake uneaten in his hand.

It astonished her that he did not know. "I was going to my lawyer, but he wasn't there. The whole firm had traveled to a wedding. I was at a loss, but I encountered the marquess resting there on his journey south. He brought me here."

"A Kat with nine lives," he said with a wry smile.

"Do try the cake," Ellen said. "It's a special recipe." She took a bite of her own.

He smiled and raised it to his mouth. And something clicked in Caro's mind.

Ellen knew she didn't like caraway.

Ellen was watching Christian.

It was ridiculous. . . .

But Caro said, "Don't eat that!" and reached to grab it. "You don't like caraway any more than I do."

He began to speak, but then put the cake down, obviously understanding her unspoken meaning. "You remembered. How touching. My apologies, Mistress Spencer. Caraway makes me ill."

Ellen put down her own cake. "Caro," she said, "you are beyond all hope."

She might mean Caro's strange behavior. It had to be so. Ellen was an even less likely assassin than she was. Christian picked up his cake again, but he wrapped it in his table napkin and put it in a pocket.

"Why did you do that?" Ellen asked sharply.

"I think I'll have it tested."

"Tested? For what?" But her voice had turned shrill.

"What might I find, Mistress Spencer?" He spoke calmly, but he might well have been a judge.

Ellen's lips quivered, but she firmed them, saying nothing.

Caro wanted to interrupt the silence, but she knew she mustn't.

Ellen broke at last. "Foxglove," she said defiantly, "of a particularly potent kind. You, sir, have ruined the lives of a good man and a woman more sinned against than sinning." She turned on Caro. "Why did you interfere? With him dead, everything could have been as it should be!"

"Ellen, what are you saying? What good man? Major Grandiston is the hero. He rescued me from a vile man."

"He murdered Moore in cold blood!"

"You know that's not true."

"I know you're deluded. Snared by carnal desires. I saw the way you just looked at him. I heard what happened at that indecent revel. He's a brute who'll make you miserable all your days, but you're too besotted to see it!"

"Ellen, you just tried to *murder* someone. What sin is worse than that?"

"I tried to *save* you, save Eyam, save all of us!" But her eyes were darting now. "Oh dear, oh dear. Will they hang me? Oh, no." She grabbed a cake off the plate and shoved it whole into her mouth.

Caro dashed around the table, forced Ellen over the back of an upholstered chair, and thumped her back. The cake flew out, almost complete.

Heaving for breath, Caro straightened to see Christian looking at her.

He shook his head. "Life with you, Lady Grandiston, is never tedious. What now?"

"Lord knows!" Caro put an arm around the weeping Ellen and helped her into the chair. "Summon Diana. I don't know. . . ." She abandoned the attempt to make sense.

Ellen had tried to commit murder.

Christian could have died!

Foxglove was a poison. It was used as a medicine as well, but it could easily kill, especially some types. Where had Ellen found it? Was it sold in apothecary shops?

Diana came quickly, Rothgar with her.

Ellen shrank back. "Caro, don't let them hang me!"

"No, of course not." But Caro had no idea what to do and she felt dizzy.

Then Christian was at her side, guiding her to the settee. He didn't sit beside her, but he stood behind. She felt his support like the shawl he'd once found for her, and wished she could be in his arms.

Diana sat beside Caro and addressed Ellen. "No one will hang, Mistress Spencer. Perhaps no one need know anything about this. But you must tell us why you attempted to kill Lord Grandiston."

Ellen shook her head.

Caro leaned forward. "I know this wasn't your idea, Ellen. Was it Lady Fowler?"

Ellen started at that. "No, no! I'm sure she would never . . ." She struggled for a moment and then said, "It was Janet Silcock."

Caro exclaimed, "*Silcock?* How do you know her?"

Christian said, "Thorn discovered she was attached to the Fowler woman. We didn't

541

think anything of it because we didn't know your companion was of the same cabal."

"Tell us everything," Caro demanded.

Ellen sniffed into her handkerchief again. "Janet and I became acquainted through Lady Fowler's Fund. We corresponded."

"I don't remember letters from America," Caro said.

"They came enclosed from Lady Fowler. Lady Fowler said that Janet had requested to be in correspondence with other women in the north of England. In fact, Janet recommended me as likely to support the cause."

Caro looked at Diana. Was she, too, seeing a long plot?

"And when you came to London," Caro said to Ellen, "you found Mistress Silcock also here?"

"Yes. So sad that she's ill and seeking treatment, but a most interesting woman. She has sound ideas about the evils of society and the way they harm women." Perhaps she recollected what had just happened, for she faltered and went silent. Some coals shifted in the grate, sending flames and sparks, and a puff of smoke.

"What happened today?" Diana asked.

Ellen shot her a frightened glance. "When I arrived at Lady Fowler's, I received a message from Janet asking me to visit her at her residence. That's in the City. I knew she'd understand all my feelings about last night's events and my distress about poor Caro and Sir Eyam."

"Sir Eyam," said Christian. "That was the man you eloped with."

"I did not!" Caro protested.

"Not you, her."

"Ellen?"

"I did not!" Ellen exclaimed.

"Silence," said Rothgar from where he'd been quietly listening. "Pray continue, Mistress Spencer. What did Mistress Silcock suggest?"

If Ellen looked faint with fright, it wasn't surprising. "She . . . she agreed that it wasn't right. That it was all Mr. Grandiston's fault. I mean Lord Grandiston . . . Major Lord Grandiston . . . oh, dear. . . ."

Caro went over to pat her shoulder. "Just tell us what happened, Ellen, and why you came to do what you did."

Ellen fixed her eyes on her. "She agreed that it was wrong that any woman be imprisoned with a brute, especially when she'd been forced into it when a child. But the law offers no recourse because it is designed only for the interests of men."

Christian muttered something.

"Then she suggested how it could be made right. It *seemed* right when she explained it! No woman should be so confined."

"You yourself advised submission to the will of God," Caro pointed out.

"This was the will of Abigail Froggatt! Janet showed me that sometimes we must act violently in the cause of justice." Though Caro could see the courage it took, Ellen looked across at Lord Rothgar. "You killed a man in a duel in a similar cause, my lord."

"So I did," he agreed.

"And you in war," she said to Christian.

"A point," he said, "but not sneakily by poison."

"We women are weak and must use what weapons we have," Ellen said, but looking down at her soggy handkerchief. "Janet gave me the foxglove and told me how to include it in the cakes." She looked up at Caro. "I put the seeds in to be sure you didn't eat any. Why did you have to interfere!"

Caro shook her head and looked around. "What do we do now?"

"Where do the Silcocks lodge?" Rothgar asked Ellen.

Ellen pursed her lips, clearly ready to be a martyr in the cause.

"Ithorne knows," Christian said. "If I'm

not needed here, I'll go to him."

He didn't address Caro directly, but she said, "Yes, please. Heaven knows what the madwoman will try next."

He left, and she felt his absence.

Ellen protested, "You can't put her on trial or I'll be dragged into court, too!"

"You *did* try to kill someone," Caro pointed out again.

"I tried to free *you.* You have to take care of me."

"You were also trying to secure the future you wanted for yourself," Caro said. "Ellen, for heaven's sake, how did you think it would go if you'd succeeded?"

"Janet said Lord Rothgar would conceal the crime. That's what the great lords do all the time."

Caro sighed and abandoned it. "Come, Ellen, you need to lie down in your room."

Once she had Ellen there, she promised her again that she'd try to keep her out of court. Then she locked the door and asked Martha to sit nearby so she'd hear if Ellen called out for anything.

She found Diana alone in her boudoir. Diana said, "Rothgar's gone to Ithorne to join forces. The Silcocks have no chance."

"No," Caro said, collapsing into a chair, "but I feel a little sorry for her. I assume she loved her brother. . . ."

"She contrived that whole elopement to try to seize your fortune," Diana pointed out.

"Even so, her only brother died and she was forced to flee the country. My aunt was not a forgiving woman. Ten years ago, though. It's as if tendrils have grown out of Moore's grave to attempt to strangle us all."

"It's all over now," Diana said.

"I hope so, but as Ellen said, if Janet Silcock is charged with a crime, Ellen will be, too. She deserves it, but I want to prevent that."

"Rothgar understands that," Diana said. "They'll find a way. I very much doubt Ellen Spencer is likely to attempt murder on her own. Do you agree?"

"I think so. Self-righteous people can be dangerous, though."

"True." Diana smiled. "I think Lady Fowler should pay for her part in all this."

"You think she knew of it?"

"Oh, no. But sometimes our plans have unintended consequences. They are still consequences and we should take responsibility. I think I shall arrange that Lady Fowler take Ellen under her wing and keep her very busy with harmless work in the cause of reforming society."

"That might work."

"Which leaves only your marriage, I think."

Caro eyed Diana. "I still want my separation."

"But Mistress Spencer's idea was sound. You should speak to Grandiston before leaving Town."

"We did speak."

"Interrupted by poison. May I invite him to call again tomorrow morning?"

Caro pulled a face at her friend. "The threat to his life weakens me, and you know it. But I won't be a fool. He's a wonderful man in many ways, but he's an inveterate rake who was making me promises of marriage when he knew he had a wife already."

"But —"

"I can't trust a man like that, Diana," Caro insisted, knowing she was arguing as much with herself as her friend. "I'll see him, but it will merely be a gentler farewell."

Lord Rothgar returned later with an account of affairs. "Janet Silcock is dead. She seems to have taken poison not long after Mistress Spencer left her. By her doctor's account she was very ill and in pain, and taking a lot of laudanum. Perhaps that affected her mind, but avenging her brother had become an obsession.

"I believe her husband is mostly innocent of anything but loving his wife. He never doubted the essentials of her version of the story and agreed that her brother's murderer should suffer in some way. However, his intent here in England was to look into the circumstances and see if charges could be laid. He had no idea that his wife had recognized the thief in Doncaster as her brother's bride. He thought her outraged by the attempted theft and was accustomed to her overreactions.

"He confesses to burning down the house in Sheffield. According to him, his wife was in such distress and so insistent that he did it, hoping it would satisfy her. It was a mean house in his opinion, and he'd already discovered that no one but servants lived there. He made sure they got out. A crime," Rothgar said, "but hardly worth the prosecution unless you insist, Caro."

"No, as you say, it's not worth the cost or effort, and the poor man must be grieving. Janet Moore was not an evil person, as best I remember. Perhaps we can put her recent action down to sickness and laudanum."

Rothgar nodded. "Silcock claims to know nothing about the poison, and I believe him, but his wife was skilled in the stillroom. He was away from the house all day on business. I suspect he's actually involved with those Americans trying to change the tax burden they see as unfair, but as long as he commits no crime there, I have no quarrel with him."

Caro sighed. "As I said, a seed sown in a grave ten years ago, which grew unobserved but bore poisoned fruit. Janet Moore was wrong to try to marry me off to her brother, but if he'd been half the man I imagined he was, the events at the Tup's Byre would never have happened. I'd have married him and thought myself blessed. For a while, at least. If there was a true villain of the piece, it was Moore."

"And he, we hope," said Rothgar, "is roasting as he deserves."

# CHAPTER 31

Caro organized her packing for the stay at Rothgar Towers, but her mind wouldn't leave Christian.

What if . . . ?

No.

If only . . .

No.

But without Ellen she was alone in the world. She had friends, including Diana and Phyllis, but they had their own full lives and she had a hollow shell.

She was increasingly aware of a temptation to fill that shell by making her marriage to Christian a true one, but she feared that would be to live on crusts.

She hadn't been able to resist reading the newspapers and had even sent Martha to find some scandal sheets. The rumors swirling about the events at the Revels were mortifying, but they triggered other revelations.

Christian was clearly a rake of the sort who didn't even try to hide his sins. There was mention of Lady J——ham, whose hopes had been dashed, but who had probably been Lord G——ston's mistress. The said lady had certainly been mistress to a Most Noble Duke. Did that mean Christian and Ithorne had *shared* her? One scurrilous cartoon suggested that. There was speculation about an actress called Betty Prickett and another called Mol Madson.

She was almost ready to join the Fowl Flock!

She slept badly and woke determined to cancel the appointment for fear of weakening, but she was already too weak to do that. Nothing could happen, after all. This wasn't an inn, and she wasn't under an assumed name.

But when she was told that Christian had arrived, she went to Diana. "Will you come down with me?"

"No."

"Don't I need a chaperone?"

"With your husband?"

Caro glared and tried to resist, but helplessly, she rushed toward the flames.

When she entered the room, Christian was looking outside. He turned sharply from the window and their eyes met.

Caro took refuge in formality. "Please be seated, my lord."

She sat on one chair, but he picked up a basket and brought it over. A gift?

"I thought I should return the cat."

"Tabby?" Caro felt suddenly hollow. This was a parting gift, a clearing of obligations. Why had she even imagined he might want to make their marriage a reality? He was a dedicated bachelor.

"Thorn thinks 'Tabitha' is more dignified." He removed the covering cloth. "For a mother."

"Oh," said Caro. "The kittens!"

Tabby looked up. *Ah-ee-ooh.*

Caro had to laugh. "And I've missed you, too." She smiled up, to see Christian glowering.

He met her eyes and laughed. "Would you believe she's said not a word to me since you left?"

"Oh. That was unfair." But Caro was fighting the giggles. This wasn't how the interview was supposed to go. Another clever, rakish trick?

She looked down at the cat again. "What lovely babies. But" — she glanced at Christian — "only two?"

"There were a few more, but born dead."

"Poor Tabby, but the two are charming." She peered closer. "Does one have a tail?"

"It seems one might be all cat," he said, taking a nearby chair. "Various scientists have visited and inspected at Ithorne's house. There's much debate about the possibility of a union of cat and rabbit, but at least one believes Tabitha is a cat-rabbit."

"Are you trying to tell me there are fanged rabbits in Hesse?"

His lips twitched. "I doubt it. But similar cats are apparently known in Cornwall and the Isle of Man."

Caro turned Tabby's scowling face up to her. "I wonder how you ended up adrift in Yorkshire."

*Ay-ah-oh.*

"Perhaps truly sent to travelers in need?" he said.

Caro gathered herself and posed a serious question. "If I'd revealed myself in Froggatt Lane, what would you have done?"

"I'm not sure, but you would have been a very pleasant surprise."

There was perhaps just a hint of a rakish twinkle in his eyes. Caro looked back at the kittens, but they didn't help her regain control and distance.

"Would you have compelled me to live with you?"

"How? Keep you in a locked room for the rest of your life? I always meant to let my wife choose how to manage our strange arrangement, as long as it posed no legal hazard to me or my family."

Caro considered him, but she saw truthfulness. "Does that still hold?"

"You know it does. If it's your wish, I'll sign the documents giving you as much freedom as possible. But first, I think we should become better acquainted."

She narrowed her eyes at him. "Why?"

"We're married, apparently until death do us part. We also, I think, found aspects of each other pleasing. Is it not worth seeing how broad those aspects are?"

"You're a handsome man and skilled in bed," she said.

She expected anger, but if any stirred, he hid it. "Not to be ignored, of course, but I believe I have other virtues."

Caro looked down again, hoping to conceal the war raging inside her. He wanted to be truly married to her, and that was a powerful force. In addition, she was assailed by temptation and lust. Add to that the bleak future she envisioned for herself and she was ready to crumble.

He was the only husband she could have unless he died, and she couldn't bear that thought. Perhaps the crumbs, such rich and generous crumbs, would be enough, and the pain of his wanderings not too unbearable, especially if she had children.

But her defenses rose again.

He needed money. Had he learned of her fortune and come here to try to gain it?

"You know I'm rich?" she asked.

Now she did see anger, in a tightening of his lips and jaw, but he answered steadily. "Yes, but not the extent of it."

"That paper you signed at the wedding doesn't cover anything acquired by me after the ceremony."

"I'll sign anything else you want. I am not here because of your money, dammit."

"Don't swear at me."

He stood, hands clenched, and turned away. But then he turned back to her. "Our time together, though intense, was short. That's why we need to become better acquainted now."

"What sort of acquaintance did you have in mind?" Something sparked in his eyes and she quickly added, "Nothing physical."

The spark didn't die. "Not yet, at least. I am asking that we spend time together without the barriers of disguises or deceits."

Caro wanted that so much, but she made sure to speak coolly. "If I consider this, it will only be out of dislike of the alternative."

His brows rose. "That being?"

"A very peculiar life."

"And you always wanted a very ordinary one." He grimaced slightly. "Caro, I can't promise you that."

A foolish bud of hope withered. "Why not?"

He spread his hands. "I'm heir to an earldom. I'm foster brother to a duke."

"You mean I'm too lowborn for you?"

*Ah-ee-wow-ooh!*

"For once the damn cat speaks sense. I mean that I'm not ordinary, and can't offer you the sort of life you once had. As well, my life is in the south. Your roots are in the north."

She raised her chin. "We could live in the north."

"I have responsibilities here."

"And I have responsibilities in the north."

*Ah-ee-ah-o.*

"The cat knows better."

"Be quiet," Caro snapped at Tabby, then rolled her eyes.

But the truth was, she didn't have responsibilities in Yorkshire. The sale of the business was in hand. Luttrell House wasn't an estate, needing management. There were her charities, but they only truly required her money.

"If you do need to spend considerable time in Yorkshire," he said, "so be it. I'd travel north with you as often as I could. But my home — our home — would be in Devon."

"Devon?"

This discussion was sliding rapidly toward possibilities and probabilities before Caro was ready for that.

Before she could think how to apply the brakes, he said, "My family home. My family aren't ordinary, either, and you would be spending a great deal of time with them."

Caro wrinkled her brow at this. "The mother who keeps bees and has strange ideas about cats?"

*Ow-ee-a?*

"Exactly," he said. "You could discuss strange cats with her."

"With your mother? She's in London?"

"No, but I have to travel to Royle Chart, my father's house in Devon."

"The simple manor house?" she asked with a touch of acid.

"I didn't lie. That was my early home. My father only inherited the earldom recently."

"Perhaps you didn't lie, but you concealed the truth. Why?"

His lips tightened. "Commanding men in the army hones an instinct for truth and lies. You were lying about almost everything — don't deny it — which didn't incline me to be honest with you. But also, the whole idea is still strange to me. I returned to England after years away, to learn I was no longer Major Hill, but Major Lord Grandiston. Instead of a future of my own deciding, I would end up, willy-nilly, as Earl of Royland with estates to manage and a seat in Parliament. Instead of traveling north to Raisby Manor in Oxfordshire, where I'd been born and lived until ten, I had to turn west into Devon to a place I'd never known. I suppose," he said, "I found being a simple man again comforting."

Caro considered sleeping kittens who didn't have a care beyond milk, lucky things. She looked up at him. "We are not so different, are we? We've both had our freedom wrenched from us."

"So we have. Come to Royle Chart with me, Caro."

A shiver went down her spine. "Why?"

"To spend time together."

"You're trying to rush me into commitment."

"On my honor, I'm not. But I must go there before the gossip reaches them."

Another journey together, and hope. "How would we present ourselves to them?" she asked.

"Perhaps by the time we arrive, we'll know."

She looked into his distinctive eyes. "And if we arrive knowing that we cannot live together?"

"Then we'll tell them that. At least if it comes from you as well as me, they might believe it. Whatever you decide, you'll like my mother. Everyone does. But I warn you, the place is a madhouse. Did I tell you I have twelve brothers and sisters?"

*"Twelve?"*

"And most of them are boys."

"Lud! I know enough of the species from the orphanages to know what that means." She weighed her words. "Why did you say 'whatever I decide'? It is for both of us."

"No," he said. "I know what I want."

"And what is that?"

"Don't be foolish, Kat."

"You pledged yourself to me once before, when you knew it wasn't possible."

He frowned. "When?"

"On the road to Adwick."

"Oh." He pulled a face. "Believe it or not, I forgot I was married. It was new to me. I meant what I said."

Now was the time to ask if he'd be a faithful husband, but Caro wasn't sure she'd reject him if he said no. There was so much about him that she liked, and her alternative was so bleak. Whom was she trying to deceive with logic? She was in danger of throwing her heart over the moon.

He came to her, taking something from his pocket. "You'll have to wear this, I think."

It was her wedding ring.

He made no attempt to put it on her finger and she was grateful. It had nothing really to do with them. It was not the ring he'd put on her finger at their wedding.

She took it, but uneasily. "There are two conditions."

"Yes?"

She looked at him. "On the journey, we do not so much as kiss."

"Agreed," he said, but added with a smile, "even if you want to."

Impudent rascal.

She slid the ring back into its familiar place. "And we travel by coach."

# CHAPTER 32

It took five days to travel to Royle Chart, and they were days to test any marriage.

Rothgar and Diana had not seemed shocked at the plan. They had, however, insisted that Caro take Martha. Caro knew she should have expected this, but the presence of the middle-aged maid had been limiting. She and Christian had been able only to talk of everyday matters.

She sometimes wished they'd brought Tabby, but mother and babies had been returned to the Duke of Ithorne's care.

But perhaps talk of everyday matters was what was needed. She'd learned about his military life and adventures abroad, and she'd told him stories from her tamer life.

In the evenings they'd sometimes been able to stroll near the inn, escaping their chaperone, but there the weather had been unkind. On two evenings it had poured with rain and they'd had to stay indoors. They'd played cards and draughts while Martha Stokes sewed, never nodding off for a doze.

The rain had made the roads soupy, slowing them down, and Caro had seen how restive Christian was in the coach. In the end she'd told him to join Barleyman on horseback, and he hadn't argued. She'd watched him mount Buck, smiling. She could watch him for hours, but rarely had opportunity to do it without him watching back.

A wheel loosened near Salisbury, bringing them to a halt in a steady drizzle. Christian and Barleyman worked with the coachman and groom to try to fix it well enough to take them on to the city.

Caro leaned out to call, "Mind your back, husband!"

He looked up, muddy and sodden, and grinned.

A repair proved impossible. Martha refused to travel on horseback, even as pillion behind Barleyman, so she remained in the coach, while Caro happily mounted behind Christian for the short journey to the next inn. Even without a pillion saddle she felt perfectly safe, and she had an inarguable excuse to wrap her arms around him and lean against his back.

"This is very nice," she said.

"It's cold, it's damp, and we'll probably

be stuck in the middle of nowhere for a day while the wheel's fixed."

"This is very nice," Caro repeated, and he laughed.

They were going to remain married. She felt sure of it by now. She knew he was honest about loving her, and she was coming to believe he'd be faithful. Her practical part warned that was folly, but most of her wasn't practical at all.

She was determined, however, on reaching Royle Chart and meeting his family before the final commitment, for she knew that once it was made, there'd be no turning back.

He seemed to truly feel she might dislike his family, and that worried her.

Perhaps they were not so much unconventional as insane. They certainly seemed wildly extravagant, for he'd explained that was the reason he was going to have to become a country gentleman and learn to manage the earldom's estates — because his family had no ability to manage money.

She had no intention of having the hard-earned Froggatt money frittered away and yet she had no defenses. Their long-ago marriage had not been preceded by those precious trusts and settlements. Instead of the third she'd intended to give Eyam,

Christian possessed all. Nor did she have the arrangement agreed upon in lieu of the separation from bed and board.

She knew she could trust Christian on the matter of choice. If she decided not to go forward with their marriage, but to sign the documents of legal separation, he wouldn't stop her. If she chose otherwise, however, and became his wife in all ways . . .

She must not do that until all legal safeguards were in place. Circumstances change; people change. It hurt to even imagine denying her heart for such practical reasons, but her Froggatt ancestors loomed in her mind like Banquo's ghost, howling in protest at the fruit of their hard labor being tossed away on fripperies. Care for her fortune was a duty, plain and simple, as unrelenting as a soldier's duty to fight the enemy.

As they rode along between well-tended fields, Caro considered the minor challenges of her situation. Christian had confessed to knowing nothing about estate management, and nor did she. They could both learn, but it threatened to be a strange life for her. She came from the industrial northeast, and Devon was deep in England's rural southwest. There'd already been times when she hadn't been able to understand the local dialect and they still had a day or two to go.

Despite Luttrell House, she was a city woman, accustomed to manufacture and trade rather than agriculture and tenants.

She was not, and could never pretend to be, of the aristocracy. Around Sheffield, she'd had the worth of being a Froggatt. That would mean nothing in Devon. She would have brought money to the marriage, of course, but having money meant less than nothing by itself.

Caro's heart sank lower and lower, but by good fortune, they drove onto the Royle Chart estate in sunshine, and it was a pretty sight. A few leaves were turning golden and some lay on the ground like blossoms. White sheep wandered, cropping the grass.

"That's economical," she said to Christian, who was in the coach for their arrival.

"Yes." But then he winced as the coach lurched into and out of a hole in the drive and various bits of wood and metal screamed. "The place is still a money-eating monster."

Caro wasn't willing to talk about money at that moment.

The house stole her breath. It was a vast array of golden stone clad in climbing plants, some of them turning russet and scarlet. It looked both enormous and comfortable.

"Not bad, is it?" Perhaps he sounded anxious.

"It's lovely."

But then people began to pour out of the door. There were a great many boys, who ran whooping to meet the coach, and some servants and other people.

The coach drew up. The boys kept running around and whooping. A portly man hurried forward to open the door himself. "Welcome, welcome!" he said to Caro, beaming. "What a glorious day!"

She heard Christian mutter, "Here we go."

Caro climbed down to be embraced by the earl, by the countess, equally portly, with bright green-gold eyes. For some reason, a young child was put in Caro's arms, and he kissed her, too, hooking his arm around her neck.

She looked desperately for Christian, but he was swarmed by boys, so she let the tide carry her into a grand but untidy hall. Stairs rose straight up to the next floor and there seemed to be a landing there with more people hanging over.

Young women were exclaiming and questioning. Orders were called to servants. . . .

Christian appeared at her side, removed the child, and put him in the arms of the nearest person. "She'll run away if you treat her like this," he said.

Silence fell. Caro thought there was hurt in it.

"What a lovely welcome," she said, smiling brightly, "but if I could be shown my room, just for a while?"

This delicate hint of bodily necessity had her swept upstairs by the countess and two young women who must be sisters-in-law, and into a handsome chamber.

Christian followed.

"Ah, yes," he said. "We'll need separate rooms, Mother."

The countess turned to him. "Separate rooms? Why?"

"I'll explain later." He might be blushing. "Even our family can't be using all the bedchambers here."

"Well, we are, as it happens," she said, still staring at him as if he'd declared he needed toads for dinner. "You must have seen that Mary and Claughton are here. With the new baby!" she added with a beam. "And Sara is to arrive tomorrow, especially to see you. And didn't I mention that my parents have come to live with us?"

"No," he said with a sigh. "Never mind. It'll be all right."

"Of course it will. Everything always is."

567

She turned her beam on Caro. "We have been praying he'd find you, dear. We'll just be off, but you must come down quickly so you can meet everyone properly over tea."

She shooed young women and boys out of the room — "No, dears, Christian will play with you later" — and the door shut.

Christian leaned back against a wall, his eyes shut. "Now you see."

Caro collapsed on the sofa in giggles. When she collected herself, he was looking at her, smiling ruefully. "This isn't a riot for your benefit," he warned. "It's like this all the time."

She bit her lips and managed to stay calm. "Perhaps one becomes accustomed?"

"I've never tried. Thorn actually likes it, but he doesn't have to live here."

"Nor do we. Isn't there some other house nearby?"

He moved away from the wall. "I think there's a dower house, and there are probably others. But if we were to live here, the others could be let."

With even a third of her money, that wouldn't be necessary, but she wasn't ready to talk of such things yet.

"That's all for later," she said. "Now I really do need the convenience."

He opened a door. "Through here."

Caro went into the small dressing room, made cozy by a fire, and used the chamber pot. She considered the matter of the shared bedchamber. Specifically, the shared bed.

They'd had separate rooms at every inn and they'd kept to their rule about no intimacy, not even a kiss. It had been hard, and now an ache was starting that would only get worse. But she knew they had to keep to their plan, their pledge, if they were able. It was the structure for a rational decision, for they spun too easily into passion, and passion could lead to a child that would bind them forever.

She didn't remember clearly, but she suspected that he'd completed the act that night on their travels. She'd had her courses since, so nothing had come of it, but they could not take such a risk again.

She returned to the bedchamber to find him looking out at the estate. She went to his side. Evening was adding extra gold but softening the distance with mist. It was exquisite.

"What are you going to tell your parents?" she asked.

"It will have to be the truth," he said, turning to her. "They'll pressure us."

"They won't want us, you in particular, to live in the limbo of a legal separation. That's reasonable."

"You understand them already?"

"Is that presumptuous? I'm sorry."

"No, no. It's just . . . I don't. I don't understand them at all." He looked at the bed. "I'll find somewhere else to sleep. There has to be a nook or cranny somewhere."

"Or a truckle bed, or a mattress. This is a large room."

"That's a large bed." A heat in his eyes sent a sizzle through her.

Hunger growled in her, but she found the strength to say, "Too dangerous."

"Do you know how much I want you?"

She licked her lips. "I know my own hungers."

"Why are we starving each other?"

"You are doing it because I insisted," she said. "I am doing it because I need to be free to make the right decision."

"And you'd no longer be free?"

"I'd be bound to you with steel."

He took her hand and kissed it. "A slight break in the rules, but no farther, I promise. What are the barriers, Caro?"

It was an honest question that she could not ignore. "Will you be faithful to me?" she asked, watching him. "Always and completely?"

"Yes. Will you?"

"What? Of course!"

"Why, of course? You did once romp with a stranger at an inn."

Caro's face flamed, but she had to bite her lips on a smile. "So I did, but I suspect you've made more of a career of it than I have."

He laughed. "True enough, but I'll keep my long-ago marriage vows, Caro, if our marriage is a true one. I promise you that."

She looked away for a moment, and then faced him again. "Which brings us to worldly goods. I never promised them to you, but the law gives them to you anyway."

"But you're here."

"What does that mean?"

"That you trust me this far. I can completely understand you needing to know more of my family before venturing farther. Let's face the bounteous Hills."

It was as chaotic as he'd said, but Caro began to find her feet, and as she did, she discovered a greater peril than even lust. Christian's family, even the noise and confusion and endless demands, was like a heady brew that she might never tire of. Yes, she'd want a sanctuary, a place to escape and be just with him, but she wanted this, too, and might be willing to pay a fortune for it.

As well as people, there were dogs and cats. Tabby would be absorbed as easily as they were. When Caro saw that one boy had a pet rabbit, she couldn't help but laugh at thought of the the fanged rabbits of Hesse.

Everyone sat to supper at the long table in a gilt-paneled dining room that had surely been designed for more-elegant assemblies. Lisa, Christian's youngest sister, led the family in grace, and it seemed to be a tradition that the honor rotate.

Caro was seated at the countess's right hand. The youngster, Ben, was on his mother's other side, seated on a block of wood. Lady Royland's conversation was entirely about Christian and included many questions. It was as if she was hungry for information about him. There was more to this situation than Caro had realized. Christian had claimed not to understand his family, and clearly he didn't visit or even write as much as his parents wished. There was work to be done.

If she was going to stay.

After supper, the women and children went to the drawing room, which was treated with no more dignity than the dining room. Caro learned the rules of a game of marbles played on the carpet and had a wonderful time. The men soon joined them and Christian got down on the floor to try to beat her at it.

He failed.

Children departed at regular intervals, and Caro saw that there was order here in some respects. In the respects, she decided, that Christian's parents thought important.

Eventually, as if by some silent arrangement, she and Christian went with his parents to the book-lined room that the earl used as his sanctuary. There, Christian attempted to explain the situation.

"So we are on trial, are we?" said his father, looking at Caro, but his eyes twinkled.

"If so, so am I, sir."

"Not at all! For you are our daughter now, come what may."

"We quite understand how difficult this must be," said Lady Royland. "Ten years, and you were both so young. And *such* an unpleasant situation when you wed. I didn't think about that. Will it be so very difficult for you to share a room?"

Caro winced. She'd never imagined Moore's rough treatment of her being part of this conversation. What could she say?

"It's always best to let nature take its

course," said her father-in-law, whatever that was supposed to mean.

"Not if Caro gets with child," said Christian bluntly.

Oh, that was what he meant.

"But you're married, dear," said his mother without a blink, "so a child would be no problem, and I'm sure Caro must want one."

"It would be a problem if we were supposed to be separated," he said.

"I don't see why, unless you think people would assume she'd taken a lover."

Caro saw Christian close his eyes.

"In other circumstances," Caro said quickly, "I would be delighted to have a baby."

"There, see," said the earl. "Off you go, then. You must be tired after such a long journey."

Christian's strangled expression strained Caro's self-control. She rose. "Yes, I'm very tired."

"Exhausted," said Christian, and he guided her out of the room.

Outside, she covered her mouth to stifle laughter. "It was as if we were ordered to . . . to . . . ," she whispered.

"Yes." He cast a harried look around. "Let's get to our room before even worse happens!"

But when they were there, of course, the bed loomed.

A mattress lay upon the floor, neatly made up, but the bed still loomed.

"You want children?" he said.

"Yes, but not now."

"I didn't mean . . ." He ran a finger over the pineapple carving of the bedpost. "I've always been resolved not to add to the overabundance of Hills."

"Oh." Caro sat on a hard chair, pondering that. She wanted children. "But if we hold to this marriage, would that be possible? Not . . . I mean."

He turned to her. "Having children with you seems to be different."

She couldn't help but smile. "Any child would be blessed to be raised as part of this clan."

"Oh, struth, you're beginning to sound like them!"

"I like them."

He laughed. "So do I."

He came to her, his hands extended. "You're like a lens that makes things seem different, Caro, and you're a companion I don't want to live without. It won't be an easy life, but there will be blessings, many blessings. Will you share it with me?"

She put hers into his and stood. "I truly want to, Christian, but I'm sorry. We must talk of money."

She thought he'd be angry, but he nodded. "Yes, we must." He led her to a settee and they sat side by side. "You see, I think, that my family needs money."

"They don't seem extravagant."

"They're not. My brother Tom's been reckless in some way, but I have faith enough in him to believe he'll learn by it. But my parents want the best for all their children, and so do I."

Caro wanted to slide closer, into his arms, and ignore all this, but it was necessary. "As it stands, you own all I possess."

"If you keep saying that, you'll anger me."

"I'm sorry, but . . . my money is like a sacred trust, Christian. Have you any idea how hard my family worked for it?"

"I can guess. What arrangement do you want, love?"

The word, the look in his eyes, almost undid Caro, but she managed to speak calmly. "I intended one-third to you outright, and the rest in a trust. At least, that's what I intended with Sir Eyam."

"Fair enough. And now?"

She saw he expected something more stringent, and spoke quickly. "A third to you, a third in a trust for me but with complete access, and a third in a restricted trust that will provide for our children. In case we both run mad with generosity. And did I say I'm selling my share of Froggatt and Skellow, so there'll be no more income from there?"

He put a finger to her lips, smiling. "My very business-like Kat. I think I'll call you Kat in private. You know, your Froggatt side is exactly what the Hill family needs. The earldom will probably be bringing in a handsome income in no time."

He'd kept his finger on her lips and Caro couldn't help but kiss it. "I'd like that," she said. "Helping make the earldom efficient and profitable."

"But now I have a money matter to discuss," he said, taking his finger away. "A confession, I'm afraid."

Caro made herself not shrink back, but if he revealed huge debts at this point, it would break her heart.

"Lady Fowler," he said.

"Lady Fowler?"

"I need to donate a thousand guineas to her fund."

*"What?"* Caro exclaimed. "That's madness!"

"It feels like it, but you see, I once took a

vow. . . ."

Caro gaped, then said, "You're one of the ones that took that vow about marrying? Along with the Earl of Huntersdown?"

"How on earth do you know about that?"

"We stopped there on our way south. I met Lady Huntersdown. She's charming."

"When not fiery and dangerous," he said. "You liked her?"

"Yes." Caro smiled. "When we left, I hoped we might be friends but couldn't imagine how."

"Now you know how, but the vow requires the absurd donation."

But Caro frowned. "Why? Surely we were married long before you took that vow."

"Isn't that picking at the truth?"

"No," Caro said firmly. "We'll have no nonsense like that, sir. A thousand guineas to that idiotic woman? Perhaps the spirit of the vow does require some donation, but I have many worthy causes. Some almshouses, an orphanage. Or," she added with a wicked smile, "an asylum for the insane."

He stared at her. "Struth, you were Carrie the maid!"

At the look on his face, Caro burst out laughing. "I was. I was terrified you'd realize, but it was fun, too."

"And the house in Doncaster?"

"My friend Phyllis's home. From which I sallied forth as Kat, to hunt you down, sir."

"And you have found and captured me, my lady, heart and soul. What is your will? We can keep to our recent vows. Not kiss. Not share that bed."

"Can we truly?" she asked, rather breathless now. "I mean, are we able?"

"*I'm* not a beast," he said with an emphasis that made her smile.

"Even if you were a beast, I might succumb, only to be part of the wondrous Hills."

He moved closer. "Alas, you only love me for my family."

She swayed closer to him, put a hand on his chest. "And you are not a beast."

"I could become one," he suggested, tilting her chin and brushing his lips over hers. "In that bed."

"Would I like that?" she breathed.

He smiled. "Yes."

"Then could you do it rather quickly?"

He laughed. "The first time, at least." He pulled her to her feet, but then left her to lock both doors, the one to the corridor and the one to the dressing room. "See, I learn."

Caro chuckled. "So I should hope."

Still by the door, he looked at her seriously. "Are you sure? There's no going back from this, you know."

"Yes. Get undressed."

She had already unfastened her gown and shed it, and was untying her petticoat. He pulled off his boots, stripped off his coat, waistcoat, and shirt, then came to her, pulling a folding knife out of his pocket. "Quickly, you requested?" He sliced the laces of her corset, bottom to top.

Caro laughed in shocked excitement, but shed her shift, reveling in being naked before him. She raised her foot on the chair to undo her garter and roll down her stocking, watching him watch her as he completed his own undressing.

By the time she tossed down the second stocking, he was magnificently naked, as she'd never seen him before.

"You've turned pink all over," he said, leading her to the bed. "Our true marriage bed, I think."

"Yes."

He drew back the covers, picked her up, and laid her there, then lowered himself slowly over her, kissing her breasts. But she could see how hard he was, how ready, as she was, aching deep. She spread her legs wide. "Quickly, quickly."

With a laughing groan he slid deep and hard into her.

It was hot and fast and perfect because there were no fears, no doubts, no need for guilt or restraint. She locked her legs around him as she had in that room, because she wanted to seal him to her forever and evermore as they reached their shuddering delight.

But then she had to let go, relax, recover, and they lay in silence, skin to skin, heart to heart.

"I can't regret anything that happened ten years ago," she said, rubbing her head against his chest, "or we'd not be here to-night."

"And I can never regret that youthful folly, or I might never have found you, my heart, my soul." He rolled onto his back, carrying her to lie over him. "You see how it is. With the Hills, things always turn out for the best."

The employees of Thorndike Press hope you have enjoyed this Large Print book. All our Thorndike, Wheeler, and Kennebec Large Print titles are designed for easy reading, and all our books are made to last. Other Thorndike Press Large Print books are available at your library, through selected bookstores, or directly from us.

For information about titles, please call:
    (800) 223-1244

or visit our Web site at:
    http://gale.cengage.com/thorndike

To share your comments, please write:
    Publisher
    Thorndike Press
    295 Kennedy Memorial Drive
    Waterville, ME 04901